CHRONICLE: VOLUME III

Written by
CHRIS METZEN, MATT BURNS,
and ROBERT BROOKS

Full-color illustrations by
ARTHUR BOZONNET
COLE EASTBURN
STANTON FENG
ROMAN KENNEY
PETER C. LEE
DARYL MANDRYK
YEWON PARK
DAN SCOTT
ROBERT SEVILLA
ABE TARAKY
KONSTANTIN TUROVEC
BAYARD WU

Additional art by
JOSEPH LACROIX

BLIZZARD ENTERTAINMENT

Written by CHRIS METZEN, MATT BURNS, and ROBERT BROOKS
Additional Story ALEX AFRASIABI, STEVE DANUSER, KEITH R.A. DECANDIDO,
EVELYN FREDERICKSEN, CHRISTIE GOLDEN, JEFF GRUBB, WILLIAM KING,
RICHARD A. KNAAK, DAVE KOSAK, MICKY NEILSON, BILL ROPER,
AARON S. ROSENBERG, LOUISE SIMONSON, WALTER SIMONSON, JAMES WAUGH •
Creative Direction and Design ELY CANNON, DOUG GREGORY, GLENN RANE,
CHRIS ROBINSON • *Editors* CATE GARY, ALLISON MONAHAN, ROBERT SIMPSON •
Lore SEAN COPELAND, EVELYN FREDERICKSEN, CHRISTI KUGLER, JUSTIN PARKER
• *Production* PHILLIP HILLENBRAND, BRIANNE M LOFTIS, JEFFREY WONG,
MICHAEL BYBEE • *Licensing* MATT BEECHER, BYRON PARNELL

Special thanks to: the *World of Warcraft* game team,
Frank Mummert, Tommy Newcomer, Max Ximenez

Maps, cosmology chart, borders, and spot art by JOSEPH LACROIX

Paintings by ARTHUR BOZONNET (89, 126, 202) • COLE EASTBURN (49, 206)
STANTON FENG (72, 110, 117, 189) • ROMAN KENNEY (28, 62)
PETER C. LEE (8-9, 42-43, 82-83, 106-107, 134-135, 168-169, 192-193)
DARYL MANDRYK (97) • YEWON PARK (155, 212) • DAN SCOTT (35)
ROBERT SEVILLA (33, 176) • ABE TARAKY (33, 147)
KONSTANTIN TUROVEC (165, 173, 179) • BAYARD WU (24, 99, 124, 161)

DARK HORSE BOOKS

Publisher MIKE RICHARDSON • *Editor* DAVE MARSHALL • *Assistant Editor* RACHEL
ROBERTS • *Designer* DAVID NESTELLE • *Digital Art Technician* CHRIS HORN

World of Warcraft® Chronicle: Volume III

Published by
Dark Horse Books
A division of Dark Horse Comics, Inc.
10956 SE Main Street
Milwaukie, OR 97222

DarkHorse.com
International Licensing: (503) 905-2377
Comic Shop Locator Service: Comicshoplocator.com
First Edition: March 2018
ISBN 978-1-61655-847-5

1 3 5 7 9 10 8 6 4 2
Printed in China

CHRONICLE

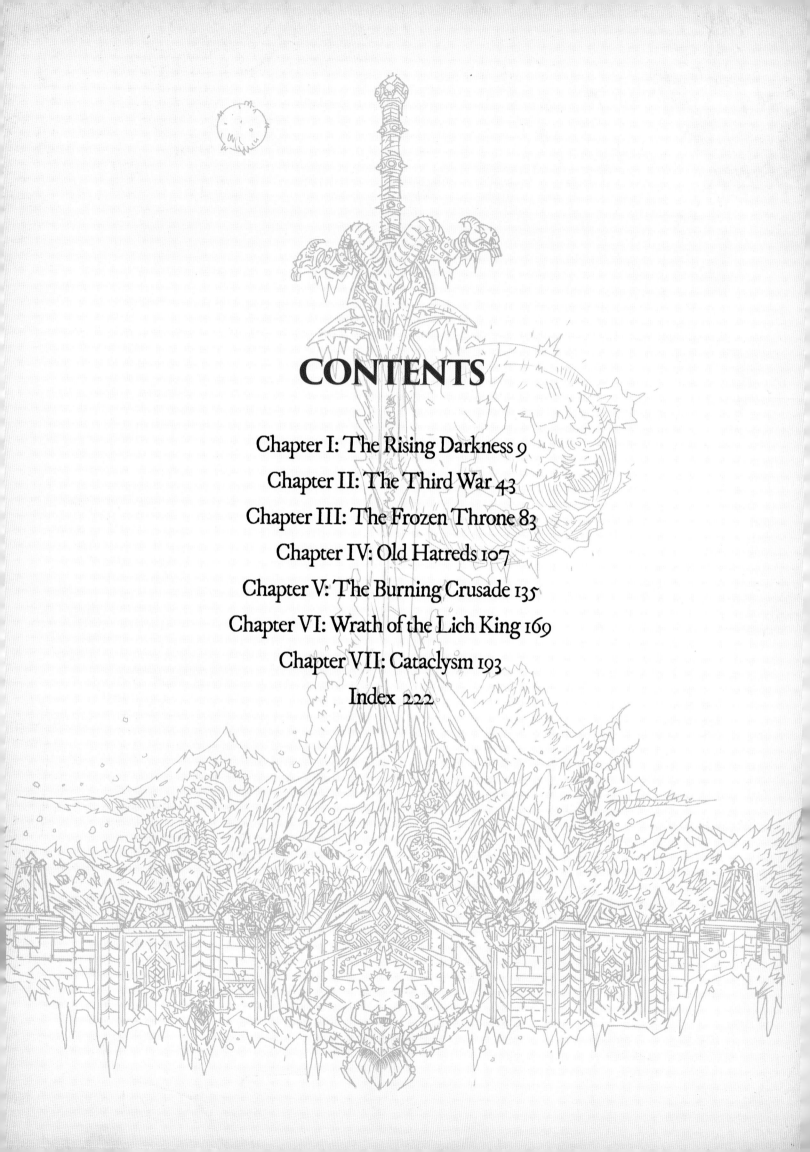

CONTENTS

THE RISING DARKNESS

THE RISING DARKNESS

ENVIOUS EYES

Long ago, across the vast expanses of the Great Dark Beyond, a powerful race known as the titans protected the cosmos from the forces of corruption and chaos. They searched for worlds that harbored nascent titan spirits, and they nurtured them. Once these world-souls had matured, the titans raised them into the order of the Pantheon.

The mightiest among the titans of the Pantheon, Sargeras, was once their greatest champion. He fought tirelessly to defend the cosmos from savage beings called demons. These creatures originated from a warped realm known as the Twisting Nether, where they reveled in fel magic, a destructive and highly addictive force.

And yet, after repelling countless invasions by demons, Sargeras became convinced that it was for naught. He had learned of a threat even greater than demons: void lords. These beings hungered to corrupt one of the defenseless world-souls, hoping to raise it as a champion of their own. Such a creature would shroud the entire cosmos in Void energies, laying waste to all creation.

Sargeras refused to let that happen. He refused even to allow it as a possibility. He embraced fel magic and enslaved demons to his will, forging them into an army called the Burning Legion. Sargeras's decision to ally with his ancient enemies was extreme, but he believed it was necessary. Demons were the only creatures in existence who he was certain would join his Burning Crusade, a campaign to burn all life from the cosmos. It was the only way Sargeras imagined he could spare the denizens of the Great Dark Beyond from the void lords.

In his eyes, a dead universe was better than one that had fallen to darkness.

No civilization was strong enough to oppose Sargeras and his fiery army. Even the other titans of the Pantheon fell before the might of their former champion. It seemed that nothing in all the universe would be able to stop him.

Eventually, Sargeras learned of a world that the other titans had once visited and shaped with their own hands. Its name was Azeroth, and it contained a world-soul with more potential power than any titan spirit the Pantheon had ever known. It also harbored a darker presence. When the titans had discovered Azeroth, they had found it infested with physical manifestations of the Void known as the Old Gods. These massive entities had forged a civilization called the Black Empire on the world's surface.

The titans and their servants later shattered the Black Empire, but they did not destroy the Old Gods. They feared that doing so would harm Azeroth itself, and they instead imprisoned the vile entities deep below the ground.

Sargeras could not ignore Azeroth's potential, nor could he ignore the presence of the Old Gods.

Ten thousand years ago, he sent his army to corrupt and destroy the creatures of Azeroth. After that, he planned to conquer the world-soul before the powers of the Void could. But an unlikely alliance of night elves, ancient spirits of the wilds, mighty guardians called the Dragon Aspects, and other brave races repelled the demons' invasion.

This brutal conflict, the War of the Ancients, was the Legion's first true defeat.

Yet Sargeras did not abandon his crusade. He took his time preparing for another assault. His most powerful lieutenants, Archimonde the Defiler and Kil'jaeden the Deceiver, led these efforts. In time, they found a way to attack Azeroth from another world—a place known as Draenor.

Kil'jaeden manipulated the proud orcs of Draenor into embracing fel magic and drinking demon blood. This last act cursed them and shackled their wills to the Legion. United as a war-hungry army called the Horde, the orcs invaded Azeroth. This force of destruction had one purpose: to weaken the world in preparation for a full-scale Legion invasion. The Horde nearly succeeded. Only by the courage of Azeroth's heroes were the orcs defeated.

The Legion had failed again. But the demons did not rest. These setbacks only proved how powerful Azeroth was. Sargeras commanded Kil'jaeden and Archimonde to seek out fresh allies and plan new methods of attack.

THE ASHES OF TWO WARS
8 YEARS AFTER THE DARK PORTAL

For a time, the races of Azeroth allowed themselves to believe that the worst had passed. They had certainly earned a respite. The past eight years had been filled with horrors.

The First War against the Horde had seen the human kingdom of Stormwind betrayed and razed to the ground. Its greatest champion, a mage known as Guardian Medivh, had been possessed by Sargeras. It was Medivh who had opened the Dark Portal, the gateway to Draenor that had exposed Azeroth to the Horde's wrath. The Guardian was slain, yet Stormwind could not be saved.

The Second War ended with the Horde's defeat—but just barely. The nations of the Eastern Kingdoms had joined together in the Alliance of Lordaeron and successfully rebuffed the orcs' invasion. Victory had come at great cost, requiring the sacrifice of countless heroes.

Most of the Horde's soldiers were either killed or captured. Some of the survivors had fled back to Draenor, but they knew there was no future there. When they had accepted the dark power of fel magic, they had unwittingly doomed the cycle of life and the balance of the elements. Draenor was dying. The orcs would not survive for long.

Their leader, Ner'zhul, engineered a desperate escape plan. He would open rifts to new worlds, new places to conquer. Perhaps somewhere in the cosmos, there was another realm his people could call home.

Azeroth's champions had no intention of letting the Horde harm other lands. An expedition of Alliance heroes, the Sons of Lothar, invaded Draenor through the Dark Portal, aiming to stop Ner'zhul. They were led by some of Azeroth's greatest defenders: Archmage Khadgar; Turalyon, the high general of the Sons of Lothar; Alleria Windrunner, the ranger-captain of Silvermoon City; Danath Trollbane, a seasoned warrior; and Kurdran Wildhammer, thane of the Wildhammer dwarves.

The brave endeavor forced Ner'zhul to act too recklessly. His spellwork caused unimaginable chaos, and his unstable rifts ripped apart the fabric of reality on his world. The Sons of Lothar tore down the Dark Portal before the destruction unfolding on Draenor could spread to Azeroth. Nearly all of the expedition's members were trapped in the apocalypse.

Azeroth could not regain contact with those left on Draenor. Presumably, all had perished. They were enshrined as heroes who had died to protect their world.

It would be many years before Azeroth learned their true fate.

FATE OF THE LOST

In the chaos of Draenor's collapse, Khadgar and his comrades fled through one of the volatile rifts to evade the brunt of the cataclysmic energies. When the destruction had finally come to an end, they returned to what was left of the world.

They discovered a shattered realm. The barriers between Draenor and the Twisting Nether had collapsed. The shredded reality had left open paths to all the various corners of the cosmos. This twisted place would be known thereafter as Outland.

Fortunately, some parts of old Draenor had survived. The Sons of Lothar established a permanent base at their main outpost—Honor Hold—and launched search missions for their missing allies.

Two of the highest-ranking members of the expedition were never found. They were feared dead, but in truth, fate simply had different plans for them.

Alleria Windrunner and Turalyon had been trapped in the Twisting Nether following the Dark Portal's destruction. They were unable to find a way back to Draenor or Azeroth on their own, but they were rescued by an unexpected force: Xe'ra, the naaru prime.

The naaru were creatures of Light who often tried to guide and cultivate mortal life. Xe'ra was one of the most powerful among her kind, and she had gathered a holy army—the Army of the Light—dedicated to fighting back against the Burning Legion's crusade. Most of Xe'ra's loyal soldiers were draenei, the sworn enemies of demons.

The draenei had a long and violent history with the Legion. They once were members of a highly intelligent race known as the eredar. Long ago, Sargeras had discovered their world, Argus, and transformed it into the Legion's seat of power. In the process, he had corrupted the eredar into demons. Those who escaped Argus took on the name *draenei*, meaning "exiled ones," and fled across the stars. The Legion never stopped hunting them in retribution for defying Sargeras. Some of the draenei, led by the wise Prophet Velen, had eventually settled on Draenor. Others found refuge with the Army of the Light.

The Army of the Light was always outnumbered and outgunned, but its soldiers waged their war against the Legion for thousands upon thousands of years. They did not despair. Xe'ra had foreseen that the demons' crusade would one day be brought low by those of mortal birth.

When Alleria and Turalyon had left their world to make war upon another, Xe'ra had received another glimpse of destiny from the Light: those two children of Azeroth would be the key to unveiling the Burning Legion's weakness.

Xe'ra told Alleria and Turalyon everything she could. They discussed the prophecy, the threat of the Burning Legion, and even the Horde, which had been corrupted as an instrument of the demons' will. She asked them to join the Army of the Light and the ongoing war against the Legion.

It was a difficult decision. Alleria Windrunner and Turalyon had a child, Arator, on Azeroth. It would be crushing to leave him—to say nothing of all their friends and family—behind. But they had come to Draenor knowing it was likely a one-way trip. They had been willing to make the ultimate sacrifice if it meant protecting Azeroth and their son's future.

Xe'ra told them that the Horde was not the last threat Azeroth would face, and thus, their war needed to continue. They left Outland and joined the Army of the Light. They would not be heard from again for quite some time.

STRUGGLE FOR A BROKEN WORLD

When the dust settled on Outland, the survivors slowly realized that this battered realm had become one of the most important strategic places in all the cosmos. Many of Ner'zhul's portals were permanently open. The world was now a crossroads for any force that wished to travel quickly from one end of the universe to the other.

The Legion saw Outland as the perfect staging ground to launch assaults against other worlds. The demons dispatched a pit lord named Magtheridon, a cruel and powerful commander, to seize the location and its inhabitants. He hunted down the remnants of the Horde, enslaving those who surrendered and butchering those who still had the will to resist. The orcs who died opposing him had the easier fate.

Those who surrendered were forced to drink Magtheridon's demonic blood. For most, it was the second time they had been subjected to the Legion's corruption. But unlike what happened more than a decade ago, the Legion's intention was not merely to bend their wills but to shatter them entirely. The orcs were transformed into crimson-skinned, barbaric creatures, and their minds could do little else but obey the Burning Legion.

Magtheridon's new "Fel Horde" established its home in Hellfire Citadel and then struck out to claim other locations with important confluences of power. Foremost among them was the Black Temple.

Once a sacred house of worship for the draenei, the Black Temple had fallen to corruption under the Horde's control, but it still held residual power. Ner'zhul had chosen it as the site of the ill-fated ritual that had destroyed Draenor. Built at the end of a peninsula, the Black Temple was approachable from only one direction, and thus it was easily defensible. It proved to be an excellent staging ground for Magtheridon's campaign of conquest against the remnants of Outland.

BLADE'S EDGE
MOUNTAINS

ZANGARMARSH

Shattrath City

NAGRAND

TEROKKAR
FOREST

Auchindoun

NETHERSTORM

OUTLAND

Hellfire Citadel

The Dark Portal

Honor Hold

HELLFIRE
PENINSULA

The Black Temple

SHADOWMOON
VALLEY

The pit lord's actions did not go unnoticed. The survivors of the Sons of Lothar mustered what soldiers they could to oppose the demons' incursion. Khadgar, Kurdran Wildhammer, and Danath Trollbane quickly realized they would never be able to defeat this Legion strike force on their own, but they *could* slow it down. Whenever Magtheridon sent his armies deep into Outland, the Alliance was there to carve up their flanks and pick off any stragglers. The two forces would skirmish intermittently for years.

The draenei who had survived Draenor's destruction could do little to aid the Alliance in these battles. Prophet Velen knew that the Legion would go to tremendous lengths to exterminate any draenei the demons found—a suspicion that was confirmed by the few unfortunate souls who had crossed their path and lived to tell of it.

Scouring the draenei was a personal quest for Kil'jaeden. He hated Velen and his followers, and he had hunted them throughout the cosmos ever since they had fled Argus. Every demon knew they would be rewarded for each draenei head they collected. Velen kept his followers hidden in small, isolated enclaves so that if one was discovered, it would not mean doom for his entire people.

Velen's followers lived a meager existence, but they were the lucky ones. The draenei had suffered terrible losses from the Horde's rise to power on Draenor. During the destruction of their grandest city, Shattrath, a fel plague had been unleashed upon their people.

Not every draenei afflicted with the Horde's corrupting magic had died. Many had survived, but they had undergone horrific mutations.

These draenei became known as *Krokul*—"Broken." Riddled with painful deformities and no longer able to access the power of the Holy Light, most of them lived in small, scattered tribes far from the rest of the draenei. Some fell to violence and despair, and there were brutal skirmishes between the tribes.

The former leader of the draenei's holy warriors, Akama, took command of the Ashtongue tribe. As one of the Broken, he, too, had lost his ability to call on the Light. Though he nurtured a small nugget of hope that he and his fellow outcasts would one day rise to their former glory, he first had to lead his people through a period of darkness and disturbing alliances.

The last notable faction on Outland was the Sethekk arakkoa. The once-proud creatures had been brought to ruin by the Horde, and the survivors had been thrown into the corrupting pools of Sethekk Hollow, an ordeal that robbed them of their ability to fly and weighed down their minds with an oppressive sense of darkness. The few who had survived the destruction of Draenor took refuge in the draenei mausoleum of Auchindoun. Dark forces had claimed the area years ago, and the arakkoa spent their time studying them, worshipping them, and eventually falling under their sway.

These factions would battle for years, their hidden war locked behind the destroyed Dark Portal. The denizens of Azeroth knew nothing of this struggle for control, and they would soon be occupied with their own troubles.

OVERLEAF: OUTLAND FOLLOWING DRAENOR'S DESTRUCTION

THE LICH KING

When the Horde was defeated in the Second War, the Legion's plan to conquer Azeroth had fallen apart. But the demons were not deterred. To the contrary, Kil'jaeden had learned an extremely valuable lesson.

The Horde had failed because of internal conflict and disloyalty. The Legion's next strike against Azeroth would not suffer from the same weaknesses. Kil'jaeden conceived of a dark, disturbing way to raise a new puppet army that would be utterly incapable of diverging from the Legion's will. All he needed was a powerful spirit, skilled in the art of wielding magic, to control it.

The decimation of Draenor had given him exactly what he needed.

During Draenor's destruction, Ner'zhul and his closest followers had escaped into the Twisting Nether. Kil'jaeden's minions had been waiting for them there.

Ner'zhul suffered unimaginable torture at the Legion's hands. The orc's physical body was torn apart bit by bit, but his spirit was kept alive, intact, and utterly aware of what was happening. A group of dreadlords—Tichondrius, Balnazzar, Detheroc, Mal'Ganis, and Varimathras—took turns subjecting Ner'zhul to the most horrific agony.

The orc soon begged for death. Kil'jaeden agreed to grant it to him, but only in return for absolute servitude as the Legion's new weapon. Death would be just the beginning.

Ner'zhul, his sanity cracking, finally agreed. Kil'jaeden passed the orc's spirit through death and revived him as a spectral entity. The orc's consciousness expanded a thousandfold, granting him extraordinary psychic powers. The dreadlords bound his disembodied spirit to a specially crafted set of armor and a mighty runeblade called Frostmourne. These items were locked in a diamond-hard block of ice to imprison Ner'zhul.

The armaments served a dual purpose: they kept Ner'zhul's spirit contained, and they were a tantalizing reward. Kil'jaeden promised his servant that if he proved his loyalty to the Legion, he would be allowed to roam free in a new body. His armor would mark him as a king, and he would rule Azeroth. However, if Ner'zhul disobeyed, his spirit would be tormented forevermore.

Kil'jaeden had no desire—and no need—to make good his promise. However, the demon lord believed the lie would keep his servant more eager to serve than if he relied on threats alone to motivate him.

Ner'zhul's loyal followers were also transformed. Their bodies were torn asunder and reshaped into powerful undead liches who would serve without question.

Ner'zhul's past life had vanished. A new one arose in its place. This being was called the Lich King, and he woke into an existence of unending servitude and indescribable power.

17

CHAPTER I: THE RISING DARKNESS

ICECROWN AND THE FROZEN THRONE

When Kil'jaeden's dark work was done, he explained his plan to his new minion. The Lich King would conjure a necromantic plague that would choke all resistance away from Azeroth. The living would die and be reborn as loyal, undead soldiers. These mindless servants would weaken Azeroth's defenses in preparation for a demonic invasion by the Legion.

Kil'jaeden remained suspicious of the Lich King. The demon lord had long since lost interest in trusting his minions. The dreadlords who had helped torment Ner'zhul and craft his armor would accompany him to Azeroth. They would be both jailors and executors, meant to hasten the Lich King's task by any means necessary.

Through a tremendous expenditure of power, the Legion opened a small portal from the Twisting Nether into Azeroth. The Lich King's icy cask streaked across the night sky and smashed into an isolated part of Icecrown Glacier in the frigid continent of Northrend. His prison, warped by the descent, came to resemble a throne. The Lich King's dreadlord caretakers soon joined him and began to construct fortifications around this Frozen Throne.

The Lich King let them do their work while he started his own. His expanded consciousness reached out to the scattered native inhabitants of Northrend, darkening their thoughts and afflicting them with terrible nightmares.

The Lich King treaded carefully at first, testing his powers. Kil'jaeden had been adamant that the nations of Azeroth not know what was coming until it was too late.

Isolated tribes and powerful beasts fell under the Lich King's command. First came fierce creatures called wendigo and the savage ice trolls. Then came lost tribes of mighty vrykul.

The vrykul were a war-hungry breed. Millennia ago, they had sought to conquer the world, but their campaign was cut short by Azeroth's foremost guardians, the Dragon Aspects. The majestic creatures had placed the vrykul in a deep, unending slumber to spare the world from their barbaric ways. The Lich King's servants slew the vrykul in their sleep, and they were raised into undeath as powerful new warriors.

Pleased with his initial successes, the Lich King crafted an early strain of the plague of undeath. There was a remote human settlement on the fringes of the Dragonblight, unaware of the dangerous force that was rising nearby. The Lich King controlled the plague with his will alone, sending it into the village while the humans slept.

Within three days, everyone in the settlement had died. Soon after, they rose again as undead minions. Their thoughts and awareness were added to the Lich King's own. He felt himself ascending higher and higher into realms of power he had never dreamed of. The more minds he controlled, the mightier he became.

As he continued to experiment with his manipulation of the undead, a fearsome stronghold rose around him. The dreadlords had constructed an impenetrable fortress called Icecrown Citadel. It would serve as the Lich King's base of operations, from which his campaign of terror would flow.

Kil'jaeden was deeply satisfied with the way events were progressing. He ordered the Lich King to quietly keep amassing his power. Once he had control of Northrend, he could begin his real work on the rest of Azeroth's living, starting with the Eastern Kingdoms. The nations there had suffered through years of conflict with the Horde. They were vulnerable and beset by internal

THE VAL'KYR

From the vrykul, the Lich King learned of intriguing creatures called Val'kyr. These spectral beings could corral spirits and even delve into the Shadowlands, the realm of death. The Lich King tried to create his own Val'kyr, but the task proved difficult even for him. After several missteps, he finally succeeded. The Val'kyr greatly enhanced his ability to control the dark powers of undeath.

strife. They would fall in short order to the plague of undeath. The Legion could then use the region as a staging point for gathering the full might of its armies on Azeroth.

Kil'jaeden's plan appeared sound. Yet the Lich King was plotting against him. Though the entity played the part of a loyal servant, he was secretly determined to break away from the Legion's control. He held no allegiance to the demons. Kil'jaeden had forced him into servitude through acts of brutality. He knew the demon lord's promise that the Lich King would be allowed to freely roam the world was a lie.

The Lich King would never forget what Kil'jaeden had done to him. *Never.* One day, he would make the demon lord pay for it.

The main obstacles to the Lich King's vengeance were the dreadlords. Under Kil'jaeden's orders, they carefully watched the entity for any signs of disobedience. The dreadlords were highly intelligent and crafty, but their cunning paled in comparison to the Lich King's. With great caution, he manipulated the demons. The Lich King masked the true scope of his power. He made the dreadlords believe that they were in complete control of him. All the while, he watched his prey and learned their individual strengths and weaknesses.

THE FRAGMENTED HORDE

The nations of the Eastern Kingdoms knew nothing of what was transpiring in Northrend. They were busy with efforts to rebuild their war-torn lands. Most of Stormwind's refugees had not returned home, and the unity between nations was fraying as the realities of post-war life set in. The orcs who had been captured needed to be imprisoned indefinitely. Huge internment camps were built to hold them, and these prisons became increasingly expensive to maintain. Kingdoms shifted the costs onto neighbors, inflaming tensions and sowing discord.

Though many of the orcs remaining on Azeroth had been captured, plenty of dangerous clans were still on the loose. The Warsongs, led by the legendary chieftain Grommash Hellscream, had refused to surrender. He and his people kept to the dense forests around Lordaeron, only emerging to raid local villages and farmsteads for food and supplies. The remnants of the Blackrock and

Black Tooth Grin clans, led by Dal'rend and Maim Blackhand, had declared themselves the "true Horde" and dwelled in Blackrock Mountain.

Dal'rend and Maim had a tenuous alliance with the Dragonmaw clan orcs, who occupied the ancient fortress of Grim Batol and retained a dark secret from the Second War. They possessed an artifact called the Demon Soul, which contained the powers of four great Dragon Aspects: Alexstrasza, Nozdormu, Malygos, and Ysera. The orcs had used the relic to enslave the Aspect of Life, Alexstrasza, and force her dragonflight to obey their commands.

Most of these clans kept to the shadows. None wanted to attract the attention of the Alliance. The Alliance, in turn, was too busy rebuilding to spend much time hunting them.

The situation changed dramatically due to Orgrim Doomhammer, the Horde's former warchief. The Alliance of Lordaeron considered him the most dangerous orc in captivity, and he had been held under close guard.

Orgrim's jailors thought he was broken, physically and mentally. Such was not the case. He outwitted his captors and escaped his internment camp.

Rage swept through the Alliance. Orgrim Doomhammer's capture in the Second War had sealed the Horde's defeat. Now he was free to rally what was left of his army and ignite a new conflict. This colossal embarrassment strained relationships among most of the Alliance nations. Trust was in short supply, and each kingdom became suspicious that the others were utterly incompetent.

The Alliance dedicated more time and resources to hunting down the orcs who freely roamed the land. The unfortunate ones they found were usually killed on the spot rather than captured. Even so, the orcs too often slipped away, making the Alliance's efforts feel wasted.

At the internment camps, the Alliance redoubled the guards and fortifications to make sure no other orcs would break free as Orgrim Doomhammer had. Escapes were virtually eliminated, but much to the surprise of the human wardens, escape *attempts* had vanished as well.

In imprisonment, the orcs were nothing like the battle-crazed warriors who had invaded the world. They had gradually become withdrawn, unable to muster the energy to retain their aggression . . . or even their pride. They accepted their confinement without much resistance at all.

This was a symptom of their withdrawal from fel magic. Archmage Antonidas of Dalaran was one of the few who studied the orcs' condition in depth, but despite his best efforts to discover a cure, there was no magical solution. Their ordeal had left deep wounds in their collective psyche. It was up to them to find a cause to live for.

In truth, many in the Alliance were perfectly happy with the prisoners' lethargy. As long as the imprisoned orcs remained aloof, they were no threat.

A Warchief in Exile

Once Orgrim Doomhammer escaped from his internment camp, he quietly traveled as far away from human cities as he could. Despite what the Alliance feared, he had no intention of rallying the Horde to continue his war against Azeroth.

Demons had treated the orcs like puppets, and after they had failed, they had been discarded. During his internment, Orgrim had seen the fire slowly disappear from the eyes of the other orcs. They had not simply been beaten. They had been broken.

Some blamed Orgrim for their plight, even though he had not led them into the demons' clutches. In truth, he had never approved of the Horde's use of fel magic. He knew of its destructive power and the way it had slowly corrupted his race.

Orgrim lived alone for years. On occasion, he would meet with the only clan he was certain would not regard him as an enemy: the Frostwolves.

He had been lifelong friends with the Frostwolf clan's former chieftain, Durotan, and with his mate, Draka. The two of them had spoken out against the Horde's formation and its use of fel magic. In retribution, Durotan and Draka had been cut down by assassins loyal to the Legion. Orgrim believed that their infant son, Go'el, had also been killed.

During his time in exile, Orgrim silently fought off the lethargy that plagued most of his kind, but he was only partially successful. His dreams of restoring his people's pride and honor went unfulfilled, and he scraped out an existence as a hermit, trying to draw as little attention as possible.

Legacy of Deathwing

The Horde's defeat devastated more than Orgrim Doomhammer and his people. It also dealt a blow to the corrupted Dragon Aspect, Deathwing, and his black dragonflight.

Long ago, the titans had empowered Deathwing—then known as Neltharion—and the other Dragon Aspects to serve as guardians of the world. Each of the majestic creatures was given a specific role. As the Aspect of Earth, Neltharion was imbued with the strength of Azeroth itself. This gift granted him immense power and fortitude, but it also inadvertently made him susceptible to the influence of the Old Gods.

After destroying the Black Empire, the titans and their servants had imprisoned the Old Gods deep underground, but that had not neutralized their power. Their dark tendrils gradually burrowed through the earth, and their influence reached into the mind of Neltharion. The Old Gods slowly transformed the Dragon Aspect into their greatest weapon and urged him to engulf the world in chaos.

During the War of the Ancients, he did exactly that.

Neltharion crafted the Demon Soul and convinced the other Aspects to sacrifice a portion of their strength to empower the artifact. He claimed that the relic would help them drive the Legion from Azeroth. Only later did he reveal his true intentions. Neltharion betrayed his fellow Dragon Aspects and turned the Demon Soul against them. Thereafter, he was known by a more fitting name: Deathwing.

In the millennia that followed, the other dragonflights had hunted Deathwing's children to the brink of extinction. Nowhere on Azeroth seemed safe for black dragons. Yet when the Horde invaded the world, Deathwing saw an opportunity. If he cultivated it properly, he could use the orcish army to destroy those who wanted him and his flight dead.

The Old Gods approved of Deathwing's intentions. Though they were enemies of the Legion, they knew the Horde would bring immense suffering and death to Azeroth. With the world and its peoples weakened, the Old Gods could assert their dominion over all and restore the Black Empire.

Deathwing proved himself to be a highly effective agent of destruction for the Old Gods time and time again. It was he who had manipulated the nations of the Eastern Kingdoms in the First War so that Stormwind was left to face the Horde alone. It was he who had led the Dragonmaw clan to the Demon Soul—albeit without revealing his true nature to the orcs. And it was he who had told them how to capture Alexstrasza and her dragonflight.

Deathwing had taken a clutch of eggs to Draenor in the hope of rebuilding his flight in peace. In the end, his plans fell to ruin. The future of his flight had been destroyed along with Draenor.

But all was not lost. The Dragonmaw orcs still held Alexstrasza captive, as well as many of her eggs and young offspring. Deathwing could claim those dragons for himself and enslave them to his will. They would become his new dragonflight.

First, he had to ensure that the Dragonmaw would not be wiped out by Alliance forces. Shortly after the destruction of the Dark Portal, Deathwing took on the guise of a human lord named Daval Prestor, a persona that he had used before. Pretending to be a charming member of the nobility, he had kept the court of Lordaeron in disarray with lies and misdirection, hampering the humans' awareness of how the First and Second Wars were unfolding. His efforts had been so effective that, even now, none of the nobles suspected that he had been actively working against them.

Lord Prestor rejoined the court, claiming that he wanted to help the Alliance recover from the war. Deathwing secretly called upon his son and daughter, Nefarian and Onyxia, to accompany him, also disguised as human nobles. Together they spread distrust and resentment among the nobility like a plague. Old rivalries flared bright among the Alliance's nations. Almost daily, fierce arguments erupted between nobles concerning the future of their faction.

The escape of Orgrim Doomhammer only added fuel to the fire. It was an unexpected gift to the Prestor family, who saw it as the perfect opportunity to chisel away at the very foundations of the Alliance.

After Orgrim's disappearance, it was easy to play upon the humans' mutual distrust. Deathwing and his children made sure Alliance scouts and raiding parties always had bad information. The hunt for the remnants of the Horde seemed constantly beset by laziness, incompetence, or both. None of these problems were ever connected back to the Prestor family.

Meanwhile, the threat posed by the Dragonmaw clan in Grim Batol remained hidden from the Alliance. Now Deathwing could focus on stealing the orcs' power away from them.

Deathwing kept his involvement with the clan a secret, believing that the orcs would never trust him or obey his commands. He sent dark dreams to Nekros Skullcrusher, the Dragonmaw's leader, offering premonitions that the Alliance was preparing a strike on Grim Batol that would wipe the clan off the face of Azeroth. To sell this fiction, Deathwing arranged for a small Alliance party—led by the powerful mage Rhonin—to stumble upon the Dragonmaw's hidden lair.

Nekros panicked. He ordered his clan to abandon Grim Batol and move to a new cave complex concealed within the mountain pass of Dun Algaz.

Drawing the orcs out of their mighty fortress was exactly what Deathwing had hoped for. Yet he was no longer the only powerful dragon with his attention on the Dragonmaw.

The Battle of Grim Batol
10 Years After the Dark Portal

During the Second War, the red dragon Korialstrasz was deeply concerned when Alexstrasza disappeared. He was the Dragon Aspect's consort and closest confidant, and he vowed to do whatever he could to find her. When he finally discovered that she was being held captive by the Dragonmaw, he found that he was utterly helpless. The Dragonmaw had enslaved Alexstrasza with the Demon Soul, an artifact that could destroy any dragon. Korialstrasz could not free her. He pleaded for help from the Dragon Aspects Ysera, Nozdormu, and Malygos, but they were wary of intervening. Like Korialstrasz, they feared that the orcs would use the Demon Soul to destroy them, or even Alexstrasza.

Soon it became clear that Deathwing planned to steal some of the red dragonflight's unhatched eggs for himself, and Korialstrasz nearly fell to despair.

After Rhonin stumbled upon the Dragonmaw, the red dragon found hope once again. Taking on the form of a powerful high elf mage named Krasus, the dragon promised the human all the aid he could muster to free the red dragonflight.

Rhonin had been stunned to find that an orc clan still had this much power after the Second War, and he was determined to break its strength. He rallied a small group of friends—including the high elf ranger Vereesa Windrunner and the dwarf gryphon rider Falstad Wildhammer—and rushed to Grim Batol to free the red dragons.

When they arrived, the battle was already under way.

The moment the Dragonmaw had left Grim Batol and set out for Dun Algaz, Deathwing attacked and slaughtered countless orcs. He had no desire to keep them or the adult dragons alive. Only the red dragonflight's eggs were of use to him.

Unfortunately for Deathwing, his brazen assault had unintended consequences. As the battle unfolded, Alexstrasza broke free of her chains. Before Nekros could kill her with the Demon Soul, she devoured him whole, taking vengeance for the horrors inflicted upon her. Then she turned her wrath upon Deathwing.

And she was not alone. Ysera, Nozdormu, and Malygos soon joined her in the fight against Deathwing. Though they had rebuffed Korialstrasz's calls to help Alexstrasza, the Dragon Aspects had not ignored him. They had decided to keep a close watch on Grim Batol in case an opening presented itself. Deathwing's attack against the orcs gave them one.

As the five Dragon Aspects grappled in the sky, Rhonin and his mortal allies focused their attention on the orcs and the Demon Soul. Rhonin found a flaw in the ancient artifact and destroyed it. In that moment, the power trapped within the relic escaped, returning to the Dragon Aspects.

Deathwing could not stand against the newly empowered dragons. He suffered terrible wounds and was forced to flee. He would not be seen again for many years to come.

The red dragonflight was free again. Many of the Dragonmaw orcs had died in the battle, and the terrified survivors had scattered into the wilds. They would remain a threat on Azeroth, but they would never truly regain their former power.

When Deathwing retreated, Lord Daval Prestor suddenly vanished from Lordaeron's royal court. His daughter, Onyxia, was left behind to carry on his work, and she relished it. The relationships between Lordaeron and other Alliance nations were continuing to deteriorate. Onyxia decided to spread her influence to the southern kingdom of Stormwind.

ALEXSTRASZA BREAKS FREE OF HER BONDS AND UNLEASHES HER VENGEANCE ON THE ORC NEKROS SKULLCRUSHER

She took on the guise of a noblewoman named Katrana Prestor and infiltrated Stormwind's royal court. Lady Prestor worked to tangle up the city's rebuilding efforts, and she meddled in local politics to keep the kingdom isolated from Lordaeron and the northlands.

Deathwing's son, Nefarian, chose to work from the shadows. He contacted the so-called "true Horde" in Blackrock Mountain, manipulating the orcs into allowing the black dragonflight to use the location as their new base. Nefarian established a hidden laboratory there, hoping to achieve his father's dream of rebuilding the black dragonflight. To that end, he conducted grotesque experiments with the blood of different dragonflights, much of which he harvested from living dragons.

FORGOTTEN OATHS

For ten thousand years, Deathwing's fellow Dragon Aspects had lived without the full measure of their power, and the sudden return of their strength was physically and mentally exhausting. As they acclimated to this change, they came to a troubling conclusion. For too long, the Aspects had withdrawn from the world. They could not afford to do so anymore. It was time to take up the charges that the titans had bestowed upon them once again.

Nozdormu, the Aspect of Time, returned to safeguarding the sanctity of the timeways. He was soon horrified to learn that a mysterious force was trying to change momentous events in history; the ripple effects of this could lead to the destruction of reality itself.

Ysera, the Aspect of Dreams, spent more time in the Emerald Dream, the mystical vision of an untouched, wild Azeroth that helped guide nature in the physical world. But with her returned power and senses, she noticed that darkness and despair were creeping into hidden parts of the Dream, in the form of corruption called the Emerald Nightmare.

Neither of them knew it, but both threats were sparked by the Old Gods. The touch of Yogg-Saron (and later, N'Zoth) was gradually corrupting the Emerald Dream, and the timeways were under assault by the infinite dragonflight. These shadowy creatures came from one of Azeroth's potential futures, though their identity remained a mystery to Nozdormu.

Malygos, the Aspect of Magic, was the least affected by the return of his power. During the War of the Ancients, Deathwing had slain most of his followers and driven the blue Dragon Aspect to the brink of madness. Malygos had hidden himself away in his lair, the Nexus, engulfed by grief and pain. With the return of his strength, his addled mind regained a sliver of clarity. It was not enough to completely break him out of his lethargy, but it did change him. For the first time in ages, Malygos began roaming the Nexus, surveying the state of his lair and his followers.

Alexstrasza, the Aspect of Life, needed time to recover after her traumatic ordeal. She and her flight sequestered themselves away to heal, both physically and emotionally.

Though most of the Dragon Aspects were eager to put the past behind them, it would be many years before they fully recovered.

The forces of evil would not wait for them to be ready.

CALL OF THE OLD GODS

During the Second War, betrayal had split the Horde in two. The orc warlock Gul'dan had broken away from the faction and sought out forbidden power in a place called the Tomb of Sargeras. He had taken two clans with him, the Stormreavers and the Twilight's Hammer, the latter led by the two-headed ogre mage Cho'gall. Gul'dan's treachery severely weakened the Horde, leading to its eventual defeat. In the end, the Legion would punish him for his greed.

When Gul'dan ventured into the Tomb of Sargeras, demons were waiting. They ripped apart the warlock and many of his followers and left their bones to rot in the massive tower.

Cho'gall and some of the Twilight's Hammer clan narrowly survived and fled from the tomb. They had no reason to continue their allegiance to the Horde or the Legion. In truth, they answered to different masters.

They answered to the Old Gods.

The Twilight's Hammer were unlike the Horde's other clans. They wielded shadow magic rather than fel, and they worshipped the powers of the Void. The Twilight's Hammer were fanatics who believed in the Hour of Twilight, a dark prophecy that foretold the end of all things. Cho'gall and his followers saw themselves as the agents of this apocalypse. The only questions were where and how it would happen.

On Azeroth, they found answers. Cho'gall and his followers heard the whispers of the Old Gods. These entities shared visions of the past with the Twilight's Hammer. They revealed how the world had once been—they revealed the Black Empire and its terrible glory.

Cho'gall and the Twilight's Hammer could help restore the Old Gods. They could break their shackles and build the Black Empire again. Its rise would herald the Hour of Twilight.

Cho'gall had once believed that the Horde was the key to bringing about the apocalypse. After Gul'dan's death in the Tomb of Sargeras, he realized that was not the case. The two-headed ogre abandoned the Horde and led his followers on a pilgrimage to Kalimdor. He sensed the presence of an Old God somewhere on the distant continent, and he was eager to meet the entity and bask in its terrible power.

It was a slow, dangerous journey from the Tomb of Sargeras to Kalimdor. The Twilight's Hammer gradually worked their way toward the southern edge of the continent, where dark whispers emanated from beneath the surface. Cho'gall did not know the land, and many threats lurked in Kalimdor. He meditated for months, submerging both of his minds in the chaotic will of the Old Gods. Though they were locked in enchanted prisons, millennia of inattention had allowed them to extend their influence across the world in small ways. The Old Gods urged Cho'gall onward, guiding him through the strange land and helping him avoid its dangers.

Cho'gall and his servants established a base in a cave system beneath the deserts of Tanaris. To the east lay Ahn'Qiraj, the prison that housed the Old God C'Thun. Cho'gall sensed he was close to his master. Unfortunately for Cho'gall, he would not reach the entity any time soon.

Before long, important members of the Twilight's Hammer began to disappear. Then others were found dead. At first, Cho'gall had suspected treason from within. And then he finally discovered the truth: he caught a glimpse of someone cutting the throat of one of his most trusted lieutenants.

It was the half-orc assassin named Garona.

Long ago, Gul'dan, Cho'gall, and their closest followers had ensorcelled Garona and used her as their personal weapon. During the Second War, she had escaped and broken free from their control. Garona harbored unending hatred for her former masters, and she had tracked Cho'gall across an ocean to seek her vengeance. The Twilight's Hammer bolstered their defenses and laid traps, but Garona had been studying the region for months. The cave complex was not their home; it was her hunting ground.

Night after night, new victims were found. Cho'gall was furious, but he had no choice. His clan fled the area and searched for a new place to continue their dark work.

NEW LEGACIES

Despite the machinations of the black dragonflight, the human kingdoms slowly returned to their old prosperity, even if their relationships with one another were not as strong as they had once been.

Varian Wrynn, the young prince who had escaped the Horde's destruction of Stormwind City in the First War, was now king, and he was widely considered to be a strong, fair, and visionary leader. He oversaw the rebuilding of Stormwind and married a noblewoman, Tiffin Ellerian. They had a son, and they named him Anduin in memory of the hero Anduin Lothar, the venerated commander who had perished in the Second War.

Grand Admiral Daelin Proudmoore, one of the commanders who had defeated the Horde at sea, still felt grief for the losses he had suffered in the Second War. He maintained order on the high seas with an iron fist and hunted down pirates and brigands who dared to prey on his territory. His young daughter, Jaina Proudmoore, grew weary of his darkened disposition and opted to receive her schooling in Dalaran. After several years, she began to study arcane magic with the Kirin Tor, and she eventually became an apprentice to the legendary archmage Antonidas.

King Terenas Menethil II of Lordaeron had a son named Arthas, and he saw that he was trained in the ways of warfare and righteousness. Arthas Menethil became a master swordsman under the tutelage of the dwarf Muradin Bronzebeard, Ironforge's ambassador to Lordaeron. The young man was also tutored in the ways of the Holy Light by the revered paladin Uther the Lightbringer. When the prince turned nineteen, he was inducted into the Order of the Silver Hand to become a paladin himself. Though he was headstrong and stubborn, he distinguished himself as a brave hero and never shirked even the most dangerous of tasks. When Amani trolls sent warbands to raid the borders of Quel'Thalas, an allied nation, Arthas was there to hunt them down and bring them to justice.

Arthas was often the center of attention among Lordaeron's nobility, especially when he courted Jaina Proudmoore. Their romance created rumors and gossip, but in the end, Jaina was committed to her arcane studies, and Arthas was focused on his future as king.

They parted ways to pursue their individual ambitions, but they never let go of their feelings for each other.

JAINA PROUDMOORE AND ARTHAS MENETHIL IN THE GARDENS OF LORDAERON'S CAPITAL

The War of the Spider

Far from the human nations, the Lich King was rapidly growing his power and building a truly terrifying army. Most of Northrend's inhabitants were easily corrupted by the plague of undeath, and his forces swelled in number.

But it wasn't long before the Lich King faced his first real test. An ancient race of insectoids called nerubians lived in Northrend, and they were monstrously fierce in battle. Their grand kingdom, Azjol-Nerub, stretched far beneath the frozen tundra. The nerubians were aware of the Lich King's presence, and they had no intention of allowing him to conquer them. Any attempts to spread the plague of undeath in their home were ruthlessly snuffed out by the nerubians' leader, a powerful warlord named Anub'arak.

The Lich King saw no way to subvert their defenses. So he settled on smashing the nerubians into rubble instead.

For years, the Lich King's undead army fought a war of attrition against the insectoids. Each one who fell was added to the Lich King's ranks, and when the end came, he was delighted to raise Anub'arak himself as a powerful undead minion. The former ruler was now a slave, and though he chafed at his leash, he could not free himself from it.

The Lich King was so impressed by the nerubians' resistance that he adopted their architectural style as his own. He infused their jagged ziggurats with magic, causing them to soar in the skies over Northrend. In time, these necropoli would become feared sights across Azeroth.

Now the Lich King was unopposed in Northrend. And yet, it was still not time to unleash the plague of undeath on the Eastern Kingdoms. Adding creatures like Anub'arak to his ranks had taught him the value of corrupting powerful minds. He would need such allies to complete the work ahead. Moreover, the Lich King secretly hoped that he could win these servants to his side and use them to break free of the Legion.

The Lich King spread his consciousness across the world, seeking individuals who would be tempted by the power he could offer. Several answered his call.

Kel'Thuzad
15 Years After the Dark Portal

One of the most powerful creatures who heard the Lich King's call was formerly a leader among Dalaran's ruling magocrats, the Kirin Tor. Kel'Thuzad had once been a respected and admired scholar of the arcane arts. In recent years, his studies had veered into the dark realm of necromancy—the manipulation of life and death.

His actions weren't simply frowned upon; they were expressly forbidden by laws almost as old as the Kirin Tor itself. He had been censured repeatedly, stripped of much of his formal power, and was on the verge of being exiled from Dalaran altogether.

Kel'Thuzad was enraged by what he saw as the Kirin Tor's closed-mindedness and outdated precepts. Azeroth had just been invaded by creatures from another world. Dalaran itself had been raided in the aftermath of the Second War. The Horde's death knights, undead warriors infused with necromantic power, had infiltrated the city. Kel'Thuzad had seen them firsthand. He had no intention of leaving that form of power unstudied, now that he knew what it could do.

The Lich King offered answers to all his questions, as well as access to the deepest secrets of the necromantic arts. He initially concealed his ties to the Legion, presenting himself as a being in command of his own destiny.

Kel'Thuzad was in awe of the entity. He abandoned his duties in Dalaran and made the journey to Northrend to witness the power of the Lich King. He saw the ruins of Azjol-Nerub; he met the conquered ruler Anub'arak; he even observed the terrors that lay within the corrupted ziggurat called Naxxramas.

It was more than he had bargained for. Kel'Thuzad briefly thought to escape, but the Lich King's servants made it *very* clear that the time for second thoughts had passed. Kel'Thuzad would serve the Lich King; the only choice left to him was whether he would do so alive or undead.

Kel'Thuzad was forced to crawl to the Frozen Throne in Icecrown to accept his "reward." The Lich King promised that loyalty would be repaid with power beyond imagining. He charged Kel'Thuzad to go to Lordaeron and gather an army of loyal followers. In time, they would be called on to spread the plague of undeath among the region's populace.

Kel'Thuzad obeyed. His reluctance fell away, and his desire to serve the Lich King grew. The power he had received was truly awe-inspiring.

When Kel'Thuzad arrived in Lordaeron, he did so as a holy man, preaching the hope of a new religion. He won over the lower classes with demagoguery, playing on their disillusionment with Lordaeron's government. He proclaimed that he could ease the pain of the downtrodden, give hope to the hopeless, and lead the destitute to eternal life. The lies came easily to him. He had seen the power of undeath. Now that he was bound to the Lich King, he no longer feared it. He even hungered for the day when he would cast off the shackles of life and ascend to a greater undead form.

For the rich, Kel'Thuzad took a different approach. He enticed nobles and landowners with offers of great power—and *immortality*—if they joined his cause. Some voiced concern about what seemed like a "people's movement" geared toward toppling the established order, but Kel'Thuzad eased their fears. He said the lower classes were no threat; they were simply a tool that the privileged could use to destroy their rivals and secure more wealth.

As the years passed, Kel'Thuzad recruited more and more people to his cause. Few truly understood the horrors that awaited them all. Only individuals whom he was certain he could turn to darkness learned the truth about the plague of undeath and what it would do to humanity.

In time, Kel'Thuzad's followers would become known as the Cult of the Damned.

The cult's headquarters were established in the catacombs beneath an ancient human fortress called Scholomance. There, Kel'Thuzad tutored his most loyal cultists in necromancy. The dark sorcerers quickly honed their craft. They conducted gruesome experiments, animating the skeletons dug up from beneath the fortress. Some necromancers hacked apart the unearthed corpses and used the pieces to create mindless undead giants called abominations.

While this work progressed, Kel'Thuzad occupied himself with the most important experiment. He had brought samples of the Lich King's plague of undeath from Northrend to Scholomance. He worked feverishly to create a strain of the disease that was both effective and subtle. He planned to spread the plague through Lordaeron's grain supplies, and he wanted its incubation period to be long enough that the humans would consume the tainted food before any symptoms surfaced, thus maximizing the number of victims.

After many long months, he succeeded.

KEL'THUZAD ARRIVES AT THE FROZEN THRONE

THRALL

South of Scholomance, the Alliance of Lordaeron continued funneling resources into its network of internment camps. Leadership over the prisons fell to a human noble named Aedelas Blackmoore, a distinguished veteran of the Second War.

Privately, Aedelas considered his position as warden of the internment camps to be an insult from the Alliance leadership. His father, Aedelyn Blackmoore, had become a pariah for committing treason against Lordaeron years earlier. Aedelas believed that the leaders still saw him as "the son of a traitor" and had burdened him with a thankless job that held no glory.

But Aedelas, like his father, was a clever military strategist. He had a secret weapon in his possession that he believed could restore his rightful position within the Alliance . . .

Just before the First War ended, Aedelas Blackmoore had stumbled across something astonishing. He had found a baby orc, alone and abandoned, lying in the snow next to his dead parents and some of the assassins who had killed them. Aedelas had resisted his instinct to slay the creature right then and there, instead deciding to raise the orc.

He named the orc "Thrall" and trained him to be a gladiator. Once Aedelas had determined that the orc would not simply be a dumb brute, he began to teach him strategy, philosophy, and the finer points of leading others into battle. He often put Thrall to the test, throwing him into fights against numerous opponents. Fighting pits were a common feature in the internment camps, and the guards would force the orc prisoners to face each other in bloody combat. Aedelas subjected Thrall to these gladiatorial arenas not just to improve his fighting skills; the man was a drunkard who liked to gamble on the outcomes of the matches. Thrall learned that his master was volatile, cruel, and occasionally brilliant.

Aedelas Blackmoore's strategic thinking was complex, bold, yet fatally flawed from drink. He saw the imprisoned orcs as a potential army, and he intended for Thrall to become their leader—while remaining loyal to his human master, of course. Aedelas planned to upend the Alliance and rule it himself, remaking the human kingdoms in his image. But his cruelty undermined any connection he might have had with the young orc. Thrall saw him not as a surrogate father but as an arrogant, brutal master who would never let him know freedom.

The one friend Thrall had during his enslavement was a human named Taretha Foxton, who regarded him as a younger brother. She secretly maintained correspondence with the orc, and when Thrall was on the verge of succumbing to despair, she helped him escape the internment camp.

Thrall evaded Aedelas Blackmoore's guards and found his way into the nearby wilderness, chasing rumors that a clan of orcs was still living there. He first encountered Grommash Hellscream and the remnants of the Warsongs, who recognized that this orphan was of the Frostwolf clan. They told him to travel to the Alterac Mountains, where the Frostwolves were known to roam.

When Thrall arrived, he found the Frostwolves and learned the truth about his parents, Durotan and Draka. They had stubbornly resisted the demonic corruption of the Horde, and they had paid for their defiance with their lives.

He also learned that he had little in common with the Frostwolves or the rest of the orcs on Azeroth. Free or imprisoned, they had lived their lives as *orcs*. Thrall had been raised as something less. Not a human, not even a despised orc. He had been groomed as a tool of conquest, nothing more.

To rejoin his people, he would need to discover who they were—and who *he* was.

AEDELAS BLACKMOORE AND HIS PRIZED SLAVE, THRALL, IN DURNHOLDE KEEP

LORD OF THE CLANS

Thrall spent time learning the basics of what it meant to be an honorable orc. Most of his race had abandoned their shamanic heritage when they embraced fel magic, but there was one among the Frostwolves who had returned to their roots. The elderly orc Drek'Thar had rekindled his connection with the elements, and he instructed Thrall in the ways of shamanism.

Thrall also learned from Orgrim Doomhammer. Meeting Thrall dredged up painful memories for the former warchief, but it put his heart at ease. Orgrim had been close friends with Thrall's parents, and he had believed that their son had died alongside them. His survival warmed the older orc's spirit. Orgrim taught Thrall how orcs fought and, more importantly, how they lived.

He might not have been raised as an orc, but Thrall's brutal upbringing had given him exactly what the Horde needed: a love of freedom, admiration for the nobility the clans had lost, and the desire to see them all made whole again.

Thrall's optimism and resilience reignited Orgrim's hopes of restoring the orcs' pride and honor. He made the young shaman his second-in-command. They joined with Grommash Hellscream and his Warsong clan, and they launched a campaign to free the orc prisoners from their internment camps. The lethargy that made the orcs submissive began to fade before the raw energy of Thrall's sense of purpose, and with each toppled camp, the new Horde grew bigger and stronger.

Orgrim Doomhammer fell in battle while liberating one of those camps, and with his last breaths, he declared that Thrall should carry on as the new warchief of the Horde. Thrall took up Doomhammer's eponymous weapon, his armor, and his responsibilities, and he sought to dismantle the entire system of internment in one fell swoop.

The Horde marched on Aedelas Blackmoore's fortress, Durnholde Keep. Thrall offered to parley peacefully. Aedelas responded by executing Taretha Foxton. Enraged, Thrall and the Horde stormed the keep, and in a bloody battle, Thrall personally struck down Aedelas.

With Durnholde conquered, the administration of the internment camps ended instantly. The new Horde had little trouble liberating the rest of the smaller, more isolated camps across Lordaeron. Thrall did not use his numbers to wage war against Lordaeron itself. Instead, he took his people across the Eastern Kingdoms in search of a place they could call home.

THE ALLIANCE SPLINTERS

The destruction of the internment camps proved to be the tipping point for many among the Alliance of Lordaeron. Lady Katrana Prestor made sure of it, speaking passionately to every person of noble birth she could reach. The orcs had all escaped. The money spent to imprison them had been wasted. What was the point of this faltering Alliance?

The high elves of Quel'Thalas were the first to leave the Alliance. The human nations of Gilneas and Stromgarde soon followed. They had always believed they were better off on their own, and the "incompetence" of Lordaeron only seemed to confirm it.

King Genn Greymane of Gilneas had an idea to stop the Horde—and any other enemies—from threatening his kingdom ever again. His nation was on a peninsula and surrounded on most sides by water. He formally cut off all military pacts with the Alliance, and he built the massive

THRALL HONORS ORGRIM DOOMHAMMER AT THE FALLEN ORC'S FUNERAL PYRE

TIRION FORDRING AND EITRIGG

The news that the Horde had re-formed had unexpected effects on human society. The initial reaction was fear, but those who encountered the orcs often reported that they were no longer the battle-hungry barbarians the Alliance had once fought.

One of these voices was Tirion Fordring, a paladin of the Silver Hand. He had encountered an old orc named Eitrigg, and Tirion believed that he was sincere in his desire to live in peace. Thus, the paladin stood against the humans who sought to kill the orc. This was considered treason, and Tirion was cast out of the Silver Hand for his crime. Despite this, Tirion found he still had access to the Holy Light, and so he knew he had done the right thing.

Eitrigg would go on to join Thrall's new Horde. Tirion would live alone, outside of human civilization, for years.

Greymane Wall to isolate his kingdom. It was clear that he had no interest in aiding the other nations. Gilneas was self-sufficient, and it needed little in the way of food or resources from the rest of the Alliance.

Several kingdoms made it known that they had no intention of letting the Alliance collapse. King Varian Wrynn of Stormwind, King Terenas Menethil II of Lordaeron, the Kirin Tor of Dalaran, Grand Admiral Daelin Proudmoore of Kul Tiras, King Magni Bronzebeard of Ironforge, and Gelbin Mekkatorque of Gnomeregan all reaffirmed their commitment to unity against whatever trials would come.

This did not please Lady Prestor at all. She had hoped the Alliance would disintegrate.

But if the nations would remain vigilant against external threats, Lady Prestor decided to inflame internal conflict wherever she could. Her secret meddling in the rebuilding of Stormwind City had left the nobility unsatisfied with the craftsmanship of the Stonemasons' Guild; meanwhile, the workers were enraged that the nobility were threatening to withhold payment for honest labor.

Lady Prestor played both sides, encouraging them to dig in their heels and never compromise, until the disagreements escalated into unrest. When the nobility announced that they would not be paying the Stonemasons' Guild for their work, riots erupted.

The queen of Stormwind, Tiffin Wrynn, was killed during the chaos.

King Varian Wrynn vowed to punish those responsible, and he cracked down hard on the rioters. The stonemasons fled the city and hid in the rural areas of Westfall until the situation settled down. Most of them had to stay in hiding, for they knew Varian's anger would never fade.

Their anger never vanished, either. Led by a gifted mason named Edwin VanCleef, and secretly supported by nobles like Lady Katrana Prestor, they formed the Defias Brotherhood. This order of bandits would continue its armed rebellion against Stormwind for years.

THE DARKNESS PREPARES

The Alliance had been diminished. Stormwind was struggling with internal conflict. The high elves and the humans of the Eastern Kingdoms no longer trusted one another.

The nations of the world were more vulnerable than they had been in years. Kil'jaeden finally whispered into the Lich King's ear that now was the perfect time to unleash the plague of undeath on Lordaeron.

The Lich King was ready. So were his servants. In recent years, Kel'Thuzad and the Cult of the Damned had spread their influence throughout Lordaeron's breadbasket, the Eastweald. The secret order held sway in many important locations, most notably in Andorhal. The city was the main agricultural distribution point in the region. Any grain that was tainted by the plague in Andorhal would eventually make its way to the far corners of the Eastweald.

Kel'Thuzad and his necromancers infused the city's granaries with the plague. Andorhal's citizens knew nothing of the danger lurking in their food supplies. Even many of the cultists were unaware of exactly what had been done. The grain showed no outward appearance of corruption. Only after it was consumed would the plague activate and run its course.

Merchants transported their lethal cargo along the usual trade routes, and innocent citizens consumed the newly arrived grain. Days passed before the first signs that something was wrong appeared in the towns and villages closest to Andorhal. There were complaints of fatigue and mild fevers, mostly from the young and the old. Then entire families became ill. Then entire villages.

None of the victims knew the dark source of their affliction, nor did they know that it was a precursor to the Legion's invasion.

Yet there was someone who did know what the demons were planning. His name was Medivh, and he had died years ago. As his spirit drifted beyond the borders of reality, he watched the plague slowly creep over the Eastweald like a dark tide. Medivh wanted nothing more than to warn the world of what was coming, but he had no way of communing with the people of Lordaeron.

There was only one person he could reach on Azeroth, someone with whom he shared a connection more powerful than magic.

His mother, Aegwynn.

FALLEN GUARDIANS
18 YEARS AFTER THE DARK PORTAL

Across the Great Sea, on Kalimdor's eastern shores, a solitary human wandered the land. Few knew her name. Fewer still knew of her extraordinary, tragic past. She was Aegwynn, one of the greatest Guardians of Tirisfal who had ever lived.

Long ago, Sargeras had dispatched an avatar infused with a portion of his spirit to Azeroth, hoping to draw Aegwynn into battle. She had met the challenge and faced the demon, its monstrous form wreathed in fire. In what had seemed like a momentous victory, Aegwynn had struck down her foe. The Guardian had not simply triumphed over a Legion agent. No, she had triumphed over the Legion's *ruler*.

Aegwynn never suspected Sargeras's true plans. Just before his avatar fell, he had transferred its spirit into the Guardian. A portion of Sargeras's own power—a portion of his very soul—now lurked within Azeroth's greatest defender.

When Aegwynn later gave birth to Medivh and passed on her Guardian powers to him, she also transferred Sargeras's spirit to her son. As the years wore on, the Legion's ruler imposed his will on the new Guardian and molded him into a weapon. He eventually used Medivh's immense power to create the Dark Portal and bring the orcish Horde into Azeroth. The terrible war that followed claimed thousands of lives.

Medivh was later slain, and his Guardian power was no longer a threat to Azeroth. But this thought gave Aegwynn little comfort. She blamed herself for everything Medivh had caused. The Horde's invasion. The carnage of the First and Second Wars. And most of all, she blamed herself for robbing her son of a fulfilling life, of a chance to reach his true potential as a force of good.

It was during these dark days that Aegwynn had a strange dream. In it, she saw Medivh dressed in a cloak lined with raven feathers. He told Aegwynn that he had a message for the world, and he pleaded for his mother to help bring him back to Azeroth. Aegwynn was initially suspicious of the dream, believing it to be the work of the Legion. But some part of her knew otherwise. She felt Medivh's soul drifting beyond the veil of reality, and she sensed that it was free of Sargeras's touch. This was her chance to make up for her failures, to both Azeroth and her son.

Aegwynn called on what little magical power she had left and sought out Medivh's spirit. Months passed without results, but she stubbornly refused to give up. She searched for magical artifacts to help her with the summoning. The quest to bring her son into the world became an obsession. The work was hard, but it was also fulfilling. For the first time in years, Aegwynn had a purpose. She felt like her old self again.

Aegwynn finally succeeded in summoning Medivh to Azeroth. A ghostly form took shape before her. Just like in her dream, he wore a robe lined with raven feathers. The moment Aegwynn looked her son in the eyes, she knew her intuitions had been right: Medivh was free of Sargeras's influence.

The reunion between mother and son was a somber affair. Aegwynn apologized for everything that had happened, and Medivh was quick to forgive her. He knew they were both victims of Sargeras. He also knew that now was not the time to dwell on the past.

Medivh told Aegwynn that while his spirit was wandering beyond the physical realm, he had witnessed many things. His vast power had allowed him to glimpse into the Twisting Nether and touch the minds of the Legion's demons. From them, he had learned of the Lich King and the plague of undeath. He had also learned what the Legion was planning after this affliction had weakened the world.

In the War of the Ancients, the Legion had tried harnessing a fount of magic called the Well of Eternity to bring the demons to Azeroth. By using its energies, they had nearly created a gateway into the world for Sargeras himself. Their plans had failed, and the Well of Eternity had been destroyed. However, another fount of magic existed. This second Well of Eternity was nestled atop Mount Hyjal, protected by the enormous World Tree Nordrassil. With the fount, the Legion could finish what it had started—it could create a portal through which Sargeras and the full might of his armies could invade Azeroth.

Aegwynn urged her son to use his Guardian powers against the Legion, but Medivh had other ideas. His corruption had taught him the dangers of relying on a single Guardian to protect the world. The possibility of that individual being turned to evil was too great. No, the age of Guardians was over. If the world's kingdoms were to survive the coming storm, they would have to unite and protect Azeroth themselves.

Medivh vowed to act as a catalyst for unity. He would travel the world and warn its inhabitants of the Legion's plans, unifying them in purpose.

Aegwynn longed to join her son's quest, but she was in no condition to do so. The summoning spell had pushed her to the edge of death. In the moments after the spell had finished, her body had begun to age and become frail. It would take her years to recover. Even then, she would never be as youthful or as powerful as she had once been.

Medivh was on his own, and time was against him. The plague of undeath was enveloping Lordaeron.

FROST AND SHADOW

In Northrend, the Lich King brooded over his enslavement. He dreamed of a day when he would make the undead *his* servants and turn them against the Legion. Yet the time for that was not right. The plague had only begun to take root in Lordaeron.

For now, the Lich King focused his attention on other things. Trapped in the Frozen Throne, he needed a way to extend his will to the outside world. He had full control over undead creatures, but their strength came in numbers. Individually, they were weak, mindless things. There was Kel'Thuzad, but the necromancer served a very specific purpose, leading the Cult of the Damned. The Lich King sought something else—something more. A mighty champion who would act as his direct surrogate beyond the Frozen Throne.

The Lich King did not yet know who this surrogate would be, but he did know how he would create his servant. The key lay within his icy prison. *Frostmourne*. It was a fearsome weapon, capable of consuming souls. If someone were to take up the blade, it would shackle them to the Lich King's will.

Yet the dreadlords would never allow the Lich King to create this new servant on his own. He had to make the demons believe it was in the Legion's best interest.

Over the years, the Lich King had discovered what the dreadlords feared most: Kil'jaeden. If the plague failed, the demon lord would punish them. The Lich King used this knowledge to his advantage. He played on the dreadlords' fears and gradually convinced them that finding other mortal champions like Kel'Thuzad was the key to victory. The Lich King's overtures were subtle and strategic; he made the demons believe that locating a new servant and arming them with Frostmourne was *their* idea.

Only Kel'Thuzad was privy to the Lich King's true intentions. The entity had revealed to the necromancer that the Legion was behind the plague of undeath, but Kel'Thuzad remained firm in his allegiance. He secretly promised to rebel against the demons in the future.

With the dreadlords' approval, the Lich King moved forward with his plan. He channeled his power within the Frozen Throne and broke away a chunk of ice containing Frostmourne. The blade fell to the base of Icecrown Glacier, where it would await its victim.

All that remained was for the Lich King to find him.

THE LANDS OF AZEROTH
BEFORE THE THIRD WAR

Icecrown Citadel

NORTHREND

Azjol-Nerub

Mount Hyjal

KALIMDOR

THE MAELSTROM

The Veiled Sea

TANARIS

The South Sea

Ahn'Qiraj

PANDARIA

Ulduar

Wyrmrest Temple

The North Sea

QUEL'THALAS

AMANI
EMPIRE

LORDAERON   *Andorhal*

Scholomance

THE BROKEN
ISLES   *Alterac Mountains*

Durnholde Keep

GILNEAS

Grim Batol

Tomb of Sargeras

Ironforge

Gnomeregan   EASTERN
KUL TIRAS   KINGDOMS

Blackrock Mountain

The Great Sea

Stormwind City   The
Forbidding
Sea

CHAPTER II

THE THIRD WAR

CHAPTER II
THE THIRD WAR

THE SCOURGE OF LORDAERON

In Lordaeron, the plague of undeath continued to spread. Healing salves and potions had little effect on the disease. Not even local priests could ease the victims' suffering with holy magic unless they treated the infection in its earliest stages. Reports of the plague soon reached Lordaeron's capital, but no one knew what to make of them. Disease was not rare, especially in the wake of the Second War. Lordaeron's population had suffered through many bouts of famine and sickness.

King Terenas Menethil II demanded more information before he would commit resources to investigating the plague. He was loath to send soldiers to quarantine villages when there were liberated orcs on the loose in other areas of the kingdom. In his eyes, the Horde was the more immediate danger.

The plague soon claimed its first lives in Lordaeron. Friends and family grieved over the victims, unaware that it would not be the last time they would see their loved ones. Had death been the end, it would have been a mercy. The number of deaths increased, and reports of strange occurrences spread to the far corners of Lordaeron. Some said that the bodies of plague victims were disappearing overnight. Others claimed that the dead were rising from their graves as mindless walking corpses.

Though these tales seemed outlandish, they were true. The final symptom of the plague was taking effect. Victims were rising into undeath as zombies, enslaved to the Lich King's will.

Kel'Thuzad watched the Eastweald's doom unfold with cold approval. He believed he had sacrificed more than most to bring the Lich King's grand designs to fruition. A fearsome army was forming before his eyes, one composed of undead minions and the Cult of the Damned's fanatical members. Kel'Thuzad named this force the Scourge, for it would act as the flail with which the Lich King would scour the whole of Lordaeron and bring humanity to its knees.

In the months ahead, the name *Scourge* would come to define all who served the Lich King.

OVERLEAF: ARCHIMONDE ASSAULTS NORDRASSIL AT THE BATTLE OF MOUNT HYJAL

The Prophet's Warning

The plague of undeath was spreading much faster than Medivh had anticipated. Though it was difficult to admit, he knew that he could not save those who had contracted the disease. There was no time. The true threat to Azeroth was the Legion's plan to harness the second Well of Eternity. Medivh needed to focus every resource he could muster on protecting the fount of power, even if it meant abandoning Lordaeron to the ravages of the plague.

Medivh decided to gather as many of Lordaeron's unaffected citizens as possible and guide them to the second Well of Eternity. He channeled his lingering Guardian powers and reached out to influential individuals across the region. Some he visited in dreams, appearing as a raven. Others he met in person, taking on the form of a hooded figure known only as "the Prophet." To all, he offered a dire warning: they must depart the Eastern Kingdoms and journey west to the ancient lands of Kalimdor, or else the entire world would fall to ruin. Medivh never revealed his true identity. Those who recognized his name would know him as a villain, the sinister mage who had brought the Horde to Azeroth.

Two of the most influential humans Medivh approached were Lordaeron's king, Terenas Menethil II, and the ruler of Dalaran, Archmage Antonidas. Neither of them paid heed to the Prophet's warning.

For Terenas II, the liberated orcs remained a constant thorn in his side. The other Alliance nations were up in arms about the prospect of their great enemies freely roaming the countryside. Terenas had dispatched his military forces, including the holy paladins, to defeat the orcs. He considered Medivh's words little more than the ravings of a madman.

Antonidas had other reasons for dismissing Medivh. He and his magi had learned of the mysterious plague spreading across the Eastweald. Unlike Terenas, they were deeply concerned about reports of this mounting epidemic. Antonidas theorized that the plague was magical in nature, but only evidence could confirm his beliefs. He sent his most promising student, the sorceress Jaina Proudmoore, to observe and gather information about the outbreak.

Medivh had little success with the humans, but he did find hope among the orcs. The irony wasn't lost on the former Guardian. The bloodthirsty savages who had invaded Azeroth and almost ruined the world might be the very creatures who would save it from destruction.

Chasing Visions

The new Horde faced an uncertain future.

Warchief Thrall had liberated many of his people from the internment camps, but they were without a home. They lived as nomads, seeking out other orcs in Lordaeron and the surrounding lands while constantly moving to avoid human military forces. Another war with the Alliance seemed all but inevitable.

The orcs looked to Thrall for answers, but he had none. Worry gnawed at his thoughts, and nightmares plagued his sleep. Night after night, he envisioned the orcs falling to the Alliance in a brutal battle. He saw his people once again herded into prison camps and left to waste away.

It was in this time of uncertainty that Medivh visited Thrall. He told the orc of a dark storm approaching Azeroth, a demonic invasion that would reduce *all* civilizations to ash. Medivh said that the only way for Thrall to stop the Burning Legion was to set out across the Great Sea, to a land known as Kalimdor.

The encounter with Medivh deeply troubled Thrall. Though he was too young to remember when the Legion had enslaved his people, he knew of demons. Older orcs like Orgrim Doomhammer and Grommash Hellscream had told him stories about how the Legion had nearly destroyed their race. Thrall feared that if he did not make a stand against the demons, the orcs might once again fall into slavery or suffer an even worse fate.

But Thrall was hesitant to put his trust in a stranger. He consulted the elemental spirits of fire, earth, air, and water for answers. Their response was urgent and immediate: *trust the stranger*. For a shaman like Thrall, that was all the assurance he needed.

Thrall hid nothing from his people. He told them of the journey that lay ahead and the enemy they would face. Many orcs were wary of embarking into the unknown, but they trusted their warchief. If not for him, they would all still be languishing in prison camps.

Thrall rallied the new Horde and set out to find a way across the sea.

RAVAGES OF THE PLAGUE

Though the Horde was still roaming Lordaeron's countryside, Terenas Menethil could no longer ignore the plague. He knew that the Kirin Tor was sending the sorceress Jaina Proudmoore to investigate the disease, and he thought it would be wise to aid her. The king dispatched envoys led by his own son, Arthas Menethil. They would accompany Jaina and search for the plague's source together. With any luck, they would find a way to stop the disease from spreading further.

Despite the grim circumstances, Arthas and Jaina looked forward to spending time together. They had ended their romantic relationship, but they still harbored feelings for each other. They didn't yet know that this quest would destroy what remained of their youthful innocence and change them both forever.

Crossing into the Eastweald was like stepping through a portal into another world. Gone was the tranquility that the region had once enjoyed. A shadow had crept over the land, bringing fear and paranoia. Arthas was heartbroken by the suffering he witnessed. These were his people, and protecting them was his responsibility. If he failed, what kind of ruler would that make him? He vowed to do whatever he could to deliver his people from doom.

From the outset, Arthas had little success. He called on his powers to cleanse the plague-stricken victims he met, but the Holy Light was largely ineffective and unreliable. For many of these poor souls, Arthas could do little else but offer words of reassurance that he would end the plague.

As time passed, Arthas and Jaina unraveled one mystery after another concerning the plague, and each revelation was more troubling than the last. The affliction was being transmitted across the region through grain shipments from Andorhal. Even more unsettling was the discovery that the plague didn't simply kill its victims; it raised them into undeath and turned them into shambling corpses.

Arthas and Jaina saw these monstrosities firsthand. They were forced to fight their way through the tide of walking corpses that surged over the countryside.

None of this was happening by chance. A human cult led by Kel'Thuzad was responsible for the plague's spread, and they had an army of undead at their command. An army called the Scourge.

Discovering that humans were behind the plague stoked the fires of Arthas's rage. He channeled his fury into the quest to hunt down Kel'Thuzad and his followers, eager to make them pay for the innocent lives they had destroyed.

In Andorhal, Arthas Menethil would have his chance.

THE SHADOW PATH

Through the eyes of his Scourge minions, the Lich King had been watching Arthas. The young human intrigued him. He was a natural leader, charismatic and confident. Judging by the mounds of undead the prince left in his wake, the Lich King knew that Arthas Menethil was also a gifted fighter and tactician. Most importantly, his anger and desperation were slowly consuming his mind.

Once again, the Lich King subtly manipulated the dreadlords and drew their attention to Arthas. They saw him as the perfect champion to corrupt, but luring him to Frostmourne in Northrend would be no easy task. The young human had just started down his path of self-destruction. The Lich King and the dreadlords would need to guide him the rest of the way.

The demons crafted a plan based on the Lich King's advice. They commanded Kel'Thuzad to face Arthas in battle and reveal that he was merely a servant of a higher power: the dreadlord Mal'Ganis, who lurked in the holy city of Stratholme. It wouldn't be enough for Kel'Thuzad to tell Arthas this information; he would need to give his life in the process. Only with the necromancer dead would the prince then focus his attention on reaching Stratholme and vanquishing Mal'Ganis.

Stratholme was chosen for specific reasons. It was heavily populated, and it was the region's most important city, strategically and economically. It was also a holy site, the birthplace of the paladin order. If Stratholme fell to the plague and became overrun by undead, it would be disastrous. Lordaeron would lose control of the Eastweald.

When Arthas arrived in Andorhal, Kel'Thuzad did not flee. He knew the Lich King would raise him as an undead creature more powerful than he could imagine. He faced the prince in battle and revealed Mal'Ganis's presence in Stratholme.

Just as planned, Arthas Menethil unleashed his fury on Kel'Thuzad and crushed the life from the necromancer. He then set out to save Stratholme, even more desperate and unhinged than before.

THE CULLING OF STRATHOLME

As the days wore on, Jaina Proudmoore noticed a change in Arthas Menethil. Hate dominated his thoughts. He pushed Jaina and his soldiers to the breaking point, forcing them onward and giving them little time to rest. Though the sorceress wanted to stop the plague just as much as Arthas did, she feared that the quest was taking a heavy toll on his psyche.

She urged him to show restraint, but her words fell on deaf ears. The prince would not rest until his people were safe.

En route to Stratholme, Arthas and Jaina were joined by the one person in Lordaeron who had the power to talk some sense into the prince: Uther the Lightbringer.

Uther was a renowned paladin and a founding member of the Order of the Silver Hand. At King Terenas Menethil II's behest, he had trained Arthas to become a holy warrior. Uther demanded much of the prince, but only because he saw greatness in the boy. As time passed, he'd even begun to see him as a son, and he considered Arthas's well-being his responsibility.

When Uther joined Arthas on his quest, he sensed that something was amiss with the young paladin, but it did not concern him. He knew the prince could be headstrong at times. Arthas simply wanted to do what was best for his people, and Uther believed he would come to his senses.

At Stratholme, Uther discovered how wrong he was. The citizens had already received and consumed tainted grain from Andorhal. Their fate was sealed. It was only a matter of time before the plague transformed them into mindless undead.

Arthas believed there was only one way to prevent Stratholme from becoming a bastion of the Scourge. He ordered his comrades to purge the entire city before its inhabitants succumbed. For Arthas, this was as much an act of mercy as it was a strategic decision. If the people of Stratholme knew they were about to turn into undead monsters that would attack everything and everyone they had loved in life, what would they prefer? If Arthas had contracted the plague, he would rather die a clean death as a free-willed human than allow the affliction to raise him from the grave as a walking corpse.

Some of the prince's allies obeyed his order. Many did not. Uther and the paladins under his command were disgusted at the thought of killing innocents. They would take no part. Their disobedience only pushed Arthas to even darker extremes. He turned his back on the other paladins, calling their refusal an act of treason.

Arthas called on Jaina to join him, but she also refused. She could not bear to see the prince commit such an atrocity. Along with Uther and the paladins, she left the prince to his grim work.

Arthas and his loyalists swept through Stratholme, and the killing commenced. Fire engulfed the city, and a storm of ash and ember billowed through the streets. Screams cut like daggers through the air. The blood of innocents ran thick along the cobblestones.

Amid the carnage, Arthas found Mal'Ganis. The dreadlord was eager to destroy the human, but that was not his purpose. He issued a challenge to the prince: come to Northrend and face him in a *true* battle. Then Mal'Ganis shrouded himself in magic and vanished from the city.

Arthas wasted no time in following. He believed if he could vanquish the dreadlord, he could shatter the Scourge and stop the plague of undeath forever. While fire still licked at the ruins of Stratholme, he gathered his followers and set sail for the frozen continent of Northrend.

Days later, Jaina and Uther returned to Stratholme. Much of the city was burned to a husk. Bodies littered the streets. It was even worse than what they had expected.

PRINCE ARTHAS MENETHIL IN STRATHOLME

As she looked over the ruins, Jaina cursed herself for not doing something to prevent the carnage. She could have used her magic to restrain Arthas, but she didn't. Her inaction had allowed the prince to commit an act that would haunt him for the rest of his days. And her own regret would weigh on Jaina in the years ahead.

Jaina Proudmoore and Uther the Lightbringer went their separate ways. The paladin journeyed to Lordaeron's capital to inform King Terenas Menethil II of what his son had done. Meanwhile, Jaina set out for Dalaran to report back to Antonidas about the plague.

Neither Jaina nor Uther knew that the next time they encountered Arthas Menethil, the prince they had known and cared for would be gone.

THE CURSED BLADE

The Culling of Stratholme was the point of no return for Prince Arthas Menethil. His heart had darkened, and his sanity was unraveling. He was almost ready to become the Lich King's greatest servant. *Almost.*

First, Arthas needed to find the cursed runeblade Frostmourne. The Scourge couldn't simply lead him to it. That would make the prince suspicious.

The Lich King turned his attention to dwarf explorers who were trekking across Northrend. Led by the great warrior Muradin Bronzebeard, they had come from the mountain city of Ironforge in search of ancient artifacts. During Arthas's youth, Muradin had served as ambassador to Lordaeron, and he had trained the human in martial combat. He would be the perfect messenger to inform Arthas of Frostmourne.

With the Lich King's guidance, Mal'Ganis and the other dreadlords manipulated the dwarves. The demons secretly planted clues about Frostmourne and its location in the explorers' encampment, including maps and ancient histories that spoke of a legendary runeblade. None of the dwarves could remember where this information had come from. They assumed that they hadn't noticed it before. The runeblade intrigued Muradin, and the dwarves set out to find it.

Meanwhile, Arthas and his soldiers made landfall in a region of Northrend called the Howling Fjord. The wintry conditions were harsh, and the Scourge were mysteriously evasive—a far departure from their aggressive tactics in Lordaeron.

The Lich King used the Scourge to attack Muradin Bronzebeard and herd him toward Arthas. When the dwarf and the prince finally crossed paths, it seemed like nothing more than a chance meeting, and a fortuitous one at that. Muradin told Arthas of his purpose in Northrend, and of his more recent quest to find Frostmourne. The story of the blade enticed the prince. It could prove useful in the fight against Mal'Ganis.

Arthas's hopes swelled, only to be crushed by news from Lordaeron. A royal emissary tracked down the prince and delivered orders from King Terenas: Arthas and his soldiers were to return to Lordaeron immediately. As much as the prince's loyalists wanted to stay by his side, disobeying the king's command would amount to treason.

Arthas knew that if he turned back now, he might never have another opportunity to find Mal'Ganis. He saw only one recourse. In secret, he burned his own ships. Every one of them. None of his soldiers knew that their prince was responsible for it. They had no choice but to remain in Northrend, at least until they could construct more vessels.

With the prince and his forces trapped, Mal'Ganis and the Scourge attacked en masse. The undead came in numbers Arthas had never seen before, and they threatened to overwhelm his soldiers. His only hope was to seek out another power.

Frostmourne.

As the prince's forces held the Scourge at bay, Arthas and Muradin tracked the runeblade to a small cavern. There, suspended within a block of gleaming ice, hung the sword. The blade radiated not only power but also something ominous and otherworldly. Muradin urged Arthas to leave Frostmourne be, but the prince could not. He had come too far to turn back now.

The Lich King sensed Arthas's determination. Energy burst out from Frostmourne, shattering its icy prison in a violent explosion. Jagged shards shot across the cavern, one of which impaled Muradin and struck him down.

Arthas rushed to heal his friend. Though the Holy Light had been fickle and unreliable in the Eastweald, it answered the prince's call. The scintillating energy coursed over Arthas and flared bright at his fingertips. All he needed to do was embrace it.

But he did not. His thoughts turned to Frostmourne and its promise of salvation. The blade held *true* power. *It* was the key to defeating Mal'Ganis, not the Light. After all, what good had the prince's holy power done him back in the Eastweald? It hadn't stopped the undead. It hadn't saved all those innocents whom Arthas had watched die before his eyes.

In that moment, Arthas Menethil forever turned his back on the Light and took hold of Frostmourne. Its terrible power surged through him. It chilled his veins to ice. It devoured his soul.

Through Frostmourne, the Lich King could now speak in Arthas's mind and guide his actions. He did not yet transform the prince into his slave. For the time being, he allowed Arthas to believe that he was in control of his own fate.

Arthas had one last act to perform before he took his place among the Scourge.

MURADIN'S FATE

Despite what Arthas Menethil believed, the ice shard that struck Muradin Bronzebeard didn't kill him. It had only knocked him unconscious.

After Arthas left the cavern, Muradin awoke. His wounds were grave, and he had no memory of who he was or why he had come to Northrend. Muradin wandered the snowy wastes on the verge of collapse. He would have died if not for the intervention of the Frostborn, a faction of dwarves who called Northrend home.

The Frostborn discovered the injured dwarf and later nursed him back to health. It would be many years before Muradin recovered his memories and returned to Ironforge.

CHAMPION OF THE DAMNED

Arthas Menethil returned to his base camp just as the Scourge were closing in around his forces. The Lich King's voice whispered from Frostmourne, urging the prince to feed the blade. And feed it he did. Arthas carved through the undead with the fury of a winter storm.

The humans rejoiced at the sight of their prince and his newfound power. No one knew how high a price he had paid for it.

Arthas didn't give his troops a chance to rest. The Lich King told him that Mal'Ganis was somewhere among the undead. The prince believed that if he could find the dreadlord—*if he could kill him*—then he would save Lordaeron. Arthas rallied his soldiers and launched a counterattack. Casualties soared among the humans, but the prince ignored the losses. He forged onward until he had found Mal'Ganis.

The Lich King did not command Arthas to stand down. This was the entity's first step toward freedom, a chance to eliminate one of his most powerful Legion handlers. The Lich King issued a single order through Frostmourne. Arthas plunged the runeblade into the dreadlord and vanquished his foe.

The remaining Scourge scattered into the wastes. The human survivors celebrated the victory, but Arthas did not join them. He wandered alone into Northrend's frigid wilds, where the Lich King stripped away the last shreds of his humanity. Dark knowledge flared through the prince's mind, and he learned to wield necromantic powers just as his new master did.

Days later, Arthas returned to his camp. His skin had become deathly pale, and his hair had turned bone white. Gone was the prince of Lordaeron. In his place stood something else. The first of the Lich King's newest undead creations: death knights.

Arthas Menethil slaughtered his followers, and Frostmourne feasted on their souls. Some arose from death as simple Scourge minions like those that roamed the Eastweald. Others were granted a different fate. Arthas transformed them into fearsome death knights like himself.

The prince didn't linger in Northrend. He rallied the rest of the Scourge to his side and prepared to return to Lordaeron.

It was time to go home.

THE DEATH KNIGHTS

The Lich King's death knights shared the same name as the infamous undead soldiers who had served the Horde in the Second War. They had much in common, such as command over necromantic magic. Yet their origins were far different. Gul'dan had forged the first generation of death knights by fusing the spirits of fallen orc warlocks to the decomposing bodies of human knights.

THE FATE OF MAL'GANIS

Mal'Ganis's death infuriated the other dreadlords, but they did not punish the Lich King. The entity convinced the demons that the slaying was an unfortunate accident. Arthas Menethil had not been under his full control yet. Now he was, and the Lich King promised that the death knight would never again raise a hand against the dreadlords.

As far as Arthas and the Lich King knew, Mal'Ganis had perished. Such was not the case. When the dreadlords crafted Frostmourne, they had shielded themselves from its power. The blade had not devoured Mal'Ganis's soul; it had simply hurled it back into the Twisting Nether. In time, the dreadlord would be reborn into a new body.

THE DARKSPEARS

Far from Northrend, Thrall and the new Horde searched for a way across the Great Sea. The orcs had used ships in the Second War, but their fleet had long since vanished beneath the waves. Building new vessels would require time and resources that the Horde didn't have. Their only option was to steal ships.

Southshore was the perfect target. Its port boasted a number of large galleons, and it was sparsely defended. Under cover of night, the Horde stormed into the town, but the orcs did not massacre its inhabitants. Wanton slaughter was the way of the *old* Horde. With little blood spilled, the Horde commandeered the Alliance ships and set sail.

Word of the theft reached Grand Admiral Daelin Proudmoore, commander of the Alliance navy. He vowed to hunt down the orcs, and he had no intention of capturing them alive.

Daelin Proudmoore and his navy were masters of the open water. They quickly tracked down Thrall and were poised to devastate the Horde fleet, but fate had other plans. A monstrous storm boiled across the sky, and the seas churned in angry unrest. The tempest battered the Horde and Alliance ships, tossing the vessels about as if they were little more than toys.

Thrall and his people took refuge on a nearby chain of islands. The clouds eventually parted and the seas calmed. The Alliance navy was nowhere in sight, but that did little to ease Thrall's anxiety. A large portion of his fleet had vanished in the storm, including Grommash Hellscream and the bulk of his Warsong orcs. Whether they were dead or alive, Thrall did not know. Of more immediate concern was the condition of the ships the warchief still had. The storm had damaged the vessels, and the orcs would need to repair them before continuing west.

The days ahead were not easy for Thrall and his people. They found themselves fighting enemies old and new. The storm had blown part of Daelin Proudmoore's fleet to the islands, and humans had fanned out across their shores. Moreover, the caverns beneath the isles were home to a naga sorceress known as Zar'jira. The hateful serpentine creature commanded an army of primitive fishlike beings called murlocs.

But Thrall did not face these dangers alone. He forged an unexpected alliance with another race that called the islands home: the Darkspear trolls.

The Darkspears had been part of the fragmented Gurubashi empire in Stranglethorn Vale. For centuries, near constant famine and warfare had plagued the trolls. The Darkspears were not savage and ruthless like the other tribes, and that made them easy targets. They had suffered immense cruelty at the hands of their fellow Gurubashi before finally abandoning Stranglethorn. The Darkspears sailed west and settled on a remote string of islands.

Thrall felt an immediate kinship with the Darkspears and their wise and elderly chieftain, Sen'jin. He sensed the goodness in their hearts, and he saw many similarities between his people and the trolls. They had both suffered oppression, and they were both in need of help to survive in a world that seemed determined to eradicate them.

The Horde and the Darkspears fought shoulder to shoulder on two fronts: one against the humans, the other against Zar'jira and her scaly followers. Thrall and his allies prevailed, but not without great cost. Blood was spilled on all sides. Among the fallen was Sen'jin.

In honor of the late chieftain, Thrall invited the Darkspears into the Horde. The trolls accepted, seeing little future on their war-torn island home.

After repairing their vessels, the orcs continued across the Great Sea. Many Darkspear trolls joined them, but others remained behind for the time being. Leadership of the tribe fell to Sen'jin's son, a young shadow hunter named Vol'jin. He rallied what was left of his people and gathered as many supplies as he could. Then he struck out west after the Horde, hoping against hope that he and his tribe would find peace in the distant lands of Kalimdor.

HEIR TO THE THRONE

While Thrall and his Horde were sailing the Great Sea, the undead mysteriously pulled back from the Eastweald and vanished from sight. The citizenry didn't know the cause, but they had theories. Most humans believed that their beloved prince had succeeded in his quest to destroy the Scourge in Northrend.

In truth, the Lich King had ordered the Scourge to retreat in preparation for Arthas's homecoming. If the people believed their prince had defeated the undead, they would welcome him into Lordaeron's capital as a triumphant hero. By the time anyone suspected that something was amiss with Arthas, it would be too late.

Arthas Menethil soon arrived in his homeland with an army at his back. He had brought more than his undead soldiers and death knights on the voyage to Lordaeron. His forces included all manner of Scourge monstrosities: human necromancers, the lumbering patchwork creatures called abominations, undead spiderlike crypt fiends, winged gargoyles, and even frost wyrms, dragons raised into undeath and imbued with icy magic.

The prince ordered his army to stay hidden for the time being. Only a handful of death knights accompanied him on his march to the capital. To hide their deathly pale skin and gaunt features, they shrouded themselves in long hooded cloaks.

Word of Arthas's approach spread across Lordaeron. His presence seemed to confirm what many people had hoped: the prince had saved them from the Scourge.

Hundreds of citizens gathered in the capital to welcome Arthas. The bells tolled at his arrival, and the adoring crowds showered his entourage with rose petals. But Arthas ignored the masses. In eerie silence, he marched to the throne room, where his father eagerly awaited him.

At the foot of the throne, Arthas and his father reunited, but there was no embrace. No tears of joy. Frostmourne's hunger stirred, and Arthas indulged it with Terenas Menethil's soul.

Before the city even knew the king was dead, Arthas and his death knights rampaged through the streets. So many well-wishers had come to the capital that the overcrowding quickly led to chaos and confusion. The citizens had no chance against Arthas and his servants. Simultaneously, the Scourge emerged from hiding across Lordaeron and launched attacks against the living.

The Third War had begun in earnest.

The other Alliance nations could hardly believe the news coming out of Lordaeron. None of them had ever imagined that such a nightmare scenario could come to pass. Most were unprepared to deal with it, but that didn't stop them from trying. Magi from Dalaran, dwarves from Ironforge and Aerie Peak, gnomes from Gnomeregan, and soldiers from neighboring human kingdoms converged on Lordaeron to vanquish the Scourge. Even Quel'Thalas, which had cut its ties to the Alliance, dispatched high elf priests to help defeat the undead.

But nothing could stand against the Scourge. The undead were more than just an army of mindless zombies. Under the Lich King's command, every creature had a purpose. Necromancers empowered their allies with dark magic and reanimated the corpses of fallen enemies. Abominations trampled over Alliance soldiers like walking siege engines. The crypt fiends burrowed beneath the ground and ambushed their unsuspecting foes. Gargoyles and frost wyrms grappled with the Alliance's gryphon riders and other aerial support.

By far, Arthas and his fellow death knights were the Scourge's most effective weapons. They were skilled in physical combat as well as in necromancy. One death knight could turn the tide of battle in the Scourge's favor and singlehandedly lay waste to countless Alliance soldiers.

And that was exactly what Arthas did. Lordaeron was his home, and he knew the terrain. His years of martial and paladin training also gave him insight into the Alliance's tactics.

In time, he used this knowledge to seize the kingdom. Small pockets of Alliance resistance remained, but they were little more than stubborn holdouts.

Lordaeron belonged to the Scourge.

THE INVASION OF GNOMEREGAN

Though all the Alliance races had sent soldiers to aid Lordaeron, one was largely absent from the fighting: the gnomes.

The gnomes were a highly intelligent people, renowned for their skills in science and engineering. They supplied the Alliance with its most advanced weaponry and war machines.

When the Third War was under way, the gnomes dispatched these armaments to Lordaeron, but they offered little in the way of soldiers. This came as something of a mystery to the other Alliance nations. Some members of the faction even questioned the gnomes' loyalty.

What the rest of the Alliance didn't know was that Gnomeregan was under siege—not by the Scourge but by brutish creatures called troggs.

Troggs had emerged as a threat only in recent times. For thousands of years, they had slept in the deep, dark reaches of an ancient fortress called Uldaman. They would have kept slumbering forever if not for a chance encounter with dwarves from Ironforge.

The dwarves had delved into Uldaman to gather artifacts and knowledge, and they inadvertently woke the monsters that slept in its belly. The troggs brutally slaughtered the explorers with glee. The survivors scrambled out of Uldaman in terror and fled back to Ironforge. The dwarves were relieved to find that the troggs didn't follow them. Their observation was only partially correct.

The troggs weren't hunting them on the surface; they were hunting them from *below*.

Most of the troggs loathed traveling aboveground, and they used their jagged claws to dig through the earth and carve out tunnels. As they neared their prey in Ironforge, strange noises caught their attention. Something unnatural. Something artificial.

What the troggs heard were the great factories in the heart of Gnomeregan, the gnomes' wondrous capital. The churning of machines and the grinding of gears were an irresistible lure for the creatures. The troggs tunneled toward the city and its unsuspecting populace. When they finally breached the lowest levels of Gnomeregan, they encountered no resistance.

Physically, the gnomes were no match for the much larger and stronger troggs. Mentally, however, they were far superior. The brilliant leader of the gnomes, High Tinker Gelbin Mekkatorque, approached the trogg invasion as he would any other problem. He didn't allow fear or anger to overwhelm him. He remained calm, relying on his people's ingenuity and technical know-how to find a solution.

Mekkatorque stationed soldiers and war machines at choke points to hold the invaders at bay. But the troggs were not so easily contained. Again and again, they burrowed through the earth and bypassed the defenses.

Even with the gnomes' technology, their army simply wasn't large enough to fight off the invaders. Mekkatorque briefly considered calling on the Alliance for help, but he abandoned the idea. Protecting Lordaeron from the Scourge was of the utmost importance, and he didn't want to divert any resources from that front. In fact, he considered the northern campaign so important that he kept news of the trogg invasion a secret from his allies.

It would be years before the world learned of what had transpired in Gnomeregan, and of the sacrifices the gnomes had made in the name of the Alliance.

EYE OF THE STORM

Lordaeron had fallen. The Alliance was crippled.

The Burning Legion could now gather its forces in the Eastern Kingdoms with little resistance. From there, the demons would cross the Great Sea and seize the second Well of Eternity. Though Kil'jaeden had laid the foundations of this invasion, he would not lead it. That honor fell to Archimonde the Defiler.

Whereas Kil'jaeden was a master of manipulating enemies from the shadows, Archimonde was a seasoned battle commander and tactician. He handpicked the members of his assault force, filling it with demonic soldiers who had waged war on Azeroth before. Among those who joined him was Mannoroth, the pit lord whose blood had been used to enslave the orcs to the Legion.

By necessity, Archimonde's force was small. There was simply no way to create a portal powerful enough to bring the full might of the Legion to Azeroth—not until Archimonde had harnessed the second Well of Eternity's energies. But even just transporting him to the world would be a monumental undertaking. One of the Legion's servants would need to create the portal *on* Azeroth and anchor it there.

When the Lich King learned of this predicament, he proposed a solution to the dreadlords. He had knowledge of an artifact called the Book of Medivh, which was now under lock and key in the city of Dalaran.

Many years ago, Medivh had infused the book with some of his immense Guardian power. He had also recorded details of the spells he had used to create the Dark Portal, the gateway connecting Draenor to Azeroth. The energies stored in the book, along with its instructions for creating portals, would be sufficient to bring Archimonde and his vanguard into the world.

Retrieving and using this book would not be easy. The Lich King knew that Kel'Thuzad was the key to success. Not only was he a gifted mage, but he had been one of Dalaran's rulers. If the Scourge resurrected Kel'Thuzad, he would be able to bypass the city's defenses and find the Book of Medivh.

THE BOOK OF MEDIVH AND THE SKULL OF GUL'DAN

At the end of the Second War, Archmage Khadgar and his magi destroyed the Dark Portal on Draenor. As the gateway buckled under the weight of their spellwork, Khadgar dispatched an ally to take two powerful artifacts through the portal, to Dalaran, where he believed they would be safe in the hands of the Kirin Tor. One of these relics was the Book of Medivh, and the other was the Skull of Gul'dan. The messenger only narrowly succeeded, escaping through the gateway just as it slammed shut and severed the way between Azeroth and Draenor.

Kil'jaeden and the dreadlords were pleased with the Lich King's plan. The demons never suspected their loyal slave's true motives. The Lich King's claims about Kel'Thuzad were true, but recovering the Book of Medivh was not the main reason he wanted to reanimate the human. The necromancer was one of the few servants he could rely on when he decided to rebel against the Legion.

PATH OF THE DAMNED

Recovering Kel'Thuzad's remains fell to his killer: Arthas Menethil. The death knight had no reservations about helping his former enemy. His only concern was to serve the Lich King's will, and serve it he did. He rallied a force of undead and marched on Andorhal, the site of Kel'Thuzad's death.

A shroud of decay had settled over the city and the surrounding region. Plague energies choked the land in toxic fog and blotted out the sun. Plants had withered. Livestock and wild animals had died. The once fertile breadbasket of the Eastweald was no more. It had become a warren of undead known as the Plaguelands.

Despite the horrifying conditions, Andorhal was one of the few places in Lordaeron still under Alliance control. Uther the Lightbringer and many of the surviving paladins had gathered in the city. They used it as a headquarters from which to launch attacks against the Scourge.

Arthas saw the paladins as easy prey, and most of them were. He stormed into Andorhal and cut down the holy warriors, the men and women he had trained with and fought alongside.

Uther did not fall so easily. He held his own against Arthas and did what no one else ever had: he bested the death knight in combat and sent the unholy warrior sprawling to the ground. Victory was within Uther's grasp. One blow from his Light-infused hammer—that was all it would take to end Arthas.

But the blow never came. Though Uther was mighty, he was not as swift as Arthas. The prince recovered and struck at the paladin again and again. Arthas gave no quarter to his foe. The apprentice who had once trained under Uther, who had once been like a son to him, finally plunged Frostmourne into the great paladin's heart.

As he watched his former mentor die, Arthas felt nothing. Uther was just an echo of some other life. A ghost from some murky, half-remembered past.

Uther's death heralded the end of Andorhal's resistance. The city fell under Scourge control. Arthas recovered Kel'Thuzad's remains and set out for the next leg of his journey.

The Lich King had convinced the dreadlords that they could do more than simply resurrect Kel'Thuzad. They could transform him into a lich, a spectral being infused with magic. The dreadlords believed that this new and more powerful form would help Kel'Thuzad bring the Legion to Azeroth. It would. But for the Lich King, it would also make his servant a formidable weapon.

Granting Kel'Thuzad this new form would require a potent source of arcane energy. The Lich King and the dreadlords knew of one deep within the high elven kingdom, Quel'Thalas.

Quel'Thalas's culture revolved around a fount of arcane energy called the Sunwell. It empowered the high elves and bathed their homeland in eternal light. It was *everything* to them, and they would fight to the last to protect it.

And Arthas would fight to the last to take it.

EASTERN KINGDOMS IN THE THIRD WAR

The Sunwell

Silvermoon City

Stratholme

THE PLAGUELANDS

LORDAERON   *Capital City*

Andorhal

SILVERPINE FOREST

Dalaran

Gilneas City

Ironforge

KUL TIRAS

Gnomeregan

Uldaman

CURSE OF THE WORGEN

As Arthas Menethil and the Scourge marched north toward Quel'Thalas, other undead lingered in Lordaeron. Some shambled to the edges of the Plaguelands in the east. Others spilled south into a region called Silverpine Forest.

The undead in Silverpine Forest made quick progress until their campaign ground to a halt in the shadow of the Greymane Wall. The enormous wood and stone barrier stretched across the top of a peninsula that was home to the human kingdom of Gilneas.

King Genn Greymane hadn't sent any Gilnean soldiers to fight the Scourge. He saw the fall of Lordaeron as confirmation that he'd made the right choice in isolating his kingdom from the world. Because of the Greymane Wall, the people of Gilneas were safe.

The Scourge's numbers were small at first, and Greymane was confident his people could simply wait them out. The undead would pull back once they realized they could not breach the wall. But the Scourge never flagged. They had no need of rest or food. More and more undead appeared outside Gilneas, and the army battered the wall day and night.

On Greymane's orders, his army amassed. The gates to the kingdom swung open, and a tide of Gilnean soldiers poured into Silverpine Forest.

From atop the wall, Greymane watched disaster unfold. The Scourge crushed the Gilneans. Soldiers who fell in battle arose as undead and turned against their former comrades. Greymane knew it was only a matter of time before the Scourge would completely overrun his forces. The king turned to his royal archmage, Arugal, to find a solution.

Arugal had just the thing in mind. He had learned of mythical creatures called worgen. They were wolflike in appearance, but they walked on two legs as a human would. Arugal didn't know the worgen's full origins, but he did know where to find them. He had sensed the beasts slumbering in another dimension—the ethereal realm known as the Emerald Dream. Summoning the creatures to Gilneas would be a challenge, but that wasn't what concerned Arugal. According to legend, the worgen were a savage race, driven by primal fury. Controlling them would be difficult and dangerous. The question wasn't *could* he bring the worgen to Gilneas; it was *should* he.

Arugal warned Greymane of the worgen's unruly nature, but the king had no other option. The wolf-beasts seemed like his only hope.

As battle raged outside the wall, Arugal performed his summoning. He opened a rift connecting the physical world and the Emerald Dream, drawing the worgen into Silverpine Forest. The wolf-beasts wasted no time in turning their fury on the Scourge. They tore through the undead in a storm of fang and claw. The creatures were even more powerful than Arugal had expected.

Before long, the Scourge buckled. The undead fled before the worgen and disappeared into Silverpine Forest. Then the wolf-beasts turned on the Gilneans to satisfy their bloodlust.

It was just as Arugal had feared. Concepts of friend and foe were lost on the worgen. They simply wanted to kill.

The surviving Gilnean soldiers retreated behind the wall, and the gates slammed shut. Greymane breathed a sigh of relief. It seemed, at first, that all was well. The Scourge were gone, and the worgen were trapped outside the wall.

Then the first reports reached Greymane of worgen inside the wall.

What the king and Arugal hadn't known was that the worgen carried a curse. It had spread to Gilnean soldiers who had been bitten by the worgen—Gilneans who had retreated behind the wall. Over time, the affliction transformed the human victims into wolf-beasts. These new worgen stalked through Gilneas and spread the curse to even more citizens.

In trying to save Gilneas, Greymane had traded one monstrous enemy for another.

THE FALL OF SILVERMOON

Far north of Gilneas, Arthas Menethil and the Scourge marched into the tranquil woodlands bordering Quel'Thalas. Much to their surprise, they met no resistance. The forests were oddly silent and deserted. It seemed as if the kingdom's high elves had fled in terror before the approaching undead, but nothing could have been further from the truth.

The elves were busy preparing for the Scourge. King Anasterian Sunstrider rallied his people into action, but he left the task of organizing the defenses and leading the military to Ranger-General Sylvanas Windrunner.

Sylvanas came from a distinguished family of high elves. Her sisters, Alleria and Vereesa, had both earned praise for bravery in battle. Sylvanas was no exception. Like her sisters, she had fought on the front lines in the Second War, when the orcish Horde had invaded Quel'Thalas and burned its woodlands. Even before that, she had garnered a reputation as a fearless and cunning ranger while battling trolls from the nearby Amani empire.

Sylvanas ordered most of the kingdom's magi and priests to gather in Silvermoon City. They would serve as the last line of defense if the Scourge made it to the capital, but the ranger-general hoped that it wouldn't come to that. Sylvanas took the rangers into the woods outside Silvermoon City, where she planned to mount a resistance so fierce that the undead would turn back.

Known as the Farstriders, the rangers were lightly armored and highly mobile troops. Historically, they stood as the first line of defense against any intruders that threatened Quel'Thalas. It was a dangerous job, but one that carried great honor and prestige.

As Arthas and the Scourge plunged deeper into the forests, Sylvanas and her rangers launched their attack from all sides. The fighting was fierce and frenzied. The undead moved steadily toward Silvermoon City, but Sylvanas made them pay dearly for every step taken. She was a brilliant tactician, and her dogged persistence infuriated Arthas.

The Scourge outnumbered the rangers, and they would inevitably reach Silvermoon. Sylvanas knew her only hope was to buy the capital's defenders time to prepare for a siege. She ordered her rangers to make a final stand outside the city. Sylvanas herself would deal with Arthas.

In full view of Silvermoon's glorious spires, the death knight and the ranger-general clashed. Sylvanas was fearsome, but she was fatigued from days of hard battle. Her strength faded, and Arthas found an opening.

Frostmourne tore through the ranger-general and spilled the life from her veins.

Death was not the end for Sylvanas Windrunner. Arthas punished the ranger-general for her defiance. He ripped the high elf's spirit from her body and converted it into a spectral banshee. This act chained Sylvanas to the Lich King's will. She could not disobey him, even though she

ARTHAS MENETHIL'S VICTORY OVER SYLVANAS WINDRUNNER IN QUEL'THALAS

wanted to. She was forced to take part in the assault on Quel'Thalas and murder her own people—the very people she had sworn to protect to the end of her days.

Sylvanas's sacrifice had been valiant, but it did not save Silvermoon. Arthas Menethil and the Scourge shattered the capital's defenses and cut a path north toward the Isle of Quel'Danas, home of the Sunwell.

King Anasterian Sunstrider and the surviving elves gathered aboard their fleet and retreated to the island. Protecting the Sunwell became their primary focus. They could always rebuild their capital, but the fount of arcane magic was irreplaceable. The Scourge had no ships, and the elves believed it would take time for the undead to find a way to cross the sea.

They were mistaken.

Arthas did not need a fleet. He had Frostmourne. When he reached the northern coast of Quel'Thalas, he dipped the runeblade into the foaming sea. The water around the weapon froze, and the ice gradually spread across the ocean until a makeshift bridge formed.

As Arthas and the Scourge marched toward Quel'Danas, King Anasterian steeled himself for battle. If the elves had any chance of surviving, it lay with him. Anasterian was elderly, but he was wise and crafty. And like Arthas, he wielded a great weapon: an ancient sword known as Felo'melorn.

The king dueled Arthas on the frozen shores of Quel'Danas. The keening of their two blades shook the sky like thunder. Anasterian lasted much longer against Arthas than most others had. But he was no match for the death knight. Neither was Felo'melorn.

With one brutal strike, Arthas Menethil shattered the king's blade. His next blow ended Anasterian's life.

THE TREACHERY OF DAR'KHAN

Silvermoon City was protected by a number of magical barriers. Two were the elfgates, which were positioned at strategic points on the main road to the capital. The third and most powerful barrier was called Ban'dinoriel. It was an impenetrable shield that derived its power from the Sunwell. Arthas Menethil and the Scourge might have never bypassed these defenses if not for the high elf magister Dar'Khan Drathir.

Dar'Khan was a talented mage, but unbridled ambition made him arrogant and vindictive. He never felt that he received the recognition he deserved. Bitterness filled his heart and darkened his emotions. Arthas sensed Dar'Khan's inner turmoil, and he saw him as a critical ally for the invasion of Quel'Thalas. The death knight whispered in the elf's mind and made an offer: if he served the Lich King, all the power and recognition Dar'Khan craved would finally be his.

Dar'Khan could not resist. He betrayed his entire race and helped the Scourge destroy and bypass Quel'Thalas's magical barriers.

Morale crumbled among the remaining high elf defenders, and the Scourge swept over Quel'Danas. Very few elves escaped.

Victorious, Arthas reached the Sunwell and submerged Kel'Thuzad's remains in its shimmering depths. The death knight drew on the fount's boundless magic and wove a spell that remade the fallen necromancer into a terrifying incorporeal lich. This transformation came at great cost to the elves. Turning Kel'Thuzad into a lich befouled the Sunwell. The fount would never be the same again. The Sunwell's corrupted energies gradually permeated Quel'Thalas and the elves who still lived there.

Arthas Menethil did not linger in the kingdom. His work was done. He gathered the Scourge and marched south toward Dalaran, leaving only ruins and death in his wake. The land in Quel'Thalas where he and the undead had set foot festered and died. This wound in the world later became known as the Dead Scar, and it would remain for many years.

THE FLIGHT TO KALIMDOR

With the Scourge approaching Dalaran, Archmage Antonidas and the Kirin Tor readied themselves for battle. They evacuated most of the city's civilians, leaving behind only a small resistance force. Though these defenders were few, they were some of the greatest magi in the world. Not only that, but Dalaran itself was a weapon. Magic coursed through the streets, and arcane barriers blanketed the city. Many of these wards would destroy any undead that touched them.

Despite these preparations, a sense of impending doom fell over Dalaran. The Scourge had brought Lordaeron to its knees. They had ripped out the heart of Quel'Thalas. These two nations were perhaps the mightiest in the Eastern Kingdoms, perhaps the mightiest in the entire *world*. If they had fallen so easily, what hope did Dalaran have?

This question plagued Antonidas. His thoughts turned to the hooded figure who had urged him to flee from the Eastern Kingdoms. Antonidas now realized that this stranger was no madman; he had been right all along.

It was too late for Antonidas to go west. As the Kirin Tor's leader, he could not abandon Dalaran. Protecting the city and its vaults of arcana was his duty. However, there was someone who could act on the stranger's advice and save innocent lives: Jaina Proudmoore.

The sorceress was initially hesitant to leave. She wanted to stay by Antonidas's side and defend Dalaran. She also wanted to see what had become of Arthas. Jaina sensed the death knight among the approaching Scourge. She still wrestled with guilt about abandoning him at Stratholme, and she wondered if there were some way to save him.

It was only after much debate that Jaina relented. She understood, just as Antonidas did, that the city could not hold out against the Scourge. If she and the archmage died, who would be left to heed the stranger's warning?

The master and apprentice parted ways. Though neither of them said it, they both knew that this was the last time they would ever see each other.

In the days to come, Jaina worked tirelessly to rally as many refugees as she could. Not everyone she met agreed to go with her, but many did. When she finally set sail for Kalimdor, her force included members from nearly every Alliance race. Some were survivors from Lordaeron and

Quel'Thalas. Some were dwarves and gnomes from the Alliance military. And some were humans from Stromgarde, Kul Tiras, and other nations in the region.

Though they came from different places, they followed Jaina Proudmoore for the same reason. She represented something that had almost entirely vanished from the Eastern Kingdoms.

She represented hope.

UNDER THE BURNING SKY

En route to Dalaran, Kel'Thuzad confided in Arthas Menethil and revealed some of the Lich King's plan to rebel against the Legion. He told the death knight that the demons were not to be trusted. They viewed the Scourge as disposable weapons, something to cast away once Azeroth was in the Legion's hands. Kel'Thuzad did not tell Arthas when this rebellion against the demons might occur or how it would unfold, but he warned him to be ready for it.

And Arthas would be. Even before Kel'Thuzad's revelation, he had distrusted the dreadlords. The demons were always following him, always watching him. He found their presence insufferable, and he looked forward to striking them down as he had done to Mal'Ganis. But the dreadlords would have to wait. For the time being, Arthas would do his part to recover the Book of Medivh from Dalaran and help bring Archimonde into the world.

In Dalaran, Arthas and the Scourge met resistance every bit as formidable as that of Lordaeron or Quel'Thalas. Perhaps even more so. The city's magi battered the undead with barrage after barrage of arcane energy, wreaking havoc on the invaders. But this frontal assault was nothing more than a diversion. While the defenders focused their attention on the main undead army, Arthas led Kel'Thuzad and a small force of Scourge into the city itself. The dreadlord Tichondrius accompanied the infiltrators, eager to keep watch over Arthas and ensure that he did what had been commanded of him.

Using Kel'Thuzad's knowledge, Arthas overcame Dalaran's inner defenses. He cut a path toward the vault containing the Book of Medivh, only to find Antonidas waiting for him.

Like so many other brave souls before him, Antonidas fought with all his heart to hold Arthas back. And like so many other brave souls before him, he failed. Frostmourne claimed another soul. This time, it was one of the world's wisest and most gifted magi.

Arthas had expected to find Jaina Proudmoore at Antonidas's side, and he was surprised to discover that she was not there. In fact, it didn't seem she was in Dalaran at all. That thought sent a strange emotion flitting through Arthas, some lingering fragment of his past life. He was *relieved* Jaina was gone. The feeling passed just as soon as it had come.

Kel'Thuzad shattered the enchanted vault holding the Book of Medivh, and he retrieved the artifact. Many other relics lay alongside the tome, one of which was the Skull of Gul'dan. Tichondrius was drawn to the item and its aura of fel energy, and he pilfered it from the vault before withdrawing from the city.

Arthas ordered the Scourge to pull back from Dalaran. He had what he needed. Archimonde and his demons were waiting.

As Kel'Thuzad prepared to open the way for the Legion, he marveled at Medivh's spellbook. The lich had never seen the tome before. It was one of the most closely guarded artifacts in

Dalaran, and even he hadn't had permission to touch it. Now Kel'Thuzad understood why. The book contained an extraordinary amount of power and knowledge. Kel'Thuzad drew on all of it, weaving a spell greater than anything he had been capable of in life.

The influx of power created a rift that linked Azeroth and the Twisting Nether, and demons poured from the fiery maw. The first to arrive were the bestial felhounds and mindless constructs called infernals. They were followed by even greater demons, such as Mannoroth and the battle-hardened doomlord named Kazzak. Then came the towering form of Archimonde.

After more than ten thousand years, the demon lord stood on Azeroth again.

Archimonde immediately turned his ire on Dalaran. If left alone, the magi would remain a constant thorn in the Legion's side. Archimonde wouldn't allow that to happen. He gathered the latent energies permeating Dalaran and wove a spell to bring the city toppling down. One after another, its glittering spires cracked and crumbled into rubble.

The demon lord then transferred control of the Scourge to the dreadlords. Archimonde saw no further need for the Lich King. The entity had served his purpose, creating a loyal army of undead for the Legion. Archimonde distrusted the Lich King even more than Kil'jaeden did.

Archimonde ordered his forces to gather in the heart of Lordaeron and crush the last vestiges of the Alliance. This would ensure that no enemies would follow the Legion when the demons launched their invasion of Kalimdor. Not all of Archimonde's followers took part in the pacification of Lordaeron, however. The demon lord sent Mannoroth and Tichondrius ahead to Kalimdor so that they could clear the way for the Legion's arrival.

THE LONG MARCH

Medivh sensed the Burning Legion on Azeroth, and he knew the demons would soon begin their assault on Kalimdor. Fortunately, the remnants of the Alliance and the Horde had nearly arrived at the continent. Though Thrall and his people had left first, Jaina Proudmoore and her followers had closed the distance. The Alliance had enjoyed calm seas and full sails; they did not have to endure the angry storm that had battered the Horde's fleet and blown most of it off course.

Though Medivh had succeeded in bringing the Horde and the Alliance to Kalimdor, he knew an even greater challenge awaited. The factions needed to join forces, but he could not simply ask them to do so. Too much enmity lingered between them. He would have to subtly draw them into a face-to-face meeting. Only then could he reveal himself and convince them to put aside their differences for the good of Azeroth.

Medivh chose to lure Thrall and Jaina to a specific place in Kalimdor: Stonetalon Peak. The mountain, located south of the World Tree Nordrassil, was considered sacred by local cultures. Magic suffused the peak, lending the site a certain air of significance and gravitas.

The only question was whether Thrall and Jaina Proudmoore would survive the journey to the peak. They reached Kalimdor at different times and in different places, but they both faced hardships as they marched inland from the eastern coast.

The terrain was harsh, a red wasteland that offered little in the way of food or water. The wildlife was just as inhospitable. Savage piglike quilboar and poisonous scorpids prowled the jagged hills. As the days wore on, both Jaina and Thrall wondered whether they had made the right decision in coming to Kalimdor.

Was there really any hope here? Or had they merely traded one land of conflict for another?

The march inland was difficult, but it was also rewarding in unexpected ways, particularly for the Horde. Shortly after arriving, Thrall discovered wreckage from the missing ships in his fleet. It seemed that Grommash Hellscream and the other orcs had survived the storm and reached Kalimdor first. They were nowhere to be found, and Thrall assumed they had forged ahead on their own.

Galvanized by the discovery, Thrall led his followers deeper into Kalimdor, eager to track down the rest of the Horde. But instead of finding Grommash, the young warchief found himself in the middle of a war.

Conflict raged between two of Kalimdor's native races: the tauren and the centaur. Though both were rugged and mighty, they were different in almost every other way. The tauren were enormous bovine creatures, but their imposing size belied a gentle spirit. They had deep ties to nature through their deity, whom they called the Earth Mother. The tauren also communed with the world's elements through their long tradition of shamanism.

The centaur viewed these mystical pursuits as weak. They were a brutal, warlike people who hunted the tauren for sport. With powerful equine lower bodies and humanoid torsos, the centaur were well suited to warfare on Kalimdor's open plains.

For generations, the tauren had weathered intermittent attacks from the centaur. The battles took a heavy toll on both sides. Though the tauren were kindhearted, they did not shy away from combat. They made the centaur pay for every unprovoked attack.

Yet they had no love for war. Whenever the centaur appeared, the tauren opted to find a new place to call home rather than throw their lives away. They lived in a constant state of upheaval, and they never stayed in one place for long. A year of peace was always followed by another of war. The tauren came to accept this great cycle of conflict as inescapable. It was the only life they knew, but that was about to change.

Thrall became fast friends with the tauren's wise leader, High Chieftain Cairne Bloodhoof. The warchief admired that many tauren practiced shamanism and respected the land. The tauren had noble hearts and yearned for a better future, but they were constantly drawn into bloody conflict. Thrall would not ignore the injustice he was witnessing. His Horde stood as a beacon of hope for races just like the tauren: the misunderstood, the oppressed, and the forgotten. And his Horde would fight to protect those in need.

In a land of dust and cracked earth called the Barrens, the Horde stood shoulder to shoulder with the tauren in battle. Their combined might crashed down on the centaur warbands like a hammer and scattered them to the wind.

The defeat shocked the centaur and sent them limping out of the Barrens in disgrace. They would never again see the tauren as easy prey.

For the first time in memory, the tauren saw the promise of a new future. The centaur would always be a threat, but not as much as they had once been. The tauren's nomadic existence was over. At last, they had broken the cycle of conflict.

In the wake of the battle, Cairne Bloodhoof offered Thrall supplies and even some of his mightiest warriors to help the Horde reach Stonetalon Peak in the north. Most of the other tauren ventured west, into a grassy plain known as Mulgore. There, they would finally settle and build a permanent home.

CRY OF THE WARSONGS

While Thrall and his Horde were aiding the tauren, Jaina Proudmoore and her expedition trekked toward Stonetalon Peak. She didn't know exactly what she would find there, but she expected to discover some new weapon or knowledge that would help her save the world from the Scourge. At least, that was what she assumed the hooded stranger would grant her.

Finding food and water became a daily struggle. The unforgiving terrain slowly wore down the Alliance refugees. The only thing keeping their hopes alive was Jaina. Though she had her own doubts about the future, she hid them well. No matter how dire the conditions became, she remained determined.

After days of travel, the Alliance forces reached a lush woodland known as Ashenvale. The region was filled with resources, pristine rivers and lakes, and wild game. Yet it was not without its dangers.

Just as Jaina reached the foothills of the Stonetalon Mountains, Warsong orcs emerged from the forest undergrowth with sharpened blades and murder in their eyes. Leading them was Grommash Hellscream.

Grommash and his people had wandered the Barrens for many days before stumbling across Jaina in Ashenvale. Rather than launch an immediate attack, the Warsong chieftain had decided to follow the Alliance at a distance. Finding his old enemy in this exotic land was a mystery, and Grommash spied on them for a time before finally indulging the urge to spill their blood.

The Alliance forces repelled the surprise attack with minor losses, but the encounter left them shaken. No one had expected to find orcs in Kalimdor. Jaina was eager to avoid a prolonged battle, and she led the refugees up the slopes of the Stonetalon Mountains. Some of Jaina's followers remained behind and erected defenses to stop the orcs from pursuing them.

Thrall and the rest of the Horde arrived in the foothills shortly thereafter. They were shocked to discover Alliance forces in the area, but they were also elated to reunite with Grommash and his Warsongs. Like Jaina Proudmoore, Thrall was reluctant to bog down his people in a needless war, especially after what they had gone through in the Barrens. Defeating the Alliance was not his purpose here.

Thrall ordered the Horde to ignore the Alliance, but his command went unheard by many orcs. Something strange was happening to his people. Ever since they had reached Ashenvale, they had become more aggressive and bloodthirsty. More like the Horde of old.

Grommash Hellscream and his Warsongs were the worst offenders. They repeatedly defied Thrall and wet their blades with Alliance blood.

Thrall could only tolerate so much. He sent Grommash and his Warsongs deeper into Ashenvale and ordered them to establish an outpost. Thrall believed the hard labor would keep them distracted until he returned from Stonetalon Peak.

Begrudgingly, Grommash and his Warsongs obeyed. They considered it a grave insult to be relegated to manual labor. They were great warriors, perhaps the greatest in all the Horde. Nonetheless, they went to work and unleashed their rage on the woodlands. Their axes bit deep into Ashenvale's ancient trees, and they chopped down large swaths of the forest to build their outpost.

This defilement of the wilds did not go unnoticed, nor would it go unpunished. Ashenvale was not orcish land.

It belonged to the night elves.

WAR OF THE ANCIENTS

The night elves were members of one of the oldest races in the world. Over ten thousand years ago, they built a glorious empire that reached the far corners of Azeroth's single landmass. This grand achievement was made possible only by the Well of Eternity, the mystical fount of arcane energy that was the lifeblood of night elven society.

For generations, the night elves had experimented with the Well of Eternity. As they mastered its energies and unraveled the mysteries of the arcane, they became gifted and ambitious sorcerers. The greatest of these magic users were Queen Azshara and a sect of night elven society known as the Highborne. Their unbridled pursuit of magic led to wondrous accomplishments, but it also brought their empire to ruin.

In search of ever greater power, Azshara and the Highborne did the unthinkable. They made a pact with the Burning Legion and summoned demons into the world.

Divisions formed among the night elves, and a resistance emerged to banish the Legion from Azeroth. These brave night elves were joined by other native races, as well as by the ancient Wild Gods, primordial creatures who dwelled in the woodland deeps. The conflict that unfolded became known as the War of the Ancients.

The war saw the rise of many heroes, but none were more famous than the priestess Tyrande Whisperwind, the druid Malfurion Stormrage, and his twin brother, the sorcerer Illidan.

Amid the fighting, Illidan abandoned his allies and sided with the Legion. He believed that by feigning allegiance to the demons, he could gain unimaginable power and use it to destroy them—and in doing so, he would prove his greatness.

Illidan Stormrage did find power, but it came at a terrible price. His eyes were burned out and replaced with smoldering pits of magic, and his skin was scarred with fel tattoos. What was more, his fellow night elves saw him as a traitor.

To cut off the Legion from the world and end the war, the resistance launched an offensive against Azshara at the Well of Eternity itself. The subsequent battle caused the fount to unravel. The Well of Eternity imploded, leading to a catastrophe known as the Great Sundering. Tectonic plates buckled. Azeroth's sole landmass ripped apart into separate continents. The world changed forever.

The resistance fled to Hyjal Summit to escape the devastation. When they arrived, they made a startling discovery. Illidan was already atop Hyjal, and he had created a second Well of Eternity.

Unbeknownst to the other night elves, he had gathered some of the original Well of Eternity's energies and used them to create a new Well. Illidan believed that if the Legion ever returned to Azeroth, the elves would need the fount's magic to fend them off.

More than his feigned allegiance to the Legion, it was this act that earned Illidan Stormrage the name "Betrayer." Malfurion recommended that Illidan be locked away in a barrow prison to prevent him from doing any more damage to the rest of his people.

The night elves feared that the Legion might use the second Well of Eternity to invade the world again. These concerns were shared by the ancient Dragon Aspects. Alexstrasza, Ysera, and Nozdormu had learned of the new fount, and they were determined to protect it. Alexstrasza planted an enchanted seed at the second Well of Eternity, which sprouted into a colossal World Tree called Nordrassil. The tree acted as a cap over the fount and prevented anyone from abusing its power.

The Dragon Aspects saw the night elves as the guardians of Nordrassil. To help them with this task, Alexstrasza and her allies infused the World Tree with potent enchantments. So long as Nordrassil stood, the night elves would enjoy immortality and immunity to disease and sickness. The World Tree would also act as a gateway to the Emerald Dream, allowing Malfurion and future druids an easier way to access the ethereal realm.

Malfurion Stormrage spent most of his time training and leading new druids. They studied nature magic, and they dedicated themselves to maintaining the health and vitality of the wilds. Malfurion and the other druids often slumbered in the physical world while their spirits roamed the primal forests of the Emerald Dream.

The task of leading night elven society fell to Tyrande Whisperwind. Gone were the days of empire building and reckless magic. Such pursuits had only led to death and ruin. Tyrande fostered a culture that was far more insular and cautious than before. The night elves kept to Hyjal's woodlands, only rarely straying into far-flung lands. To protect her borders, Tyrande forged a military order called the Sentinels. The force was mainly composed of night elf priestesses, many of them hardened veterans of the War of the Ancients. The Sentinels established outposts throughout Ashenvale and at the borders of night elven territory.

Defending the forests was not without its dangers, but the Sentinels could summon other creatures for aid. Sometimes, they would awaken the druids from their sojourns in the Emerald Dream or call on the fay spirits who dwelled in the wilds. The woodlands teemed with these potential allies: fierce chimaeras, faerie dragons, wise treants, dryads, and the ancient keepers of the grove.

By far, the most powerful of these creatures was a Wild God known as Cenarius. He had taught night elves the art of druidism, and he cared deeply for their well-being and prosperity. Cenarius shared the night elves' quest to protect Nordrassil and the second Well of Eternity. He had fought in the War of the Ancients. He had seen his fellow Wild Gods ripped apart by demons. He had witnessed the forests burning in towering walls of fel fire. Cenarius knew that to prevent such a catastrophe from *ever* happening again, the elves and the forest spirits needed to work in unison.

And with Cenarius's help, they did. The night elves and woodland creatures overcame every foe that threatened their lands.

This vigil did not extend to the Eastern Kingdoms. Tyrande Whisperwind and her people were partially aware of events transpiring across the Great Sea, but they rarely intervened. When they did, their activities were always subtle and unseen.

The druids were the first to notice the plague of undeath killing the wilds as it spread across the Eastern Kingdoms. From within the Emerald Dream, their spirits reached out to the physical world to stop the blight. Yet they had little success. Some of these druids told Tyrande of what was happening. Though she maintained her isolationism, she sensed a familiar force at work behind the plague.

She sensed the Legion.

THE SPIRITS OF ASHENVALE

When Sentinels reported that strangers were barging into Ashenvale, Tyrande Whisperwind expected the worst. She was somewhat relieved to find that these outsiders were not demons. Tyrande correctly assumed that the Horde and Alliance refugees were fleeing the plague across the Great Sea. From the way they fought each other, she also guessed that they were bitter enemies.

Tyrande ordered her Sentinels to observe the newcomers from a distance. She hoped that the refugees were merely passing through Ashenvale en route to other lands. She was wrong. Some of the Horde's green-skinned orcs made war on the forests. They *stole* from the woodlands without asking, felling trees with reckless abandon. Tyrande had no love for these creatures. They were brutish and violent. And Tyrande would suffer their presence no more.

The Sentinels struck Grommash Hellscream and his Warsongs. Some night elves, perched high in the trees, unleashed a storm of arrows on their prey. Others, armed with razor-edged glaives, descended on the backs of winged beasts called hippogryphs or giant felines called nightsabers.

The Sentinels were as deadly as any foe the orcs had faced. That didn't frighten Grommash and his warriors; it excited them. They had been longing for a chance to fight a worthy enemy.

Before long, the orcs found themselves severely outmatched. Cenarius had also been watching the newcomers, and he smelled the demon blood in their veins. Thinking that the green-skinned creatures were Legion servants, Cenarius attacked them alongside the night elves.

The orcs stood no chance against the night elves and their forest allies. Though their battle lust remained undimmed, defeat seemed imminent. It was in this moment of desperation that a dark and familiar form of energy called to Grommash and his followers. They tracked this source of magic to a pool of emerald liquid, hidden in a dense corner of the forest.

It was blood. *Demon* blood.

THE BLOOD OF MANNOROTH

Grommash Hellscream and his orcs had not stumbled across the demon blood by chance. On Archimonde's orders, Mannoroth and Tichondrius had come to Kalimdor to weaken its defenses in preparation for the demons' invasion. The continent teemed with creatures who were hostile to the Legion. The demons considered most of them harmless, little more than minor annoyances. But Cenarius and the other Wild Gods were different. During the War of the Ancients, they had fiercely resisted the Legion. If the Legion had any hopes of reaching the second Well of Eternity, the demons would have to get through Cenarius and his woodland allies first.

To blunt the might of the wilds, Mannoroth and Tichondrius had brought the Skull of Gul'dan to Kalimdor. The artifact had changed since falling into the Legion's hands. The demons had infused it with even more fel magic, making it far more powerful than it had been before. Mannoroth and Tichondrius could draw out these energies to poison Ashenvale's woodlands and weaken Cenarius. The process would be slow, but it would be effective.

Before the demons could begin, another opportunity presented itself. The orcs.

Years had passed since the orcs had drunk Mannoroth's blood, but the curse still lingered in their veins. It bound them to the pit lord and made them susceptible to his influence.

CENARIUS BATTLES GROMMASH HELLSCREAM IN ASHENVALE FOREST

Mannoroth's mere presence in Ashenvale had already started affecting the orcs, particularly Grommash Hellscream and his Warsongs. Being near the pit lord had made them increasingly violent and aggressive. Their unbridled fury had drawn them into a war with Cenarius. The orcs stood no chance of winning, unless they had more power.

And that was exactly what Mannoroth would give them. By drinking his blood, the orcs would become mighty enough to defeat Cenarius. They would also become slaves to the Legion once again. Mannoroth spilled his blood in the forest, and then he retreated from sight.

As expected, Grommash found the pool. He suspected the dangers of drinking the blood, but he knew it was the only way his orcs would survive the battle against Cenarius. Unable to resist the temptation of power, Grommash drank deep. His followers did the same.

With otherworldly power surging through their bodies, the orcs rampaged across Ashenvale. Scores of night elves and forest creatures fell to their hungry blades. Grommash Hellscream himself clashed with Cenarius. The Wild God fought with all his primal fury, but even he could not withstand the orc's supernatural might. Grommash's axe sank into Cenarius, and the Warsong vanquished his foe.

At the moment of Cenarius's death, the wilds around Hyjal darkened and trembled. Dryads, chimaeras, treants, and other fay creatures retreated in horror. Though some would return to aid the night elves, many would remain in hiding for the duration of the war.

Only later did Grommash discover where the source of his new power came from. By then, it was too late for the orc or his followers to resist. They were bound to Mannoroth's will.

BOUND BY DESTINY

While Grommash Hellscream was battling Cenarius and the night elves, Thrall and Jaina Proudmoore led their followers into the Stonetalon Mountains. They took different paths up the rocky slopes, and only when they had ventured into the caverns at the peak did they come face-to-face.

In an instant, blades were drawn and battle lines formed. Jaina and Thrall had wanted to avoid open conflict with each other, but now violence seemed inevitable.

Before blood was spilled, Medivh revealed himself. Jaina and Thrall froze at the sight of the hooded figure. It was the man who had lured them to Kalimdor through dire warnings.

Medivh had only one chance to win Jaina and Thrall to his side, and he held nothing back. He told them of the Burning Legion's plans, and that the demonic invasion had already begun. The world teetered on the edge of oblivion. Alone, the races of Azeroth were doomed to annihilation. But together . . . together they stood a chance of saving their world.

To convince them of exactly what was at stake, Medivh revealed the fate of Grommash Hellscream and his Warsongs. They had drunk Mannoroth's blood and were once again the pit lord's slaves. This was the fate that awaited all orcs unless a united front was formed against the Legion.

This news about Grommash horrified Thrall. He had vowed that his people would never again live through the dark days of the Horde. If uniting with his enemies in the Alliance was the only way to make good on that promise, so be it.

Jaina Proudmoore considered it madness to join forces with the Horde, but she eventually saw the wisdom in Medivh's words. During her studies in Dalaran, she had learned fragments of knowledge about the Burning Legion. All of it had terrified her. If a demonic invasion was truly unfolding, it would be foolish not to do everything in her power to stop the Legion. Failure would mean more than Jaina's own death; it would mean that everyone who had sacrificed their lives to defend Lordaeron had died for nothing.

Thrall and Jaina brokered an uneasy truce. They did not completely trust each other, but they were willing to put aside old hatreds and work together for the time being.

The first test of this tenuous alliance was dealing with Grommash Hellscream and his Warsongs.

THE BLOOD-CURSE

After descending the Stonetalon Mountains, the united Alliance refugees and Horde moved against Grommash Hellscream and his blood-crazed followers. The Warsongs were so lost to the depths of rage that they could not differentiate friend from foe. They cut down Alliance and Horde with equal ferocity, spilling the blood of orcs whom they had once seen as brothers and sisters.

As the battle raged on, Thrall led a daring assault through Warsong lines and captured Grommash. In unison, Horde shaman and Alliance priests called on their magics to purge the bloodlust from his veins. It worked. For the first time in days, the cloud of hate lifted from Grommash's eyes. He saw the monster he had become, and shame overwhelmed him.

And then he remembered who had done this to him. Mannoroth was out there, somewhere, stalking through the forests, reveling in the carnage he had unleashed. Grommash and Thrall both knew that if they did not confront the demon, their people would be doomed.

While the Horde and the Alliance refugees worked to pacify the rest of the Warsongs, Grommash Hellscream and Thrall tracked Mannoroth to a fel-corrupted canyon in southeastern Ashenvale. The pit lord found the two orcs more amusing than threatening. He saw Thrall as little more than a harmless pup, and he cast aside the orc with ease. The pit lord expected no retaliation from Grommash. He would never dare raise a hand against Mannoroth, his *master*.

The pit lord was only partially right. The blood-curse burned bright in Grommash's soul, but there was something else that burned even brighter: the desire to set his people free.

Grommash Hellscream buried his axe deep into the pit lord's chest, a mortal blow that caused the demon's body to rupture and disintegrate. Mannoroth exploded in a blinding flash of light, and searing fel energy washed over the canyon.

The pit lord was no more, but his defeat had come at a price. The explosion had mortally wounded Grommash.

He drew his last breath with Thrall at his side, content in the knowledge that he had redeemed himself by destroying Mannoroth. By vanquishing the demon, he had finally purged the blood-curse from the orcs.

They were free.

DEMON FALL CANYON

The orcs would regard Grommash Hellscream as one of their greatest heroes. The site of his noble sacrifice would become known as Demon Fall Canyon. Many orcs would make pilgrimages there to honor the warrior who had liberated them from the Legion's curse.

THE INVASION OF KALIMDOR

Though Mannoroth had fallen, he had accomplished his mission. Cenarius was dead. The forest spirits would still resist the Legion's invasion, but their primal strength was greatly diminished.

The time to invade Kalimdor had come.

Archimonde left some of his demons and undead in the Eastern Kingdoms to ensure that the nations there remained pacified. He launched the rest of his forces into Ashenvale. As infernals rained from the sky, thousands of undead and demons appeared at the eastern edges of the region. Archimonde and his followers soon met resistance from the night elves, forest spirits, and the combined Horde and Alliance armies. But these defenders fought on separate fronts, scattered across Ashenvale. The Legion easily overwhelmed them. Archimonde's unyielding army marched steadily inland toward Hyjal Summit, trampling the woodlands and all who stood in its path.

Progress was swift, but Archimonde would leave nothing to chance. He had led wars beyond count, and he knew the value of securing every advantage that he could, even when facing an inferior foe. There was one weapon he had not used: the Skull of Gul'dan. Tichondrius still had the artifact in his possession. He no longer needed it to kill Cenarius, but he could use it to weaken the forests and clear a path to the second Well of Eternity.

Tichondrius forged ahead of the main Legion army and found a tranquil corner of the forest near Hyjal. The dreadlord drew out the Skull of Gul'dan's fel energies and infused them into the earth. Toxic magic seethed across the land, mutating trees and local wildlife into monsters that served the Legion. The pristine river that snaked through the wilds turned a sickly green. This poisoned forest became known as Felwood.

The fel magics continued to spread up Hyjal's slopes, corrupting everything they touched. Soon, the energies would reach the very shores of the second Well of Eternity. This would allow the Legion to march through the darkened wilds with little resistance.

THE AWAKENING

The sight of Archimonde and his vanguard defiling Ashenvale filled Tyrande Whisperwind with shock and fury, but she knew it was only the beginning. The Legion was not in Kalimdor to conquer the forests; the demons wanted to consume the entire world. With the second Well of Eternity, they would have the power to do so. They could open gateways for the rest of the Legion. Perhaps even for Sargeras himself.

Tyrande needed every weapon at her disposal to defend Hyjal. That meant rousing the druids from their sojourn within the Emerald Dream. It troubled her that Malfurion Stormrage and his followers had not yet emerged from the Dream. They must have sensed the corruption spreading across Ashenvale. What reason could they possibly have for remaining in the ethereal realm?

The reason was Cenarius. When he had fallen, his death had sent a shockwave through the Dream, weakening the druids and throwing them into a state of confusion. Malfurion and his followers sensed fragments of what was happening in the physical world, but they were effectively trapped within the Emerald Dream.

When Tyrande finally managed to wake Malfurion, he was stunned to see what had become of Ashenvale. Fel fire consumed his beloved forests, while a toxic undead blight choked all life from the land. Malfurion hurried to awaken the other druids, eager to save the wilds.

He and Tyrande trekked across Hyjal and into the snowy hills of Winterspring in order to visit the underground barrow dens where the other druids slept. Malfurion dispatched some of the newly awakened druids to join the Sentinels in battle against the Legion. He sent others to rally the forest creatures and rouse the remaining Wild Gods. These beings were elusive even at the best of times. Without Cenarius to command them, it would be near impossible for the druids to find and convince them to join the fight. Even so, the night elves tried.

The quest to wake the druids was long and arduous, but it gave Malfurion Stormrage and Tyrande Whisperwind time to reconnect. Centuries had passed since they had last met. Malfurion found that the long years of defending the night elves had changed Tyrande. She was fiercer than before, and more willing than ever to make any sacrifice if it meant protecting her people from danger. Malfurion didn't realize just how far Tyrande would go to safeguard the land until they stumbled across an ancient gateway within one of Hyjal's barrow dens.

It was the prison of Malfurion's twin brother, Illidan the Betrayer.

Tyrande saw Illidan Stormrage as a potential weapon. He was a great sorcerer, and his knowledge of demons was without equal among the night elves. If she were to set him free, he could unleash his might against the Legion.

Malfurion vehemently opposed liberating his brother. Time had not changed his opinion of the Betrayer, and he believed Illidan was still a danger to the world.

After weighing the risks, Tyrande made her choice to free Illidan, and she set out on her own. All that stood in her way were the Watchers, an order of night elves who had guarded the Betrayer for millennia. When Tyrande called on them to release Illidan, they openly defied her.

And for that, they paid the ultimate price.

With the fate of Azeroth itself hanging in the balance, Tyrande Whisperwind would not suffer dissent. Not from anyone. She struck down the Watchers who stood in her path and cleared the way to Illidan's prison.

From the darkness of the barrow emerged the Betrayer.

THE BETRAYER

During his ten thousand years of imprisonment, Illidan Stormrage had languished in darkness. The endless solitude had tugged at the threads of his sanity. As time wore on, he had focused his thoughts on finding a way for Azeroth to defend itself against the Legion. Mulling over these scenarios led Illidan to a single conclusion.

Azeroth could never defeat the Legion by fighting a defensive war.

If the demons were turned away, they would come back again. And again. And again. On and on until they finally overwhelmed the world. Even the "victory" during the War of the Ancients had been nothing more than a momentary reprieve.

The key to the Legion's strength was its resilience. If demons were killed on Azeroth, they would merely rematerialize in the Twisting Nether and fight another day. In effect, this made the Legion's numbers endless. The only way to permanently destroy demons was to kill them *within* the Nether or in areas inundated with its energies. And that meant taking the war to the Legion's own domain.

When he finally emerged from his prison, Illidan was desperate to begin his war against the Legion. He had no intention of working with the other night elves. He hadn't forgiven them for his imprisonment. What was more, he knew they would never trust him. Even if he explained the revelations he'd had about defeating the Legion, the elves would either treat his wisdom with suspicion or see him as a madman.

Illidan stormed into Hyjal's war-torn forest. He had no specific destination in mind, but he had a purpose. To bring the Legion to its knees, he needed even greater knowledge and power. Illidan sensed both emanating from northern Ashenvale, where immense fel energies rippled out from the wilds. He followed the magics to their source, and he soon found himself in Felwood.

The first creature to bar his way was not a demon. It was a human who reeked of death.

A DESTINY OF FLAME AND SHADOW

On the Lich King's orders, Arthas Menethil had joined the Legion's invasion of Kalimdor—not to help the demons but to secretly hamper their efforts. The death knight worked from the shadows, always careful not to alert the demons of his intent. He subtly influenced the Scourge, sometimes causing the undead to disobey their Legion masters and run amok. This slowed the demons' progress to Hyjal Summit. Occasionally, it even allowed their enemies to escape.

Yet these measures were only minor nuisances. As Arthas pondered another way to hurt the Legion, he found himself drawn to Tichondrius and the Skull of Gul'dan. The dreadlord had used the artifact to corrupt a large swath of Ashenvale with fel magic. These dark energies spread farther by the day, slowly creeping up Hyjal's slopes.

If Arthas could strike down Tichondrius and destroy the Skull of Gul'dan, it would stop the spread of fel magic and deal a significant blow to the Legion's war effort. Yet slaying the dreadlord was easier said than done. Arthas himself could not destroy Tichondrius without alerting Archimonde to the Lich King's treachery. But what if someone else did the killing for him?

CHAPTER II: THE THIRD WAR

That thought crossed Arthas's mind when he discovered Illidan Stormrage carving a path of destruction through the woodlands. Fel magic suffused the strange night elf, but he was no friend of the Legion. Nor was he a staunch supporter of his own people.

Arthas sensed Illidan's insatiable yearning for power. It would be an easy thing to use the night elf's ambition as a weapon.

In Felwood, Arthas confronted Illidan and enticed the night elf with knowledge. The death knight revealed that a powerful artifact called the Skull of Gul'dan was nearby. Yet finding the relic would not be easy. Arthas warned Illidan that a cunning dreadlord named Tichondrius prowled Felwood.

Illidan was deeply suspicious of Arthas, but he had already sensed the great power emanating from within Felwood. It was too enticing to ignore. Illidan went in search of it and left Arthas behind. It would not be the last time they would meet.

A trail of fallen demons stretched behind Illidan Stormrage by the time he found the Skull of Gul'dan. He was pleased to discover that the artifact was filled with not only energy but knowledge. The skull contained the memories of the orc warlock. Rather than simply draw power from the relic, Illidan consumed its energies entirely. Fel magic surged through his flesh and blood. Massive horns sprouted from Illidan's skull, while leathery wings unfurled from his back. Illidan transformed from a night elf into something else. A demon.

As power flooded into Illidan, so did Gul'dan's memories. He learned of the creature's homeworld, Draenor, and of the mysteries and ancient artifacts locked within the Tomb of Sargeras.

Imbued with this new power, Illidan hunted down Tichondrius and destroyed the dreadlord.

By claiming the Skull of Gul'dan, Illidan had struck a grave blow to the Legion. Felwood would remain tainted, but its corruptive energies would not spread into the rest of Ashenvale or Hyjal.

Despite the fact that he had helped the night elves' war effort, Illidan faced scorn from his brother, and even from Tyrande Whisperwind. He had gone too far in consuming the Skull of Gul'dan. He had become a demon—one of the very creatures that the night elves were struggling to defeat. Malfurion Stormrage banished his brother from night elven lands. Illidan obeyed, but only because he knew that staying in Hyjal was meaningless. If the night elves thwarted the Legion's invasion, it would not matter. A single defeat would not stop the Legion from coming back.

Illidan Stormrage had his own war to fight. For him, it was the only war that mattered.

OPPOSITE: THE LEGION'S WAR PATH THROUGH KALIMDOR IN THE THIRD WAR

Mount Hyjal

FELWOOD

Stonetalon Peak

ASHENVALE

Demon Fall Canyon

THE BARRENS

MULGORE

The Legion's War Path

THE BATTLE OF MOUNT HYJAL
21 YEARS AFTER THE DARK PORTAL

As the Legion steadily ascended Mount Hyjal and approached the second Well of Eternity, thousands of night elf Sentinels and druids gathered near the mountain's summit. They did not fight alone. Though the druids had been unable to summon the Wild Gods, they had rallied many other forest spirits to their cause, such as the dryads and the keepers of the grove. The Horde and the Alliance refugees also hacked away at the demonic army with all their strength.

This gathering of races had not been seen since the War of the Ancients. Even so, the defenders were outnumbered. Worse still, most of them were not working together. The night elves and the forest creatures were wary of the Horde and the Alliance refugees. Tyrande Whisperwind in particular believed that the two factions were responsible for leading the Legion to Kalimdor.

With Hyjal's defenders in disarray, Archimonde sensed that victory was within his grasp. But he did not know of Medivh's presence or of his grand designs.

Medivh brought Thrall, Jaina Proudmoore, Tyrande Whisperwind, and Malfurion Stormrage to his side. The meeting was tense. Tyrande balked at the idea of unifying with the Alliance refugees and the Horde. But Medivh eventually convinced her to put aside her prejudices for the good of Azeroth. The disparate factions unified, but they knew they could not defeat Archimonde through brute force.

Malfurion proposed a solution. A dangerous and costly one. The World Tree Nordrassil was imbued with powerful enchantments from the Dragon Aspects, enchantments that granted the night elves immortality and immunity to sickness and disease. Malfurion believed that he and his fellow druids could ignite these magics, causing an explosion that would annihilate Archimonde and the Legion invaders. But doing so would also destroy the enchantments, leaving the night elves vulnerable to aging and sickness for the first time in over ten thousand years. The impact on night elven society would be devastating, but the defenders had little other choice.

As Malfurion and his druids prepared to draw out Nordrassil's enchantments, the rest of the defenders dug in around Hyjal's summit to buy them time. Orcs and humans, night elves and tauren, trolls and dwarves—all fought a bitter battle against a relentless tide of undead and demons.

Thousands of defenders died that day, but they did not give their lives in vain. By the time Archimonde reached Nordrassil, Malfurion and his druids had completed their work. Countless incorporeal spirits known as wisps emerged from the forests around Hyjal. They closed in around Archimonde, but they did not attack him. At Malfurion's urging, they instead channeled their energies into the World Tree and ignited the enchantments within.

A shockwave of blinding energy erupted from Nordrassil, shaking Kalimdor to its roots. Archimonde was instantly destroyed. So were most of his undead and demons. The Legion's hopes of seizing the second Well of Eternity were shattered.

The defenders immediately launched a counterattack against the surviving Legion forces. Their furious assault destroyed almost all of what remained of the demons and undead in Kalimdor. Arthas Menethil only narrowly escaped the attack. He rallied as many of the Scourge as he could before he retreated to the Eastern Kingdoms.

Following the victory, the Horde and the Alliance refugees departed Hyjal in search of new lands to settle. Their tenuous pact would remain, but it would be tested in the years to come.

Tyrande Whisperwind and Malfurion Stormrage remained in Hyjal and began rebuilding. Most of the surrounding woodlands were in ruins. Worse yet, Nordrassil had been damaged by the explosion. Many of its great roots, which had provided life-giving energies to the world, withered and died. Though Nordrassil would heal in time, the enchantments from the Dragon Aspects were gone. The night elves would no longer enjoy immortality or immunity to sickness. They would grow old and infirm. They would die, just like all other mortal races. The damage wrought by the explosion also made it far more difficult for Malfurion and the other druids to reach the Emerald Dream.

From afar, Medivh surveyed the war-torn world and was relieved by what he saw. The Legion's invasion had failed. Azeroth was safe . . . for now. Medivh knew that other threats, like the Lich King, yet lurked in the dark corners of the world, but he could not stop them. His powers were waning, and he felt that his time on the physical plane was coming to an end.

The task of safeguarding Azeroth now fell to its inhabitants, just as he had intended. Medivh had shown them that there was strength in unity. All he could do was hope that they would continue fighting together as they had on Hyjal.

And with that, the Last Guardian of Azeroth vanished.

THE FROZEN THRONE

CHAPTER III
THE FROZEN THRONE

UPRISING

Once more, against impossible odds, Azeroth's defenders had turned back the Burning Legion. Despite the crushing defeat, the demon lord Kil'jaeden did not believe that all was lost. He still had the Lich King, some of his dreadlords, and the Scourge at his disposal. The undead had suffered heavy losses in Kalimdor, but thousands of the monstrous creatures remained in control of Lordaeron. The Scourge could quickly replenish their ranks and mount another attack.

But when Kil'jaeden reached out to the Lich King, his hopes died. The entity *refused* the demon lord's command.

The Lich King had seen the defeat at Mount Hyjal as an opportunity to break free of the Legion, and he wasted no time. He rallied Arthas Menethil, Kel'Thuzad, and the rest of the Scourge in Lordaeron. With his forces amassed and completely under his control, he sent them against his remaining dreadlord handlers: Balnazzar, Varimathras, and Detheroc.

The dreadlords stood little chance against the seething mass of undead. The demons fled into the Plaguelands and used their dark magics to shroud themselves from sight.

Now the Legion could not oppose the Lich King. The Scourge was his, and his alone.

Kil'jaeden had always suspected that the Lich King might rise against him. What the demon lord hadn't expected was how devious his weapon had become. The Lich King had hidden his true might from Kil'jaeden and the dreadlords. He'd played the part of a loyal servant, all the while manipulating the demons. As the Scourge had grown, so, too, had the Lich King's strength. His psychic power was far beyond what it had once been.

The opportunity to use the Lich King to launch another Legion assault against Kalimdor had slipped away. Far worse, the entity now posed a direct threat to the demons. If the Lich King conquered Azeroth, any future demonic invasions would be nearly impossible.

There was but one thing left to do: destroy the Lich King. Kil'jaeden sensed a new demon on Azeroth who was strong enough to complete the task. Someone who had allied with the Legion during the War of the Ancients...

SERVANT OF THE LEGION

In consuming the Skull of Gul'dan, Illidan Stormrage had acquired otherworldly knowledge and strength. But transforming into a demon had also made his presence known to Kil'jaeden.

From afar, Kil'jaeden reached out to Illidan with an offer. If the former night elf destroyed the Lich King, he would be granted anything his heart desired. Illidan was intrigued. Given his history of fighting the Legion, he would have expected Kil'jaeden to see him as an enemy, not a potential ally. Clearly, the demon lord needed him, and he thought the former night elf would simply bend the knee for a few scraps of power.

Kil'jaeden knew nothing of Illidan's singular quest to annihilate the Legion. Though it took great effort, the former night elf buried his true thoughts deep within his mind and hid them from the demon lord.

Illidan feigned allegiance to Kil'jaeden and accepted the offer, seeing it as an opportunity to learn more about the Legion. He was also eager to rid the world of the Lich King. In his view, the entity was nothing more than a Legion-forged weapon. The sooner he culled the creature from Azeroth, the sooner he could focus all his attention on the Legion itself.

From what Illidan knew of the Scourge and its vast numbers, a frontal assault against the Lich King would be impossible. He had something else in mind, something more suited to his sorcerous abilities.

The Skull of Gul'dan had granted him knowledge of an artifact called the Eye of Sargeras. It could act as a conduit for Illidan's own magic, amplifying it and allowing him to strike the Lich King from a great distance. There was only one hurdle to overcome, and it was immense. The artifact lay across the sea in the Tomb of Sargeras, an ancient structure on an archipelago known as the Broken Isles.

The Broken Isles had once been part of the night elven empire, but that was over ten thousand years ago. Illidan knew little of what dangers might await him there now. He needed allies to help him recover the Eye of Sargeras, but he could not ask for assistance from the night elves, not after Malfurion Stormrage had banished him from their lands.

Moreover, Illidan was being hunted. The night elf Watchers who had guarded him for millennia were furious that Tyrande Whisperwind had set him free—none more so than the order's leader, Warden Maiev Shadowsong.

The epitome of the Watchers, Maiev was a militaristic proponent of the law who dedicated her life to watching over prisoners and hunting down dangerous criminals. She saw Tyrande's liberation of Illidan as more than an act of recklessness. She saw it as treason. Tyrande had killed many of the Watchers to unleash the Betrayer. Maiev would never forgive her for that. *Never.* Nor would she allow Illidan Stormrage to walk free.

Illidan knew that it was only a matter of time before the Watchers found him. With little other choice, he reached out to creatures from his past: the Highborne sorcerers.

LEGACY OF THE HIGHBORNE

Ten thousand years ago, when the original Well of Eternity imploded during the War of the Ancients, the Highborne sorcerers were sucked into the depths of the sea alongside their queen, Azshara. There, in the darkness beneath the waves, they found salvation from the Old Gods.

In exchange for servitude, the Old Gods spared the Highborne from their watery doom. But there was a price. The elves were twisted into scaly serpentine creatures called naga. Their hearts became as black as the deepest ocean trenches, and hate enveloped their thoughts.

Illidan Stormrage had heard only rumors of the Highborne's fate. Whether they were true, he did not know. But when he cast a powerful spell to reach the Highborne in the ocean deeps, they answered. A group of naga led by Lady Vashj emerged from the depths, an army of scale and fang. One and all, they pledged themselves to Illidan.

The naga did not come because of the history they shared with the former night elf. Nor did they respect his power as a demon. They came because the Old Gods willed it.

The Old Gods had taken notice of Illidan. His hunger for power and his chaotic past intrigued them. His quest to destroy the Lich King could spark a new war on Azeroth, one that would likely envelop the undead, the world's nations, *and* the Legion. With that kind of turmoil consuming Azeroth, Cho'gall and his cultists could awaken the Old Gods relatively unopposed.

Illidan had the potential to be very useful, and the Old Gods had sent the naga to make sure his campaign against the Lich King succeeded. If the former night elf became troublesome, so be it. The Old Gods would simply command the naga to cut out his fel-corrupted heart.

Either way, the Old Gods were confident that they could use Illidan Stormrage to bring a new age of conflict to the world.

THE EYE OF SARGERAS

With the help of his new allies, Illidan Stormrage crossed the Great Sea and reached the Broken Isles. He had grown up in the region, but that had been long before the Great Sundering. Time and isolation had changed the Broken Isles. Illidan sensed and saw many intriguing creatures prowling the shores, but he did not indulge his curiosity. Maiev Shadowsong and her Watchers were on his heels.

Illidan outmaneuvered his hunters and plunged into the Tomb of Sargeras. He felt forbidden magic stirring in the depths of the ominous tower, along with other things. This was a cursed place, a monument to death and betrayal. Danger lurked in every corner. Gul'dan's memories helped him safely navigate the tomb's winding, water-logged corridors. He found the Eye of Sargeras not a moment too soon. A number of Watchers had closed in around him, but whatever chance they might have had to restrain Illidan was gone. With his sorcerous power magnified by the Eye of Sargeras, he was beyond their control.

Of those Watchers who confronted Illidan in the tomb, only Maiev survived.

Severely wounded, she retreated to the surface and rallied the rest of her Watchers. Her brush with death did not frighten her into abandoning her hunt. To the contrary, she was desperate to destroy Illidan as soon as possible. He had slaughtered many of her loyal Watchers. Vengeance burned hot in Maiev's soul.

She dispatched a messenger to Kalimdor, imploring Malfurion Stormrage for aid. No matter what, she would not run again. Maiev and the remaining Watchers on the Broken Isles prepared to make a final stand against Illidan.

Illidan later emerged from the tomb, though somewhat reluctantly. There was more power he could gain from the structure, but he knew that Maiev was still alive. Something else consumed his attention as well. The Eye of Sargeras was not quite as powerful as he had expected. Even when he channeled his own magic through the artifact, he could not assault the Lich King. The distance was too vast. He needed an additional source of magic to amplify his spellwork. Once more he sifted through the knowledge in Gul'dan's memories. And, once more, he found an answer.

In his mind's eye, he saw a glimmering city to the east. Not only was it filled with magic, but it was also constructed on a nexus of potent arcane ley lines. The city's name was Dalaran.

Illidan sent Lady Vashj and most of her naga ahead to scout out Dalaran and its surrounding ley lines in preparation for the attack. The former night elf would deal with Maiev Shadowsong himself. As long as she was living, she would be a thorn in his side. It was time to tear out that thorn and crush it beneath his heel once and for all.

Illidan and his remaining allies assaulted Maiev and her Watchers. The night elves were wounded and exhausted. They knew the battle to come would be their last, but they faced it with grim determination. Maiev's only desire was that with her dying breath, she might have the chance to strike down Illidan Stormrage.

She would not get her wish.

As the battle unfolded, a force of night elf Sentinels and druids arrived. Leading them were Malfurion Stormrage and Tyrande Whisperwind. When Maiev's messenger had reached them with news that Illidan had gathered an army and was seeking out demonic artifacts, they both had been horrified. Tyrande felt personally responsible for Illidan's treachery. She didn't regret releasing him. Given the circumstances, that had been necessary. But the Illidan she'd known, her friend and confidant from ten thousand years ago, was no more. In his place was something else. A monster little better than those that had invaded Mount Hyjal.

The night elf reinforcements turned the tide of battle against Illidan, and he escaped to the east, desperate to reach Dalaran. He could have used the Eye of Sargeras against Tyrande and Malfurion, but he could not bring himself to do it. Even though the two night elves saw him as a traitor, he still harbored feelings for both of them.

CURSE OF THE BLOOD ELVES

Much had changed in the Eastern Kingdoms since Lordaeron's fall. The Scourge continued roaming the land, hunting down survivors and clashing with Alliance resistance forces. Yet Lordaeron was not the only nation struggling to cope with the aftermath of defeat. The high elves of Quel'Thalas had suffered just as many losses as their neighbors to the south. Not only had the death knight Arthas Menethil left the once-beautiful lands a blighted graveyard, but he had also tainted the Sunwell, the fount of arcane magic that was the beating heart of high elven society. Grieving for the decimation of their homeland, the high elves decided to call themselves blood elves in honor of their fallen people.

Arthas had also killed Quel'Thalas's king, Anasterian Sunstrider. By right of succession, rule over the elves fell to the sorcerous prince Kael'thas Sunstrider, but at first he was nowhere to be found. The heir to the throne had been in Dalaran during his homeland's downfall. When he received word of the attack, he rushed to Quel'Thalas. By then, the battle had already been lost.

The surviving elves greeted Kael'thas with thinly veiled resentment. Rather than fighting to protect Quel'Thalas, he had been in Dalaran. To many elves, it seemed that Kael'thas enjoyed spending his time in that distant city more than in his own homeland.

Kael'thas made no excuses for being absent in Quel'Thalas's hour of need. His people had every right to be bitter. He resolved to prove himself to the elves and do whatever he could to rebuild their kingdom. It was not easy for him. In truth, Kael'thas *had* always felt distant from his people. They were largely insular and isolationist, but he had been quite the opposite. He had wanted to see the world, to interact with different races and learn new ideas.

He surveyed Silvermoon City's ruins and attended his father's funeral, but he struggled to connect with the elves. Nonetheless, Kael'thas continued trying. He did love his people and his kingdom, more than some elves might have known. And this love was what drew him to the tainted Sunwell.

Kael'thas was horrified at the sight of the Sunwell and the twisted energies swirling through its depths. Through his attunement to magic, he sensed that the fount's dark power was gradually enveloping Quel'Thalas. In time, it would seep into the hearts and minds of the blood elves and kill them all. There was no means to cleanse the Sunwell with any certainty. Quel'Thalas's other senior blood elves had come to the same conclusion. Along with Kael'thas, they decided there was only one way to stop the spread of the Sunwell's toxic energies.

Kael'thas gathered the most powerful magi in Quel'Thalas at the fount. In unison, they conducted a great ritual that destroyed the Sunwell. A burst of energy cascaded out from the fount, obliterating the remaining Scourge in the area.

The loss of the fount was immediately felt by the blood elves. They had lived their entire lives bathed in the Sunwell's energies, so much so that they had become addicted to arcane magic. Now cut off from the fount, they began suffering from withdrawal. The pangs of addiction would only grow more debilitating as time passed, and many elves would fall ill and become lethargic.

Though Kael'thas was troubled by this new development, more immediate dangers consumed his attention. The Scourge were still in firm control of Lordaeron. As long as the undead roamed the nearby land, the blood elves would never know peace. If Kael'thas and his people were to rebuild their kingdom, they needed to help the remnants of the Alliance defeat the Scourge.

BATTLE BETWEEN SCOURGE AND ALLIANCE FORCES IN THE THIRD WAR

Kael'thas's father had seceded from the Alliance, but that did not stop the prince from lending aid to the faction. He gathered his healthiest soldiers and journeyed into Lordaeron to join the fight against the undead. The prince appointed a seasoned ranger named Lor'themar Theron to serve as regent lord in Quel'Thalas and watch over the rest of the blood elves in his stead.

Kael'thas's departure did not surprise most blood elves. Once again, he was leaving behind his homeland and venturing to distant lands.

CHILDREN OF BLOOD AND STARS

Though many pockets of Alliance resistance were scattered across Lordaeron, the largest group had gathered in Silverpine Forest. This force was led by a human, Grand Marshal Othmar Garithos. As the highest-ranking survivor of Lordaeron's military, Garithos was leader of the army by chance, not because of merit. He was far from the ideal commander. Garithos was an ill-tempered and xenophobic man who scorned the non-human races in his ranks.

Prince Kael'thas Sunstrider and his blood elves were not spared from the grand marshal's bigotry. When the prince pledged his loyalty to the Alliance resistance, Garithos accepted it purely out of necessity. He made no attempt to hide his disdain for the elves.

Despite the chilly reception, Kael'thas committed himself and his people to the war effort. The blood elves quickly proved themselves to be one of the most effective fighting forces in the Alliance army. They seized large swaths of land in Silverpine Forest and slowly worked their way toward the ruins of Dalaran. The broken city was still partially under the control of the Kirin Tor, but the surrounding land was swarming with undead.

As Kael'thas approached Dalaran, he made an unsettling discovery. The air crackled with unseen arcane energy, and the earth trembled beneath his feet. Somewhere near Dalaran, a storm of magic was brewing.

Whatever this disturbance was, it threw the Scourge into a frenzy. Undead streamed into the region in greater numbers than ever before. The blood elves braced against the tide of undead, and each day was a struggle to hold their ground. Kael'thas was in the midst of pulling his soldiers back from the front lines when he crossed paths with strangers from a distant land. After braving foul weather and rough seas, Maiev Shadowsong, Tyrande Whisperwind, Malfurion Stormrage, and other night elves had reached Lordaeron's coast in pursuit of Illidan.

Blood elves and night elves shared a common ancestry, but their cultures were vastly different. However, Kael'thas did not find this off-putting. There was much he could learn from his distant cousins, perhaps even something to help ease his people's magical withdrawal. When Kael'thas discovered that the night elves were hunting a powerful demon named Illidan, he theorized that the creature might be responsible for the anomaly in Dalaran. That would explain why the Scourge had suddenly become so frenzied.

Kael'thas agreed to aid the night elves in their hunt for Illidan Stormrage. After more than ten thousand years of separation, the divided elven societies were working together for a common good.

ASSAULT ON THE LICH KING

The night elves were not the only ones hunting Illidan Stormrage. Through the eyes of the undead, the Lich King had seen Lady Vashj and her naga skulking around Dalaran. Their intentions did not become clear until Illidan later appeared in the city's ruins and began his spellwork. He drew on Dalaran's ley lines to amplify the Eye of Sargeras's destructive potential. A rising storm of arcane energy slowly coalesced around Illidan, growing more powerful by the day.

The Lich King had always known that Kil'jaeden would retaliate against him. It seemed the demon lord had found a new agent to do his bidding. And a mighty one at that.

It was clear that Illidan would soon direct his immense spell at the Frozen Throne. Not for the first time, the Lich King was reminded of his one true weakness. He was trapped in ice, which made the entity an easy target for the likes of Illidan. The Lich King's only recourse was to unleash the Scourge on Dalaran and stop the spellwork. The undead flooded through southwestern Lordaeron, but they reached Illidan too late.

He had finished his preparations. Illidan directed the tempest of arcane energy at the roof of the world, channeling its fury into Icecrown Glacier. Even Lady Vashj and her naga were awed by the display of raw power. The influx of magic caused the land itself to buckle. Massive fissures erupted, not only near Dalaran but in regions across the world.

Illidan ignored these unintended effects as well as the Scourge army closing in around him. While his followers held the undead at bay, he focused his mind on Icecrown. Wave after wave of magic pummeled the ice. The bombardment finally cracked the Lich King's prison, leaving the entity exposed. A few more strikes were all that Illidan needed to extinguish the lord of the Scourge. But as he prepared his final barrage, chaos engulfed him. The combined night elf and blood elf armies crashed into Illidan's forces.

The fighting soon reached Illidan himself, and the night elves threw his spellwork into disarray. The Eye of Sargeras crumbled before him. The quaking earth stilled. The roaring storm of magic above Icecrown Glacier went silent. In an instant, Illidan's victory had turned into disaster.

He was furious that the night elves had inadvertently saved the Lich King, but they felt no remorse for their actions. Illidan's spell had devastated the land, and it would have led to even more destruction if they hadn't stopped him. In Illidan's view, the night elves were being shortsighted. They didn't understand that they would need to be ready to sacrifice *everything* to destroy the demons and their creations. The elves didn't have the will to fight Illidan's war against the Legion.

And Illidan did not believe they ever would.

THE DEAD WORLD

Illidan Stormrage knew Kil'jaeden would show him no mercy for his failure. He still had much planning to do in his war against the Legion, and drawing the demon lord's ire at this fragile time could destroy his plans forever. He needed a refuge to escape Kil'jaeden's wrath and gather his forces, and he settled on the world of Draenor. He had first glimpsed it in Gul'dan's memories, a realm left mostly dead and barren by the rampant use of fel magic. Its grim state had not bothered Illidan. If most of Draenor's creatures had died off, it would make it easier for him to carve out his sanctuary there.

But that would only be possible after he replenished his ranks. Most of his forces had perished at the battle within Dalaran's ruins. Lady Vashj and her surviving naga had managed to slip away from the fighting and take shelter deep within nearby Lordamere Lake.

Illidan ordered Lady Vashj to find new allies for his army. In the meantime, he would scout the lands of Draenor himself.

He had discovered a tear in the fabric of reality near Dalaran. Unbeknownst to him, this was where Kel'Thuzad had opened a portal to summon Archimonde and his Legion vanguard into the world. The bridge between Azeroth and the Twisting Nether had long since vanished, but a small rift had been left behind. Illidan used it and the knowledge from the Skull of Gul'dan to weave a new portal, one that led to Draenor.

Illidan expected to step into the world from Gul'dan's memories, a dead place ripe for the taking. What he found was the shattered realm known as Outland. Numerous portals shimmered across the wasted landscape, each one leading to an unknown corner of the cosmos. Through these rifts, the pit lord Magtheridon and a host of demons had reached Outland and laid claim to much of its lands.

The presence of demons troubled Illidan, but he could not return to Azeroth. The night elves would cast him back in his old barrow prison the first chance they had. Illidan's only hope was to stay on Outland and bring it under his control. The broken realm could still serve as a staging ground in his war, but only after he cut off the Legion from the world and dealt with Magtheridon.

As Illidan scouted the Legion forces on Outland, he sensed that someone was hunting him. But by the time he made this discovery, it was already too late.

Maiev Shadowsong and her Watchers had followed Illidan from Azeroth. Without his naga or the Eye of Sargeras, he was easier prey. Maiev outmaneuvered her nemesis and imprisoned him in an enchanted cage, one specially crafted to hold the former night elf and neutralize his sorcerous powers. After so many months of hardship, vengeance was hers.

A Dark Covenant

After Illidan Stormrage's defeat in Dalaran's ruins, Tyrande Whisperwind and Malfurion Stormrage returned to Kalimdor. Though the night elves sympathized with the plight of Lordaeron's defenders, it was time for them to go home. Nordrassil was in a weakened state, and the elves needed to do everything in their power to rebuild the wilds and secure the second Well of Eternity.

With their departure, Kael'thas Sunstrider and his blood elves rendezvoused with Othmar Garithos and the rest of the Alliance forces. They took control of Dalaran and transformed it into their base of operations. Efforts began to rebuild the ruined city.

Reclaiming Dalaran should have been a momentous occasion for Kael'thas, but it was overshadowed by the effects of his people's addiction to magic. He and his elves tried to draw on the city's convergence of ley lines, but they could not gather enough power to satisfy their cravings. The pangs of withdrawal became more pronounced and debilitating. Even Kael'thas struggled to bear the burden.

Serving under Grand Marshal Garithos only increased Kael'thas's aggravation. The human constantly belittled the elves and relegated them to menial tasks. A rift formed between Kael'thas and his commander, and it grew wider by the day.

Lady Vashj and her naga were aware of this rift. From the shadows, they had been watching the blood elves. Lady Vashj had seen the fatigue set in on Kael'thas and his people as they struggled to cope with their addiction. She had also seen their morale dwindle under Garithos's mistreatment. They were almost ripe for conversion to Illidan's cause.

Lady Vashj approached Kael'thas, and she convinced him that the naga meant no harm. She explained that her kind were eager to destroy the undead and that their battle outside Dalaran had been the result of a grudge between Illidan and the night elves. The naga had no ill intentions toward Kael'thas, she assured him.

Kael'thas was initially wary of Lady Vashj, but he would soon see her as a more trustworthy and dependable ally than Garithos.

Before long, the Scourge launched a counterattack to take Dalaran and crush the Alliance resistance. The battle would be one of the largest waged in Lordaeron since the kingdom's fall. For Kael'thas and his blood elves, it would be the last they would ever fight under Garithos's banner.

As the Scourge advanced, part of the undead army began amassing on the Alliance's flank. Garithos dispatched blood elves to the new front and commanded them to stop the undead before they reached Dalaran. Kael'thas and his people obeyed, but victory seemed impossible. Garithos had divided the blood elf forces, keeping most of their soldiers under his own command on the main battlefront. The Scourge were poised to overrun Kael'thas when aid arrived from Lady Vashj and her naga.

Kael'thas had little choice other than to accept their help. His decision saved his life. With the naga, the blood elves halted the Scourge advance, protecting the main Alliance army's flank and allowing it to drive back the undead assault.

When Garithos learned what had happened, he did not praise Kael'thas; he condemned him. Like most humans, the grand marshal considered the naga to be sinister creatures, little better than the Scourge. Kael'thas's alliance with them was seen as an act of unforgivable treason.

93

Garithos bound the blood elves in chains and locked them within Dalaran's dungeons to await execution. Kael'thas was stunned by his treatment. He had weathered his commander's bigoted ramblings, but this was too much for him to bear. Down in the dark corridors below Dalaran, he lost all faith in the Alliance.

Once again, Lady Vashj appeared in Kael'thas's moment of need. She slipped into the dungeons under cover of night and extended him an offer. The Alliance had nothing to give the blood elves, but Illidan . . . Illidan could give them everything they wanted: freedom from their chains and their addiction to magic.

Seeing no future for his people in the Alliance, Kael'thas Sunstrider agreed to join Illidan Stormrage. He could think of no better alternative. Even if Kael'thas somehow escaped from Dalaran's dungeons, he would return to Quel'Thalas as an outlaw and a failure. He could not face his people again until he had found a way to help them.

The path to saving Quel'Thalas did not lie on the world of Azeroth. It lay beyond.

CIVIL WAR IN THE PLAGUELANDS

The Lich King had survived Illidan Stormrage's attack, but he would never be the same. His essence was bleeding through the crack in the Frozen Throne. As his power escaped, his hold on the Scourge weakened. His once-oppressive will slowly faded from the minds of many undead in Lordaeron. They felt something familiar returning to them, something they had lost in death. *Free will.*

Most of the undead were perplexed by this change. They wandered the fallen kingdom in confusion, unsure of what to do. But there were other Scourge who saw the Lich King's weakness as an opportunity for revenge. Among them was the banshee Sylvanas Windrunner.

Ever since her death, Sylvanas had thrashed against the Lich King's control. Her efforts had always been fruitless. The Lich King's will had been as strong as steel, and the entity had forced her to make war against the living. Her hatred of the Lich King and his foremost servant, Arthas Menethil, had swelled. Vengeance and rage consumed her soul, but she'd had no means to channel them at her enemies.

Now she did. Sylvanas rallied other free-willed undead and gave them a purpose. They would never again have the lives that had been stolen from them, but they would have revenge. Their first victim would be the creature who had devastated Sylvanas's beautiful kingdom, he who had ripped away her future and made her into a monster: Arthas.

Sylvanas wasn't the only one seeking to destroy the death knight. Varimathras and the other dreadlords had learned of the Lich King's weakness. They took control over part of the Scourge with the hope of eventually launching an invasion into Northrend to vanquish the lord of the undead. Much like Sylvanas, they knew that eliminating Arthas was the first step toward this goal.

Arthas was in no condition to quell these uprisings. As the Lich King's power faded, so, too, did his own. The once-feared and nearly invincible death knight found himself hunted on multiple fronts by Sylvanas and the dreadlords. Though Arthas was willing to fight, he had a more pressing purpose. The Lich King had commanded him to abandon Lordaeron. The entity needed all those Scourge that were still loyal to him to be at his side in Northrend, for he knew it was only a matter of time before Kil'jaeden struck at the Frozen Throne.

The Lich King was right to expect a reprisal from his enemies. But it would not come from the dreadlords or Sylvanas Windrunner. It would come from Outland.

SERVANTS OF THE BETRAYER

After reaching Outland, Kael'thas Sunstrider and Lady Vashj led their people through the cracked, barren expanse of Hellfire Peninsula. Illidan Stormrage was nowhere to be found. For days, the blood elves and naga wandered the desolation until they spied Warden Maiev Shadowsong and her Watchers.

Though Maiev had captured Illidan, she had been unable to find a way back to Azeroth. The gateway she had used was gone. Many other portals existed on Outland, but none of them led home. Maiev did not know the geography of the shattered realm, nor what dangers awaited her. She and her Watchers treaded carefully until they discovered something quite unexpected: soldiers from the Alliance.

The remnants of the Sons of Lothar had established a bastion known as Honor Hold in Hellfire Peninsula. Maiev saw these refugees as her best chance of finding a way out of Outland. But before the Watchers could reach Honor Hold, Kael'thas and Lady Vashj struck. The blood elves and naga emerged from the dust-blown wastes with blades drawn. Fierce though the Watchers were, they were hopelessly outnumbered. Kael'thas and Lady Vashj liberated Illidan and drove Maiev and her surviving followers into the wilds.

Illidan suppressed the urge to hunt down Maiev. Chasing after the warden on the Broken Isles had ultimately been a waste of time, and he would not repeat the same mistake twice, no matter how much he wanted to destroy her.

Illidan appraised his new forces with satisfaction. The blood elves were highly trained and loyal fighters. Their leader, Kael'thas Sunstrider, was a gifted sorcerer, albeit wrestling with inner demons. Illidan immediately sensed the turmoil gnawing at the elves' hearts. He bluntly told Kael'thas that there was no cure for their addiction to magic. However, that did not mean they were doomed to live in torment. Illidan promised to find a new source of magic for Kael'thas, one even greater than the Sunwell.

It was not the answer Kael'thas had been hoping for, but it enticed him nonetheless. It wasn't often that he met someone with a greater mastery of magic than he had. Kael'thas had already come this far. He would cast his lot with Illidan.

Following his liberation, Illidan formed a plan to seize Outland from Magtheridon and the Legion's forces. First, he would shut down the numerous gateways on Outland, portals through which the Legion sent reinforcements to the realm. Then Illidan would launch his army at Magtheridon's seat of power: the Black Temple in Shadowmoon Valley.

The campaign was unforgiving. Illidan asked much of his followers, and he gave little in the way of praise. But his unwavering sense of purpose and the sheer force of his will energized his soldiers and pushed them forward.

As Illidan Stormrage closed in on the Black Temple, he found new allies among the Broken. The twisted creatures were part of the Ashtongue tribe, and they were led by a former draenei exarch named Akama. He also sought to liberate the Black Temple from Magtheridon, albeit for different reasons. The stronghold had once been a sacred draenei site. Akama saw reclaiming it as a means to redeem the Broken in the eyes of the draenei race.

THE BINDING OF MAGTHERIDON

Illidan Stormrage's army crashed against the Black Temple and drew the wrath of its defenders. Magtheridon had infused orcs with his blood, transforming them into crimson-skinned, battle-crazed warriors called fel orcs. Demons fought alongside these soldiers, training the Legion's war machines on the invaders. They bathed the terrain outside the walls in emerald fire, but it wasn't enough. Illidan and his followers cut their way through the Legion's defenders and confronted Magtheridon himself.

Illidan, Lady Vashj, Akama, and Kael'thas Sunstrider were formidable on their own. But together, they were unstoppable. For all his terrible strength, Magtheridon succumbed to his enemies with alarming speed.

Illidan could have killed Magtheridon, but the pit lord was more useful to him alive than dead. He had seen what the demon's blood had done to the fel orcs. It had transformed them into bloodthirsty creatures who lived for only one thing: war. Illidan could use such single-minded soldiers in his own army. And with Magtheridon's blood, he could create even more.

Illidan appeared before the rest of the Black Temple's defenders. He offered them a simple choice: bend the knee or face oblivion. Some chose death, but most accepted Illidan as their new master. Though many were fel orcs, demons also bowed their heads in subservience.

The fact that Illidan allowed demons into his army appalled Kael'thas and Akama, but he assuaged their fears. Forging a pact with demons was an opportunity. They could reveal much about the Legion's strengths and weaknesses. This knowledge could aid Illidan and his allies when Kil'jaeden inevitably retaliated against him.

That retaliation came much sooner than Illidan expected. On the heels of victory, the fiery visage of Kil'jaeden appeared before him and his followers.

The demon lord had learned of Illidan's insurrection on Outland. He trusted Illidan even less than he had before, but he believed the former night elf was useful. Illidan had gathered new allies like Kael'thas, and his army had grown.

Kil'jaeden was still confident he could manipulate Illidan. Demons were conniving creatures, and it was not uncommon for them to betray each other in search of power. That was exactly how Kil'jaeden saw Illidan's recent transgression: his servant had claimed Outland as a prize. Kil'jaeden demanded that Illidan return to Azeroth and finish off the Lich King. If he obeyed, Outland would be his to do with as he pleased. If he disobeyed, Kil'jaeden would do everything in his power to rip the broken realm from Illidan's control and destroy the former night elf.

ILLIDAN STORMRAGE, AKAMA, LADY VASHJ, AND KAEL'THAS SUNSTRIDER BATTLE MAGTHERIDON

For Illidan, this ultimatum was a stroke of good fortune. He needed more time before he could begin his true war against the Legion, and Kil'jaeden had given him just that. Illidan Stormrage once again feigned subservience and rallied his army to invade Azeroth. Using one of the many portals on Outland, he crafted a new gateway back to that world.

He did not take the full might of his forces with him. Illidan left behind Akama and some of his other followers to secure Outland in his absence.

THE ASCENSION

When Illidan Stormrage and his army arrived on Azeroth, the Lich King's worst fears were realized. Kil'jaeden had sent his servants to vanquish him for good. They were determined, and they wielded formidable magics that helped them reach Northrend with astonishing speed.

Arthas Menethil had no such way to hasten his journey. By the time he set foot in Northrend, Illidan's forces were already marching toward Icecrown Citadel.

There was only one route by which Arthas could reach the Lich King before his enemies did. He plunged into the forgotten corridors of Azjol-Nerub, the nerubian kingdom that stretched below the earth. It was not an easy path, nor was it a safe one. Azjol-Nerub was ancient, a place built when the world was young. Minions of the Old Gods lurked in its depths, and they were determined to stop Arthas from helping his master.

And Arthas was just as determined to find a way through the forgotten city. In desperation, he cleaved through the Old Gods' servants and emerged at Icecrown Glacier before Illidan. In preparation for war, the death knight rallied every undead he could find in the frozen wastes.

Illidan was surprised at the sudden appearance of Arthas and the Scourge, but he was not deterred. Battle erupted in the shadow of Icecrown Citadel. Neither side took prisoners. This was not a war of conquest; it was one of total annihilation.

As the fighting wore on, Arthas rode out to meet Illidan in one-on-one combat.

Though his energies were dissipating, the Lich King infused some of his remaining power into Arthas. It was a dangerous gamble that pushed the entity even closer to the edge of oblivion, but it was the only chance he had to survive. If Arthas failed, the Lich King would fall, and so, too, would the rest of the Scourge. But if the death knight succeeded, it would turn the tide of battle against the blood elves and the naga.

In full view of the two armies, Arthas Menethil fought Illidan Stormrage. Frostmourne crashed against the former night elf's legendary warglaives, the Twin Blades of Azzinoth. Bolstered by the Lich King's infusion of power, Arthas gained the upper hand.

Frostmourne sliced into Illidan's flesh and nearly killed him. Yet Arthas never delivered the final blow. The Lich King's will urged him to go to the Frozen Throne as soon as possible.

As Arthas sought out his master, the Scourge slaughtered as many of the blood elves and naga as they could. Illidan and what was left of his army retreated to Outland in disgrace.

Illidan was gone, but that did not change the fact that the Lich King's power was continuing to bleed through the crack in the Frozen Throne. The Lich King would eventually fade from existence altogether, his energies dissipating into Northrend's frigid air. There was but one way to escape this fate: to merge with his greatest champion.

ILLIDAN STORMRAGE CONFRONTS THE DEATH KNIGHT ARTHAS MENETHIL IN NORTHREND

Through this act, the Lich King could do more than save himself from oblivion. He could finally claim a physical vessel and use it to free himself from the Frozen Throne. The Lich King knew of the inner doubts that had long plagued Arthas, and he believed the death knight's mind would be easy to subdue.

At his master's command, Arthas stepped before the Frozen Throne and shattered it with a single strike from Frostmourne. The enchanted helm containing the Lich King's spirit tumbled to the death knight's feet.

If Arthas took up the helm, the Lich King promised him that he would ascend to *true* power, but the death knight hesitated. Was his master merely seeking to use him? Would the Lich King destroy his mind after he donned the helm? He did not know for sure, but one thing was certain: if he did nothing, his master would fade away, and Arthas would be weakened. His enemies were many, and they would do anything to end his existence. Without the Lich King's power to draw on, Arthas feared he would eventually fall to his hunters.

Thus, Arthas embraced the unknown and placed the helm upon his head. The Lich King's power flooded into him. Their spirits merged, becoming one of the mightiest entities the world had ever known.

THE BANSHEE QUEEN

Arthas Menethil's departure from Lordaeron did not bring peace to the region. Undead that were still loyal to the Lich King roamed from the center of the fallen kingdom to the eastern edge of the Plaguelands. From the southwest, Othmar Garithos and the remnants of the Alliance were launching offensives into these lands. And trapped between these sides were two rebel undead factions: one led by Sylvanas Windrunner, and the other by the dreadlords Balnazzar, Detheroc, and Varimathras.

The dreadlords sensed the hatred burning within Sylvanas, and they saw her as a useful ally. They offered her a place in their army.

In response, Sylvanas gave them war. She had only recently regained her freedom from the Lich King, and she was not about to pledge herself to a new master. What was more, the dreadlords had helped bring the plague of undeath to Azeroth. They had helped create Arthas. And, by extension, they had made *her* into a monster.

Varimathras was the first to succumb to Sylvanas. To escape defeat, he kneeled before her and promised to act as her obedient servant. Loyalty meant little to demons, a fact that Sylvanas understood well. But she saw Varimathras as a potential weapon. He was powerful, and he knew what tactics the other dreadlords would use against her. As long as he remained useful, she would allow him to draw breath.

Sylvanas gave no quarter to the other dreadlords. Though her undead were few, she had gained formidable new powers in undeath. Moreover, her years as a ranger-general had made her a master of strategy and battlefield tactics, and she methodically dismantled the dreadlords' forces.

Detheroc was the next dreadlord to fall before her wrath. Balnazzar barricaded himself behind the walls of Lordaeron's fallen capital and prepared for the inevitable siege. His efforts were in vain. Sylvanas and her forces stormed through the city, defeating the dreadlord and seizing the stronghold for themselves.

With the capital under her control, Sylvanas now had a refuge to protect herself from her enemies. She named her followers the Forsaken and proclaimed herself their Banshee Queen. Sylvanas ordered the Forsaken to establish a new kingdom in the city's subterranean crypts, dungeons, and sewers. This putrid warren became known as the Undercity. In its toxic corridors, Sylvanas Windrunner and her Forsaken planned their vengeance against the Lich King.

THE FRACTURING OF THE LIGHT

After Arthas Menethil merged with the Lich King, he remained in Northrend. The task of commanding the Scourge in Lordaeron fell to Kel'Thuzad. Though Sylvanas Windrunner and her Forsaken were entrenched in the Undercity, the lich's undead still dominated much of the Plaguelands. Yet there was one troublesome enemy that constantly vied for control of Kel'Thuzad's domain.

The Order of the Silver Hand had been devastated by the war with the Scourge, but its remaining paladins banded together and vowed to drive the undead from the land. Among these pious warriors was Alexandros Mograine, wielder of the Ashbringer. The weapon, crafted in Ironforge and infused with the Holy Light, had become a thing of legend. It destroyed any undead that it touched, leaving only ash in its wake. As the paladins waged battle against the Scourge, word of Alexandros's deeds spread. He soon took on the same name as his sword.

THE FATE OF GARITHOS

Sylvanas Windrunner did not lay siege to Lordaeron's capital alone. Detheroc had ensorcelled Othmar Garithos and many Alliance soldiers. When Sylvanas defeated the dreadlord, she also liberated the human commander and his forces. Garithos distrusted Sylvanas and her undead, but he saw the dreadlords as an even greater threat. He agreed to help Sylvanas assault the capital, and she promised to give him control of it in return.

Only too late did Garithos learn what a promise from Sylvanas truly meant. After conquering the city, Sylvanas rewarded Garithos with death. Her ghouls feasted on the human's remains. All they left behind were bones.

THE BROKEN
ISLES

Tomb of
Sargeras

The Sunwell

Silvermoon City

QUEL'THALAS

LORDAERON

The Undercity

THE
PLAGUELANDS

SILVERPINE
FOREST

Dalaran

The paladins were elusive and resourceful, and the Scourge had little luck defeating them in open combat. While these holy warriors focused their attention on the undead, another foe infiltrated their ranks unseen: Balnazzar.

The dreadlord had succumbed to Sylvanas's forces in the siege on Lordaeron's capital, but he had not been destroyed. He had used the last of his power to flee into the Plaguelands. Without the help of the other dreadlords, his command over the undead was limited. He kept to the shadows, fearful that the Scourge might one day discover his presence. In the paladins, Balnazzar saw a means to protect himself—a means to create a new army.

Balnazzar killed a venerated paladin named Saidan Dathrohan, and then he assumed his form. In the guise of such a respected holy warrior, the dreadlord was confident that he could twist most of the paladins into his service. Yet there was one he believed was beyond his reach: Alexandros Mograine. The wielder of the Ashbringer embodied piety and valor. The sooner he was gone, the sooner the other paladins would fall under Balnazzar's influence.

Over time, the dreadlord manipulated Alexandros's eldest son, Renault Mograine. He turned the young human to darkness and forced him to commit one of the gravest of acts.

Renault murdered his father with the Ashbringer.

Alexandros's corpse and the Ashbringer sword were later recovered by the Scourge. Kel'Thuzad saw a use for both of them. The lich raised the legendary paladin into undeath and transformed him into an obedient servant. The Ashbringer itself, having been used for such an atrocious purpose, was distorted into an unholy shadow of the sword it had once been.

Alexandros's death rocked the paladins. Some of them suspected that a dark force had taken hold of Saidan Dathrohan and his closest followers, but they could not prove it. Their suspicions created divisions between the paladins. The holy warriors splintered into two separate factions: the Argent Dawn and the Scarlet Crusade.

The Argent Dawn held true to the tenets of the Light, but its counterpart did not. Balnazzar retained control over the Scarlet Crusade. It was just the army he had been searching for, and it soon became synonymous with corruption and extremism.

HUNT FOR THE SUNWELL

North of Lordaeron, the repercussions of the Sunwell's destruction continued to unfold. When Kael'thas Sunstrider and his people destroyed the Sunwell, the massive explosion did not destroy its power. The fount's energies scattered across the land. The red dragon Korialstrasz discovered this unprotected magic, and he was deeply concerned that it would draw the attention of differing factions and ignite a conflict.

His fears were proved correct. Malygos, the Aspect of Magic, sensed the presence of the Sunwell's energies. He dispatched one of his servants, the blue dragon Kalecgos, to investigate just how far the power had spread. The Lich King also felt the ripples of energy cascading from the fount. He ordered Dar'Khan Drathir, the traitor who had delivered Quel'Thalas to the Scourge, to collect this power in the name of the Frozen Throne.

Korialstrasz scoured the ravaged lands around Silvermoon City and gathered every scrap of power he could. Knowing that time was short, he molded a human avatar named Anveena Teague and imbued her with the Sunwell's energy. He gave her false memories and even created an illusion of a human family for her. He hoped that she would escape the notice of anyone hunting the Sunwell's might. Anveena had no idea what she was, nor did she know that dark forces would do anything to claim her power.

Kalecgos and Dar'Khan soon encountered Anveena, but her true nature remained hidden from them for quite some time. Eventually, Dar'Khan unraveled the truth and abducted her, taking her to the site of the ruined Sunwell to siphon the power from her. Kalecgos and Korialstrasz each gave chase, but they found Anveena too late. Dar'Khan had already begun to take the power of the Sunwell for himself.

Using his newfound might, Dar'Khan took control of Korialstrasz and forced him to battle Kalecgos. When all seemed lost, Anveena finally awakened to her true potential. She realized that the power of the Sunwell was within her. She was capable of wielding it herself.

Anveena turned her full fury on Dar'Khan Drathir and defeated him.

After the dust of battle had settled, Anveena Teague remained in Quel'Thalas under the protection of Lor'themar Theron, one of the blood elves' highest-ranking rangers. Kalecgos stayed with her, living under the guise of a half-elf named Kalec. For years, he personally watched over her and kept her presence a secret from the world at large.

HERALDS OF SHADOW

Far from Quel'Thalas, Garona was on the hunt.

She had hounded Cho'gall and his Twilight's Hammer cultists across southern Kalimdor, slowly whittling away at their numbers. Her prey was cunning, but so was she. Garona gave no quarter to her foes. She vowed not to stop killing until she had sunk her daggers into Cho'gall's heart.

Garona's persistence infuriated Cho'gall. She struck from the shadows, disappearing as soon as she'd slain one of his cultists. Cho'gall set traps and laid ambushes for Garona, but she always escaped them. As the days wore on, the Old Gods' whispers thundered in his mind. They were angry—he was taking too long to deal with the meddlesome assassin.

Deep within the dense rain forests of Feralas, Cho'gall found a way to draw Garona out of hiding. At great risk to himself, he sent away his cultists and waited for the huntress. He knew she wanted him dead, and he knew she would never pass up the opportunity to face him, especially when he was without the protection of his followers.

Just as expected, Garona struck. The ogre mage and the half-orc assassin grappled in the misty wilds. Garona gravely wounded Cho'gall, but it was not enough to defeat him.

Cho'gall bested the assassin in combat and brought her under his dominion. Long ago, the Shadow Council had woven mental shackles around Garona's mind, making her into their unwilling servant. The human archmage Khadgar had unraveled these bonds and given the half-orc freedom. Yet Cho'gall knew how to remake them. He forged new mental shackles and transformed Garona into his pet. *His* assassin.

With Garona under his control, Cho'gall returned to his original quest to awaken the Old Gods. He took what remained of his Twilight's Hammer cultists and ventured into the sun-scorched desert of Silithus. Cho'gall sensed an Old God somewhere beneath the golden sands. He felt the entity calling to him, its power stirring in his veins.

And he heard its name whispered in his mind: *C'Thun.*

CHAPTER III: THE FROZEN THRONE

CHAPTER IV
OLD HATREDS

CHAPTER IV
OLD HATREDS

THE NEW WORLD TREE

The Third War had unleashed terrible damage upon the night elves. Their World Tree, Nordrassil, had protected them for thousands of years, but now its enchantments were gone. The night elves would be subject to disease and aging. The damage to Nordrassil also made it more difficult for druids to enter the mystical Emerald Dream.

Archdruid Fandral Staghelm believed he had a solution. He proposed planting a new World Tree, one that would restore the night elves' immortality. He had attempted a similar feat thousands of years ago, when he had planted the World Tree known as Andrassil. That had ended in failure, but Fandral had learned from his mistakes. More importantly, he felt there was no choice but to act.

Malfurion Stormrage rejected his plan. He remembered Fandral's last attempt to plant a World Tree. Corruption had taken hold in Andrassil and spread throughout the land, driving innocent creatures to madness. Malfurion and other druids had been forced to fell the great tree, which they renamed Vordrassil. Its dead stump was a cold reminder of the danger of meddling with powers that only the Dragon Aspects could wield.

Fandral seethed with rage. In his eyes, Malfurion was refusing to take bold steps to ensure the future of their people. Fandral dreamed of what could be possible with the power of a revitalized World Tree, and he secretly hoped to resurrect his fallen son, Valstann Staghelm. Malfurion was an obstacle to that goal.

One night, while Malfurion slept in his barrow den, Fandral Staghelm ambushed him, plunging the druid into a deep coma and trapping his spirit within the depths of the Emerald Dream.

When Malfurion did not wake, other druids searched the Dream for his spirit, but they could not find it. At first, that was not cause for serious concern. Malfurion had spent millennia within the Emerald Dream before, and after the destruction of the Third War, there was much to be done to restore the druids' connection with the ethereal realm and nature itself. It was easy to assume he was engrossed in important work.

In Malfurion's absence, Fandral Staghelm took control of the druids of the Cenarion Circle and led them to the coastal region of Darkshore, where they joined together to plant a new World Tree. The druids named it *Teldrassil*, or "Crown of the Earth." It soared high over the ocean, its trunk so large that it resembled an island. Fandral had indeed learned from his errors

THE NIGHTMARE'S SERVANT

The corruption of Teldrassil was largely the work of Fandral Staghelm, but he was guided by dark forces. He had fallen under the sway of Xavius.

In the War of the Ancients, Xavius had served as Queen Azshara's trusted advisor until Malfurion Stormrage had struck him down. Like many of Azshara's inner circle, he now obeyed the will of the Old Gods. Xavius, who had become known as the Nightmare Lord, planned to spread the Nightmare far and wide, even beyond the borders of the Emerald Dream.

Xavius had won Fandral to his cause by exploiting the night elf's sorrow. The Nightmare Lord tricked him into believing his fallen son, Valstann Staghelm, was still alive. Xavius used a false visage of the long-dead elf to speak to Fandral, guiding his actions and convincing him to infect the World Tree Teldrassil with the Nightmare's touch.

Xavius's influence would gradually drive Fandral to madness.

in planting Vordrassil. This new World Tree was bright, powerful, and apparently uncorrupted. Brimming with hope, the night elves established a city, Darnassus, among the World Tree's massive boughs.

Unfortunately, Fandral's decision to create the tree without the Dragon Aspects' help proved to be a terrible mistake. Without their blessings, Teldrassil was vulnerable to the dark influence of the Emerald Nightmare.

From the heart of the Emerald Dream, the Nightmare reached out to Teldrassil. Before long, it seeped into the World Tree's essence.

Fandral went to great lengths to hide the emerging darkness from the rest of the night elves. It was easy enough to keep the others occupied. Satyr and furbolg raiders were igniting small conflicts across night elven territory, and the Horde had established new nations south of Ashenvale. The faction had allied with the night elves against the Burning Legion in the Third War, but not long before that, they had been fierce enemies.

Trust would be a long time coming, if it ever came at all.

ORGRIMMAR UNDER CONSTRUCTION

THE FOUNDING OF DUROTAR

A great weight had been lifted from Warchief Thrall's heart. He and his people had defended Azeroth against the Burning Legion, their former master. The crimes of the first Horde could never be erased, but the recent battles stood as proof that the orcs deserved to make a home for themselves on this world.

Shortly after the Battle of Mount Hyjal, Thrall led his people to a desolate desert region along the eastern coast of Kalimdor. He named the land Durotar, after his late father, Durotan.

The Horde soon forged a capital in Durotar. Thrall named the stronghold Orgrimmar in honor of his friend, the former warchief Orgrim Doomhammer, who had taught him that the Horde could become something greater than a weapon. Though Orgrimmar would serve as the Horde's capital, some of the faction's other members settled in different areas. The Darkspear trolls carved out a home to the south, on the Echo Isles. To the west, the tauren built a permanent settlement called Thunder Bluff, nestled amid the verdant grasslands of Mulgore.

Durotar stood in stark contrast to the lush plains of Mulgore. It was a rugged area, and the orcs' first years there were filled with hardship. Thrall considered those difficult times to be penance for the damage that the orcs had wrought on this world decades ago.

The settling of Durotar drew the attention of Rexxar, an old beastmaster who had invaded Azeroth alongside the first Horde. He had later abandoned the army after growing disgusted with what it had become. For years, he had lived alone, learning how to survive and thrive in Azeroth's wilds. Thrall's Horde seemed like a force of pride and honor, and Rexxar cautiously joined the orcs in their new home.

As the Horde built its nations, some of their former allies in the Third War moved farther south. The Alliance refugees, led by Jaina Proudmoore, settled in Dustwallow Marsh and established a seaside city named Theramore Isle.

Jaina and Thrall continued to communicate, and their uneasy truce developed into something more permanent. Both leaders declared that they would respect the other's territory and refrain from any acts of aggression.

THE FLEET OF KUL TIRAS

Though the Horde and the humans of Theramore Isle maintained peace for years, it did not last. Yet it was not Warchief Thrall or Jaina Proudmoore who reignited war.

A massive Alliance naval armada arrived on the shores of Kalimdor. It was led by Jaina's father, Grand Admiral Daelin Proudmoore. The fleet immediately launched attacks against the orcs and nearby troll settlements. Admiral Proudmoore had fought in the Second War, and he had even lost a son to the Horde. He had no intention of letting the creatures who had nearly destroyed the human kingdoms regain their strength. His goal was nothing less than extermination.

Thrall hoped to make peace with the humans and convince them that his new Horde was not like the one of old that had decimated the Eastern Kingdoms. Yet he never had the chance to make his plea.

Admiral Proudmoore dispatched assassins disguised as "emissaries" from Theramore to lure Thrall into a trap and end his life. The ruse failed, and war became inevitable. Thrall rallied the orcs, the Darkspear trolls, the tauren, and even the nearby Stonemaul ogre clan for battle.

Time was not on their side. Despite the impassioned urging of his daughter, Jaina, Admiral Proudmoore had taken over Theramore and now had control of both the sea and a defensible city. If given time to fortify his position, he would be able to launch strikes across Kalimdor with impunity.

The Horde's armies traveled to Theramore and quietly reached out to Jaina. Thrall asked her to do the impossible: let the Horde into Theramore so they could kill her father. Otherwise, Daelin Proudmoore would extinguish the Horde forevermore.

Unlike her father, Jaina knew that Thrall's Horde was different from its predecessor. She had seen proof of that with her own eyes. She had stood alongside the Horde against the Burning Legion and witnessed the valor and honor of its soldiers. They wanted the same thing she and many of her followers did: an end to the cycle of hatred between the Horde and the Alliance.

She saw the bloodshed between the factions as a distraction. The Scourge and other threats still lingered on Azeroth. The world's noble races needed to be united in strength to focus on their true enemies. She had tried to convince her father of that, but he refused to listen.

Devastated by the seemingly impossible choice, Jaina stood aside, asking only that the Horde spare as many of her people as they could. The armies of the Horde assaulted Theramore and cut their way through the city.

Rexxar himself inflicted the mortal blow on Grand Admiral Daelin Proudmoore. He was no stranger to how blind prejudice and hatred could darken the hearts of good soldiers. He had seen that fate befall many members of the old Horde. He urged Jaina Proudmoore to remember her father for the proud warrior he had been, not for the person he had become.

The Horde left the city in Jaina's hands after the deed was done. Most of the survivors of Daelin's fleet sailed back to the Eastern Kingdoms.

THE ANGER OF KUL TIRAS

Not only was Grand Admiral Daelin Proudmoore a military commander, but he was also ruler of the human nation of Kul Tiras. His people cried out for vengeance for his death, but the rest of the Alliance did not seek it. The plague of undeath in Lordaeron had already left the Alliance reeling, and its other leaders had little pity for Daelin Proudmoore, who had launched a war of aggression on his own authority.

In fury, the people of Kul Tiras isolated themselves from the rest of the Alliance. But their anger was not focused on King Varian Wrynn or any of the other Alliance leaders. Instead, they grew to hate Jaina Proudmoore, the daughter who had betrayed her family.

Following the battle, Rexxar decided not to remain with the Horde. He had grown accustomed to hunting alone, and he returned to the wilds, where he felt at peace. However, he made it clear that he would fight to defend the Horde whenever it needed him.

THE FORSAKEN AND THE HORDE

Across the sea from Kalimdor, Queen Sylvanas Windrunner and her Forsaken were beset by enemies on all sides. The Scarlet Crusade did not care that these undead had reclaimed their wills from the Lich King; the fanatical sect had vowed to eradicate them no matter what.

Sylvanas reached out to her former people in Quel'Thalas, asking them for sanctuary. She had given her life to protect them, and she expected something in return for her sacrifice. Yet her request was refused. The blood elves feared the undead and treated them as monsters.

Growing more and more desperate, she sent ambassadors to both the Alliance and the Horde. Her emissaries to the Alliance never returned. Sylvanas suspected they hadn't survived long enough even to make it past the gates of Stormwind City.

The first sign of hope came from an unexpected place: the tauren. An archdruid named Hamuul Runetotem looked past the undead's monstrous exterior and believed that they could be redeemed and revived—perhaps not physically, but spiritually. He brought the Forsaken ambassadors to meet with Cairne Bloodhoof, high chieftain of the tauren tribes, and Cairne agreed that the undead should be given a chance to thrive.

Thrall invited Sylvanas Windrunner to Orgrimmar. He had sympathy for her followers—the orcs had once been corrupted as well, and that had been a hard legacy to overcome—but he also recognized the strategic value of the Forsaken. They lived in the ruins of Lordaeron. The city would be a valuable foothold in the Eastern Kingdoms should the Alliance ever provoke war again.

More importantly, the Scourge had not been eradicated; it had been only temporarily defeated. The Horde needed every ally it could find to protect its lands from the Lich King's undead army.

After much consideration, Thrall made his decision. The Forsaken were allowed into the Horde.

FALL OF GNOMEREGAN
25 YEARS AFTER THE DARK PORTAL

Throughout the Third War, the savage troggs had besieged the gnomes of Gnomeregan. Over time, the gnomes had slowly lost ground in their own home.

Clever solutions could not solve the problem of the troggs' overwhelming numbers. They eventually dug around the gnomes' defenses and breached Gnomeregan's engineering quarters. Not only did this cut off the gnomes from their best inventions, but it also placed unstable materials and machines into the hands of creatures that could not understand how dangerous they were. It was only a matter of time before a mistake would lead to the wholesale destruction of the city.

The gifted engineer Sicco Thermaplugg proposed a solution: Bathe the overrun sections of Gnomeregan in lethal radiation. The gnomes would take shelter and wait for the troggs to die. It was a brutal, desperate ploy, but it seemed as if it might work. The gnomes' leader, High Tinker Gelbin Mekkatorque, eventually agreed to the plan. It seemed better than waiting for an inevitable disaster to destroy the city.

Unfortunately, Thermaplugg had ulterior motives. He envied Mekkatorque's position and prestige, and he wanted to use the war to seize both for himself. Thermaplugg also chafed at how the gnomes never used their inventions to expand the power of their nation, a failing he laid squarely at Mekkatorque's feet.

Mekkatorque learned the truth only when Thermaplugg's bomb irradiated the troggs—and most of the gnomes.

In a matter of days, nearly eighty percent of the gnomish race perished. The survivors had no choice but to evacuate their own city. Thermaplugg was left behind, trapped in the horror he had wrought.

The dwarves of Ironforge took in the refugees, and the gnomes created a small home for themselves inside the mountain, calling it Tinker Town. The future of the gnomes was uncertain, and opinion was divided over what to do next.

Some gnomes argued that they should focus all their attention and resources on reclaiming Gnomeregan as soon as possible. Mekkatorque did not agree. Though he did plan on eventually returning to the capital, he believed the gnomes had more immediate obligations to the Alliance. The Third War had decimated the faction, and the gnomes' allies needed all the help they could get to survive the days ahead. Mekkatorque urged his people to research new technologies that would bolster the Alliance.

In his mind, the fates of the Alliance and the gnomes were intertwined. If the faction crumbled, Gelbin Mekkatorque and his people would never have the support they needed to restore Gnomeregan to what it once was.

THE LOST KING

After the Third War, the balance of power among the human kingdoms shifted. Lordaeron was in ruins, and the nations of Gilneas and Kul Tiras had isolated themselves. In their place, Stormwind arose as a new bastion of leadership and military might in the Alliance. This granted the kingdom immense prestige and influence on the world stage, but it also made it a target.

The black dragonflight still desired to crush the last remnants of Alliance power in the Eastern Kingdoms, but they wanted to do so quietly. Onyxia, in the guise of a noblewoman named Katrana Prestor, had devoted herself to weakening Stormwind. She had enlisted the help of the Defias Brotherhood, a group of human rebels who opposed the kingdom's nobility.

The Defias learned that King Varian Wrynn was sailing to Theramore on a diplomatic mission. They ambushed his ship, killing everyone aboard except the king, and delivered Varian to a remote island. Onyxia was waiting for them.

She wove a dark ritual to sunder Varian's spirit, stripping away the traits that would allow him to defy her: his strength, his stubborn resolve, his unyielding will. She intended to destroy this half of Varian, leaving a malleable shell that would appear to be a charming, regal king . . . who would serve blindly as her puppet.

Before Onyxia could destroy the embodiment of Varian's will and strength, he escaped her grasp and plunged into the sea. The waves swallowed him whole, and darkness closed in around him. Varian later regained consciousness on the distant shores of Kalimdor. Onyxia's spell had left his mind in tatters. He had no memory of what she had done to him. He could not even recall his own name. In the days to come, he would wander the world with no notion that he was supposed to be a king.

Onyxia was furious that this half of Varian had escaped, but her plans had not entirely fallen to ruin. She would eventually return to Stormwind with her puppet king, but only once she was sure he would serve as her unquestioning servant.

In the interim, the people of Stormwind agonized over Varian's disappearance. Many feared he had been killed. Varian's young son, Anduin Wrynn, was crowned king. The legendary paladin Bolvar Fordragon was named regent lord to handle the day-to-day duties of administering the kingdom until the child was older.

Neither Bolvar nor Anduin believed that Varian had died, and they never lost hope that they would see him again.

CHAMPIONS ARISE

The troubles of the world were multiplying at a rapid pace.

The armistice between the Alliance and the Horde was tenuous at best. Major battles gradually erupted in strategic locations like Alterac Valley, Warsong Gulch, and Arathi Basin, bringing the two factions closer to all-out war.

Of greater concern were threats from outside the Horde and the Alliance. In Mulgore, the tauren dealt with encroaching bands of primitive creatures called quilboar. In Elwynn Forest, human villages were besieged by kobold thieves and diseased wildlife. In Durotar, centaur warbands plotted to take over the outlying orcish lands. The crises seemed endless. On every continent, in every nation, in every region, chaos was spreading, threatening to become catastrophe.

What the Horde and the Alliance did not realize was that this explosion of disorder was partially the work of the Old Gods. The entities were subtly fanning the flames of conflict to weaken the world's nations. If left unchecked, those small sparks would have spread to ignite a roaring wildfire of destruction.

But they never had a chance to spread. It was not the legendary heroes of past wars who rose up to fight for their world; it was the ordinary citizens of Azeroth who intervened. They began their journeys for different reasons. Some fought for adventure or for the noble cause of justice. Some fought for vengeance and to join the war against a hated faction. Some even fought for money and looked for ways to profit from the conflicts. Still others fought for glory, so that their names would be remembered by the entire world. And some traveled alone, while others formed mighty guilds that worked together to fight against the darkness.

As the years passed, these extraordinary champions would be called upon to do the impossible. Without them, Azeroth would surely have succumbed to evil.

THE SUFFERING OF THE DARK IRONS

More than two centuries ago, the sorcerer-thane of the Dark Iron dwarf clan condemned his people to enslavement when he summoned Ragnaros the Firelord back to Azeroth. The violent eruption killed many and formed a volcano that became known as Blackrock Mountain. The surviving Dark Irons carved out a stronghold in its depths called Shadowforge City. For generations, they were forced to serve Ragnaros and his lieutenants.

The Wildhammer and the Bronzebeard dwarf clans were unable to save their distant cousins, nor were they inclined to do so. The Dark Irons had earned their fate by launching a war of aggression against the other dwarves. Now they had to live with the consequences.

Emperor Dagran Thaurissan, a descendant of the long-dead sorcerer-thane, now ruled the Dark Irons on behalf of the Firelord. A charismatic but hard leader, he bristled at his servitude but delighted in the power Ragnaros had bestowed upon him.

When Ragnaros ordered Dagran to prepare the Dark Irons for a new war, the emperor was overjoyed. He had long dreamed of conquering the other dwarf clans, not only to rule over them but to wield their combined power in order to break free of the Firelord's control.

His first act of aggression was kidnapping Princess Moira Bronzebeard, the daughter of Ironforge's king, Magni Bronzebeard. He had intended to use her as a hostage of last resort once the war began. He believed that Magni would do anything to protect his daughter's life, and thus would never consider any assault on Blackrock Mountain that would put her in harm's way.

Dagran was surprised to find that he fell in love with her. Moira had a sharp wit and a strong will, and she was not intimidated in the slightest by her predicament. The two dwarves began to speak at length about their hopes for the future. Moira was the rightful heir of Ironforge, yet her father had never believed that a woman could rule as well as a man. Dagran confided in her that he wanted to free his people from enslavement, and he was willing to do anything to achieve that. In a few short months, Moira and Dagran joined together in marriage.

King Magni could hardly believe the rumors that his daughter had willingly married an enemy. He recruited a covert team of Alliance champions to infiltrate the Dark Iron stronghold and rescue Moira.

MAJORDOMO EXECUTUS LORDING OVER THE DARK IRON DWARVES IN BLACKROCK MOUNTAIN

The Alliance team cut their way through Shadowforge City until they reached the Imperial Seat. The ensuing battle shook the mountain, but in the end, Emperor Dagran Thaurissan was slain.

Much to the surprise of the Alliance infiltrators, Moira Bronzebeard was furious. She refused their offer of rescue and announced that she was pregnant with Dagran Thaurissan's child.

She had come to believe in Dagran's plan to free the Dark Irons. She intended to carry on his work without him.

THE MOLTEN CORE

To honor her husband's memory, Moira Thaurissan put aside her anger at his death. The strike on Shadowforge City had left her clan in absolute chaos, and for the moment, that was an advantage. Ragnaros's lieutenants were deeply suspicious of how loyal the wife of Dagran Thaurissan would be to the Firelord, but they were too busy trying to reestablish control over the Dark Irons to keep a close eye on her.

She used the opportunity well. Moira quietly let out word that the Dark Iron dwarves were being forced to create a massive army for the Firelord. Dagran Thaurissan's death had delayed the creation of that army, but not for long. Ragnaros and his forces would only become stronger as time went on. To draw as much attention as possible, Moira made sure the rest of the world knew that there were riches and artifacts of untold power hidden deep within the mountain. She hoped that some adventurous (or greedy) heroes would band together to shatter Ragnaros's defenses and banish the Firelord back to the Elemental Plane.

Her plan worked better than she could have ever dreamed. Before the Alliance or the Horde acted on the rumors, another force did: the Hydraxian Waterlords, elemental beings of water who were natural enemies of the fire elementals. They offered aid and rewards to anyone who would challenge Ragnaros.

Before long, the Waterlords had recruited scores of powerful champions to invade Ragnaros's domain in the heart of the mountain: the Molten Core. They carefully moved through the fiery stronghold, engaging and killing the greatest of the fire elementals.

As the Molten Core's defenders fell, the champions used the gifts of the Waterlords to destroy Ragnaros's protective runes, leaving no barrier between them and the Firelord.

Ragnaros's strength was legendary, but it was not enough to slaughter the invaders. In defeat, he was banished back to the Elemental Plane.

The Dark Iron dwarves were finally free. Any among them who had doubted Moira's intentions begged her for forgiveness. As the widow of Emperor Dagran Thaurissan, she'd always had the *right* to rule them. As their liberator, she now had their *loyalty*.

But her victory did not mean that times would be easy for the Dark Irons. Nor did it mean that Moira Thaurissan had given up on her husband's dream of conquest.

Mysteries of Maraudon

For more than a millennium, tauren tribes and the centaur had fought a vicious war, leaving countless dead on both sides. The only respite had come recently. When the tauren had joined the Horde, Warchief Thrall had made sure that his new allies were protected. Any centaur who defied their borders were taught a very painful lesson.

For years, that had curtailed hostilities. Most of the centaur had retreated to the lifeless region of Desolace. Meanwhile, the tauren looked toward a bright future in their new home, Thunder Bluff.

Yet the reappearance of the centaur shattered any hope of peace. Their warbands swarmed out of Desolace and laid waste to the surrounding regions. Thrall called on the emerging heroes of his faction to handle this disturbance and put it to rest for good.

The Horde's forces quickly discovered that the various centaur tribes were slaughtering each other just as often as they were attacking outsiders. When they investigated further, they encountered a centaur named Warug, a leader of the Magram tribe.

Warug told the Horde that Desolace had been corrupted, and that the source of the corruption lay in a place called Maraudon. It was sacred ground to the centaur. It was also home to the earth elemental known as Princess Theradras and the spirit of her fallen mate, a keeper of the grove named Zaetar. Legends told that these two beings were the progenitors of the barbaric centaur race.

Theradras loved the centaur, and she worried that the Horde's rise to power might eventually drive them to extinction. After years of hostilities with the orcs and their allies, she had acted to save her progeny. She had infused the centaur with her power, driving them to make war and claim new territories outside Desolace.

Most of the centaur tribes were deeply loyal to Princess Theradras. Yet the Magram had no such loyalty, and thus they were perfect allies for the Horde.

The Horde helped suppress the other, violent tribes, and then its champions turned their gaze on Maraudon itself. They journeyed into the depths of the burial ground and defeated every creature inside it, including Theradras.

Their victory ended the spreading corruption in Desolace and erased the violent bloodlust in the centaur. With the Horde's blessing, Warug and his Magram tribe became the rulers of the united centaur and led them to an age of tranquility.

Yet no one knew how long they would stay on the path of peace.

The Ruins of Dire Maul

Scarcely had the Horde settled the crisis in Desolace when a new source of darkness emerged. Deep within the southern forests of Feralas, ogre raiding parties were razing settlements and villages, as well as waylaying any travelers unfortunate enough to cross their path. Druids also sensed corruption and decay twisting the wilds.

After a series of skirmishes throughout Feralas, the Horde learned that the source of both troubles was in Dire Maul, the ruined elven city once known as Eldre'Thalas.

Almost fifteen years earlier, an ogre leader known as Gordok had led his clan, the Gordunni, to Dire Maul. Not only had they survived the aftermath of the Second War, but they had thrived.

THE OGRE CLANS ON AZEROTH

After the defeat of the Horde in the Second War, the ogre clans dispersed in all directions. Some escaped through the Dark Portal to Draenor, but others had no intention of remaining near the orcs and their legendary bloodlust. The ogres who made the difficult journey across the ocean to Kalimdor found plenty of space to inhabit. Those who remained in the Eastern Kingdoms were hunted ruthlessly by Alliance patrols.

The Gordunni had turned Dire Maul into a gladiatorial arena, which proved to be quite popular among the mercenaries and miscreants of the world.

Gordok had always been a cruel and ruthless leader, but terrible whispers now plagued his mind, urging him to madness and slaughter. He had commanded his clan to indiscriminately murder anyone they could find.

The Horde dispatched its forces to scour the Gordunni from Dire Maul. They had expected only to kill Gordok and end his reign of madness, but once they arrived, they discovered two different sources of corruption lurking in the city. The first was the Emerald Nightmare. The dark energy of the Old Gods had slipped past the Emerald Dream's borders and manifested in the physical world. It was this power that had driven Gordok to insanity, and the Horde's champions knew that eradicating it was the only way to spare Feralas.

The second source of corruption shocked those who explored Dire Maul. A secretive group of elves—the Shen'dralar—were living deep in the bones of their old city. Their presence did not raise alarm at first, for they did not seem hostile. Yet when the Horde discovered that the elves had imprisoned a demon named Immol'thar and were feeding on his power, there was no choice but to act.

The Horde banished Immol'thar to the Twisting Nether. In doing so, they cut off the elves' source of power and incurred their wrath.

The Shen'dralar's leader, Prince Tortheldrin, personally led the counterattack against the Horde, but he could not restore Immol'thar or claim vengeance. He fell to the Horde's blades, and Dire Maul became his tomb.

The remnants of the elves fled Dire Maul for good. They spent years wandering the wilds, trying to wean themselves off demonic power and feel whole again.

ASSAULT ON BLACKWING LAIR

Far from Dire Maul, uncertainty reigned over Blackrock Mountain. Ragnaros was defeated. He and his elemental minions had been banished back to the Firelands. The adventurers who had triumphed over him returned home to enjoy the spoils of victory, believing that the dangers within Blackrock Mountain had been extinguished.

Moira Thaurissan knew better. Her people had been freed from the elementals, but now they were exposed to a frightening new foe.

Ragnaros had controlled only the lower half of Blackrock Mountain. The upper half belonged to Deathwing's son, Nefarian, and other members of the black dragonflight. Though both sides served the Old Gods, they were not truly allies.

For more than a decade, a tenuous truce had prevented the minions of fire from warring with the remnants of Deathwing's brood. Nefarian had kept his presence shrouded, relying on unusual allies to protect his territory.

The "true Horde," led by Dal'rend Blackhand, had never accepted Orgrim Doomhammer's rule after the First War and *certainly* had no interest in recognizing Thrall as the Horde's new leader now. Unable to openly make war against the armies of Orgrimmar, Dal'rend's Horde had bided their time in the stronghold of Blackrock Spire.

In exchange for the true Horde's allegiance, Nefarian had promised that the powers of the black dragonflight would fight on their behalf against Thrall and his Horde. It was an empty promise. Nefarian had little interest in trifling in a meaningless civil war. He had much more frightening goals.

Nefarian had carried on his father's work of revitalizing and empowering the black dragonflight. He subjected captured dragons to torturous rituals, hoping to tease out unexplored power by combining the blood of the different flights. His experiments were horrific, brutal, and eventually effective. For years, the spawn of this new *chromatic* dragonflight—consisting of blood from all five flights—had died before hatching. Eventually, a few began to survive. Then a few more. Nefarian believed he was on the verge of ensuring their survival, and he eagerly set his minions to preparing a clutch that would hatch an entire generation of this flight. The potential within them was greater than anything he could have hoped for, but for the moment, they were still vulnerable. Only a few had reached maturity and could defend themselves.

As the black dragonflight stirred, Moira Thaurissan plotted to save her people. She knew she did not have long. Before Nefarian would turn his power upon the region, he would certainly conquer Ragnaros's old lair and wipe out the Dark Irons.

Moira had been impressed by the ferocity of the champions who had ended the Firelord's reign. Once again, she had her people send information to the far corners of Azeroth, telling the world that Dal'rend's Horde had allied with the black dragonflight. Her spies made sure that this knowledge found its way to Orgrimmar.

As she suspected, it immediately caused an uproar among the leadership of the Horde. Thrall had known about the "true Horde" for years, but he had never imagined that they posed any real danger. If Dal'rend Blackhand was foolish enough to trust the son of Deathwing, there was little time to waste.

Some of the Horde's emergent champions traveled to the Eastern Kingdoms to settle the matter for good. Dal'rend personally joined the defense of Blackrock Spire. Though he was a mighty warrior, the heroes he faced were mightier still. The self-proclaimed leader of the true Horde died in his stronghold. The rest of his followers scattered, depriving the black dragonflight of their protectors.

Nefarian turned his wrath on the Horde intruders, but they did not flee. They cut their way through endless waves of Nefarian's twisted creations until he, too, fell to their strength and persistence.

The Horde champions took Nefarian's head as proof of their victory and returned to Orgrimmar as conquering heroes. As far as the citizens of Azeroth knew, the black dragonflight's last bastion of power had just been erased, never to return.

DRAGONS OF NIGHTMARE

Off the western coast of Kalimdor, Fandral Staghelm struggled to hide the corruption that was spreading in Teldrassil from the rest of the night elves. Yet the emergent Emerald Nightmare soon began to touch the physical world in different places across Azeroth.

Druids were the first to recognize the growing threat, even if its origins were unclear. Fandral reluctantly allowed the members of the Cenarion Circle, even the ones who were not elves, to join the fight against the Nightmare.

The Cenarion Circle's investigations took them across the world. An underground cave system known as the Wailing Caverns became one of the first points of conflict. After an order of druids became trapped—and some, corrupted—in the caverns' depths, the Horde mounted a rescue mission, cleansing the caves of the Nightmare and saving several of the druids.

But more terrifying dangers were emerging elsewhere. An old threat was stirring once again.

More than a thousand years ago, Ysera and her green dragonflight had intervened when a group of fanatical trolls—the Atal'ai—had tried to summon a dark god to Azeroth. His name was Hakkar, the Loa of Blood, and he sustained himself on living sacrifices. The green dragonflight had sunk the Atal'ai's temple deep beneath the boggy mires in the Swamp of Sorrows and set a watch to make sure it would never again be used for evil.

But the green dragons were subtly being affected by the Emerald Nightmare. The descendants of the Atal'ai trolls returned to the Sunken Temple and found that its guardians were disoriented and vulnerable. Both the Nightmare and the trolls dragged the dragons down into the depths of madness and corruption. In firm control of the temple, the Atal'ai began their gruesome rituals to summon Hakkar into Azeroth again.

A green dragon named Itharius called for help from the Cenarion Circle, and the druids sent an Alliance force to cleanse the temple. These champions slaughtered many Atal'ai adherents and put an end to their rituals, but the ripple effects of the Nightmare had only begun. Corrupted green dragons emerged from the Emerald Dream across Azeroth. Driven mad, they murdered innocents by the hundreds, indiscriminately targeting whatever living creatures were nearby.

The Cenarion Circle's members were mournful but resolute. Very few of the green dragons could be saved. Many were killed. There was no other way to stop their rampages. The memory of that day would haunt the green dragonflight for many years.

And still, even though the druids and their allies had succeeded, the danger had not yet passed.

THE LOA OF BLOOD

The Zandalari trolls were shocked to learn about the attempt to summon Hakkar. They saw themselves as the spiritual leaders and guardians of their entire race, and they believed the Loa of Blood's return would herald a dark time for their people. The Zandalari were pleased to hear that the Atal'ai had been defeated in the Sunken Temple, but their relief soon turned to horror.

Some of Hakkar's adherents had survived, and they were continuing their quest. They had quietly infiltrated Zul'Gurub, the capital of the Gurubashi trolls, and enslaved the minds of many of their most powerful priests. Together, the Atal'ai and their unwilling servants were performing grisly rituals to draw Hakkar into the world.

Not all trolls in the region fell under the Atal'ai's sway. Some launched an offensive to retake Zul'Gurub, but it ended in failure. The mighty trolls who fearlessly stormed the capital never returned. Instead, the Atal'ai captured and enslaved them, too.

The Atal'ai and their leader, Jin'do the Hexxer, were growing more powerful by the day. The Zandalari knew that they did not have the resources to scour them from Zul'Gurub.

They sent word through the Darkspear trolls that the Horde needed to act immediately. If the Atal'ai completed their summoning of Hakkar, it would throw the world into chaos. Thrall ordered a large strike force to respond to the threat.

The battle for Zul'Gurub was costly and brutal. The Horde charged into the temple city, hacking through masses of Atal'ai and their enslaved followers. Though they slew Jin'do the Hexxer, his death came too late to stop Hakkar from entering the world.

The Loa of Blood manifested as a force of death and insanity. He poisoned the blood of some of the Horde's champions and tried to drag their thoughts into absolute madness. Yet it was Hakkar's own power that proved to be his undoing. In desperation, *all* of the Horde invaders allowed themselves to be poisoned, and then they let the loa feed on their corrupted blood.

In his frenzied state, Hakkar paid little attention to the tactics of his seemingly harmless enemies. His every thought was filled with an overwhelming urge to consume blood. Hakkar gorged on his prey, unaware of the poison flooding his veins until it was too late. The Loa of Blood succumbed to his own dark magic. The survivors staggered out of the now-silent city of Zul'Gurub, exhausted, weary, but victorious.

THE EMERGENCE OF C'THUN

The touch of the Old Gods was being felt in every major corner of the world, though few could identify its origins. The Emerald Nightmare's spread, for all the damage it had caused, was only a symptom of the Old Gods' reemerging power, and it was only a fraction of what they might be capable of doing should their servants release them from their prisons.

While the Horde and the Alliance were fighting to protect their lands, Cho'gall and the Twilight's Hammer cult continued their work to usher in the Hour of Twilight, the apocalyptic end of all things. Their journey had led them to the desert of Silithus, home to the ancient city of Ahn'Qiraj. The Old God C'Thun was imprisoned within, but the ogre mage had no way to reach it. An enchanted barrier known as the Scarab Wall stood between him and his unseen master.

HAKKAR, THE LOA OF BLOOD, IN ZUL'GURUB

Centuries ago, a combined force of night elves and dragons had erected the Scarab Wall to contain Ahn'Qiraj's inhabitants: vicious insectoids called the silithid and the qiraji. None could pass the barrier. Not by flying over it. Not even by tunneling under the ground.

But Cho'gall did not need to physically pass it. Outside the wall, he and his cultists performed a great ritual. Their magic extended beyond the barrier, piercing into the prison chamber where C'Thun was chained. The influx of power shattered the Old God's bonds. C'Thun's liberation came at a price for Cho'gall's followers. The energies unleashed by the ritual destroyed most of the cultists who had taken part. The few who survived were left catatonic, unable to speak or even move. Cho'gall abandoned them in the desert. He had no more use for them.

Once C'Thun was free of its bonds, Cho'gall departed. There were other Old Gods imprisoned beneath Azeroth's surface. The ogre mage needed to loosen their bonds, whatever the cost.

Under C'Thun's orders, Cho'gall also set out to recruit new members for the Twilight's Hammer, willingly or by force. Its cultists would secretly spread to every corner of Azeroth. They would infiltrate every city, guild, and faction like an unseen plague. Then, when the time came, the Old Gods would call on the cult to rise up and herald the Hour of Twilight.

Meanwhile, C'Thun made preparations of its own. Thousands of qiraji and silithid lay dormant in Ahn'Qiraj and beneath the sands of Silithus. Both races were remnants of the Black Empire, loyal servants forged by the blood of the Old Gods.

C'Thun awakened the insectoids and rallied them for war.

THE GATES OF AHN'QIRAJ

The disturbance in Ahn'Qiraj was noticed immediately. Druid outposts in Silithus fell under attack from swarms of silithid and qiraji. Their desperate cries for help were heard by both the Horde and the Alliance, who sent many to aid them in the land's defense. Soon the truth of the insectoid aggression was revealed by the bronze dragonflight.

Anachronos, a dragon who had fought the qiraji centuries ago, sensed that C'Thun had awoken. There was no doubt that only the Old God itself could have launched such a war against Azeroth, but this was but a sliver of C'Thun's potential.

The Old God had been imprisoned for too long. It needed time to gather its full strength. Once it did, Anachronos did not believe that any army in the world would be able to stop the entity.

Warchief Thrall and Regent Lord Bolvar Fordragon—acting on Anduin Wrynn's behalf—quickly came to an unprecedented agreement. Both factions would combine the might of their armies to strike back against the threat of C'Thun. Varok Saurfang, a seasoned orc warrior, was granted command of the campaign.

Together, the heroes of Azeroth stood strong against the tides of qiraji and silithid. But the insectoids seemed to have endless numbers; eventually, they would win a war of attrition. The Horde and the Alliance's only hope of victory was striking into the heart of Ahn'Qiraj and challenging the Old God directly.

No one knew if it was possible to defeat C'Thun, but there was no alternative—and no shortage of volunteers.

THE OLD GOD C'THUN IN THE TEMPLE OF AHN'QIRAJ

The Scarab Wall around Ahn'Qiraj was impenetrable, and the only instrument capable of opening it had been destroyed, its pieces scattered across the world. The champions of Azeroth scoured the continents for fragments of this artifact, the Scepter of the Shifting Sands. They gathered each shard until finally it had been assembled.

Varok Saurfang marched his armies to the gates of Ahn'Qiraj and decreed that the scepter be used.

The gates flung open. It was as if a dam had burst, releasing a seemingly endless tide of qiraji against the forces of Azeroth. Countless heroes fell to the insectoids that day, but the line did not bend, and it did not break. The bulk of C'Thun's armies had just been matched, and when they crumbled, the way into Ahn'Qiraj was finally open.

Varok wasted little time. He had no intention of letting an Old God regain its footing and spawn a new army. He ordered a dual strike upon C'Thun's forces. The first attack would raid the ruins of Ahn'Qiraj, which held the bulk of the qiraji. Varok knew the insectoids would show no mercy. He deployed his most elite Horde champions in this fight, believing that only they could endure such a brutal battle.

While the Horde held the line against the qiraji, the Alliance would storm beneath Ahn'Qiraj. They would not face swarms of insectoids, but they would fight C'Thun's most powerful minions . . . and then they would confront the Old God itself.

With the Horde occupying the qiraji army above, the Alliance soldiers descended into the maw of madness. The whispers of C'Thun slithered into their minds, seeking to turn them against one another.

And yet, they succeeded. Through blade, shield, and magic, an Old God was defeated.

Few mortals could grasp the sheer magnitude of the victory inside Ahn'Qiraj. Even the Dragon Aspects, who had lived for so long, did not truly understand how dangerous it had been to challenge C'Thun.

The triumph of Azeroth's defenders was a warning to the remaining Old Gods: when mortals joined forces, they were strong enough to overcome them.

THE ASHBRINGER

Far from Silithus, the Scourge still held sway over the fallen kingdom of Lordaeron. The toxic Plaguelands were rife with shambling undead, deadly poisons, and the vengeful spirits of those claimed by recent years of violence.

Two opposing groups of paladins remained focused on eradicating the Lich King's influence. The Scarlet Crusade was growing ever more belligerent and corrupt, resorting to brutal tactics against anyone who dared to question its members' methods. But as they prosecuted their zealous war, another order of paladins grew in strength and determination. The Argent Dawn was founded by those who were sickened by the Scarlet Crusade but had refused to give up their holy mission of protecting Azeroth.

One of the newest recruits to the Argent Dawn was Darion Mograine, the youngest son of the late Alexandros Mograine. His father's death had left Darion shaken. It was not the Scourge that had sealed Alexandros's doom, but his own blood.

Darion's brother, Renault Mograine, had fallen to darkness and murdered their father.

For a time, Darion had questioned his faith in the Holy Light, but recent events had renewed

IN THE WAKE OF
THE THIRD WAR

NORTHREND

TELDRASSIL

**AZUREMYST
ISLE**

KALIMDOR

Orgrimmar

*The
Veiled Sea*

THE MAELSTROM

Thunder Bluff

Maraudon

Theramore Isle

Caverns of Time

The South Sea

Ahn'Qiraj

PANDARI

his hope. He had learned that Alexandros's spirit was held captive inside the floating Scourge necropolis of Naxxramas. When Darion joined the Argent Dawn, he asked them to aid him in his quest to free his father's tortured soul.

Many volunteered to help, and together, they made a daring assault on the well-defended fortress. Darion and his allies faced some of the Lich King's most notable minions, including the fearsome Four Horsemen. The leader of the Horsemen was none other than Alexandros Mograine, raised from the grave as a death knight. Nearly all of the Argent Dawn's party perished in the fighting. Darion barely managed to defeat his father and escape with his life.

Against all odds, he had reclaimed the Ashbringer, the holy weapon that had earned his father renown across the land. After Alexandros's death, the blade had been corrupted to the Lich King's cause. Darion could hear someone speaking to him from the Ashbringer, and to his shock, he realized that it was the voice of his father. His spirit was trapped inside the weapon, and he was desperate for a way out.

Darion obeyed his father's wishes and sought out Renault Mograine. As the two estranged brothers came face-to-face, Alexandros's spirit erupted from the Ashbringer and beheaded Renault in an act of justice. But whatever satisfaction Alexandros Mograine felt did not release him from his curse. He was still trapped.

Finally, Darion sought out Tirion Fordring, an old war hero who was living in exile. Tirion knew of the Ashbringer's legacy, and he was distraught to see how it had been corrupted. Yet there was no easy means to cleanse it. The only way to break the curse and free the soul trapped within was to perform an act of compassion greater than the treachery that had defiled the weapon.

Darion nearly fell to despair. He did not know what Tirion meant. He returned to the Argent Dawn and joined them at Light's Hope Chapel in the Plaguelands. An army of Scourge was mounting an offensive against the holy site. Though the Argent Dawn were greatly outnumbered, Darion stood with them on the front lines.

The Battle for Light's Hope Chapel was a desperate last stand. If the Argent Dawn failed, the Scourge would claim the consecrated ground and all the righteous souls who had been laid to rest there.

The tide of battle soon turned against the chapel's defenders. It was then that Darion Mograine finally understood Tirion's words. His father had died due to betrayal. The only act that could free him was to make the ultimate sacrifice.

And if Darion could free him, then perhaps Alexandros Mograine could save the Argent Dawn from annihilation.

Darion took the corrupted Ashbringer and impaled himself upon it. This selfless act did more than free his father. The souls interred beneath the chapel were also awakened. Alongside Alexandros, their vengeful fury laid waste to the invading Scourge.

Light's Hope Chapel was saved, but many had fallen. Some, including Darion, were recovered by the Scourge. Though he had saved his father's soul, he had damned his own.

Both Darion Mograine and the Ashbringer were now in the Scourge's hands.

OVERLEAF: THE LANDS OF AZEROTH AT THE TIME OF AHN'QIRAJ'S REOPENING

SHADOW OF THE NECROPOLIS

The Scourge's defeat at Light's Hope Chapel did not trouble the Lich King. His agents had been watching the Horde and the Alliance. Recent conflicts in Ahn'Qiraj and other parts of the world had weakened both factions. Though the bulk of his armies were still in Northrend, he believed he had an opportunity to strengthen his position in Kalimdor and the Eastern Kingdoms.

Without warning, the Lich King unleashed his necropoli. The floating fortresses appeared over several regions of Azeroth and terrorized the local populations.

The Argent Dawn sent word that the Scourge's power was concentrated in Naxxramas, the best defended of all the necropoli. Home to the lich Kel'Thuzad and other mighty undead, it loomed over the Plaguelands.

Bolvar Fordragon recruited scores of Alliance heroes to assault Naxxramas. The twisted creatures that roamed the necropolis proved to be nearly insurmountable foes. The Alliance champions faced plagued abominations, a monstrous frost wyrm, and the Scourge's most powerful death knights. Finally, they confronted Kel'Thuzad, and the lich unleashed all his power upon them.

But in the end, Kel'Thuzad fell. The Alliance had succeeded in stopping the Scourge's short-lived invasion. Though they could not destroy Naxxramas itself, none dared stay inside the fortress. It soon began drifting back to Northrend.

With his last breath, Kel'Thuzad promised that he would return, more powerful than ever. They were not idle words.

THE UNRAVELING OF TIME

Ten thousand years ago, a group of mortals had joined together with the powerful Wild Gods to drive back the Burning Legion's invasion. It was a long, drawn-out war, filled with incredible victories, shocking betrayals, and heartbreaking sacrifices.

For creatures who could traverse the timeways like the bronze dragonflight, such a momentous period of history drew a great deal of attention. It was common for them to quietly observe the War of the Ancients in detail, for there always seemed to be new acts of heroism to witness.

But as the bronze dragons studied the War of the Ancients, they discovered that some parts of history were changing. At first, these anomalies were subtle, but they became more drastic, even to the point that the Burning Legion seemed to have won the war. Nozdormu, the Aspect of Time, could not see what force was corrupting the timeways, and that alarmed him greatly.

Since he could not discern what was altering history from the outside, Nozdormu dispatched three heroes into the past to make sure events played out correctly. They were the human mage Rhonin, the red dragon Korialstrasz, and Broxigar, an orc veteran of the First, Second, and Third Wars.

The three time-lost champions joined the night elf resistance and mounted a defense against the Legion to ensure that the demons were defeated. In the final battle, when events seemed to spiral out of control, Broxigar leapt through the Burning Legion's portal to Azeroth, slaughtering countless demons.

TIMEWAY CORRUPTION

In all known realms of the cosmos, time flows forward, ever forward. Chaotic energies in places like the Twisting Nether can affect how quickly it flows, but it only flows forward.

Once an event happens, it cannot be changed. These events and choices, made up of all creatures and forces in the cosmos, join together like a river, sharing the same reality. Different choices and different possibilities naturally spin off the river of time like small creeks and estuaries, ebbing and flowing for a while. If these shades of what could have been are left alone, they will eventually dissipate into nothing. If efforts are made to preserve them (or alter them), they can indeed remain in existence indefinitely. They can even be made to feed back into the main river—dead creatures can seemingly "live again," and the past (or future) may literally come back to haunt you. This is not a natural phenomenon, and the inhabitants of the main timeway will often find these experiences to be quite alarming.

But the only timeway that has a permanent effect on the cosmos is the main timeway. Creatures like the bronze dragons, who have command of temporal magic, can see all the countless tributaries of alternate universes and timelines, and they can even move back and forth along the stream to observe the past and the future.

If that main river is disrupted, it could spell doom and disaster. All life on Azeroth depends on time to flow ever forward. Without the surety that the sun will rise and set each day, the seasons would not pass, the cycle of life would become meaningless, and all living creatures would eventually die from being unable to sustain themselves. It is the most sacred mission of the bronze dragonflight to keep that from happening.

He died on Argus, the Legion's seat of power, while challenging Sargeras himself.

After their mission was complete, Nozdormu returned Rhonin and Korialstrasz to the present. The sanctity of the timeways had been upheld, but it would not be the last time that anomalies would appear in history. Nozdormu became obsessed with unraveling the mystery of what—or who—was responsible.

He disappeared into the timeways and would not be seen again for years.

CHAPTER IV: OLD HATREDS

CHAPTER V
THE BURNING CRUSADE

CHAPTER V
THE BURNING CRUSADE

THE LORD OF OUTLAND

Years before the assault on the Molten Core and Ahn'Qiraj, conflict raged on the broken realm of Outland.

Illidan Stormrage's failed campaign against the Lich King had cost him dearly. He had fled from Northrend, wounded and humiliated, with much of his army broken and bloodied. His defeat had also drawn Kil'jaeden's ire. The demon lord would not give him another chance to prove his worth.

But Illidan didn't need one. The time for feigning subservience to the Legion was over. The time for his *true* war had begun.

Illidan assumed Kil'jaeden would launch an attack on Outland soon, and he strengthened his defenses in preparation. To replenish his army, he transferred the captured pit lord Magtheridon to Hellfire Citadel, former capital of the old Horde. Illidan's servants bound the demon in enchanted bonds within the stronghold. They siphoned Magtheridon's blood from his veins and infused it into hundreds of orcs, transforming them into ruthless, battle-crazed soldiers.

As Illidan's army grew, so did its need for provisions. Most of Outland was a dust-blown wasteland. Food was scarce. Water, even more so. Illidan sent Lady Vashj and her naga to secure resources in one of the few regions that still had them: Zangarmarsh.

Zangarmarsh had once been a vast sea, but the destruction of Draenor had transformed it into a swampy mire of islands and waterways. The region teemed with creatures of all kinds, from lumbering fungal giants to small and primitive sporelings. Zangarmarsh was also home to a considerable population of draenei and their mutated cousins, the Broken.

Lady Vashj and her servants were well suited to the watery terrain, and they quickly spread to the far corners of Zangarmarsh. The draenei kept to their main refuge, Telredor, and used its defenses to fend off the naga.

Yet the Broken were not so lucky. In recent years, some of the twisted creatures had mended ties with the draenei and worked together with them. However, many tribes of Broken roamed the wilds in isolation. Lady Vashj hunted down these groups, and she used many of them as slave labor to forge Coilfang Reservoir in the heart of Zangarmarsh. The massive stronghold housed a complex network of machineries designed to leech water from the swamp.

Draining the water threw Zangarmarsh's delicate ecosystem out of balance. Some creatures, like the fungal giants, began to die off. Yet Lady Vashj cared little about these consequences. Coilfang Reservoir was a success—it was keeping Illidan's army alive.

From the Black Temple, Illidan Stormrage oversaw these activities. Most of the shattered realm had fallen under his sphere of influence, if not his direct control. Outland was effectively his domain.

With his defenses in place, he focused his attention on molding a new weapon to strike at the Legion. Years ago, he had envisioned making warriors in his own image, fellow elves empowered by demonic energy. A fighting force unified by their need for vengeance, willing to sacrifice everything to destroy the Legion.

He would call these new warriors demon hunters.

THE DEMON HUNTERS

Illidan Stormrage forged his demon hunters from blood elves and night elves who came from all walks of life. They were sons, daughters, mothers, and fathers. Some were trained in the arts of war. Others were simple artisans. The one thing they had in common was the hatred that burned in their souls. They had all lost someone to the Legion. And they were all consumed by a need for vengeance.

Illidan trained these elves within the Black Temple, but he kept their existence a secret from the rest of his allies. Even Kael'thas Sunstrider, leader of the blood elves, knew only rumors about what was happening. The stories that did reach his ears were grisly and almost too outlandish to believe.

The truth was even more unsettling. Illidan gave no quarter to his demon hunters during their training. He could not afford weakness in those who would stand by his side against the Legion. He forced each of his servants to eat the flesh of a demon and bind their spirit with the creature. This granted the elves great power as well as visions of the Legion's true nature. What they saw was so shocking, so terrifying, that they cut out their own eyes.

Ingesting demon flesh also infused the trainees with fel energy. The elves transformed, sprouting horns and wings much like Illidan's. From that point on, each demon hunter would fight an inner struggle against the monster that lurked in their soul. The spirits of the demons within them would constantly whisper in their minds, urging them to turn on Illidan and give in to the Legion.

Few prospective demon hunters survived the training. Most died in the process or were driven to madness. Those who became demon hunters were forever changed by their experiences.

Using the portals that remained open on Draenor, Illidan and his servants stormed into worlds controlled by the Legion and slaked their thirst for vengeance with demon blood.

For Illidan, these operations were mere overtures for what was to come. It wasn't enough for him to destroy the Legion's agents; he needed to destroy its *worlds*. Chief among these targets was Argus. It was the Legion's seat of power, home to Kil'jaeden and other high-ranking commanders. Due to its location in the Twisting Nether, any demons Illidan killed there would be gone forever.

Destroying an entire world was not beyond Illidan Stormrage. He had studied Draenor's fate, and he had learned how Ner'zhul's uncontrolled spellwork had torn the world asunder. Illidan would do the same to Argus, but first he had to find it.

He knew of only one place to look for clues: Nathreza, homeworld of the dreadlords and a repository of the Legion's arcana and forbidden knowledge. However, it would take time for Illidan to prepare for his assault.

WEB OF LIES

Kil'jaeden had misjudged Illidan Stormrage. He'd once seen the former night elf as little more than a troublesome pest, but that was not the case. Illidan had forged an army of fel-empowered warriors. He had found a way to strike at Legion-controlled worlds.

Kil'jaeden knew this was only the beginning. Illidan was unpredictable and secretive, but his true motives were now clear: he aimed to destroy the Legion. Kil'jaeden speculated that he might even try to strike at Argus itself. The only questions were *when* and *how*.

If it was a war Illidan wanted, Kil'jaeden would indulge him. The demon lord immediately dispatched an army to Outland. This force was led by one of Kil'jaeden's most trusted lieutenants, the doomguard known as Highlord Kruul. Though the demons were eager to spill Illidan's blood, they found it difficult to reach Outland. Illidan and his followers had closed many of the portals on the shattered realm. It would take months before Kruul gathered enough demons to establish a foothold on Outland.

Kil'jaeden feared that Illidan would launch new attacks on the Legion before Kruul and his forces could mount a proper campaign. Waiting for that to happen was not an option. Kil'jaeden needed another weapon, and he found one among his enemies.

Illidan's obsession with fighting the Legion was his greatest weakness. In his fervor, he had embraced fel magic and alienated the peoples of Azeroth. They did not distinguish between him and the Legion. They saw him as a monster. If the Horde and the Alliance learned that he had taken control of Outland and built an army—with demon blood fueling a large part of it—they would stop him. The only thing Azeroth's nations needed to rally their forces against Illidan was a push in the right direction. Kil'jaeden would give them that.

As this plan took shape in his mind, Kil'jaeden saw yet another opportunity. If he could manipulate the Horde and the Alliance into committing their resources on Outland, that would leave Azeroth vulnerable to a Legion invasion on a second front.

Kil'jaeden would lead this attack himself. The failures of the Lich King, and even of Archimonde, had shown him that he could not rely on anyone else to secure Azeroth for the Legion. Yet he needed a powerful gateway through which to enter the world. During the Third War, the Legion had tried to seize the second Well of Eternity on Mount Hyjal to form such a portal. The assault had failed, and the fount of magic was now under close watch by the night elves. Launching another campaign against Hyjal would draw too much attention. However, there was an alternative: the Sunwell.

The blood elf prince, Kael'thas Sunstrider, and his followers had destroyed the Sunwell and dispersed much of its power, but Kil'jaeden had discovered a means to restore it.

Following the Third War, what remained of the Legion's army had spread across Azeroth. Kil'jaeden had used these survivors to spy on the world's nations. Through one of his agents, the demon lord had learned of a source of power somewhere deep within Quel'Thalas. His most cunning servants had assumed the forms of blood elves and infiltrated the kingdom's inner circle. They soon heard about the existence of Anveena Teague, an avatar containing the Sunwell's lost energy.

She was the key to transforming the Sunwell into a gateway.

And so was Kael'thas.

Kil'jaeden's servants on Azeroth were few. Even if they could seize the location of the Sunwell, they were not familiar enough with the fount to empower it using Anveena. However, Kael'thas Sunstrider was. He also knew the region's defenses and how to bypass them.

For now, Kil'jaeden simply watched Kael'thas, waiting for the right moment to win him over to the Legion's side.

BURDENS OF LEADERSHIP

Illidan Stormrage had taught Prince Kael'thas Sunstrider and his people how to siphon energy from artifacts, creatures, and the environment to sate their cravings for magic. Yet these methods only left the prince and the other elves wanting more.

Desperate to find a more satisfactory source of power, Kael'thas looked to fel magic. The prince knew the dangers of consuming the chaotic energy, but he believed it could be controlled. By now, he had confirmed the existence of the demon hunters, and he had witnessed them using fel magic without falling under the Legion's sway. If they could bend that power to their will, then Kael'thas reasoned that he could, too.

Kael'thas convinced Illidan to show him how to feed on fel energies. The prince proceeded cautiously, only drawing on small portions of the magic. Before long, he grew hopelessly addicted to it. The more he fed on the dark energy, the more it ate away at his mind, body, and soul. His reliance on fel magic frayed the bonds between him and his people. Though he was desperate to save the blood elves, he secretly became paranoid of them. He was convinced that they saw him as a failure.

The truth was that Kael'thas's journey to Outland had not helped his people; it had only made their suffering worse. The wise option would have been to cut his losses and return home, but the thought of marching into Quel'Thalas without a lasting solution for the blood elves filled him with shame and anger. It was this pride, this inability to admit defeat, that sealed his fate.

The emotions that warred in the prince's heart made him unpredictable. Sometimes he played the part of kindhearted prince. Other times he lashed out at his followers with sudden, unexplained fury.

Kil'jaeden realized it would not be easy to manipulate the prince, and he treaded carefully. Kael'thas was aware of the Legion's role in the formation of the Scourge. He knew that the demons were responsible for destroying Quel'Thalas and tainting the Sunwell.

The demon lord eventually reached out to Kael'thas. He said nothing of Anveena Teague's existence or his plans to invade Azeroth. He focused solely on Illidan Stormrage and the promise of feeding the prince's craving for magic.

Kil'jaeden whispered in the prince's mind and claimed that Illidan was holding back the true secrets of using fel magic. The former night elf had only shared one way to siphon the chaotic energies, but there were others. The demon hunters had used these more refined techniques, and that was what made them so powerful. The reason Illidan had not granted this knowledge to Kael'thas was simple: he didn't believe the prince and his people were worthy. The former night elf saw them as tools to sacrifice in his war against the Legion. Nothing more.

Kil'jaeden promised to reveal the true power of fel magic to Kael'thas. In exchange, he simply wanted the prince to abandon Illidan's side.

The prince refused the demon lord's offer, but Kil'jaeden continued making subtle overtures. In the days to come, his words would fester in Kael'thas Sunstrider's addled mind and erode his trust in Illidan Stormrage.

LIGHT IN THE DARKNESS

The constant arrival of Legion forces on Outland drew the attention of creatures across the realm. None was more concerned than Velen, leader of the draenei. The Legion had always had a presence on Outland, but the demons were now invading on a much larger scale.

For over a decade, Velen had done whatever he could to keep the draenei hidden in settlements scattered across Outland. Despite his efforts, he feared that the demons would discover them. He feared that they would finish what they'd started all those years ago and slaughter what remained of the draenei.

Throughout his hardships, Velen had never abandoned his faith in the Holy Light. He prayed daily for guidance from the naaru. And when the Legion began its new invasion of Outland, he prayed even more.

Velen was not the only one who reached out to the naaru for help. Archmage Khadgar had remained on Outland since the destruction of the Dark Portal, eking out an existence alongside other members of the Sons of Lothar. Over time, he had used his magic to scour the Great Dark Beyond for allies to fight the Legion. Along with Velen's prayers, Khadgar's presence was felt by the naaru in the Army of the Light.

The Army of the Light had been waging a war against the Legion on Argus itself. The naaru were eager to aid Velen and Khadgar, and they saw Outland as an important battlefront against the demons. However, their current battles with the Legion were costly and ceaseless. They could not spare soldiers from their army to protect Outland, but perhaps they could still do something to help Velen and Khadgar defend themselves.

The naaru A'dal, M'uru, and O'ros volunteered to assist the peoples of Outland. Aboard a dimensional fortress known as Tempest Keep, the beings traversed the stars and arrived in an otherworldly corner of the shattered realm called the Netherstorm.

Their arrival in the Netherstorm was not by chance. Reality itself was warped in the region. The Twisting Nether constantly ate away at the Netherstorm's borders, and its chaotic magics slowly bled into Outland. This made the Netherstorm a dangerous and unpredictable place, but it also made it easy for the naaru to reach.

A'dal immediately surveyed Outland. The being sensed different enclaves of draenei scattered across the wastelands, as well as the remnants of the Sons of Lothar. These creatures were divided, but they did not need to be. They all sought to protect themselves from the Legion.

A'dal searched for a place to rally the factions of Outland and organize them into a defense force. The naaru chose Shattrath City after sensing holy rituals being performed there. An order of draenei priests, the Aldor, had moved into a temple in the stronghold's ruins and continued their worship of the Holy Light.

Calling on Tempest Keep's energies, the naaru transported itself to the city, leaving M'uru and O'ros behind to watch over the dimensional fortress.

The Aldor welcomed A'dal with open arms, and they pledged themselves to do the naaru's bidding. Soon other creatures trickled into Shattrath. Drawn by A'dal's holy power, they journeyed from the far corners of Outland. Velen brought only a handful of followers to the city, fearing a Legion trap. He was elated to discover the truth—his prayers had been answered after all.

Khadgar and other members of the Sons of Lothar also braved the wilds and traveled to Shattrath. Many draenei were wary of these outsiders, but A'dal quickly put them at ease. The naaru called on those gathered in Shattrath to find common ground and unite. Divided, they would fall to the Legion. Only together did they stand a chance of surviving.

The naaru's advice was welcomed by all. Much like the draenei, Khadgar and his followers had weathered enough hardships. They were not eager to make new enemies. Under A'dal's guidance, the Alliance forces and the draenei began rebuilding Shattrath as a beacon of hope that would one day shine across Outland.

THE SCRYERS

The draenei and the Sons of Lothar were not the only factions that noticed the naaru's arrival. So did Illidan Stormrage. He saw the resurgence of Shattrath as a potential threat to his war against the Legion. If the naaru gathered enough strength, they would likely move against Illidan's holdings and seize control of Outland.

Illidan decided to strike while Shattrath was still weak. He ordered Kael'thas Sunstrider to send his blood elves against the city and take it by force.

Kael'thas requested that the demon hunters join the assault, but Illidan refused. They had another purpose, though he remained silent about what that was.

Illidan's response angered Kael'thas, but he obeyed the command. He charged a gifted magister named Voren'thal with leading the attack. The blood elf army soon marched to Shattrath. Among its ranks were some of Kael'thas's most skilled sorcerers. They knew the ways of war, and they were eager to please their prince. In their eyes, Shattrath and its defenders stood no chance against them.

Yet the attack on Shattrath would end before even a drop of blood was spilled.

En route to Shattrath, Voren'thal experienced a vision. He saw a glimpse into the future, a time when his people would rise to their former glory and live free of addiction and despair. At the heart of this vision was a naaru. Its Holy Light radiated across Quel'Thalas and eased the torment in the soul of every blood elf it touched.

Voren'thal was forever changed by what he saw. He told his followers of the vision, and he convinced them that the naaru were somehow the key to saving their people. The blood elves embraced Voren'thal's optimistic future. It was not a difficult choice for them. They had faced hardship after hardship on Outland with little to show for it. The elves were desperate for a new path to follow, even one based on a fleeting vision.

BLADE'S EDGE
MOUNTAINS

Coilfang Reservoir

Telredor

ZANGARMARSH

Garadar

Shattrath City

NAGRAND

TEROKKAR
FOREST

Auchindoun

NETHERSTORM

Tempest Keep

THE INVASION
OF OUTLAND

Hellfire Citadel   *The Dark Portal*

Honor Hold

HELLFIRE
PENINSULA

The Black Temple

SHADOWMOON
VALLEY

Upon reaching Shattrath, Voren'thal and his army put aside their weapons and pledged their loyalty to A'dal. These blood elf newcomers would become known as the Scryers.

Voren'thal sent word to Kael'thas, urging him to join the naaru in Shattrath. He received no reply.

Kael'thas was furious that his army had abandoned him to follow the naaru. Publicly, he condemned the act as treason and an attack on his sovereignty as prince. Privately, he saw Voren'thal's defection as evidence of his own failure.

This incident widened the rift between Kael'thas and Illidan. The prince demanded that the former night elf retaliate against the naaru, but nothing was done. Illidan was so focused on his demon hunters that he paid little attention to Voren'thal's army. This only proved to Kael'thas that what Kil'jaeden had told him was true: Illidan did not care about the prince and his people.

Kael'thas would not allow Illidan to sacrifice the blood elves as pawns. He lost all faith in the former night elf, and he looked to Kil'jaeden as a new benefactor. Some small part of Kael'thas knew that he should not trust the Legion, especially after what it had done to his kingdom. But he could not resist the temptation of fel magic. The prospect of finding new ways to feed on the dark energy dominated his thoughts and made all else secondary.

With little hesitation, Kael'thas forged a pact with the demon lord, and he agreed to abandon Illidan Stormrage. In return, Kil'jaeden granted the prince what he sought most: more knowledge about using fel magic.

THE BLOOD KNIGHTS

While Illidan Stormrage was focused on his demon hunters, Kael'thas Sunstrider and most of his followers quietly left the Black Temple. The prince promised he would return, but it was a lie. He sought out a distant corner of Outland known as the Netherstorm, where he established his own base. Only much later would Illidan realize that Kael'thas had no intention of rejoining his forces at the Black Temple.

Kael'thas had journeyed to the Netherstorm before and had tried to harness the latent energies that suffused the region. Even for a sorcerer as skilled as Kael'thas, it had been an impossible task. The Twisting Nether's magics were chaotic and fickle, and the prince's efforts had resulted in little more than frustration.

Yet that was before Tempest Keep's arrival. It boasted technologies far beyond anything he had seen on Azeroth.

Kael'thas knew little of Tempest Keep's inner workings, but he believed he could deploy its machinery to capture the region's errant magic and feed on it. He and a small army of elves used their newfound command over fel energy to infiltrate the fortress and overrun its defenses. The naaru within stood no chance against the invaders. O'ros called on its magic to bar the elves from its wing of the fortress, a satellite structure of Tempest Keep known as the *Exodar*. M'uru suffered a different fate. It fell under the blood elves' control.

Despite his allegiance to Kil'jaeden, Kael'thas still cared for his people. He believed that M'uru's power could sate the elves' cravings for magic.

ANVEENA TEAGUE

Through his demonic agents in Quel'Thalas, Kil'jaeden learned that Kael'thas Sunstrider did not know of Anveena Teague's existence. Only the kingdom's regent lord, Lor'themar Theron, and a handful of others were aware of her presence and of what she truly was. They'd kept this information a secret from Kael'thas. Lor'themar and his followers understood that the prince was desperate to save the elves. They feared that if Kael'thas learned of Anveena, he might act without considering the consequences. The elves did not know what would happen if the avatar's power was infused into the site of the Sunwell. Quel'Thalas was already a wounded nation. Another disaster might destroy it forever.

Over time, Lor'themar's opinion about this secrecy changed. He and his people constantly worried about Kael'thas's fate on Outland. It was time for him to come home, and Lor'themar believed the only way to bring him back was by telling him about Anveena.

After Kael'thas dispatched M'uru to Azeroth, messengers from Lor'themar set out to inform the prince about Anveena. Yet they never reached him. Kil'jaeden's agents in Quel'Thalas made sure of it. The prospect of restoring the Sunwell would give Kael'thas hope, and that was not what the demon lord needed. He wanted the prince to be desperate and uncertain about the future until he was firmly under Kil'jaeden's control.

Kael'thas drew on Tempest Keep's ability to traverse the cosmos to form a gateway to Azeroth. He ordered some of his followers to take M'uru to Quel'Thalas, where the rest of the elves could feed upon the being. He also ordered his servants to teach the people of his kingdom how to siphon magic from other sources, like creatures and artifacts.

The blood elves of Quel'Thalas had mixed feelings about M'uru's arrival. Regent Lord Lor'themar Theron and many other elves were troubled by the idea of leeching energy from a being of Holy Light. Others did not share their concerns. Some spent months experimenting on M'uru. Eventually they learned how to force out the naaru's holy energies and wield the Light themselves.

Word of this development traveled fast among Quel'Thalas's former priests, including Lady Liadrin. When the Scourge destroyed her kingdom in the Third War, she had felt that the Light had forsaken her. Liadrin's faith had faltered, and she had lost her ability to call on her holy powers. A similar fate had befallen some of Quel'Thalas's other priests.

But through M'uru, Liadrin and her kind found a way to call on the Holy Light. They would bend the naaru's energies to their will.

Liadrin was the first to indulge in M'uru's energies. She and those who followed in her footsteps forged a new order of elf paladins known as the Blood Knights.

THE ETHEREALS

Along with M'uru, Kael'thas Sunstrider sent another source of power to Quel'Thalas. He and his blood elves had discovered how to harness Tempest Keep's technologies to siphon magic from the Twisting Nether. They dismantled parts of the fortress and built a series of devices called manaforges. The elves placed these arcane machines throughout the Netherstorm. As they rumbled to life, they harvested magic from the Twisting Nether and stored it in enchanted mana cells, which the blood elves fed on.

Kil'jaeden urged Kael'thas to continue his work and dispatch shipments of the mana cells to Quel'Thalas. His advice was far from altruistic. The demon lord believed that Kael'thas could use the cells to help craft the Legion's portal in the Sunwell when the time was right.

Over time, the manaforges weakened the fabric of reality in the Netherstorm. This attracted the mysterious ethereals, a race of gifted scientists and magi who originally dwelled on the world of K'aresh. In pursuit of knowledge and arcane technologies, they had doomed themselves and their home: the K'areshi had torn open a rift into the Void and drawn the wrath of a being known as Dimensius the All-Devouring.

Dimensius had bathed the world in volatile energies that slowly tore it apart, and the K'areshi had desperately tried to shield themselves from harm. Their efforts had only partially worked. Their magic had blocked Dimensius's shadowy power, but raw arcane energy had shattered their physical bodies. All that remained were their souls, bristling with magic. From that day forward, these incorporeal creatures called themselves ethereals.

The ethereals had splintered into different factions. Some had become nomads and traders, roaming the cosmos in search of sources of magic and powerful artifacts. Others had sworn to destroy Dimensius and the creatures of the Void to avenge K'aresh.

These factions saw Outland as a realm where they could pursue their interests. Merchants hoped to ply their trade and discover new wealth, while the more militant ethereals sought new weapons to fight their war against the Void.

THE ASSAULT ON NATHREZA

As Kael'thas Sunstrider was settling in the Netherstorm, Illidan Stormrage continued his attacks against the Legion. His obsession with the demon hunters soon alienated another ally: Akama.

Akama had joined Illidan under the expectation that the Broken would assume control over the Black Temple, a site that he and his people considered sacred ground. That had not yet occurred, and he was uncertain if it ever would. Illidan was a secretive and ruthless leader. He openly embraced fel magic, as did the mysterious demon hunters who lived in his shadow. In some ways, Illidan was little different than the Black Temple's former overlord, Magtheridon.

Akama's distrust of Illidan drove him to find new allies who could liberate the Black Temple from evil. Chief among them was Maiev Shadowsong.

Maiev and her Watchers had remained on Outland, building up their forces for another attack on Illidan. They had faced many hardships on the shattered realm, but Maiev gave them little rest.

ILLIDAN STORMRAGE AND HIS DEMON HUNTERS

Her obsession with hunting Illidan clouded her judgment and pushed her to dangerous extremes. She would not leave Outland until she had captured her prey, even if that quest put her Watchers at risk.

It took time for Akama to earn Maiev's trust. They were born on different worlds and compelled by different desires, but they shared a common goal. In secret, they planned to bring Illidan to his knees and purge the Black Temple of his servants.

Akama took great care to keep these dealings hidden from his master, but it mattered little. Illidan was far more perceptive than the Broken had realized. He learned of Akama's treachery, but he did not kill him. Illidan had another use for the Broken.

The demon hunters were nearly prepared for their invasion of Nathreza. All that remained was opening a portal to the world, but doing so required a source of immense power. The souls of Maiev's followers would do nicely.

Illidan forced Akama to lure Maiev and her allies into an ambush. She and her Watchers walked right into the trap. Maiev's followers fell to Illidan and his soldiers, and their souls were used to fuel a gateway between worlds. Of the Watchers, only Maiev survived. It was not out of mercy. Illidan ordered his servants to imprison Maiev. He looked forward to tormenting her just as she had tormented him, but that would have to wait.

The way to Nathreza was open.

Illidan and his demon hunters struck at the dreadlords' homeworld with lethal precision. They stormed Nathreza's main archive and slaughtered its guardians. None could stand between Illidan and his prize: the Seal of Argus. The artifact thrummed with potent energy and knowledge. Illidan knew it was the key to his war—it held the location of the Legion's seat of power.

After taking the artifact, Illidan and his servants cut their way through the world's defenders and slipped through the portal back to Outland. Rather than close the gateway, Illidan focused all his power on destabilizing it.

It was time to see if he could do to Nathreza what had been done to Draenor years ago.

The portal unraveled, and a tidal wave of magic surged over Nathreza. The earth roared in protest. The dreadlords' cities crumbled to dust. Illidan Stormrage quickly closed the gateway on Outland to protect his domain from the destruction unfolding on Nathreza.

He was just in time. Shortly after the portal closed, Nathreza blew apart. Every demon on its surface perished.

It was the greatest defeat the Burning Legion had suffered in millennia.

THE *EXODAR*

In Hellfire Peninsula, Highlord Kruul and his invasion force crept across the region and carved out fortresses in the barren hills. Day by day, their strength grew.

A'dal and its followers in Shattrath kept abreast of the Legion's activities. The naaru knew it was only a matter of time before the demons moved into other parts of Outland. Though many brave souls had gathered in Shattrath, the city's defenders were outnumbered by the Legion. That fact was not bound to change. There were simply not enough soldiers to draw on from Outland.

A'dal needed new allies, and it could not pull them from the Army of the Light. The naaru looked to Azeroth instead. A'dal knew of the world and its heroes, and it knew of their history with the Legion. Getting to Azeroth would be difficult but not impossible. Though Kael'thas Sunstrider and his blood elves had dismantled parts of Tempest Keep, A'dal sensed that there was one wing of the fortress that was still able to traverse the stars and reach Azeroth. O'ros had hidden itself away in the *Exodar*, and it remained untouched by the blood elves.

When A'dal proposed commandeering the *Exodar*, Velen immediately volunteered to make the perilous journey. He was tired of hiding, and he felt it was his duty to do something to protect what remained of his people from the Legion. He also knew the inner workings of naaru fortresses.

A'dal gave its blessing, and Velen rallied a force of draenei to storm Tempest Keep. Though they ventured to the Netherstorm in secret, they could not elude Kil'jaeden's ever-watchful eyes. Before long, he learned of the plan to reach Azeroth.

Kil'jaeden decided not to stop the draenei, as much as he relished the prospect of killing them. He hated Velen, and he had spent thousands of years dreaming of an opportunity to make him suffer. Though it was difficult, Kil'jaeden put aside his lust for blood, not wanting it to compromise his true goal.

It was dangerous to let the draenei reach Azeroth and potentially join forces with the world's nations. However, Kil'jaeden believed the possible benefits of such a journey outweighed the risks. If the draenei told Azeroth's inhabitants of the Legion's presence and Illidan's misdeeds on Outland, it would only urge them to take action.

And once they arrived at the shattered realm, Kil'jaeden believed they would wage war against Illidan and unwittingly end his shadowy campaign against the Legion.

Unaware that Kil'jaeden was watching them, Velen and his people began their daring raid. The blood elves assumed the draenei had come to capture the whole of Tempest Keep, and the defenders arrayed their forces across the stronghold. Only too late did they realize that the draenei had no interest in conquest.

The draenei concentrated their assault on the wing of Tempest Keep containing O'ros, smashing through the blood elves' defenses. The satellite structure broke away from Tempest Keep and vanished in an explosion of magic.

Only after the journey began did Velen realize something was wrong with the *Exodar*. During the battle at Tempest Keep, a handful of blood elves had fought their way into the *Exodar* and sabotaged it, hoping to disable the structure. They failed, but their meddling had repercussions.

Upon reaching Azeroth, Velen lost control of the *Exodar*. The fortress plummeted through a rift in the heavens like a falling star. The *Exodar* slammed into a remote area in northern Kalimdor called Azuremyst Isle. The crash nearly destroyed the *Exodar* and its helpless voyagers. Casualties were high, but many of the passengers survived.

Teldrassil's night elves saw the flash of light in the heavens, and they investigated the phenomenon. Though they were wary of the draenei newcomers, the night elves soon realized that Velen and his people were no threat. They shared a common enemy in the Legion.

From Stormwind City to Ironforge, messengers relayed stories of the draenei's arrival and the state of Outland. The Alliance voted to welcome the draenei into its ranks and give them shelter and protection. The decision was unanimous.

Though the tales of Illidan's shadowy deeds and a Legion army amassing on Outland worried the Alliance, the faction's leaders did not yet agree to act.

NEW ALLEGIANCES

Quel'Thalas was still in turmoil. Packs of undead roamed the land. On the southern borders, the Amani trolls began launching attacks against the weakened blood elves. Regent Lord Lor'themar Theron had few resources to protect his home from these threats. The kingdom's army was in tatters. Overindulgence of magic had transformed some elves into withered creatures called the Wretched. These unfortunate souls turned their backs on society and wandered the land in search of magic to feed on.

To make matters worse, Prince Kael'thas Sunstrider had still not returned from Outland. The latest news that Lor'themar and his people had heard from the shattered realm did not bode well. The Legion was gathering in great numbers for reasons unknown, and a large portion of Kael'thas's blood elves had abandoned the prince.

Kael'thas was vulnerable, but Lor'themar could not leave Quel'Thalas undefended while he launched a campaign to assist the prince on Outland. The blood elves needed allies, and they would not find them among the humans, dwarves, gnomes, or night elves. Kael'thas's decision to join Lady Vashj and Illidan had soured relations between Quel'Thalas and the Alliance.

An answer came from an unexpected source: Sylvanas Windrunner. The Banshee Queen urged the Horde's leadership to ally with the blood elves, but her reasons remained a mystery. Rumors circulated that some lingering part of her still sympathized with Quel'Thalas and its hardships. Other stories hinted that Sylvanas had ulterior motives. Whatever the truth, she arranged for Warchief Thrall and High Chieftain Cairne Bloodhoof to convene with Lor'themar and discuss such a possibility.

Despite the elves' history of bitter warfare with the orcs, Lor'themar was receptive to the idea. He knew this Horde was different than the one that had ravaged Quel'Thalas in years past. He was also painfully aware that time was running out for his kingdom and his prince.

Thrall and Cairne saw great promise in the blood elves. The people of Quel'Thalas had proved their courage and resolve while fighting to protect their kingdom from outside threats like the Scourge. Thrall and Cairne believed that the Horde and the blood elves needed each other to survive the days ahead. They extended the hand of peace to Lor'themar, and he accepted.

This alliance benefited both sides. While the blood elves now had allies to call on, the Horde gained another strategic foothold in the Eastern Kingdoms. Thrall and Cairne also saw helping the blood elves as an act of honor. Much like the other races of the Horde, they were a people on the verge of extinction. Enemies lurked on all sides. Constant war and addiction to magic had chipped away at their pride and once-glorious culture. Thrall and Cairne believed they could help the blood elves find peace.

After the blood elves were inducted into the Horde, Lor'themar Theron told Thrall and Cairne Bloodhoof of the Legion's presence on Outland and his desire to find Kael'thas Sunstrider. The news about demons was deeply troubling. Yet, like the Alliance's leaders, Thrall and Cairne were wary of venturing to Outland.

Soon Kil'jaeden would give them a reason to do so.

THE INVASION OF OUTLAND
26 YEARS AFTER THE DARK PORTAL

Kil'jaeden hadn't anticipated the blood elves joining the Horde, but he welcomed it. Word of the Legion's presence on Outland and Illidan Stormrage's conquest of that realm had spread throughout the most powerful nations on Azeroth. Leaders convened to discuss what to do, but they remained hesitant to act. The Dark Portal was closed. Outland was a distant threat.

That was about to change.

On Outland, Kil'jaeden ordered Highlord Kruul and his forces to gather at the Dark Portal. He gave the same command to his forces on Azeroth. Many demons had been trapped on the world following the Third War. The most powerful among them was the doomlord Kazzak. As the Legion's de facto ruler on Azeroth, he rounded up what demons he could find and brought them to the site of the Dark Portal in the Blasted Lands.

Kil'jaeden then guided his followers in a great ritual to reopen the rift. Though the Dark Portal had been closed, reality was permanently warped by its former presence. The Legion's spellwork tore through this weakness, and the bridge between worlds flared to life again.

Kazzak stormed into Outland and took control of the Legion army. He was a more seasoned commander than Highlord Kruul, and he inspired greater fear and respect in his followers.

Kil'jaeden had another purpose for Kruul. The highlord would be the spark that set Azeroth and Outland alight with war. Kruul gathered a small invasion force and marched through the Dark Portal. He struck at Stormwind City, Orgrimmar, and other locations throughout the world. His purpose was not to conquer but to stir the Horde and the Alliance into a frenzy. In that, he succeeded.

The Horde's and the Alliance's response was immediate. Their armies mobilized and made war on the demons. Kruul and his followers feigned retreat, gathering in the Eastern Kingdoms and luring their enemies to the Dark Portal. The highlord always intended for the Horde and the Alliance to reach Outland, but he made them work for it. His demons bled their foes every step of the way. The fiercest fighting erupted outside the Dark Portal, and the Horde and the Alliance paid dearly to push the demons through the gateway.

The defenders of Azeroth could no longer ignore the threat posed by Outland. The Dark Portal had been restored. If they closed it, the Legion might simply open it again. There was but one choice to make.

The Horde and the Alliance launched their armies into Outland. For most of these soldiers, it was the first time they had seen the broken world. Many orcs had been there before, but even they were shocked by what they witnessed.

Kruul, Kazzak, and a massive Legion army greeted them on the other side of the Dark Portal. And this time, the demons would not retreat.

The Legion and Azeroth's defenders waged a brutal war for supremacy in the Dark Portal's shadow. The Horde and the Alliance slowly pushed into Hellfire Peninsula. Casualties mounted on both sides. Not even Kruul or Kazzak was spared the fury of battle. They had expected Kil'jaeden to send reinforcements to help the demons hold back the heroes of Azeroth.

Yet that had never been Kil'jaeden's intention. The demon lord sacrificed Kruul and Kazzak to embolden the Horde and the Alliance. He needed them to carve out footholds on Outland and turn their wrath on Illidan as soon as possible. Bogging them down in a prolonged war with the Legion did not serve Kil'jaeden's purpose. It might have caused them to retreat to Azeroth.

As the Horde and the Alliance pushed inland, they established strongholds in Hellfire Peninsula. The Alliance soldiers were shocked to discover Honor Hold and its inhabitants. The Sons of Lothar had not perished as had once been thought. The commander of Honor Hold, the revered human warrior Danath Trollbane, welcomed the Alliance with open arms.

The Horde had no pre-existing fortress to call their own. They built a new settlement, Thrallmar, in the north of Hellfire Peninsula. Soon, the Horde found allies to join their cause: the Mag'har orcs.

The Mag'har were few, but they proved to be fierce fighters. They had never succumbed to the demonic blood-curse that had twisted most other orcs, turning their skin from brown to green and transforming them into war-crazed soldiers. Ever since the destruction of Draenor, small

THE ASSAULT ON THE DARK PORTAL

The Horde and the Alliance were not the only ones who fought the Legion at the Dark Portal. Secretly, Illidan Stormrage and his demon hunters had also joined the fray. They had spotted Highlord Kruul leading a small force to outflank Azeroth's defenders. Illidan and his followers struck before that came to pass. They carved through the demons' ranks until they had defeated Kruul himself.

The demon hunters did not linger in the area. Illidan was wary of making his presence known to the Alliance and the Horde. He believed they would see him and his fel-wielding followers as nothing more than agents of the Legion. After the battle, Illidan left the Dark Portal and continued preparing for strikes against the Legion on other worlds.

communities of Mag'har had clung to survival on Outland, honing their shamanic traditions and carrying on the old ways of their people. They saw the new Horde for what it was: a return to the pride and honor of the orcs' former society.

From Honor Hold and Thrallmar, the Alliance and the Horde continued their offensives against the Legion. They broke the demons' strength and pushed them to the outskirts of Hellfire Peninsula.

The champions of Azeroth then turned their attention to Outland's self-proclaimed lord: Illidan Stormrage. By now, both factions had heard disturbing rumors about the Betrayer. Stories of the naga warping the land in Zangarmarsh, of the blood elves seizing Tempest Keep and leeching magic from the Netherstorm.

And there were other tales, ones that spoke of Illidan training an army of elves infused with demonic power.

The Alliance and the Horde were unaware of Illidan's true goal to destroy the Legion, and he made no attempt to tell them. He was almost ready to launch his attack on Argus. He knew that if he tried to explain his methods to the peoples of Azeroth, they would not understand. Thus, he focused all his attention on his demon hunters and their mission.

GHOSTS OF DRAENOR

After crushing the Legion's hold on Hellfire Peninsula, the Horde launched an offensive against Illidan Stormrage's fel orcs at Hellfire Citadel.

For many members of the Horde, the assault was personal. The ferocious, red-skinned orcs were a reminder of the demonic corruption that had plagued the old Horde. Using the pit lord Magtheridon's blood, Illidan had forged an army of brutal soldiers. The infamous chieftain of the Shattered Hand orc clan, Kargath Bladefist, lorded over Hellfire Citadel. He and his fel orcs were beyond saving. They showed no mercy to the Horde, and they were offered none in return.

Horde forces defeated Kargath and marched into the heart of Hellfire Citadel. They did not rest until they cut down Magtheridon in the belly of the fortress. Though Magtheridon would never again taint the orc race, there was little celebration. The Horde's triumph had been grim work, and few soldiers rejoiced in spilling the blood of fel orcs.

Yet the Horde's time on Outland also brought hope and redemption, especially for Thrall. Born on Azeroth, he had never been to his race's ancestral home. Little was left of old Draenor, but there was a place largely untouched by the calamity that had befallen the world.

Thrall and many other members of the Horde eventually ventured into Nagrand, a region steeped in ancient orcish culture. The largest community of Mag'har called it home. They dwelled in Garadar, a village named after Thrall's late grandfather and watched over by his grandmother, Geyah. Meeting her changed the warchief's life. His parents had died when he was only an infant, and Geyah was the closest connection he had to them. She taught him much about his parents, his people, and himself.

But Thrall also had something to teach. Garadar's leader was Garrosh Hellscream, son of the legendary warrior Grommash Hellscream. Garrosh did not know of his father's deeds on Azeroth. He believed that Grommash was a monster, one of the orcs who had led his people into the clutches

REXXAR AND THE MOK'NATHAL

Rexxar accompanied the Horde to Outland, seeking to reconnect with his fellow mok'nathal. It had been many years since he'd seen his people. Rexxar found them north of Hellfire Peninsula, among the jagged peaks of the Blade's Edge Mountains. An aging warrior led the mok'nathal. His name was Leoroxx, and he was Rexxar's father.

Years ago, a rift had formed between father and son. Leoroxx was opposed to the Horde of old, and he had been against Rexxar's decision to join it. A fierce argument had engulfed the two mok'nathal, and they had parted ways with anger in their hearts.

Time had not yet healed these wounds. Rexxar could not face his father, but he did everything in his power to help the mok'nathal fend off their enemies in the Blade's Edge Mountains.

of demons. Thrall was quick to tell him that his father was a hero. He recounted how Grommash had sacrificed himself to defeat Mannoroth, how he had lifted the blood-curse that had afflicted the orcs. The truth filled Garrosh with confidence.

Thrall saw much potential in Garrosh. He was brash and quick to anger, but Thrall believed Garrosh's fierce pride and knowledge of orcish culture would serve the Horde well. The warchief convinced the Mag'har orc to act as his advisor back on Azeroth.

COILFANG RESERVOIR

Before long, the Alliance and the Horde had forged into the murky swamp of Zangarmarsh. The draenei who had joined the Alliance were eager to reconnect with those whom they'd left behind on Outland, and many of them dwelled in Zangarmarsh. The Alliance forces soon gathered at the sanctuary of Telredor, the largest draenei stronghold in the region.

From Telredor's draenei, the Alliance learned many unsettling things. Conditions in Zangarmarsh were rapidly deteriorating. Disease had spread among plants and animals alike. Food sources were vanishing, driving the local creatures into a frenzy. Nearby tribes of Broken were disappearing, never to be seen again.

Lady Vashj and her naga were the cause of Zangarmarsh's troubles. Their efforts to drain its water had upset the region's delicate ecosystem. Nature was in upheaval, and it would only continue to unravel unless something was done.

The Alliance did not hesitate. Its champions stormed into the naga's watery fortress, Coilfang Reservoir.

WARCHIEF THRALL TELLS GARROSH HELLSCREAM OF THE HEROIC ACTS OF GROMMASH HELLSCREAM

Much like the Horde's attack on Magtheridon in Hellfire Citadel, the Alliance's assault on Coilfang Reservoir exacted a heavy toll from the invaders. The stronghold was filled with diseased wildlife and Lady Vashj's most fearsome naga warriors. Enslaved Broken also roamed Coilfang Reservoir, and nearly all of them welcomed the promise of freedom. The Alliance's forces shattered their bonds as they charged through the naga's fortress.

Lady Vashj was the last to fall to the Alliance's blades. With her death, Coilfang Reservoir was no longer a threat. Though it would take time, balance would return to Zangarmarsh. Telredor's inhabitants were now safe to expand across the region.

THE FALLEN SUN

In time, the Horde and the Alliance reached Shattrath City. A'dal rejoiced at their arrival. Velen's daring escape to Azeroth had paid off. The naaru now had allies to protect Outland from the Legion.

Shattrath became a pivotal staging ground for the Horde and the Alliance. Trade flourished between the peoples of Azeroth and many of Outland's creatures. Though weapons and armor were exchanged, the most valuable thing that the Horde and the Alliance discovered in Shattrath was information.

Much of it came from Archmage Khadgar. He had become an influential figure in the city. Though he was a member of the Alliance, he knew the Horde also had a crucial role to play in determining Outland's fate. He sought to bridge the divide between the factions and arm them with knowledge about Illidan Stormrage's domain.

Some of Azeroth's defenders gradually converged on Shadowmoon Valley, site of the Black Temple. There, the Alliance rallied with other heroes from the Sons of Lothar. Kurdran Wildhammer and his fellow dwarves had forged a stronghold in Shadowmoon Valley. From it, they watched the Black Temple and reported what they saw to Khadgar.

Khadgar knew that rifts had formed between the Betrayer and his lieutenants, most notably Kael'thas Sunstrider. The blood elves had abandoned Illidan Stormrage and left him with little in the way of an army to defend himself.

That did not seem to trouble Illidan. Sightings of the demon hunter had become increasingly rare. Khadgar was unsure about Illidan's activities, but he knew the time was drawing near to attack the Black Temple. There was little opposition to this plan among the Horde and the Alliance. Illidan had almost destroyed Zangarmarsh. He had used Magtheridon to corrupt hundreds of orcs. If he were left to his own devices, it was only a matter of time before he caused some other calamity.

Yet the heroes of Azeroth were not ready to besiege the Black Temple. Most of their forces were still scattered across Outland. Many were gathering in the Netherstorm, particularly the Horde's blood elves.

In Shattrath, they had learned about Kael'thas Sunstrider's fate. It was worse than they'd expected. News had spread that their prince had pledged himself to the Burning Legion.

Some blood elves did not believe these stories. At least, not at first. When they ventured to the Netherstorm, they saw the truth with their own eyes. Kael'thas had embraced fel magic and become the Legion's pawn. He was their prince no more.

Word of this discovery reached Lor'themar Theron and the other ranking elves in Quel'Thalas. The news broke their hearts, but they came to a consensus. Kael'thas was lost. It was their duty to vanquish him and end his treachery.

The Horde made war on Kael'thas and his followers. The battle spread into Tempest Keep and engulfed every corner of the dimensional fortress. It was there where the prince made his final stand. It was there where some of his own loyal subjects spilled his blood and ended his reign.

Yet unbeknownst to the Horde, Kael'thas Sunstrider did not die.

Kil'jaeden had expected the prince's defeat, and he had prepared accordingly. Kael'thas's demonic allies spirited him away and brought him back from the brink of death. Little was left of the elf's mind. He was now Kil'jaeden's loyal servant, and he would do whatever his master asked of him.

While the Horde and the Alliance directed their forces to the Black Temple, Kael'thas and his Legion comrades journeyed through the Dark Portal and toward the Sunwell.

SIEGE OF THE BLACK TEMPLE

Illidan Stormrage was running out of time.

Alongside forces from Shattrath City, the Horde and the Alliance had arrived at the Black Temple's walls and begun their siege. Illidan's defenses were sound, but they would not hold for long. Desperation consumed him. He had learned Argus's location, but powerful enchantments surrounded the world, preventing him from opening a gateway there. A means to reach the Legion's seat of power lay in a shattered world in the Twisting Nether known as Mardum. Illidan had discovered that this broken land was home to an invaluable artifact. It was called the Sargerite Keystone, and it could open the way to Argus.

As his enemies breached the Black Temple and poured into the fortress, Illidan made a choice. He could not simply abandon Outland. After retrieving the Sargerite Keystone, he would need to return and prepare for the assault on Argus. Instead, he sent his demon hunters to Mardum, and he remained in the Black Temple to fend off his foes. He hoped that what was left of his followers would hold back the tide.

They could not. A unified army of Horde, Alliance, and Shattrath City's forces carved its way through the Black Temple. Some of Illidan's servants fought to the death. Some fled in terror. And others took the assault as an opportunity to turn on the Betrayer.

Akama was one of them. His time serving Illidan had been full of suffering and disappointment. When the siege had begun, he had freed Maiev Shadowsong from her prison and urged her to strike at Illidan. She had needed little convincing.

Maiev set out on her own while Akama helped Azeroth's champions enter the heart of the Black Temple. She eventually joined the invaders as they confronted Illidan, and she struck at the Betrayer to quench her long-held thirst for justice and vengeance.

Illidan Stormrage called on all his power and knowledge to overcome his attackers. He fought not only to save himself but to keep his war against the Legion alive. His conviction never faltered, but that was not enough to grant him victory.

In the end, he fell.

157

CHAPTER V: THE BURNING CRUSADE

GODS OF ZUL'AMAN

As the Horde and the Alliance were waging war on Illidan Stormrage's forces, Warlord Zul'jin and his Amani trolls prepared to march on Quel'Thalas. They were bitter enemies of the blood elves, and they had been waiting for the perfect opportunity to launch a full-out assault. With most of Quel'Thalas's soldiers occupied on Outland, that opportunity was now.

Zul'jin was a cunning leader, and his attack was motivated by hatred of Quel'Thalas as well as strategic reasons. The blood elves had recently joined the Horde, which had granted them more power and resources. Zul'jin believed Quel'Thalas would inevitably convince its new allies to strike at the Amani empire.

Within the Amani capital, Zul'Aman, troll priests performed rituals to harness the power of their loa. These mighty creatures roamed the city in the form of giant beasts. Their energies suffused the troll soldiers, transforming them into living embodiments of the loa.

The Horde was desperate not to fight a war on two fronts—Outland and Quel'Thalas. The faction's mightiest champions volunteered to storm Zul'Aman. They did not have the strength to face the trolls' army directly, but they had no need to. The Horde's strike force cut off the serpent's head, killing Zul'jin and his priests before their rampage in Quel'Thalas could even begin.

It was a cruel twist of fate that heroes from the very world Illidan sought to protect were the ones to kill him and cut short his war against the demons. In his final moments, his thoughts turned to his old nemesis. He knew that his defeat would ruin Maiev Shadowsong. She had spent much of her life acting as his jailor and hunter. Now that her quest was over, she had lost her purpose.

Illidan's demon hunters returned from Mardum with the Sargerite Keystone only to witness their master's fall. Maiev quickly subdued them. She froze the demon hunters and Illidan's corpse in enchanted crystals. They were too dangerous to abandon, and so Maiev transported them back to Azeroth for safekeeping. She would later lock them away in the Vault of the Wardens, a closely guarded prison on the Broken Isles.

Outland was free of Illidan Stormrage and his army. Yet before the Horde and the Alliance could celebrate, dire news reached them. Kael'thas Sunstrider was not dead. He had rallied a force of corrupted elves and demons on Azeroth.

FURY OF THE SUNWELL

North of Zul'Aman, Kael'thas Sunstrider and his forces invaded Quel'Thalas. With most of its soldiers still in Outland, the kingdom could do little to stop the fallen prince.

Under Kil'jaeden's orders, Kael'thas and his forces captured the naaru M'uru and Anveena Teague, the avatar of the Sunwell's energies. The prince leeched away their power to re-form the ruined Sunwell. A brilliant explosion of energy erupted from the fount, sparking it to life for the first time since the Third War. Kael'thas fortified his ritual with energy from the mana cells he had gathered in the Netherstorm.

Kael'thas then began weaving the Sunwell's power into a gateway for Kil'jaeden to reach Azeroth. As he worked, some blood elves fled to Outland to warn the Horde leadership about what was transpiring. One of these elves was the Blood Knight Liadrin. She had witnessed Kael'thas's assault with her own eyes. In Shattrath City, Lady Liadrin met with A'dal, renouncing her allegiance to Kael'thas and swearing to defeat the Legion. The naaru welcomed her into a new order that had been forged to stand against the prince. It was called the Shattered Sun Offensive, and it included both the draenei of the Aldor and the blood elves of the Scryers.

The Shattered Sun Offensive marched on the Sunwell and waged a fierce battle against the Legion forces in the area. Though constantly besieged by demons, Liadrin and her allies had an impact. They disrupted Kael'thas's spellwork long enough for more help to arrive.

Members of the Horde and the Alliance soon converged on the Sunwell and stood alongside the Shattered Sun Offensive. Liadrin directed the Horde's champions to hunt down Kael'thas in the Magisters' Terrace. Though the prince had grown more powerful since his defeat at Tempest Keep, so had the heroes he faced. The Horde slew Kael'thas Sunstrider and ended him once and for all.

Meanwhile, the Alliance infiltrated the Sunwell Plateau, which housed the Sunwell itself. Kael'thas's spellwork had torn a rift in the fount's depths. Before the Alliance's eyes, Kil'jaeden emerged from the portal and into the world.

The Alliance soldiers fought with all their strength to drive Kil'jaeden back through the portal, but their efforts had little effect. In the end, it was Anveena Teague who turned the tide of battle. She sacrificed her own existence, expending what was left of her energy to weaken Kil'jaeden. It was just enough for the Alliance to finally banish the demon lord and close his gateway into Azeroth.

The world was spared from the Legion once more, but there were consequences. Kael'thas's meddling had tainted the Sunwell. As before, corruptive energies coursed through the fount, and they would soon spread throughout Quel'Thalas and engulf the blood elves. Lor'themar Theron and his followers considered destroying the Sunwell again, but another solution presented itself.

Velen had come to the Sunwell to pay his respects to M'uru. Little was left of the naaru save its heart. Velen sensed a glimmer of power—of hope—in what remained of M'uru. He used the naaru's heart to cleanse the Sunwell and transform it into a fount of Holy Light and arcane magic. Its brilliant energy blazed across land and sky for all in Quel'Thalas to see.

This turn of events had a profound effect on the blood elves, particularly Lady Liadrin and her Blood Knights. They abandoned wielding holy energies by force and returned to their old ways. Through the Sunwell, they would *ask* for the Light's blessing.

The Sunwell was reborn, and its return heralded a promising future for the blood elves. With the fount to draw on, they no longer needed to look elsewhere to satisfy their cravings for magic.

KALECGOS AND ANVEENA

For years, the kindhearted blue dragon Kalecgos had watched over Anveena Teague in Quel'Thalas. When Kael'thas Sunstrider invaded the kingdom, Kalecgos fought desperately to protect the human avatar, but his foes were too numerous to hold back.

The dreadlord Sathrovarr the Corruptor possessed Kalecgos and forced him to serve the Legion in the Sunwell Plateau. Only later did the Alliance free him from the demon's control.

NETHER DRAGONS

The journey to Outland had a profound impact on the Horde and the Alliance, but it also changed the destiny of many beings who had not visited the shattered realm.

While exploring Outland, the blue dragon Tyrygosa had befriended a brood of creatures known as nether dragons. They traced their lineage to the black Dragon Aspect, Deathwing, from when he had left some of his eggs on Draenor for safekeeping. When the world had exploded, the influx of energies had warped the unhatched dragons into partially incorporeal beings. These nether dragons were powerful yet childish. They had no true leader, and that made them unruly. It also made them susceptible to outside influence.

A renegade death knight named Ragnok Bloodreaver had seen great potential in the nether dragons. He had hoped to incorporate them into his army—an army he would use to conquer Outland.

His plans fell to ruin, but his abuse of the nether dragons deeply troubled Tyrygosa. She was concerned that they would die from the injuries they'd suffered while fighting under Ragnok's command. Tyrygosa transported many of the nether dragons to the blue dragonflight's lair, the Nexus. She hoped that its energies would reinvigorate the wounded creatures. What Tyrygosa never considered was whether the blue dragons would be safe from their new guests.

The nether dragons bathed in the arcane energies of the Nexus. The magic was unlike anything they had ever experienced. They wanted it all, seeing it as a way to make themselves stronger so that no one would control them as Ragnok had. The nether dragons launched a surprise attack against the blue dragons to seize the Nexus for themselves.

The battle that unfolded drew the attention of Malygos.

Millennia ago, after Deathwing betrayed the other dragonflights in the War of the Ancients, Malygos had become a recluse. He hid himself away in the Nexus, engulfed in grief and pain. Malygos largely ignored what was happening in the outside world, relying on his servants to investigate anomalies and keep watch over Azeroth. Yet he would not ignore an attack on his own lair.

KIL'JAEDEN EMERGES INTO AZEROTH AT THE SUNWELL

Malygos lashed out at the nether dragons, absorbing nearly all of them into his being. Unexpectedly, the energies of the incorporeal creatures swept away the haze of suffering and regret that had clouded his mind.

The nether dragons' attack convinced Malygos that he needed to embrace his sacred duty of safeguarding arcane magic on Azeroth once again. He assessed the state of magical affairs on the world, and he was not pleased by what he saw. In his eyes, the foolish actions of mortal magi had led to war and chaos.

Malygos formed a plan to reestablish his dominance over magic. He would sever the link between mortals and the latent arcane energy coursing through Azeroth.

SHADOW OF THE LIGHT

As events transpired on Azeroth and Outland, Cho'gall had continued expanding the Twilight's Hammer cult. The organization had transformed into something far different from the orcish clan it had once been. The cult welcomed members from all races and walks of life. Cho'gall's followers spread throughout every major city on Azeroth, secretly evangelizing and converting others to their cause. They often preyed on survivors of the Third War, especially those who had witnessed unspeakable horrors in Lordaeron.

One of these individuals was Archbishop Benedictus, leader of the Church of the Holy Light. He had lived through the First and Second Wars. Though the suffering he'd seen troubled him, it had not shaken his faith. In some ways, he'd viewed the conflicts as a test of his beliefs. Yet the Third War had been different. The fall of Lordaeron and the appearance of the Scourge had pushed his conviction to the breaking point. Why had the Holy Light not protected Prince Arthas, King Terenas, the paladins, or the other good people of the kingdom? Why, in humanity's hour of greatest need, had it abandoned its pious servants?

The cultists learned of the archbishop's uncertainty, and they flocked to him like crows to carrion. They presented themselves as believers of the Holy Light in need of guidance. In truth, they came to whittle away at what was left of the archbishop's beliefs. Slowly but surely, they did. Some spoke of the Void, a universal force of energy that would *never* abandon its servants as the Holy Light had.

Like other priests, Archbishop Benedictus knew of shadow magic. He had not experimented with it himself, believing it was unholy and corruptive. Yet he now began to wonder if that was truly the case, or if it was merely what he had been led to believe.

And it was this curiosity that opened the way to the Old Gods. They whispered in the archbishop's dreams and showed him the Light from their perspective. The holy energy was not as benevolent as it had once seemed. It tolerated only perfect order and obedience. It served its mortal adherents when it needed to, not because of their faith.

These dreams continued for many nights, culminating in a vision of the Hour of Twilight. Benedictus was moved by what he saw. He considered the Hour of Twilight as not the apocalyptic end to all things but a chance to break free from the Holy Light's tyranny, a chance to create a new world where he would be the master of his own destiny. He came to believe that the Old Gods and the powers of the Void were the natural state of the universe, and that it was wrong to fight that reality as he had once tried as a practitioner of the Holy Light. The Light had brought him and thousands of other people only disappointment and heartache. The Void was not the source of lies but of every possible truth. It would not ignore or abandon its followers, and Benedictus pledged his life to serving it.

Benedictus joined the Twilight's Hammer cult, becoming one of its most influential members. Publicly, he remained head of the church, and through sheer willpower, he retained his ability to wield the Holy Light. The position afforded him great power and access to disillusioned priests and believers whom he could recruit into the cult.

Cho'gall saw Benedictus's induction into the Twilight's Hammer as a triumph. The number of cultists was growing at a faster pace than he had expected.

DIRGE OF THE NORTH

Though Cho'gall was pleased by the Twilight's Hammer cult's burgeoning strength, he remained troubled by C'Thun's fall. He had never expected mortals to have the power to defeat an Old God. Nonetheless, Cho'gall did not abandon his quest to initiate the Hour of Twilight.

While the Horde and the Alliance were occupied in Outland, Cho'gall visited Northrend and infiltrated Ulduar, the keeper-wrought prison of the Old God Yogg-Saron. He slipped into the depths of the fortress, and its defenders did nothing to stop him. Yogg-Saron clouded the minds of Loken and the other ancient keepers, concealing Cho'gall's presence.

Yogg-Saron had long ago enthralled the keepers who guarded Ulduar, but the entity's grasp on them was tenuous. Convincing them to directly help the Old God had proved fruitless in the past, but there would be no such trouble with Cho'gall. The two-headed ogre willingly chipped away at Yogg-Saron's enchanted bonds. He could not break them, but he managed to weaken the chains.

That was enough to increase Yogg-Saron's influence tenfold. The Old God's control over the keepers became as strong as iron. It commanded the greatest of them, Keeper Loken, to create an army from the Forge of Wills. In the right hands, this extraordinary machine had the power to make noble forms of life. In Loken's hands, it churned out legions of metal-skinned dwarves and vrykul who sought only bloodshed and war.

As Yogg-Saron's army fortified the lands surrounding Ulduar, Cho'gall left Northrend to continue guiding the Twilight's Hammer cult. He needed to give Yogg-Saron as much time as possible to prepare its forces. He also needed to keep the Old God safe from the Alliance and the Horde. By defeating C'Thun, the two factions had proved that they were unstoppable when they put aside their differences and united.

Cho'gall would not allow them to do so again. He would drive a wedge between the Horde and the Alliance. And the perfect opportunity soon presented itself.

THE GLADIATOR KING

During the invasion of Outland, Varian Wrynn lived without complete knowledge of his past. His essence had been split into two halves, inhabiting two different bodies: one was his diplomatic, amenable side, and the other was his unbending will. After his willful half had escaped from Onyxia's grasp, he had been enslaved by an orc named Rehgar Earthfury and trained as a gladiator. This part of Varian had become a warrior without equal, and he won renown for his ferocious fighting style. His exploits earned him the moniker Lo'Gosh, a name that the tauren had given to the Wild God Goldrinn. Legends told that this enormous white wolf possessed unparalleled rage and fury, just as Varian did.

Fragments of Lo'Gosh's true identity began to surface. Sensing there was something more to his life than mere blood sport, he escaped Rehgar's custody and eventually sought out someone who could help him part the mists shrouding his past. His journey led him to a powerful mage named Jaina Proudmoore in Theramore.

Lo'Gosh stumbled into the city without realizing he had been Jaina's friend. In his eyes, she was just another stranger.

Jaina did not immediately recognize the battle-scarred warrior, but she sensed something familiar about him. The magic that had sundered Varian's spirit had also enveloped him in an aura of dark magic. These energies hid his identity from everyone, even his former friends.

Jaina turned to her chamberlain, the legendary sorceress Aegwynn, for help. Together, they called on their magic to pierce the veil over Varian's mind and reveal his identity. He was no slave, no gladiator. He was the rightful king of Stormwind.

Galvanized by this knowledge, Varian returned home. He was dismayed to find an impostor wearing his crown, a man who looked just like him. In the guise of Lady Katrana Prestor, Onyxia had placed the other half of Varian's sundered essence on the throne as a puppet ruler whom she could manipulate with ease. Stormwind's populace was fooled, but many of those who had been close to Varian were not. Prince Anduin Wrynn knew that something was amiss about the man who claimed to be his father, but he had no way to act on that suspicion.

AEGWYNN'S LEGACY

Following the Third War, Theramore attracted adventurers, merchants, and even heroes from the past. One of them was a former Guardian of Tirisfal, Aegwynn. Jaina Proudmoore had convinced the legendary sorceress to stay in the city. Aegwynn had accepted, becoming Jaina's official chamberlain. The position did not carry the glory of her old life, but that was a welcome change. After she had brought her son, Medivh, back into the world, Aegwynn lost much of her power. She longed for a simpler, more peaceful existence.

KING VARIAN WRYNN AND PRINCE ANDUIN RETURN TO STORMWIND CITY AFTER ONYXIA'S DEFEAT

Varian Wrynn was not one to shy away from conflict. He confronted Katrana Prestor and brought her deception to light. Then chaos engulfed Stormwind City when Prestor took on her true form. The monstrous black dragon Onyxia seized Prince Anduin and fled the city, returning to her lair in the swampy mires of Dustwallow Marsh.

Varian's two halves were at odds, each claiming that he was the real king. Yet what they agreed on was their love for Anduin. They put aside their differences and hunted down Onyxia. As one, they marched into the dragon's lair. It was this unity, this shared commitment to sacrifice their lives to protect their son, that would change the course of Varian's life and the history of Stormwind itself.

As battle engulfed Onyxia's lair, the dragon's enchantment over Varian Wrynn crumbled. His shattered essences merged, and he was made whole again. The one true king of Stormwind brought Onyxia low and cut her head from her shoulders.

With Anduin at his side, Varian returned to his throne in Stormwind. Onyxia's head was hung from the gates of the city, a warning of the fate that awaited anyone who sought to destroy the kingdom.

Varian Wrynn had won, but he was never quite the same. His warrior spirit would remain the dominant force in his heart. In the years to come, he would struggle to control his rage, that fearsome part of him that had earned him the name Lo'Gosh.

THE PROMISE OF PEACE

Tensions had long simmered between the Horde and the Alliance, but the campaign on Outland had proved that the factions could work together. Besieging the Black Temple and the Sunwell had succeeded only due to unity. For the first time in years, hope surfaced that perhaps the Horde and the Alliance could reach a lasting peace accord.

Jaina Proudmoore championed this path. She was certain that Azeroth would face new threats in the future, either from the Legion, the Lich King, or other dark forces. Jaina organized a meeting between the Horde and the Alliance in Theramore, promising that her city would act as neutral ground.

Not everyone in the Horde and the Alliance sought peace, but most of their leaders did. Varian Wrynn and Thrall led delegations from their respective factions and convened in Theramore. This gathering was unprecedented in the history of Horde and Alliance relations. It had the potential to change Azeroth's destiny for the better.

If not for Cho'gall, perhaps it would have.

The two-headed ogre had learned of the summit. It was exactly the opportunity he had been waiting for to sow chaos between the factions. Cho'gall commanded Garona to assassinate Varian and other members of the delegation, an act that he was certain would ignite war. She had no choice but to obey her master.

As the summit was under way, Garona launched a surprise attack and brought her blades to bear on Varian. The king narrowly fended off the assault, and his would-be assassin was captured.

Varian was livid. He believed she was a *Horde* assassin, and he had good reason to think so. During the First War, Garona had murdered Varian's father, King Llane Wrynn, in Stormwind Keep's throne room. Varian saw this attack at Theramore as an attempt to repeat history.

He accused Thrall and the Horde of treachery, and he withdrew from the peace summit with war on his mind.

Though Garona had failed to kill Varian, she'd destroyed any hope of peace between the Horde and the Alliance.

Varian Wrynn thirsted for vengeance, but he never had a chance to pursue it. News from Orgrimmar and Stormwind arrived in Theramore. After a long period of eerie silence, the Lich King had stirred in Northrend.

The Scourge, in numbers not seen since the Third War, were launching attacks across the globe.

GARONA'S FATE

After the news of the Scourge attacks, the Horde and the Alliance delegations left Theramore. Jaina Proudmoore and Aegwynn were charged with watching over their new prisoner: Garona. The sorceresses knew that the half-orc was not entirely herself. A pall of dark energy hung over her. Despite their efforts, Jaina and Aegwynn failed to sever the enchanted shackles that Cho'gall had placed on Garona's mind.

However, Garona pledged to use her willpower to fight Cho'gall's mental control and work against him. She revealed what she knew of the Twilight's Hammer cult, but much about the order remained a mystery. Jaina, Garona, and Aegwynn decided to uncover more information about the cult and its true goals.

Garona would eventually set out on her own once more, eager to take revenge on Cho'gall and his cultists for what they had done to her.

Peter Lee 17

CHAPTER VI

WRATH OF THE LICH KING

WRATH OF THE LICH KING

THE BLUE DRAGONFLIGHT'S DESCENT

Troubles were stirring across the icy mountains and tundras of Northrend. Yogg-Saron was gathering its strength. The Lich King was preparing his ultimate plan to conquer Azeroth.

But among the snowy peaks at the roof of the world, an entirely new threat was rising. Malygos, the Aspect of Magic, was calling his blue dragonflight to his side. He had decided that mortal magi were bringing ruin to the world and that the only way to end their transgressions was to cut them off from magic completely.

He commanded his followers to scour Azeroth for every magical ley line and redirect its energy toward his lair, the Nexus. As they did, the Dragon Aspect took the gathered torrents of power and channeled them into the Twisting Nether.

In short, Malygos intended to siphon from every source of arcane power on Azeroth and dispose of the energy where no mage could reach, thereby erasing arcane magic from the world.

The magi of Azeroth quickly noticed that something was amiss. The natural paths of arcane power that they had grown accustomed to using were disappearing, and they could sense them being redirected to Northrend.

A few powerful magi of the Kirin Tor set out to investigate. When they arrived at the Nexus, they were confronted by Malygos himself. The blue Dragon Aspect hid nothing from them. He told them *exactly* what he was trying to do, and exactly why he was trying to do it. The use of the arcane had put the Burning Legion's eye on Azeroth—repeatedly—and now the armies of the Horde and the Alliance were abusing those energies to settle their factional disputes. He showed the magi the damage that had already been done to Azeroth, and he demanded that they join his cause.

Some high-ranking magi were swayed by his argument, and they pledged themselves to the blue dragonflight. Others were horrified and attempted to escape. None succeeded. They were killed to stop word from getting back to the Kirin Tor. The magi who joined Malygos soon became known as mage hunters, and they dedicated themselves to erasing all resistance to the blue dragonflight's new purpose.

They, like Malygos, did not know of the damage his plan might have wrought if implemented fully.

The titans had entrusted the Dragon Aspects with untold power and knowledge, but there had been one fact they had *not* shared: Azeroth harbored a slumbering world-soul that might one day awaken and become the most powerful titan ever seen.

Malygos's campaign had upset the equilibrium of the world, sparking natural disasters from Northrend to the southern tips of Kalimdor and the Eastern Kingdoms. Unless something was done, these disasters would spiral out of control and cause irreparable harm to Azeroth's world-soul.

WAR FOR THE FROZEN THRONE

No one on Azeroth had forgotten the looming danger of the Scourge. It was not long ago that the Lich King's necropoli had assaulted regions in Kalimdor and the Eastern Kingdoms, sowing terror and undeath. Yet as devastating as those attacks were, the Lich King had merely been probing for weaknesses. He had needed to conserve his strength.

Unbeknownst to the rest of the world, another battle had only recently concluded in his domain: the fight between Arthas Menethil and Ner'zhul.

When Arthas had donned the armor of the Lich King, he had feared that the entity might consume his mind in the process. That had not happened. Arthas's personality had remained intact, and he had ascended to even greater power—a power he wielded alongside Ner'zhul. Both of their spirits coexisted within the same physical body.

Over time, Arthas had concluded that sharing the Lich King's might with Ner'zhul would only lead to disagreements, confusion, and disorder. Only a single mind could wield this power with precision and harness its true potential.

Arthas had tried to overwhelm the orc's spirit, and Ner'zhul was nearly destroyed. Arthas had sat on the Frozen Throne, satisfied that he was completely in control of the Lich King's strength— the sole ruler of the Scourge. After a few years, he realized that he was wrong.

Deep within his mind, he could feel Ner'zhul struggling to wake up. The two beings went to war for permanent control of the Lich King's power.

Ner'zhul had the initial advantage, for he had lived with this power far longer than Arthas had. But Arthas was prideful, stubborn, and determined. He found the single weakness in Ner'zhul's soul: the lingering guilt over his unwitting role in enslaving the orc race to the Burning Legion. Arthas had long since buried his own guilt. The murder of his father, the innocents he had slaughtered, and all the rest of his betrayals—he no longer felt an ounce of sorrow about any of it.

Through force of will, Arthas clawed his way through the orc's mental wounds and tore apart Ner'zhul's mind. As the Lich King's body sat motionless on the Frozen Throne, Arthas took complete control. The process was agonizing for Ner'zhul. Not only did Arthas drown him in his guilt, but he deliberately snapped the bonds of his sanity, causing the orc to spiral further and further into despair.

When the final battle was through, nothing remained of Ner'zhul but a wail of sorrow in the back of the Lich King's consciousness. Arthas found it easy to ignore.

He spent a few years recovering his strength and planning his next move. As a paladin, Arthas had always sought to bring order and justice to Azeroth. That desire remained, but it was now far more twisted than ever before.

A world ruled by the undead would have no more injustice, no more wars, no more mortal flaws. Perhaps most importantly to the Lich King, he believed his Scourge would be far more capable of defending Azeroth against the threats that would try to conquer it. He had observed the awakening of C'Thun and the Burning Legion's attempts to launch other attacks on Azeroth. Neither the demons nor the powers of the Void would rest until they controlled the world. A fractured world, constantly beset by skirmishes between the Alliance and the Horde, simply would not be prepared for another incursion.

The Lich King soon had his strategy in place. He had seen visions of destiny and had plotted all the possible outcomes of his plans. It would not be enough to conquer the world through sheer force. Many others had tried that and failed. To control Azeroth, the Lich King would enslave the strongest creatures within it, the great champions who had arisen within the Alliance and the Horde.

Once they were under his will, the rest of the world would fall in a war of attrition. But the Lich King first needed to lure these champions into his clutches.

He raised his armies in Northrend and ordered his most trusted agents to prepare themselves for their final war against the world. At the Lich King's command, the undead launched brutal attacks upon both the Horde and the Alliance. They began by infecting many towns' and villages' food supplies with the plague of undeath, condemning hundreds of innocents to becoming unwilling servants of the Scourge. The heroes of both factions were forced to destroy their own infected citizens to halt the plague's spread.

For the Alliance, this reopened old wounds from the fall of Lordaeron. For the Horde, it was a new, but no less horrific, experience. Both factions were stirred to action, and as each pocket of infection was cleared, their resolve to defeat the Lich King grew stronger.

KNIGHTS OF THE EBON BLADE

The Scourge's attacks on Kalimdor and the Eastern Kingdoms were mostly feints, designed to rouse anger and provoke an assault on Northrend. But there was one part of the Lich King's plan that was not a ruse. The undead launched a full-scale offensive on a small human town called New Avalon on the edge of the Eastern Plaguelands. The Lich King left nothing to chance; he personally commanded this campaign.

The death knight Darion Mograine, wielder of the corrupted Ashbringer, served as the Lich King's right hand. He led a mission to eradicate the Scarlet Crusade and countless civilians in New Avalon. The most powerful among the fallen were raised as death knights and immediately sent to kill their surviving brethren.

As fire and ash swept over the town, Darion led his new death knights against the last bastion of justice in the region: Light's Hope Chapel. This site had special significance to Darion. On its

THE DEATH KNIGHT DARION MOGRAINE LEADS THE SCOURGE AGAINST LIGHT'S HOPE CHAPEL

hallowed grounds, he had given his life to save the tormented spirit of his father. The cruel irony of sending Darion to the chapel was a sign not of the Lich King's sadism but of his strategy. He cared little for the death knights. He was prepared to sacrifice *all of them* to draw out a single individual: Tirion Fordring.

Tirion was a seasoned paladin and a natural leader. The Lich King hoped to end him before Tirion had a chance to take a prominent role in defending Azeroth from the Scourge's new war.

As the Lich King had planned, Tirion emerged to defend Light's Hope Chapel. Along with the paladins of the Silver Hand and the Argent Dawn, he unleashed his holy fury against the invading armies of undead. The Light overwhelmed the might of the Scourge, and the death knights knew defeat.

The Lich King soon appeared and revealed that the attack on Light's Hope Chapel was merely a ploy to strike at Tirion. Darion was enraged that he had been used as fodder, and he lashed out at his master with all his wrath.

The Lich King easily cast him aside. He incapacitated Darion and the other death knights, and then he began to drain Tirion's soul with Frostmourne.

Darion Mograine resisted the Lich King's control just enough to give Tirion Fordring the corrupted Ashbringer. The paladin drew upon the power of the Light and cleansed the blade in a blinding flash of energy. With the restored Ashbringer at his command, Tirion drove the Lich King from the chapel's holy grounds.

The paladins of the Argent Dawn and the Order of the Silver Hand had a new champion to rally behind. Tirion merged both groups into a single faction that he called the Argent Crusade, and he vowed to see the Lich King destroyed.

Most of the death knights on the field that day had been liberated from the Lich King's control. Darion rallied these free-willed death knights and bestowed upon them a new name: the Knights of the Ebon Blade. They returned to their homes among the Horde and the Alliance, and they pledged to fight the Lich King alongside the two factions. Although there was plenty of uneasiness about forging a pact with these undead, the Horde and the Alliance believed the death knights would serve as valuable allies in the war to come. They eventually allowed the death knights into their ranks.

The Lich King's former servants would soon have the opportunity to seek vengeance against him.

INVASION OF NORTHREND
27 YEARS AFTER THE DARK PORTAL

The Scourge's attacks had sent the Alliance and the Horde into a righteous fury. Both factions mobilized their armies and brought war to the Lich King's doorstep.

King Varian Wrynn of the Alliance commanded the paladin Bolvar Fordragon to eliminate the Scourge. The army under his control was dubbed the Valiance Expedition. Upon reaching Northrend, it established a beachhead on the Howling Fjord, a darkened, nightmarish coast filled with hostile vrykul and dangerous spirits. The Lich King's reach quickly became frighteningly clear: many of the vrykul had fallen under the Frozen Throne's sway, and they hurled themselves at the Alliance's defenses until their numbers were spent.

Once the champions of the Alliance had secured the coastline, they found friendlier faces inland. The Frostborn dwarves, who lived in the icy Storm Peaks, were initially reluctant to join a war against the Lich King, but they eventually offered assistance to the Alliance campaign.

Warchief Thrall tasked the orc Garrosh Hellscream with leading the Horde's forces. Garrosh was hungry to prove himself to his people, and he had already developed a reputation for showing keen leadership in battle. His army was called the Warsong Offensive, named after the bold orc's ancestral clan, and it boasted many revered warriors. Two of the most famous were the seasoned fighter Varok Saurfang and his son, Dranosh Saurfang. The latter was given command over the Horde's vanguard, a task that he accepted with great pride.

The Horde made landfall in the Borean Tundra, where they immediately faced resistance. Garrosh Hellscream helped carve through the ranks of the Scourge and oversaw the construction of a massive outpost that would serve as the core of the Horde's push inland.

Nearby tribes of a noble race, distant ancestors of the tauren called the taunka, joined Garrosh's forces in driving back the Scourge. Later, these mighty yet kindhearted creatures formally allied with the Horde in gratitude.

THE FATE OF NAXXRAMAS

Through separate offensives, the Alliance and the Horde gradually marched deep into Northrend, pushing closer to the seat of the Lich King's power. After they arrived at the frozen valley of the Dragonblight and established crude outposts, the Scourge launched its first major counterattack.

Naxxramas, the dreaded necropolis, appeared in the skies above the Horde's and the Alliance's forces. Commanding the stronghold was its old master, Kel'Thuzad. He had been reborn by the power of the Lich King, and he was mightier than ever before. Kel'Thuzad directed his undead armies with lethal precision, waylaying the Horde and the Alliance with attacks from all sides. His hidden spies sowed chaos within both factions and cut off the flow of crucial information from their leaders. The Alliance and Horde vanguards, headed by Bolvar Fordragon and Dranosh Saurfang, were creeping closer to Icecrown Citadel, but Kel'Thuzad's strategy threatened to divide their campaigns and leave their armies vulnerable.

Yet Kel'Thuzad had made a critical mistake. By bringing Naxxramas so close to the front lines, he had given an opening for a daring strike on the fortress itself.

Champions from the Horde and the Alliance stormed into Naxxramas, tearing it apart from the inside and purging the evil from its halls. For some of these heroes, it was the second time they had assaulted this fortress, and they were more than prepared to face Kel'Thuzad again.

Despite the Lich King's efforts to send reinforcements to the stronghold, Kel'Thuzad was defeated. Rumors quickly spread that his soul was lost to the Shadowlands, the realm of the dead. His fall deprived the Lich King of one of his most powerful lieutenants just as the invasion of Northrend was approaching its zenith.

The Lich King's ultimate strategy was imperiled by this unexpected defeat, but fortunately for him, another threat would soon distract the heroes of the Alliance and the Horde.

THE NEXUS, LAIR OF THE BLUE DRAGONFLIGHT

THE NEXUS WAR

The fall of Naxxramas had allowed the invading armies to establish permanent footholds in the Dragonblight from which they hoped to strike at Icecrown Citadel itself.

It was not to be. The Kirin Tor had finally uncovered what was happening at the Nexus. Malygos and most of his blue dragonflight were draining away Azeroth's arcane magic, and they were killing every mage who dared to oppose them.

Archmage Rhonin and the ranking members of the Kirin Tor were shocked to learn that some of their own had defected to the blue dragonflight's cause. The danger posed by Malygos was so great that the magi of Dalaran did something unprecedented: they pooled their power and teleported their entire city to the skies above Northrend.

From their new vantage point, the Kirin Tor launched an offensive to stop Malygos's campaign, but progress was slow. The blue Dragon Aspect and his servants were too strong for even the great magi of Dalaran to contend with. In time, the Kirin Tor called upon the Alliance and the Horde to aid them. The idea of diverting resources from the war against the Lich King did not sit well with Garrosh Hellscream or Bolvar Fordragon, but both agreed that it was necessary.

Members of the Horde and the Alliance set out to probe the blue dragonflight's defenses around the Nexus. They were joined by representatives of the other dragonflights, who had also grown wary of Malygos. The mortals and dragons attempted to contact the Aspect of Magic and convince him to end his destructive crusade, but their efforts were met with open hostility.

As this conflict intensified, the Dragon Aspect Alexstrasza and ambassadors from the other dragonflights met to discuss Malygos's fate. Even some of the blue dragons who opposed the Aspect of Magic attended the gathering. Malygos had already killed too many innocents, and his

TWILIGHT DRAGONS

The black dragonflight attempted to use the war with Malygos to their advantage. One of the few nether dragons who had escaped the Aspect of Magic's wrath was captured by Sintharia, consort of Deathwing. She was determined to rebuild her flight by creating a new and fearsome breed of dragon.

Sintharia drew on the nether dragon's power to forge creatures known as twilight dragons. Her desperate attempt to restore the black dragonflight was only partially successful. A number of heroes, including the dragons Kalecgos and Korialstrasz, learned of Sintharia's experiments. They launched an attack on the black dragon, killing her and eradicating most of her progeny.

Unfortunately, not all of the twilight dragons were destroyed. Deathwing had discovered Sintharia's brood, and he had recognized the twilight dragons' incredible potential.

In the months to come, he would carry on his fallen consort's work.

siphoning of Azeroth's ley lines had upset the balance of the world. The death and destruction were bound only to worsen over time.

With heavy hearts, the dragons reached an agreement that would become known as the Wyrmrest Accord. For the good of Azeroth, they would join the side of mortals and make war on Malygos. Reaching this decision was difficult for all of them, but especially for Alexstrasza. She saw Malygos as a brother. And as a guardian of life, she abhorred the bloodshed that was to come. Yet if she did nothing, she knew the number of lives lost would be unimaginable.

The united forces of the Wyrmrest Accord assaulted Malygos's stronghold in the Nexus. Alexstrasza herself was there when Azeroth's defenders faced the Aspect of Magic and struck him down. She felt no relief or joy in ending the life of her ancient friend, only a deep sorrow.

With Malygos dead, the blue dragonflight's campaign was put to an end. Members of the Kirin Tor would spend years reversing the damage done to Azeroth's ley lines, eventually restoring them to their former power.

THE BATTLE OF THE WRATH GATE

After Malygos's death, the Horde and the Alliance refocused on Icecrown Citadel. Bolvar Fordragon and Dranosh Saurfang waged separate campaigns against the Scourge, pushing the undead armies farther and farther back into the Dragonblight.

Both commanders quickly realized that a victory for one faction was a victory for all against the Lich King. When one side attacked the undead, the other would "coincidentally" order their own forces to draw the Scourge's attention on another front. A grudging mutual respect formed between the two commanders, and their subtle attempts to coordinate attacks were remarkably effective. Though their efforts took the Horde and the Alliance in different directions, they eventually met at the southern entrance of Icecrown: Angrathar the Wrath Gate.

Once the Wrath Gate was secured, both factions would be able to mount offensives against Icecrown Citadel at the time of their choosing. The Lich King's defenses were formidable, and breaking through the bulwarks would take a brutal, costly battle.

Neither Bolvar nor Dranosh would allow the other to claim all the glory. Thus, when the day came to assault the Wrath Gate, both sides eventually gathered on the field of battle. The Scourge army that stood before them was greater than anything the Horde and the Alliance had yet faced. Vicious, close-quarters fighting ensued.

Before the combined might of Azeroth's defenders, the Scourge's lines buckled. Slowly, Bolvar and Dranosh cleaved their way to the foot of the Wrath Gate. Victory seemed within reach, but the Lich King could not allow his enemies to prevail. His plan to convert the Horde and the Alliance's champions to his side would succeed only if both factions were war-weary and exhausted by the time they arrived at the Frozen Throne. Should they come brimming with confidence and in a position of power, they might very well sweep away the Scourge entirely.

The Lich King emerged from the Wrath Gate, joining the fight himself. The very sight of him could have shifted the tide of battle in favor of the Scourge. Yet the Alliance and the Horde refused to flee before his presence. They grimly dug their heels in and fought on.

BOLVAR FORDRAGON AND DRANOSH SAURFANG BATTLE THE SCOURGE AT THE WRATH GATE

If the Battle of the Wrath Gate had reached its conclusion, it might have spelled the end of the Lich King. But that was not to be.

From a rise overlooking the Wrath Gate, a barrage of plague canisters rained down on all armies and stopped the fighting dead in its tracks. A lethal green fog, capable of killing the living and the undead alike, enveloped the battlefield. The Lich King instantly understood what was happening, and he retreated without hesitation. Everyone left on the field of battle was killed: Bolvar Fordragon and almost five thousand Alliance soldiers, and Dranosh Saurfang and over four thousand loyal Horde followers.

The plague would have spread throughout the entire region and destroyed whomever it touched if not for the red dragonflight. Alexstrasza and her servants descended from the skies and purified the land with enchanted fire. They could not save the fallen, but they did eradicate the plague.

When the smoke cleared, Dranosh's and Bolvar's bodies were missing. Their disappearance was a mystery for another day. Both factions were enraged by what had transpired at the Wrath Gate. The origin of the plague was obvious to all: only the Forsaken could create such a weapon.

And the Horde and the Alliance were ready to destroy those responsible for using it.

THE BATTLE FOR THE UNDERCITY

Following the disaster at the Wrath Gate, Warchief Thrall sent a summons to Queen Sylvanas Windrunner, but she was already on her way to meet him. She told the warchief that she had been forced to flee her home in the Undercity after a faction of undead dissidents and demons had attempted to overthrow her rule. The dreadlord Varimathras—once thought to be cowed and cut off from the Burning Legion—had apparently been scheming against her all along. He had convinced a gifted alchemist, Grand Apothecary Putress, that the Legion would have more rewards to offer than the Banshee Queen. Together, they had created a new plague of undeath. Not only was it capable of slaying the living, but it could also destroy the Scourge and perhaps even the Lich King himself.

As Thrall and Sylvanas worked together to plan a counterattack, Jaina Proudmoore convened with them. King Varian Wrynn was prepared to lay all responsibility for the Wrath Gate at the Horde's feet . . . unless Jaina could convince him otherwise.

Sylvanas told Jaina what she knew and promised that she would exterminate the traitors who had killed so many on both sides.

When Jaina brought this news to Varian, he greeted Sylvanas's explanation with suspicion. But whether or not the Banshee Queen was lying, Varian saw an opportunity. For the moment, the Undercity was not under the Horde's control. Perhaps it was time for the Alliance to reclaim the old nation of Lordaeron.

The Horde and the Alliance launched separate offensives against the Undercity. The Horde, led by Sylvanas and Thrall, targeted Varimathras, the mastermind behind the coup. The Alliance invasion, helmed by Varian, stormed through the city's sewers in search of Putress.

SYLVANAS'S ROLE AT THE WRATH GATE

Like most good lies, Sylvanas Windrunner's account of the rebellion in the Undercity contained some truth. Grand Apothecary Putress truly had attempted to overthrow her, and Varimathras truly was trying to claim the Forsaken in the name of the Burning Legion.

But the plague had been created at her direction. Sylvanas was willing to take vengeance against the Lich King at almost any cost, even by making a weapon as deadly as the plague. Whether she was aware that Putress and Varimathras were planning to use the concoction remained a mystery. Rumors persisted that she knew about the attack at the Wrath Gate beforehand, and her denials did not assuage the doubts of her detractors.

Both missions were successful. Varimathras and Putress paid the price for their treachery and were defeated.

But Varian was not satisfied. Still seething with rage, he marched to the Undercity's throne with blades drawn to confront Thrall. No matter who was truly responsible for the attack at the Wrath Gate, Varian Wrynn could not trust the Horde, and he believed the world would be a better place without it. He declared war upon Thrall and his people right then and there.

A catastrophic battle unfolded, but Jaina Proudmoore expertly used her magic to subdue everyone present and teleport the Alliance forces out of the Undercity.

For the moment, full-scale war was averted. But tensions still boiled between the two factions. In the days to come, the Horde's and the Alliance's armies in Northrend frequently clashed, though only in small, short-lived skirmishes.

SECRETS OF ULDUAR

As the war in Northrend raged on, Yogg-Saron continued amassing its forces in the depths of Ulduar. The Old God was greatly pleased by the chaos unfolding above. Not only were the Horde and the Alliance in conflict with the Lich King, but they had turned their wrath on each other. However, Yogg-Saron knew that the longer both factions swept across Northrend in search of hidden Scourge outposts, the more likely they were to discover the entity's presence in Ulduar.

Yogg-Saron had been watching closely when C'Thun was defeated in Ahn'Qiraj, and it had no desire to meet the same fate. The Old God bided its time. Its corrupted servant, Keeper Loken, had reignited the enchanted Forge of Wills and was crafting new generations of fearsome iron dwarves and vrykul, all of them loyal to Yogg-Saron.

Yet even though the Old God concealed its presence, it could not hide from mortal eyes forever. One of the founders of the Explorers' League, Brann Bronzebeard, stumbled upon the secret. He had come to Ulduar seeking revelations about his race's ancient history, and he found more than he had bargained for. Brann barely escaped from Ulduar with his life, and he immediately notified Rhonin of the Kirin Tor that a living nightmare was stirring within the forgotten stronghold.

Rhonin notified the Alliance and the Horde, hoping they would see fit to set aside their differences again, if only for one more battle. When King Varian Wrynn, Warchief Thrall, and Garrosh Hellscream gathered in Dalaran to discuss Ulduar, all hope of cooperation vanished. Garrosh and Varian almost immediately came to blows. They would have fought to the death if Rhonin had not intervened.

Though the two commanders were set firmly against each other, many of their followers recognized that ignoring the darkness in Ulduar would doom their war against the Lich King.

Members of the Alliance offered to escort Brann Bronzebeard into Ulduar to uncover more of its mysteries. They infiltrated a wing of the fortress known as the Halls of Stone, home to the Forge of Wills. Sjonnir the Ironshaper, one of Keeper Loken's most trusted servants, was waiting for them. He served as the master of the Forge of Wills and the architect of Yogg-Saron's iron army. The Alliance heroes braved countless dangers and destroyed Sjonnir, denying the Old God any further reinforcements.

Meanwhile, the Horde did not remain idle. A handful of its greatest heroes traveled to another of Ulduar's wings: the Halls of Lightning. Loken called this corner of the fortress home, and he surrounded himself with his most ardent followers. The Horde's champions were nearly struck down when they came face-to-face with the fallen keeper, but their persistence paid off, and they slew him. In his final moments, Loken gave his enemies a cryptic message: his death would herald the end of Azeroth.

The Horde's champions were deeply disturbed by the keeper's words. Through intermediaries in the Kirin Tor, they quietly reached out to the Alliance heroes who had assaulted the Forge of Wills, asking if they knew the meaning of Loken's warning. Brann Bronzebeard was instantly

THE BLOOD OF YOGG-SARON

Thousands of years ago, tendrils of Yogg-Saron's essence seeped to the world's surface in the form of a strange mineral called saronite. Blooms of the jagged substance appeared throughout Northrend.

When the Lich King first arrived in Northrend, he discovered and studied saronite. He found that it was nearly indestructible and incredibly resistant to many forms of magic. The Lich King also learned that it had the power to destroy the bodies and souls of undead creatures. Intrigued, he ordered his servants to use saronite to create armor, war machines, and even his fortresses across Northrend.

alarmed. From what he had learned thus far of Ulduar, he was convinced that Loken's death would have dire consequences for the entire world, but he did not yet fully understand why. The only way to learn more was to journey into the heart of Ulduar, where Yogg-Saron dwelled.

The Explorers' League and the Kirin Tor implored members of the Horde and the Alliance to join them in a final assault on the stronghold. Since the request came from neutral parties, the heroes agreed. They had glimpsed the evil in Ulduar, and they refused to let it spread unchecked, no matter the bitter rivalry that burned between their factions.

The assault on Ulduar was more difficult than anyone had imagined. The stronghold was defended by the remnants of Yogg-Saron's iron army along with the other mighty keepers who, like Loken, had fallen to the Old God's influence. The grueling battle against these forces raged from the fortress's frigid outer ramparts to its dark, subterranean halls.

When the invaders finally reached the prison chamber of Yogg-Saron, the Old God tore at their minds with visions of madness, betrayal, and suffering. Several of the heroes were lost to insanity, and the Old God turned them against their former allies.

But, just as when they had faced C'Thun, the mortals of Azeroth prevailed. Yogg-Saron was defeated, and its control over Ulduar vanished.

THE TITANS' FAIL-SAFE

Azeroth's defenders had once again achieved the impossible, but they would not have the luxury of even a moment's rest.

During the assault on Ulduar, Brann Bronzebeard had discovered something deeply troubling. Keeper Loken had not been exaggerating when he said his death would mean the end of the world. His demise had triggered the first steps of a fail-safe mechanism designed by the titans.

Ages ago, the titans had instructed the keepers to build two enchanted devices: the Forge of Wills and the Forge of Origination. The first was housed in Ulduar, and the second was embedded in the ground far to the south, in a land called Uldum. The Forge of Origination served a much different purpose from its counterpart to the north. If Azeroth should succumb to corruption, the machine's energies could be released to purge the world's flora and fauna. Once the scouring was complete, the Forge of Origination would trigger a process that would create a new generation of life.

To oversee this procedure, the titans had conscripted a constellar named Algalon the Observer. The entity would judge the state of Azeroth and decide whether the world needed to be scoured.

Brann Bronzebeard did not yet know the full implications of this fail-safe protocol, but he feared it would not end well. He led the champions who had defeated Yogg-Saron into a hidden chamber within Ulduar, hoping to forestall whatever fate awaited Azeroth. They were already too late.

Loken's death had summoned Algalon to Ulduar, and the guardian had concluded his analysis. The Old Gods' corruption had spread across the world and even taken root in strongholds like Ulduar. Algalon proceeded with the fail-safe protocol, believing that the only recourse was to unleash the Forge of Origination's power on Azeroth.

Azeroth's heroes fought bravely to stop Algalon, much to the constellar's puzzlement. He could not see the logic in their actions; the fail-safe had already been activated, and if he died, it would not stop the procedure.

THE RE-ORIGINATION OF AZEROTH

As part of the fail-safe protocol, Algalon sent a signal to the titans that would notify them of his analysis, allowing them to approve the Forge of Origination's activation. Neither the constellar nor Azeroth's heroes knew that the titans had fallen to Sargeras and the Burning Legion long ago.

Though the titans would never receive Algalon's signal, that would not have stopped the fail-safe. Ultimately, the Forge of Origination would have destroyed all life on Azeroth.

But the mortals did not back down. They fought for their world, for their homes, and for their friends. And in the end, they made Algalon yield.

Algalon was moved by their resolve. Azeroth was not the first world he had purged, and he had never considered that life on those other worlds had wanted to survive as desperately as these heroes did. He decided that they had earned the right to fight against Azeroth's corruption themselves. Algalon allowed the mortals to reverse the fail-safe protocol before the Forge of Origination rumbled to life.

Algalon then disappeared, but he did not go far. He would watch over Azeroth from a distance in the years to come.

THE ARGENT TOURNAMENT

Despite the chaos and carnage unfolding in Northrend, the war against the Lich King was proceeding well. The armies of the Alliance and the Horde had crushed numerous Scourge outposts throughout the continent, taking the undead's territory piece by piece.

All that was left was the final assault on Icecrown Citadel. The Lich King was holding most of his remaining forces there, almost daring his enemies to storm the Frozen Throne.

Garrosh Hellscream and Varian Wrynn were eager to see the Lich King destroyed, but neither one of them gave the order to attack. Tirion Fordring, the leader of the Argent Crusade, had sent word to both leaders, warning them to hold back. He believed that a full, overwhelming assault was *exactly* what the Lich King wanted.

The Argent Crusade and the Knights of the Ebon Blade had both carved out small footholds near Icecrown Citadel and spent weeks carefully observing the tactics and movements of the Scourge. Despite their differences, the paladins and the death knights had shared information with one another and reached the same conclusions. The Lich King was prepared to absorb heavy losses in a ground assault because he knew the Scourge would *inflict* heavy losses in return. Every one of the living who died in battle would rise again as a minion of the Lich King.

Argent
Tournament
Grounds

Ulduar

THE STORM
PEAKS

*Icecrown
Citadel*

Dalaran

Wrath Gate

NORTHREND

The Nexus

Azjol-Nerub

DRAGONBLIGHT

BOREAN TUNDRA

Wyrmrest Temple

HOWLING FJORD

WAR AGAINST
THE LICH KING

The Alliance's War Path
The Horde's War Path

Tirion believed there was only one way to conquer Icecrown: a small, surgical strike force could punch a hole in the citadel's defenses and fight its way to the Lich King.

To that end, Tirion called upon Azeroth's champions to prove themselves worthy of this crucial mission. Thus, the Argent Tournament was born.

Despite the tension between the factions, both trusted Tirion Fordring. He had shown exemplary bravery in his fight to protect Light's Hope Chapel, and the Horde remembered his commitment to justice in defense of the orc Eitrigg many years earlier. None doubted his sincerity and single-minded desire to see the Lich King destroyed. There was no shortage of heroes willing to march at his side, no matter their faction.

Countless heroes participated in the tournament's trials. Before long, Tirion had winnowed the ranks to find his chosen few. He and the Argent Crusade now had their champions. They were joined by Darion Mograine and many of his death knights under the banner of a new order called the Ashen Verdict.

Together, they would bring final judgment upon the Lich King.

FALL OF THE LICH KING

The assault on Icecrown Citadel began in the skies. Gunships from both the Horde and the Alliance swooped toward the stronghold and landed their forces at different locations. The invaders cut deep into Icecrown Citadel until they reached a wing of the fortress called the Halls of Reflection. There, the Lich King himself clashed with the mortal champions, forcing them to retreat.

Despite this defeat, Azeroth's defenders redoubled their efforts and prepared for a final assault. The Argent Crusade and the Knights of the Ebon Blade forged a staging ground just inside Icecrown Citadel's main entrance, and the champions of Azeroth leaped forward to bring down the Lich King.

The battle that engulfed Icecrown Citadel tested the strength and willpower of Tirion Fordring and his followers. Not only had the Lich King kept his most powerful and dangerous minions close to his side, but he also commanded a hero from the past: Dranosh Saurfang.

After the proud orc had fallen at the Wrath Gate, the Scourge had recovered his corpse. The Lich King had then transformed Dranosh into a death knight, and now he was forced to fight against his former allies—and they were forced to vanquish him. When Varok Saurfang learned what had become of his son, he was heartbroken. Even members of the Alliance sympathized with him, so malicious and brutal was the torment inflicted on his beloved boy.

Icecrown Citadel's guardians were many, but the strike team nevertheless persisted. They cut their way through the Scourge's ranks until they stood before the Frozen Throne.

There they found another hero who had vanished at the Wrath Gate. Bolvar Fordragon, his body disfigured by the red dragonflight's enchanted fire, was suspended by chains above the Frozen Throne. Like Dranosh, the paladin had been recovered by the Lich King, but he was not as easy to corrupt as the orc had been. Bolvar had been subjected to horrific torture as the master of the Scourge struggled to turn him to darkness.

The champions could not free Bolvar, not until they faced the Lich King. They were exhausted, battered, and enraged . . . just as the Lich King had planned. His true prize now stood before him:

the most powerful heroes of Azeroth. If they succumbed to the Lich King, he would raise them into undeath and wield them as weapons against the living.

The fate of the world rested upon this single moment.

The Lich King unleashed his full fury. Tirion Fordring and his champions fought back in a valiant battle that shook Icecrown Citadel to its foundations. The Lich King ripped several heroes' souls from their bodies with Frostmourne, but even that did not stop them. The champions trapped in the cursed blade fought on, stirring the other spirits imprisoned in the sword to action.

But despite their valor and heroism, the champions could not prevail. The Lich King's strength overwhelmed them all. Tirion Fordring was subdued in a block of ice, and his followers were slaughtered.

The Lich King had won. He began to raise his foes into undeath.

Tirion refused to give up. He broke free of his icy prison, and with a desperate blow, he destroyed Frostmourne with the Ashbringer. In an instant, the souls trapped in the blade were released. The spirits of the Lich King's victims swarmed around their tormentor, repaying his cruelty with righteous vengeance.

The spirit of Arthas Menethil's own father, Terenas Menethil II, raised the slain champions back to life, and they rejoined the battle anew. This time, the Lich King was defenseless, and he was fatally wounded.

In his dying moments, Arthas felt the corruption of the Frozen Throne fading away from him, and he was faced with the enormity of his crimes. He slipped into death, into a cold and unforgiving afterlife of darkness.

All that was left was to decide how to deal with the remnants of the Scourge. Terenas's spirit warned Tirion Fordring and his champions that without a powerful consciousness controlling the undead, the creatures would run amok and cause unimaginable damage to the world.

TRIUMPHANT RETURN

After the Lich King's defeat, the armies of the Alliance and the Horde returned home as conquering victors. They had triumphed over one of the greatest threats Azeroth had ever known. Garrosh Hellscream was greeted in Orgrimmar with the thunderous applause of his brethren. He was now seen as a worthy heir of the Hellscream lineage and a remarkable battle commander in his own right.

The Horde's other commander, Varok Saurfang, remained in Northrend to oversee his faction's withdrawal from the continent. The death of his son, Dranosh Saurfang, had deeply wounded him, and he wished to grieve in peace. His absence meant that the Horde no longer had his experience and leadership, and that would create severe problems in the days to come.

Tirion agreed, but it was not a burden he could ask anyone else to bear. He took up the Lich King's helm and steeled himself to become the jailor of the damned. But before he could don the cursed armor and seal his fate, Bolvar Fordragon intervened.

Now freed from his chains, Bolvar volunteered to take Tirion's place. The wounds he had suffered at the Wrath Gate had left his body broken and his mind scarred. He could never return to his former life—he could never walk among the living as he once had. For the sake of Azeroth, he would wear the Lich King's helm and assert his will over the Scourge to keep them in check. By doing so, Bolvar hoped that the threat posed by the Scourge would be gone forever.

THE DORMANT THRONE

As the armies of the Horde and the Alliance withdrew from Northrend, they scarcely saw the Scourge. Since most believed that the Lich King was no more, it was easy to assume that the undead were no longer a threat. This, of course, was not true.

Bolvar Fordragon was struggling to maintain control over the endless ranks of undead. The Lich King had directed them to make war upon the living, and it was difficult to quell their aggression. Bolvar fought to maintain his sanity; he had been a mighty paladin all his adult life, but the moment he had donned the Lich King's helm, the Holy Light had abandoned him. His new necromantic powers warred with his sense of justice and righteousness, and it took nearly all his strength to keep the undead contained.

Some pockets of the Scourge managed to break free of his control. Packs of undead in the Eastern Kingdoms continued to follow the Lich King's old directives, mindlessly attacking anyone who dared to trespass in the Plaguelands. The most troubling blow to Bolvar's hold over the Scourge resulted from an unexpected event: the second death of Sylvanas Windrunner.

For years, Sylvanas had been dedicated to killing Arthas Menethil, the man who had ripped her soul from her body and transformed her into his unwilling servant. Now he was dead, and she had not even had the satisfaction of killing him herself. Longing for peace from her tormented existence, Sylvanas flung herself from the top of Icecrown Citadel.

The fall itself did not end her, but the jagged spikes of saronite embedded in the ground did. Like the Lich King, the Alliance and the Horde had discovered and experimented with this mysterious element. It had many intriguing properties, one of which was that it could destroy the body *and* soul of the undead.

Sylvanas was cast into a bleak, terrifying afterlife. Spectral beings known as the Val'kyr found her soul there and gave her a glimpse of her people's future. Without her to protect them, the Forsaken would be squandered by the Horde and eventually made extinct. The Val'kyr offered a pact: they would return Sylvanas's soul to her body, but only if she would bind herself to them. The Val'kyr longed to finally be free from the Lich King's control, and they would gladly serve the Banshee Queen in exchange. Sylvanas agreed, and she returned to Azeroth to continue leading the Forsaken.

Bolvar was shocked to feel that his connection with the Val'kyr had suddenly been severed. When he tried to reestablish his will over them, they did not respond. It was as if they now served another master.

TIRION FORDRING AND HIS ALLIES DEFEAT THE LICH KING AT THE FROZEN THRONE

Bolvar considered this event a lesson learned, and he embraced his fate. Not only did he have to keep the undead from harming the living, but he must also keep others from misusing the Scourge's power.

WAR AGAINST THE NIGHTMARE

The Old Gods had been attempting to corrupt the Emerald Dream for millennia. They had extended their influence into the ethereal realm, and the effects of this were known as the Emerald Nightmare. Yogg-Saron's recent defeat in Northrend had not eradicated the danger. In fact, it had spurred the entity's minions to action.

Following the Lich King's death, the Nightmare reached farther into the outside world. People across Azeroth experienced horrific dreams. Tyrande Whisperwind was one of those affected by these night terrors. As she investigated the cause, she witnessed a vision from the goddess Elune, a being revered by the night elves. In this vision, Tyrande saw her mate, Malfurion Stormrage, dying inside the Emerald Dream.

Malfurion had been sleeping in the Dream for years, but until now, there had not been cause for alarm. Many druids spent long periods of time exploring the realm. Tyrande tried to wake him, but she could not. Then it became clear that nearly *everyone* who had recently entered the Dream, druid or not, was unable to awaken. Even Ysera, the Aspect of Dreams, was locked in perpetual slumber.

Fandral Staghelm, the leader of the Cenarion Circle in Malfurion's absence, claimed to have the answers. He downplayed the amount of corruption that had seeped into the World Tree Teldrassil, and he suggested that it was free of the Emerald Nightmare's influence. Yet that was a lie. The Nightmare had *already* spread to Teldrassil, but Fandral had hidden its presence from the other night elves.

To keep his deception alive, he declared that he could protect Teldrassil and prevent the Nightmare from having any hold upon it. Once that was done, he said he was certain there would be a way to save Malfurion.

Tyrande would not stand by while Malfurion was in danger. She entered the Dream herself to find him. In time, she discovered that Malfurion was being kept prisoner by an ancient enemy: Xavius, the Nightmare Lord.

Xavius answered to the Old Gods, but he had many servants of his own. Among them was Fandral Staghelm. Years ago, Xavius had enticed the druid to join his efforts by convincing him that his long-dead son, Valstann Staghelm, was still alive.

When Tyrande learned of Fandral's role in recent events, she finally uncovered the full, horrifying truth: Teldrassil had been corrupted by the Nightmare, and Fandral had been hiding that fact from the rest of the night elves.

Tyrande and her allies fought to free Malfurion. Once he had awakened, they launched an assault against Xavius and the Nightmare itself.

In the end, Xavius was defeated, and the Nightmare was largely cleansed from the Dream. Neither Tyrande Whisperwind nor Malfurion Stormrage could eradicate it completely, so they sealed away the corruption, along with Xavius's spirit, in a corner of the Emerald Dream called the Rift of Aln. They hoped the Nightmare would stay contained there, but they feared it might one day find a way out.

The victory inside the Emerald Dream had lasting effects on many who had suffered under the Nightmare. Ysera was freed from her endless slumber, and she took on a new name to mark her return: "the Awakened."

The Nightmare's hold on Fandral Staghelm had also been broken, but that did not heal his wounded mind and soul. The archdruid had fallen to madness, and there was little the other druids of the Cenarion Circle could do to help him. Knowing they could not let him roam the land freely, they imprisoned Fandral in a barrow den.

In the wake of the Nightmare's defeat, the Dragon Aspects Alexstrasza and Ysera decided that Teldrassil needed to be guarded. They both gave it their magical blessings, protecting it from the Nightmare's corruption forevermore.

CHAPTER VII
CATACLYSM

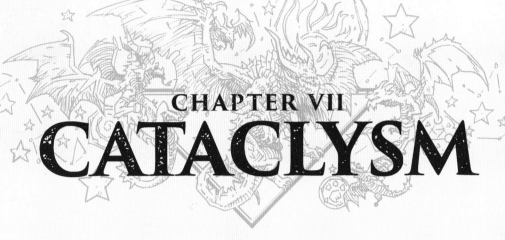

CHAPTER VII
CATACLYSM

THE UNSEEN

The Old Gods had suffered shocking setbacks in recent years, including the defeat of C'Thun and Yogg-Saron at the hands of Azeroth's defenders. They had never anticipated such fierce resistance. They had never anticipated the rise of such fearless heroes.

Shrouded in an ocean of fevered dreams, among the bones of nameless horrors, N'Zoth remained untouched by the blades of mortals. The Old God was certain that Azeroth's champions would eventually seek it out and try to overwhelm it as they had done to C'Thun and Yogg-Saron.

N'Zoth was not afraid, but it did sense that a window of opportunity was fast closing. The world was wounded by the recent war against the Lich King. The ancient Dragon Aspects were consumed by their own struggles. Ysera had recently returned from the depths of the Emerald Dream, but she was not the same as she had once been. Prophetic visions bombarded her mind, and she found it difficult to tell what was real from what was not. Meanwhile, Nozdormu had disappeared in the timeways in search of the shadowy force that was disrupting the past, present, and future. Malygos was dead, leaving the blue dragonflight leaderless. Only Alexstrasza continued safeguarding Azeroth, but she was in dire need of rest after helping the Alliance and the Horde fight in Northrend.

The time to usher in the Hour of Twilight was now.

The first hammer blow to herald the apocalypse would not come from Cho'gall or his cultists. It would come from Deathwing. Sometime after the Battle of Grim Batol, Deathwing had taken refuge in Deepholm, the realm of earth in the Elemental Plane. Ages ago, the keepers had forged the Elemental Plane to contain the world's unruly elemental spirits. For Deathwing, Deepholm was something of a second home. His innate connection to the element of earth allowed him to absorb the realm's latent energies and use them to gather his strength and nurse his wounds.

N'Zoth fed its own dark energy into Deathwing's heart, infusing the black Dragon Aspect with a power unlike any that he had ever known. This influx of strength made his form more unstable, and the magma that flowed through his veins threatened to erupt from his body and consume him entirely.

At N'Zoth's command, Twilight's Hammer cultists ventured into Deepholm to help Deathwing. They bolted elementium plates over the black Dragon Aspect's wounds to keep his body from tearing apart. The process was agonizing, and Deathwing often unleashed his wrath on the cultists.

As the cultists tended to Deathwing, N'Zoth reached out to its other ancient allies in the Elemental Plane. When the world was young, the Old Gods had enslaved Azeroth's destructive elemental spirits and used them as weapons. They would have a role to play in the Hour of Twilight as well. N'Zoth called on the elementals to prepare for war, but not all of them answered.

Two elemental rulers defied the Old God: Neptulon the Tidehunter and Therazane the Stonemother. In the ages since their enslavement, they had broken the shackles that had bound them to the Old Gods. They would not serve N'Zoth, and they would fight with all their fury against any attempts by the entity or its servants to enslave them.

The remaining elemental lords embraced N'Zoth's command. Ragnaros the Firelord and Al'Akir the Windlord relished the prospect of war, and their ties to the Old Gods remained unbroken. N'Zoth promised to release them from their prisons and let them roam free on Azeroth as they once had in ancient times.

Deathwing himself would be the key to their liberation. Once the black Dragon Aspect was ready for war, he would burst forth from Deepholm and tear a rift between the Elemental Plane and the surface of Azeroth. Deathwing would also serve as an extension of N'Zoth's will, commanding the Twilight's Hammer and the elementals and coordinating their attacks. The Old God made him believe that by doing so, he could scour Azeroth of other dragons and claim the world as his own.

In truth, N'Zoth had no plans to reward Deathwing. The Old God would use the corrupted Dragon Aspect to restore the Black Empire to its former glory and shroud the world in shadow.

Once that was accomplished, N'Zoth would dispose of its servant.

ELEMENTAL UPHEAVAL
28 YEARS AFTER THE DARK PORTAL

In Deepholm, Deathwing basked in the dual energies of N'Zoth and the Elemental Plane. He recovered at a startling pace, but it came at great cost to the world. Absorbing the Elemental Plane's power had destabilized the realm and thrown the elementals into turmoil. Their pain and confusion were not confined to Deepholm; they spread to the surface of Azeroth.

The oceans churned in anger. Freak storms howled down from the mountains and blanketed normally temperate regions in ice. The earth heaved and groaned, triggering earthquakes across the world. These natural disasters did not stop. They grew ever more frequent and severe. Travel became perilous, and many merchant vessels were lost at sea.

Warchief Thrall and other shaman sensed that something was very wrong with the elements, but what was causing this upheaval remained a mystery. On many occasions, Thrall tried to commune with the elemental spirits, but they were in no condition to give him answers. He could do nothing to calm the beings. Then an idea came to him: if he could not commune with Azeroth's elementals, perhaps he could speak to the ones on Outland and receive their advice.

Before Thrall left for Outland, he named Garrosh Hellscream as the Horde's acting warchief. The warrior still had much to learn, but he had proved himself to be a capable leader in the war against the Lich King. Garrosh's bravery and fierce pride had made him very popular, especially among the orcs.

Not all of Thrall's advisors agreed with his choice of acting warchief. High Chieftain Cairne Bloodhoof argued against passing control of the Horde to Garrosh, whom he saw as a brash warmonger. Thrall held Cairne in the highest regard, but his decision was final. He believed that this new responsibility would temper Garrosh and grant him wisdom. He was wrong.

Taking on the mantle of leadership only encouraged Garrosh to indulge his warlike ways. He believed the Horde was being too timid. Resources were scarce, especially after the war in Northrend. The elemental turmoil engulfing the world had only made things worse.

After Thrall had departed, Garrosh turned his gaze northwest, to the lush forests of Ashenvale. It was a land of plenty, and it was well within the Horde's reach. Most of the region belonged to the night elves, but that did not stop Garrosh from sending troops into the woodlands. He was not interested in asking the Alliance for resources or trading for them. Why would he do that, when he could simply *take* what he wanted by force?

The Horde's new incursions into Ashenvale enraged the Alliance. Tensions between the factions flared, and open war seemed inevitable.

Some of the Horde's members welcomed these bold and aggressive maneuvers, but Cairne Bloodhoof did not. The elder tauren did everything he could to reason with the acting warchief and prevent bloodshed. In Cairne's eyes, Garrosh was leading the Horde down a dangerous path, one that would inevitably destroy it.

Garrosh did not listen to his wisdom, and so Cairne spoke the only language the orc would understand. He challenged Garrosh to a mak'gora, a ritualistic duel.

Before a crowd of onlookers, the tauren and the orc fought for the future of the Horde itself. On one side stood the promise of a peaceful future. On the other, the promise of blood and conquest.

It was blood and conquest that won the day. Cairne Bloodhoof fought bravely, but he fell to his opponent. With the elder tauren's death, none remained to oppose Garrosh Hellscream's rule.

THE COUNCIL OF THREE HAMMERS

Much like the Horde, the Alliance was struggling with internal unrest. The elemental upheaval had hit the dwarven city of Ironforge especially hard. Massive earthquakes rocked the snowy hills outside the stronghold, causing widespread destruction and loss of life.

King Magni Bronzebeard was determined to protect his people from these disasters, even at the risk of his own well-being. He and his advisors had recently learned of an ancient ritual to commune with the earth. It originated from the dwarves' ancestors, a race of stone-skinned beings called the earthen. Magni volunteered to undergo the ritual himself so he could find out what was causing Azeroth's troubles.

The ritual did not go as he had planned. It didn't simply connect Magni with the earth; it made him *one* with it. He transformed into a seemingly lifeless diamond statue. Most believed that he was dead, and Ironforge mourned the loss of their king.

News of Magni's fate reached his estranged daughter, Moira Thaurissan, in Shadowforge City. In recent years, she had worked to free the Dark Iron dwarf clan from their ancient masters, the fire elementals, and protect them from the black dragonflight. Yet current events threatened to destroy Moira's progress. As the elemental spirits grew more chaotic, some of the Dark Irons reverted to their old ways. They bent the knee to Ragnaros and led a revolt against Moira.

Moira saw Ironforge's vacant throne as an opportunity to deliver her loyal Dark Irons to a safe place. She knew the dwarves of Ironforge would not welcome them with open arms. The Bronzebeards were bitter rivals of the Dark Irons. Yet that did not stop Moira. By the rules of royal succession, the crown belonged to her. Moira's word was law.

She marched into Ironforge with her Dark Irons and declared herself queen under the mountain. Some dwarves were furious about her return, but others accepted her as their leader. Tensions boiled in the city, threatening to ignite civil war.

To prevent the outbreak of violence, Moira took an iron-fisted stance. She barred anyone from entering or leaving Ironforge until she could complete her transfer of power. This proved to be a grave mistake. Stormwind's crown prince, Anduin Wrynn, was in the city at the time. Holding him hostage was seen by King Varian as an act of war. The only family he had left was his son, and he would do anything to protect him, even spill royal blood.

Varian Wrynn gathered a strike force of assassins and infiltrated Ironforge. They moved like shadows through the city until they cornered Moira. Varian would have cut her throat then and there if not for Anduin. The prince pleaded with his father to show mercy. It was a difficult thing for Varian to restrain himself and walk the path of peace. But in the end, he saw the wisdom of Anduin's words.

THE GRIMTOTEM COUP

Cairne Bloodhoof's death was the result of treachery. One of his fiercest rivals, the tauren Magatha Grimtotem, had seen his duel with Garrosh Hellscream as an opportunity. She had dreamed of seizing her race's capital, Thunder Bluff, and asserting control over all tauren. Only Cairne had stood in her way.

Magatha had secretly coated Garrosh's legendary axe, Gorehowl, with poison. It was this advantage that had allowed him to slay Cairne.

After the duel, Magatha led a coup in Thunder Bluff and seized the city. Yet her victory was short-lived. Cairne's son, Baine Bloodhoof, launched a counterattack that deposed Magatha. He had every right to execute his foe, but he stayed his hand. He looked to his father's teachings for guidance, and he decided that walking the path of honor and compassion was the mark of a true leader. In the end, he exiled Magatha far from Thunder Bluff.

During these events, Magatha beseeched Garrosh for help, but he gave her none. He was furious that she had poisoned his blade. It had tarnished his victory in the mak'gora and called into question whether he was truly a better fighter than Cairne.

Varian had spared Moira's life, but he wouldn't grant her sole dominion over Ironforge after what she'd done. He called for a new organization to rule the ancient city. In response, the dwarves formed the Council of Three Hammers, a governing body that included a representative from each of their rival clans.

Some dwarves welcomed it, but others chafed at the idea of the clans being ruled by a council. Though it took time, the Council of Three Hammers found its footing. Three prominent dwarves would serve on it in the years to come: Moira Thaurissan, Falstad Wildhammer, and Muradin Bronzebeard.

The three clans had not lived together for hundreds of years. Finding common ground was a daily struggle. Tensions remained high, and sporadic violence broke out between the dwarves.

Conditions were only destined to become worse in the months ahead, for both Ironforge and the rest of the world.

THRONE OF THE ELEMENTS

Thrall knew nothing of the events unfolding on Azeroth.

On Outland, he met with Greatmother Geyah and sought her advice about the elemental unrest on his world. The wise orc revealed a hard truth to Thrall: he was a gifted shaman, but he still had much to learn. If he hoped to make any difference on Azeroth, he needed to hone his connection to the elements.

There were talented shaman among Outland's Mag'har orcs. Geyah called on her brightest student to mentor Thrall. Her name was Aggra, and she gave no quarter to her new pupil. She was not impressed by the fact that Thrall had led the Horde. To the contrary, she considered that to be part of the reason he was struggling to grow as a shaman. Aggra argued that he had divided his attention between his duties as warchief and as a shaman. He would never reach his full potential in either role until he chose one to focus on.

Thrall refused to abandon the Horde, but he did devote himself to Aggra's teachings. He listened. He watched. He learned. Day by day, his connection to the elements strengthened. And day by day, he and Aggra grew closer.

Once Thrall was confident in his new abilities, he visited the Throne of the Elements. This sacred site was a home to Outland's elemental spirits and a place of worship for shaman. Four great beings called the Elemental Furies dwelled there: Gordawg, Fury of Earth; Incineratus, Fury of Fire; Kalandrios, Fury of Air; and Aborius, Fury of Water.

The Furies had suffered immensely in recent decades. When the old Horde had first risen to power, its use of fel magic had broken the elementals' strength. Then came the destruction of Draenor, which had nearly annihilated them. The Furies' recovery had been a long and painful process, but the future was bright. Peace had finally settled on Outland.

Thrall beseeched the Furies for help, for a solution to ease Azeroth's own elementals. Instead, he received a warning: the elemental unrest on the world echoed the conditions on Draenor just before it had ripped apart.

Thrall returned to Azeroth to warn his people of what he had learned. Aggra decided to accompany him. Although it was difficult for her to leave her home in Nagrand, she believed it was her duty as a shaman to help Azeroth's elements. Moreover, she didn't want Thrall to face the trials ahead alone. She had come to see him as something more than a pupil, more than even a friend.

Azeroth had changed since Thrall had left. He was shocked to learn of the renewed conflict between the Horde and the Alliance. He was even more disturbed to discover that Cairne Bloodhoof was dead, struck down by the very orc Thrall had entrusted to lead his people. Thrall had been wrong to put his faith in Garrosh Hellscream, and he blamed himself for all that had come to pass.

But he had no chance to set things right. Before Thrall's eyes, the world buckled. The ground cracked beneath his feet.

The Cataclysm had begun.

THE SHATTERING

The time had come. Deathwing's volatile form bristled with fire and shadow. The elementium plates bolted to his hide were all that kept this power from tearing apart his body. At N'Zoth's word, he gathered his rage and unleashed it. Deathwing exploded from Deepholm into Azeroth, breaking down the boundaries between the Elemental Plane and the physical world.

His return ignited a chain reaction of natural disasters across the globe, which collectively became known as the Cataclysm. Mountains crumbled to dust. Fiery chasms tore open in the earth. Towering waves slammed into the coasts, annihilating seaside towns and causing widespread flooding. Casualties numbered in the thousands, but there was more death to come. Much more.

N'Zoth stoked the fire in Deathwing's veins, filling him with excruciating pain. The black Dragon Aspect turned his fury on the world. His smoldering form darkened the skies as he bathed cities and forests in flame. His relentless destruction seemed indiscriminate, but it had a purpose.

As Deathwing was wreaking havoc on the world, he ordered Cho'gall and the Twilight's Hammer to emerge from the shadows. Most of the cultists had remained in hiding for years, but they had not been idle. Their numbers had grown, and their ranks included powerful individuals such as Archbishop Benedictus, leader of the Church of the Holy Light.

Cho'gall took many of the cultists to the Highlands, an idyllic coastal region north of Ironforge. A large population of Wildhammer dwarves inhabited these hills and mountains, yet they were not the sole power in the Highlands. After the Battle of Grim Batol, what was left of the Dragonmaw orc clan had fled to the area and established a crude fortress on the coast.

Neither the dwarves nor the Dragonmaw were prepared for the Twilight's Hammer. The cult's attack was sudden and brutal. Its members made war on the peoples of the Highlands and carved out a fortress in the heart of the region. Cho'gall named this stronghold the Bastion of Twilight, and he fashioned it into the cult's base of operations and a place for its members to worship their unseen gods. Void energies gradually bled from the spire, creeping across the terrain and mutating all life that passed beneath its shadow. The land itself warped and darkened, and the region soon became known as the Twilight Highlands.

Far to the south, other cultists established a foothold in Blackrock Mountain and used it as a place to mold new weapons. They recovered the broken corpses of Nefarian and Sintharia, then reanimated them with Void magics. The dragons retained a sliver of their former personalities, but they were now obedient servants of the Twilight's Hammer. It was not their strength that the

THE BURNING OF STORMWIND CITY

Following his catastrophic emergence from Deepholm, Deathwing descended on Stormwind and burned parts of the city to the ground. Soldiers gathered to face the black Dragon Aspect in battle, but they never had a chance to draw his blood. Almost as quickly as he had appeared, Deathwing vanished from Stormwind.

Stormwind had been at Deathwing's mercy, but destroying it was never his intention. The people of the city were worth more to him alive than dead. His true goal had been to break them so that they could be remade into his servants.

This fate befell many of Stormwind's citizens as the fearful populace sought counsel from Archbishop Benedictus, not knowing that the holy leader was secretly a member of the Twilight's Hammer. He preyed on these desperate people and subtly guided them into the cult's embrace.

cult sought, but their knowledge of how to craft monsters. Sintharia continued her work building an entire flight of twilight dragons, while Nefarian returned to his own experiments and forged a new generation of chromatic dragons.

For the Horde and the Alliance, enemies were appearing on all sides. Yet even as the world crumbled around them, they seemed determined to destroy each other.

INVASION OF GILNEAS

As the Cataclysm unfolded, Thrall found himself at a crossroads. The Horde needed his guidance as warchief, but the world also needed his help as a shaman. Aggra was right: he couldn't divide his attention between both responsibilities. He had to choose. In his heart, he knew that the path of healing the world was the right one. If Azeroth was destroyed as Draenor had been, there would be no Horde left.

Thrall and Aggra gathered with the Earthen Ring, a neutral faction of shaman dedicated to maintaining the balance between the elements. It included shaman from the Horde and the Alliance, individuals who had put aside old rivalries for the good of the world.

Thrall, Aggra, and many of the Earthen Ring journeyed to the place where Deathwing had burst into Azeroth: the Maelstrom, a churning whirlpool in the Great Sea.

At this specific location, the black Dragon Aspect's return had left a scar between the surface of Azeroth and the Elemental Plane. The instability at the Maelstrom cascaded over the world, stirring the elemental spirits into an even greater frenzy. If the Earthen Ring could not heal the rift Deathwing had made, destruction would continue to unfold across Azeroth.

With Thrall at the Maelstrom, Warchief Garrosh Hellscream had free rein. The Cataclysm had not deterred him from war with the Alliance. He believed the Horde would need every advantage to survive. He desperately wanted to expand the Horde's holdings in the Eastern Kingdoms to gather more resources and strengthen the faction's presence on the continent.

The Cataclysm had presented him with the perfect target: Gilneas, a highly defensible nation with strategic ports.

Gilneas had escaped invasion from outside forces due to the massive Greymane Wall on its northern border. But that had changed with the Cataclysm. Earthquakes had shattered part of the wall, leaving Gilneas vulnerable.

Garrosh Hellscream was not the only member of the Horde who desired Gilneas. Sylvanas Windrunner was eager to bring the kingdom under her dominion. She convinced Garrosh to give her control over the invasion force, and she led the Horde's rampage through the isolated nation.

The Horde's incursion could not have come at a worse time for Gilneas. A civil war, the Northgate Rebellion, had chipped away at Gilneas's strength. So, too, had a much darker internal struggle. For years, the worgen curse had ravaged the kingdom, transforming many of its citizens into feral wolf-beasts. These creatures became slaves to their own rage, unable to tell friend from foe. King Genn Greymane himself was a victim of the curse.

The worgen curse had first originated long ago among the night elves. Some of them had sensed Archmage Arugal's spell pulling the wolf-beasts from the Emerald Dream, and they had set out to Gilneas to investigate. The night elves felt it was their responsibility to help the human nation deal with the curse. As the Horde's invasion was under way, they performed a ceremony called the Ritual of Balance to bring harmony to many of the worgen. It did not purge the curse from their veins, but it tempered the fury in their hearts and eased their bloodlust.

The Ritual of Balance also brought peace to Gilneas's divided population. Genn Greymane rallied worgen and human alike, reminding them that they were all Gilneans. They were not a people who would give up. Not ever. The Gilnean army valiantly fought the Horde with sword and claw.

Losses were heavy on all sides, especially for Gilneas's king. Sylvanas nearly struck him dead with a poisoned arrow, but it never reached its target. Genn Greymane's only son, Liam Greymane, shielded his father from the attack. The arrow took the prince's life instead.

The fierce resistance pushed Sylvanas Windrunner to desperate measures. She loosed the plague on Gilneas City, forcing Genn and his people to retreat. They had suffered too many losses to mount a counterattack, and they found themselves trapped within their own kingdom.

It seemed that all was lost for the Gilneans, until a fleet of night elven ships appeared on the coast. Once again, the strangers from across the sea had come to help Genn Greymane and his people.

The decision to abandon the land of his ancestors was one of the hardest Genn had ever made, but it was his only option. Staying in Gilneas would have meant certain death for himself, what remained of his family, and his loyal subjects. He ordered his people to board the ships, and they set sail for the distant night elf capital, Darnassus.

Even if it took him years, even if it cost him his own life, Genn Greymane vowed to return one day and restore Gilneas to its former glory.

KING GENN GREYMANE GRIEVES AFTER HIS SON, LIAM, WAS STRUCK DOWN BY SYLVANAS WINDRUNNER

THE BILGEWATER CARTEL

Gilneas was not the only independent nation to suffer from the Cataclysm. The devastation pushed the savvy goblins of the Bilgewater Cartel to the verge of extinction.

For many years, they had lived on the Isle of Kezan, the central hub of a vast mercantile empire. The goblins were gifted engineers and accomplished seafarers, but they were best known for their unabashed avarice. They rarely picked a side in the wars between the Horde and the Alliance. Remaining neutral allowed them to trade with both factions and maximize their profits.

However, this neutrality left them with no reliable allies to call on in times of need. The Cataclysm sparked the eruption of Mount Kajaro, a massive volcano on Kezan. Molten rock rained down on the island, blasting apart the Bilgewater Cartel's factories, warehouses, and ships. A tide of lava swept down from the volcano, consuming everything left standing.

The goblins had no choice but to flee. Their home was doomed.

The Bilgewater Cartel's vainglorious leader, Trade Prince Jastor Gallywix, preyed on the desperate goblins. His gaudy pleasure yacht was the only remaining ship in Kezan, and he forced his people into slavery in exchange for safe passage aboard the vessel.

If the goblins were hoping that the danger had passed, they were disappointed. The currents carried them straight into the conflict brewing between the Horde and the Alliance.

Amid a naval battle, Alliance vessels sank the goblins' ship. This unwarranted hostility eventually propelled the goblins into the arms of the Horde. It wasn't easy for the Bilgewater Cartel to forgo their cherished neutrality, but Gallywix knew the value of adapting to the times, and he was determined to turn these unfortunate events into a profit.

The goblins officially joined the Horde and later settled in the region of Azshara. Gallywix was forced to release his people from slavery, but he managed to stay in control of the cartel. Few had his connections and charisma, and he soon proved why he was the best goblin to lead. Under his supervision, the cartel reshaped Azshara and raised a new city on its shores. Bilgewater Harbor was as much a strategic Horde port as it was a monument to vice. Gambling dens, pleasure houses, and other luxuries filled the city's streets.

Garrosh Hellscream loathed the goblins' naked greed and decadence, but he saw great promise in their war machines and other technologically advanced weaponry. At his command, the goblins deployed their iron-skinned shredders into Ashenvale and cut down vast swaths of the forest. Clearing away the woodlands gave the Horde a steady supply of timber, and it allowed Garrosh to expand his influence into night elven lands.

He would not stop until the Horde's crimson banners hung over every corner of the woodlands.

FURY OF THE WORGEN

The Horde's encroachment in Ashenvale came at a time of great uncertainty for the night elves. At the end of the Third War, they had lost the enchantments that bound them to the World Tree Nordrassil. Their immortality and protection from disease and aging were gone. They now had to face their own inevitable mortality.

Night elf culture and traditions were also in upheaval. The Highborne Shen'dralar sorcerers from Dire Maul had settled in Darnassus along with the Gilneans. Many night elves were wary of their guests. Both sets of newcomers dredged up painful memories from the past. The Highborne in particular were treated with suspicion and open hostility. During the War of the Ancients, their obsession with arcane magic had brought the Legion to Azeroth. That was not a sin easily forgotten or forgiven, even after ten thousand years.

Tyrande Whisperwind did her best to ease her people's fears and convince them of the necessity for having more allies. The night elves were in a fragile state, and with the Horde on a warpath, they needed help wherever they could find it. Now was not the time for isolation; it was the time for making new friends and reaffirming the night elves' commitment to the Alliance.

Tyrande believed that adding the worgen to the Alliance would strengthen the faction. Yet that was not a decision she could make on her own. She called a meeting of the Alliance nations in Darnassus to induct the worgen into their ranks.

As the event unfolded, it seemed it was doomed to fail.

King Varian Wrynn had no love for King Genn Greymane, and he soundly rejected an alliance with the worgen. He despised the Gilnean ruler for his decision to abandon the Alliance and close off his nation from the rest of the world. However, Varian's anger was also a product of his own internal strife. Ever since he'd been made whole again after Onyxia's spell was broken, he had suffered from bouts of uncontrollable rage. His anger had slowly pushed away his friends, his confidants, and even his own son, Anduin. Now it threatened to tear apart the Alliance.

Archdruid Malfurion Stormrage subtly mended ties between the human kings. He arranged for them to embark on a hunting excursion, where they would be forced to work together. The more Varian learned of Genn, the more he saw him as an honorable and courageous ruler. He even reached out to the Gilnean king for help tempering the fury in his heart. Genn led Varian through the same Ritual of Balance that he and other worgen had used to control their rage.

It worked. For the first time in years, Varian Wrynn felt at peace with himself.

Meanwhile, Garrosh Hellscream continued his encroachment on Ashenvale and launched the Horde deeper into the woodlands. His troops besieged the night elves' strongholds, but their brutal offensive was short-lived.

Varian Wrynn, Genn Greymane, and the worgen joined the night elves in the defense of their homeland. The combined Alliance force crashed against the Horde lines and halted their advance. The worgen proved themselves as fearsome warriors in battle. They tore through the Horde's soldiers with primal ferocity, sending their enemies fleeing in terror.

Though the Alliance reclaimed some of its holdings in Ashenvale, Garrosh stubbornly clung to much of the land he had conquered. The forest would remain a bitterly contested territory.

Following the battle in Ashenvale, the Alliance held another vote to induct Gilneas into its ranks. This time it was Varian who stood as the kingdom's most vocal supporter. The decision was unanimous. The leaders welcomed Genn Greymane and his people into the Alliance. In turn, the Gilneans vowed to fight for their faction. They vowed to die for it if need be.

THE DEFENSE OF AZEROTH

Following the events in Ashenvale, sporadic battles erupted between the Horde and the Alliance in other regions. With the factions spread thin, Deathwing unleashed the Old Gods' minions on the world.

Far to the south of Kalimdor, Al'Akir and his elementals emerged from their domain in the Elemental Plane, the Skywall, through a rift in the ancient land of Uldum. Thousands of years ago, the servants of the titans had magically shrouded the region from sight, but the elemental unrest had destroyed this enchanted barrier. Uldum was now exposed to the world, and so were its deadly secrets.

Deep within Uldum lay the Forge of Origination. The keepers had built this machine to help fortify Azeroth and protect it from corruption. The Forge of Origination could release incredible energies to purge the flora and fauna of the world, allowing life to start anew. It was this ability—the power to scour every creature from Azeroth—that Al'Akir sought to harness.

Beneath the waves, another servant of N'Zoth stirred. She was called Queen Azshara, and she had ruled the ancient night elf empire before falling under the will of the Old Gods. She sent her loyal naga to an underwater region known as Vashj'ir, where there was a rift to the elemental realm of Neptulon the Tidehunter. The water elementals had defied N'Zoth's command, and for that they would suffer. Yet Azshara and her naga sought more than just to destroy Neptulon. The elemental lord held the power to control the world's seas, and it was this that N'Zoth demanded. With it, the naga could cut off all sea travel between the continents, splintering the world's nations into isolated enclaves.

N'Zoth was confident that even if the Horde and the Alliance managed to stop some of its servants, they could never stop all of them. If *one* of the Old God's campaigns succeeded, it would usher in the Hour of Twilight.

Bogged down in their own conflict, the Alliance and the Horde were ill prepared to deal with these new enemies. Fortunately, these factions were not Azeroth's only defenders.

Neutral factions rallied to stand against Deathwing and his followers. The first were the shaman of the Earthen Ring, who gathered in areas of elemental unrest to restore balance to the world. They called for help from the Horde and the Alliance, from anyone wise enough to put aside their warmongering and focus on sparing Azeroth from destruction.

The same heroes who had fought in Northrend, Outland, and Ahn'Qiraj answered the Earthen Ring's call. They came from different lands. They held different beliefs. Some were even sworn enemies. Yet what they shared was a common desire to protect Azeroth—their *home*.

These heroes spearheaded missions across the world. In Deepholm, they destroyed the Twilight's Hammer's presence, allowing the Earthen Ring to repair the damage caused to the realm by Deathwing's emergence into Azeroth.

Campaigns in Vashj'ir and Uldum met similar success. Alliance and Horde strike forces ventured beneath the waves and broke the strength of the naga and their allies. In Uldum, they secured the ancient Forge of Origination before the Twilight's Hammer could harness its energies. It was there that Azeroth's defenders delivered a crushing blow to N'Zoth's elemental minions—through a gateway in Uldum, they infiltrated the lofty domain of the Skywall and vanquished Al'Akir the Windlord.

Al'Akir's defeat gave the world's defenders a glimmer of hope. They would need it for what was to come.

THE DEFENDERS OF HYJAL BATTLE AGAINST THE ELEMENTAL FORCES OF RAGNAROS

THE BURNING OF HYJAL

As conflict shook Vashj'ir and Uldum, another battlefront unfolded on Mount Hyjal. Shortly after the Cataclysm, Deathwing and a force of Twilight's Hammer cultists had gathered near the mountain's summit. The corrupted Dragon Aspect led a great ritual that tore a rift into the Firelands, Ragnaros's domain in the Elemental Plane. From it emerged thousands of fire-wreathed beings. At the head of this army was Ragnaros himself.

The elementals reveled in their release. They were more than pleased to set the woodlands aflame, but Ragnaros gave them another purpose. He whipped his servants into a frenzy and dispatched them up the mountain's slopes, toward the World Tree Nordrassil.

Nordrassil had not fully healed since the Third War, but it still held immense power. Its roots reached deep into Azeroth, nurturing the land and mending its unseen wounds. Due to Nordrassil's presence, much of Hyjal was finally starting to bloom again. N'Zoth believed that burning the World Tree would deal a blow to the world from which it would never recover.

As the sworn guardians of nature, the druids of the Cenarion Circle and their ancient friends, the green dragons, stood as the first line of defense against the elementals. They were soon joined by the night elf military and champions from the Horde and the Alliance. This unified front established defenses across the mountain, but even these were not enough to hold back the storm of smoke and ember.

Hyjal's defenders needed something more. They needed the Wild Gods, nature's most ferocious guardians.

The Cenarion Circle led efforts to rally the legendary Wild Gods for battle. Most of these immense beasts had either died during the War of the Ancients or gone into hiding following that conflict. Only Cenarius had played an active role in safeguarding the woodlands in recent times. In the Third War, he had fallen to Grommash Hellscream's axe, and his spirit was lost in the depths of the Emerald Dream.

As the Third War had drawn to a close, the druids had tried and failed to rouse the other Wild Gods from the Dream, asking them for help. Cenarius's death had thrown the creatures into turmoil.

By now, enough time had passed for the Wild Gods to find inner peace. Slowly and with great care, the druids and their allies drew the majestic creatures to Hyjal. They even found Cenarius's spirit in the Dream and brought him back to the physical world. The forests soon trembled with the footfalls of legends like Goldrinn, the Great Wolf, and Tortolla, the wise and unyielding turtle.

The return of the Wild Gods was a historic moment. Not since the War of the Ancients had they come together with so many other races in defense of the world.

Unified in purpose, Hyjal's guardians were unstoppable. With blade and spell, talon and fang, they destroyed the Twilight's Hammer's presence in the region and pushed back the fire elementals. Even Ragnaros fled before the fury of the Wild Gods and their mortal allies. He and what remained of his servants vanished into the rift between Azeroth and the Firelands.

For the moment, Hyjal was safe.

FALL OF THE TWILIGHT'S HAMMER

With the elemental and naga assaults thwarted, the tide of war turned. The Alliance and the Horde remained consumed by their own power struggle, but recent events had taught them that they could not ignore what was happening to the rest of the world. Though the true purpose behind the Cataclysm and the elemental invasions was still unknown, the attacks had clearly been coordinated. The Alliance and the Horde believed that Deathwing was using the Twilight's Hammer cult to organize this campaign against the world.

At one time, the Alliance and the Horde had regarded the cult as nothing more than an order of loosely affiliated fanatics and rabble-rousers. Now, they knew that the Twilight's Hammer was highly organized and extremely dangerous. The cultists had spread across the land like rats. They would only grow in power if ignored.

The Horde and the Alliance launched a counterattack against the Twilight's Hammer, targeting its most prominent holdings. This offensive culminated in a strike on the Twilight Highlands. Fleets of airships blotted out the sun, laden with war machines and soldiers. The Horde and the Alliance did not strike in unison, but they had the same goals. They wanted to bring the cult to its knees, and they hoped to secure the Highlands for themselves in the process.

The Alliance found new friends among the region's Wildhammer dwarves. They were a fiercely independent people, isolated from the rest of dwarf society and not accustomed to working with outsiders. It took time to win their support, but it proved invaluable in the battles ahead.

The red dragonflight also came to the Alliance's aid, most notably at Grim Batol. They joined forces for a unified attack on the ancient stronghold and ripped it free from the clutches of the Twilight's Hammer.

Meanwhile, the orcs of the Horde rekindled old bonds with the Dragonmaw. Since the end of the Second War, the clan had remained isolated and aloof. Warchief Garrosh Hellscream convinced the Dragonmaw's orcs to pledge themselves to *his* Horde with promises of blood and glory. Under his command, they had their fill of both.

As war raged in the Twilight Highlands, Garona emerged to scour the cult. She had not given up her quest to destroy Cho'gall and his followers. Though she had not sworn herself to the new Horde, she fought by their side. She was vengeance incarnate, and she painted her daggers with the blood of all who wore the Twilight's Hammer sigil.

The Horde eventually struck at the cult's seat of power: the Bastion of Twilight. The stronghold's defenses crumbled before the onslaught, and the Horde's greatest champions cut their way through the citadel. They did not rest until they had plunged their blades into Cho'gall's black heart. The two-headed ogre did not flee from his enemies. He embraced his fate. Despite the defeats he had suffered, he died believing the Hour of Twilight was inevitable.

The fall of Cho'gall and the Bastion of Twilight broke the cult's strength, but its influence endured. Many of its members remained active throughout the world. With Cho'gall dead, Archbishop Benedictus ascended to a position of leadership. He cast off his old identity once and for all, and he assumed his true name: the Twilight Father.

RISE OF THE ZANDALARI

Cultures across Azeroth reeled from the Cataclysm, but some suffered more than others. Earthquakes and tidal upheaval rocked the Zandalari trolls, causing widespread devastation on their island, Zandalar.

Following these natural disasters, a strange force began assaulting the trolls—an enemy from the past.

These events were only the latest in a string of hardships that had weakened the trolls. The Zandalar tribe had once reigned over an empire that stretched to the far corners of the world. Those glorious days were gone. For millennia, the trolls had known little more than war and famine.

A mysterious prophet known as Zul arose to help his people. He had seen troubling visions of his island home sinking beneath the waves, and he urged the trolls to abandon Zandalar and embark on a new destiny. The Cataclysm had caused political upheaval across the world, and Zul saw that as an opportunity. The Zandalari could take advantage of the chaos to unite the scattered troll tribes into a mighty empire and establish themselves as Azeroth's preeminent power like in ancient times.

The Zandalari's ruler, King Rastakhan, did not heed Zul's advice to abandon their home, but he did give him permission to take the tribe's fleet and bring along anyone else who wanted to join him.

Other troll tribes throughout the world embraced Zul's call. The most powerful were the Gurubashi and Amani. With the Zandalari's guidance, they rebuilt their shattered nations and readied themselves for war.

Zul reached out to Vol'jin and his Darkspear trolls as well, hoping to win their support. This proved to be a grave mistake. Not only did Vol'jin reject the offer, but he also moved to end the Zandalari's warmongering.

Vol'jin was not as hostile to the Alliance as Warchief Garrosh Hellscream. Seeing the wisdom in cooperation, he recruited heroes from the Alliance and the Horde to crush the ascendant troll empire. They succeeded, but that did not deter Zul. He would continue to search for ways to assert troll dominion over the world.

THE FRACTURED ACCORD

After the Horde and the Alliance arrived in the Twilight Highlands, Deathwing briefly appeared in the skies. So, too, did Alexstrasza, the Aspect of Life. She had been horrified by the sheer destructive power unleashed by the Cataclysm and the untold deaths it had caused. Yet when she learned that Deathwing was responsible for the disaster, she knew it was only the beginning. Alexstrasza vowed to stop the fallen Dragon Aspect and end Azeroth's suffering.

The two dragons clashed above the Twilight Highlands in a storm of fire and scales. Deathwing was severely wounded in the encounter, but he nonetheless triumphed. Alexstrasza was forced to flee before his fury.

Despite his victory, Deathwing was troubled. He had narrowly bested Alexstrasza. What if Ysera and Nozdormu had been at her side?

Unlike Alexstrasza, the other Dragon Aspects seemed harmless and in disarray, but Deathwing knew that could change. If they returned to their former glory and power, they would become the only true threat to his existence. Deathwing was eager to destroy the noble Dragon Aspects before that came to pass. He rallied an army to his side, composed mainly of the fearsome twilight dragons. Then he vanished from the Twilight Highlands, leaving Cho'gall and the rest of the cultists to their fate. Whether they lived or died was of little concern to Deathwing.

An opportunity to strike at the Dragon Aspects soon presented itself. Alexstrasza had called on Nozdormu and Ysera to gather at Wyrmrest Temple. Her hope was to bring order to the scattered dragonflights and unite them against Deathwing.

From the outset, the meeting was a disaster. Nozdormu's whereabouts remained unknown. Ysera answered Alexstrasza's call, but her mind was clouded by strange visions of the future. She had lost the ability to tell the difference between these premonitions and reality.

The blue dragons Kalecgos and Arygos also convened at Wyrmrest Temple to discuss the future of their flight. With Malygos dead, they had emerged as the two most promising candidates to succeed him. Yet they couldn't have been more different. Kalecgos was wise and even-tempered. Arygos, the son of Malygos, was brash and arrogant. He still blamed Alexstrasza for his father's death, and he had no intention of forgiving her.

A heated argument erupted between Arygos and the other dragons. It was at this moment that Deathwing's forces struck.

Twilight dragons descended from the skies and launched an attack against Wyrmrest Temple and its defenders. Unbeknownst to Alexstrasza and her allies, the assault was merely a diversion.

Members of the Twilight's Hammer infiltrated a series of enchanted sanctums beneath Wyrmrest Temple, which housed each dragonflight's eggs. The cultists shrouded the clutches with Void energies, slowly transforming the unhatched creatures into twilight dragons.

Their ritual would have worked if not for Alexstrasza's consort, Korialstrasz. The red dragon learned of the corruption seeping through the sanctums. It was too late to cleanse the eggs of the cult's magic. Korialstrasz decided to end their tortured existence before the creatures hatched as twilight dragons, and he saw only one way to do it.

He drew on his own life essence, igniting an explosion of enchanted fire within the sanctums. Every egg and cultist was destroyed in the blaze. So, too, was Korialstrasz.

The blast shook Wyrmrest Temple to its foundations. Not long afterward, the twilight dragons pulled back and vanished into the skies.

THE LEGACY OF TWILIGHT

During their campaign against the Twilight's Hammer cult, the Horde and the Alliance vanquished Nefarian and Sintharia. Yet their creations lived on. They had both produced powerful weapons to serve the cult, particularly Sintharia. She had forged hundreds of twilight dragons, and they became the backbone of Deathwing's army.

Upon investigating the sanctums, Alexstrasza and the other dragons learned that Korialstrasz was responsible for the eggs' destruction. However, they did not know *why* he had destroyed them. Rather than seeing his actions as a heroic sacrifice, the dragons believed he had fallen under Deathwing's sway.

This apparent betrayal, the loss of so much new life, shattered Alexstrasza's heart. Overcome with grief, she disappeared from Northrend. The others who had gathered at Wyrmrest gradually abandoned the temple as well. With their departure, whatever hope remained of uniting the dragonflights vanished.

Though Deathwing's plan to corrupt the eggs had failed, he was pleased with the aftermath. The bonds between the dragonflights had broken. Wyrmrest Temple fell under the control of Deathwing's forces. He commanded the Twilight Father to occupy the sacred temple alongside an army of twilight dragons and cultists.

There was still much work to be done before the Dragon Aspects could be eliminated forever.

TWILIGHT OF THE ASPECTS

South of Northrend, Thrall and the Earthen Ring continued their struggle to restore balance to the elements. Day and night, they performed rituals at the Maelstrom. All of them ended in failure. The Earthen Ring's troubles were not only due to the unruly elementals. Thrall was also to blame.

He remained haunted by Cairne Bloodhoof's death and the Horde's uncertain future. His inner turmoil disrupted the Earthen Ring's rituals. Thrall was lost, unsure of who he was and what difference he could make in a world teetering at the edge of oblivion. An answer came from a mysterious visitor at the Maelstrom.

Ysera had foreseen the Hour of Twilight. In a vision, she saw a gray world devoid of all life. Even Deathwing would perish in this dire future. Yet there was a glimmer of hope. Ysera had also seen Thrall in her dreams, playing some important role in the days to come. Ysera did not know exactly what role Thrall would play, but she was determined to find out.

Unsure how to leverage Thrall's abilities, Ysera initially asked him to embark on a simple quest to calm the elements in a distant corner of Feralas. The orc balked at the suggestion, but Aggra

YSERA'S VISION OF THE HOUR OF TWILIGHT, WITH DEATHWING IMPALED ON WYRMREST TEMPLE

convinced him to take part. Though it was difficult for him to admit, he was doing more harm than good at the Maelstrom. He needed time to reflect if he was to overcome his uncertainties.

Thrall's mission started in Feralas, but it soon grew into something far more. In the time that followed, the orc traveled the far corners of the world in a quest to help the Dragon Aspects. He would see things that few mortals had ever laid eyes on.

After visiting Feralas, Thrall plunged into the timeways and found Nozdormu. The wise Aspect of Time had become lost in his own domain—he had become trapped in *all* moments of time. Thrall helped liberate Nozdormu from his temporal prison, and the bronze Dragon Aspect returned to the present.

Nozdormu was changed by his experience. In the timeways, he had discovered that the Old Gods were responsible for Deathwing's corruption, the Emerald Nightmare, and other dark events throughout history. For thousands of years, the vile entities had chipped away at the Dragon Aspects' strength and unity.

Nozdormu had also learned that the Old Gods had orchestrated the rise of the infinite dragonflight. This shadowy force was responsible for the time anomalies that had consumed his attention for so many years. Just as unsettling was the identity of the infinite dragonflight's leader.

It was Nozdormu himself.

In some distant future, he had fallen to corruption and taken on the name Murozond. This shade of Nozdormu had forged the infinite dragonflight to unravel the sanctity of time.

Thrall later journeyed to the Nexus to aid the blue dragons in selecting a new Dragon Aspect for their flight. There was deep division between those who supported Kalecgos and those who supported Arygos. Most of the dragons tried to make their decision with reason and cold logic, but Thrall helped convince them to trust their hearts instead. In doing so, they chose Kalecgos.

In response, Arygos did the unthinkable. He attacked his own kind.

Unbeknownst to the rest of the blue dragonflight, Deathwing had won Arygos to his side. He had played on the rage that consumed the blue dragon in the wake of his father's death. Arygos had nursed a bitter hatred toward Alexstrasza and the mortals who had struck down Malygos. He saw their actions as a betrayal, and he longed for a way to exact retribution. Through his allegiance to Deathwing and the Twilight's Hammer, Arygos believed he had an army powerful enough to end those who had wronged him and his father.

THRALL'S LESSONS

Thrall changed the lives of Alexstrasza and her allies. In the process, he also changed himself. His journey to the far corners of the world brought him inner peace and strengthened his connection with the elements. He learned to focus on the present rather than worry about the decisions he had made in the past, or the uncertainties that awaited him and the rest of Azeroth in the future.

Arygos revealed his alliance with Deathwing by assaulting the Nexus with an army of twilight dragons. His attack failed, and Arygos himself was slain. He died as a traitor to his flight.

Following Kalecgos's ascension to Dragon Aspect, Thrall met with Alexstrasza. The Life-Binder had taken refuge in the wastelands of Desolace. She dwelled there alone, lost in her sadness. Thrall pulled her from the grip of despair with a vision of the past. Through the elements, he had witnessed Korialstrasz's sacrifice to spare the red dragonflight's eggs from corruption.

Thrall shared this vision with Alexstrasza, and it rekindled her hope. She found inspiration in Korialstrasz's noble sacrifice. She found a reason to fight again.

Alongside Thrall, Alexstrasza rallied the dragons and set out for Wyrmrest Temple. For the first time in over ten thousand years, the noble dragonflights were unified in purpose.

The battle to reclaim Wyrmrest Temple from Deathwing's forces was long and brutal. In the end, the combined strength of the Dragon Aspects and their followers was too much for the Twilight's Hammer to withstand, and they abandoned the temple.

RAGE OF THE FIRELANDS

The Dragon Aspects were eager to take the fight to Deathwing and the remnants of the Twilight's Hammer, but they first sought to heal the broken world. They gathered at Hyjal Summit to perform a ritual on Nordrassil. The World Tree was mending, but not fast enough. By infusing it with their power, the Dragon Aspects hoped to restore Nordrassil to its former glory. Its withered roots would grow and flourish again, strengthening the world and hastening Azeroth's recovery.

When Deathwing learned of their intentions, he unleashed Ragnaros and his fire elementals on Mount Hyjal once more. The rift to the Firelands tore open, and an army of ember and smoke poured into the forests.

As Azeroth's defenders fought to hold back the firestorm, Deathwing turned his attention to Thrall. He had never imagined that a simple orc could threaten him, but this creature was different. Thrall's meddling had unified the noble Dragon Aspects and saved them from destruction. Not only that, but the orc's connection with the elements gave him extraordinary power over earth—Deathwing's domain.

Deathwing called on a new weapon to end Thrall: the Druids of the Flame. They were led by Fandral Staghelm, the disgraced former leader of the Cenarion Circle.

Fandral had been locked in a barrow den for his attempted murder of Malfurion Stormrage and his dealings with the Emerald Nightmare. As the Cataclysm had unfolded, agents of the Twilight's Hammer had helped him escape his bonds. The cult then presented him with an offer: if he served Deathwing, he would be granted the power to take revenge on the world for the death of his son, Valstann Staghelm.

Fandral had never recovered from losing his child. After his defeat in the War Against the Nightmare, he knew that resurrecting Valstann was impossible, and that fact had darkened his mind and soul. His only desire was to bring ruin to Azeroth, and the Twilight's Hammer gave him the means to do so.

Ragnaros himself remade Fandral in flames, disfiguring the night elf but also granting him command over the element of fire. He became the Firelord's foremost lieutenant and the first Druid

THE BLACK PRINCE

Deathwing's corruption had spread to nearly all members of his black dragonflight. They embodied his malice and thirst for destruction. However, there were some exceptions. After the Cataclysm, a red dragon named Rheastrasza had embarked on a dangerous quest to capture a black dragon egg and cleanse it of Deathwing's influence. She succeeded.

The creature who hatched became known as Wrathion, the Black Prince. Though a whelpling, he was wise and powerful beyond his years. Free of Deathwing's control, he saw with clear eyes what had become of the black dragons, and he recognized the threat they posed to Azeroth. Wrathion knew of only one way to purify the flight: death. He launched a brutal campaign to assassinate the world's remaining black dragons.

When his bloody work was done, Wrathion stood as one of the last living black dragons.

of the Flame. Fandral recruited others to his side, mainly druids who were disillusioned with the Cenarion Circle. Like their new leader, these druids were reborn in fire.

Near Hyjal Summit, Fandral and his druids ambushed Thrall. They used the orc's own shamanic power to shatter his spirit and hurl the pieces across the Elemental Plane. Each sundered portion of his essence embodied one of his raw emotions.

Thrall was thought dead by many of his allies, but not Aggra. She would not abandon the orc she had grown so close to. She convinced members of the Horde and the Alliance to seek out Thrall's fractured spirit. Together, they made him whole again.

Meanwhile, Malfurion Stormrage rallied Hyjal's defenders in a massive counterattack against the fire elementals. They drove Ragnaros's army back into the Firelands, but they did not stop there. Malfurion knew that as long as Ragnaros lived, the creature would launch another invasion. There was only one way to protect Hyjal from his fiery touch.

The Cenarion Circle stormed into the Firelands and carved out a stronghold known as the Molten Front. Fire elementals constantly battered Hyjal's defenders, but they held fast. Reinforcements from the Horde and the Alliance soon joined the Cenarion Circle. Slowly, they pushed deeper into the Firelands until they reached Sulfuron Keep, Ragnaros's blazing citadel.

Secure in his own domain, Ragnaros thought himself beyond the reach of simple mortals. Yet so had Al'Akir. Like the Windlord, Ragnaros fell before the onslaught of Azeroth's defenders. His greatest lieutenants, including Fandral Staghelm and most of the Druids of the Flame, suffered the same fate.

With the Firelord's destruction, Hyjal was at last spared from his all-consuming flames.

THE SHATTERING
OF AZEROTH

NORTHREN

The Nexus

Mount Hyjal

Bilgewater Harbor

Orgrimmar

THE MAELSTROM

*The
Veiled Sea*

NORTHERN
BARRENS

*Thunder
Bluff*

KEZAN

SOUTHERN
BARRENS

KALIMDOR

The South Sea

Uldum

PANDARI

THE DRAGON SOUL

With peace restored to Hyjal once more, the Dragon Aspects finally turned to their original task. They gathered at the base of Nordrassil and channeled their energies into the World Tree. The effects were immediate. Nordrassil's wounds healed, and new life pulsed through its limbs. Its verdant crown touched the heavens, and its roots burrowed to the deep places of the world.

Nordrassil's life-giving energies cascaded over the surrounding woodlands. Among the charred trees that dotted the mountain, saplings pushed through the ash and unfurled new leaves.

The Dragon Aspects were pleased with their work, but there was much yet to do. They remained at Nordrassil and discussed how, or even *if*, they could defeat Deathwing. He was not the same creature they had fought in Grim Batol years ago. Void energies now coursed through his veins, making him nearly invincible. To defeat him, the Dragon Aspects would need to unmake Deathwing. They would need to destroy every portion of his essence.

Kalecgos theorized a way to do so. The Dragon Aspects would need to combine their powers and amplify them through some means. And he knew of an artifact that could accomplish this goal, an artifact specially crafted to contain their energies.

In the Second War, the orcs had discovered this relic and transformed it into a weapon. Not understanding its true origins, they had called it the Demon Soul, but it was known to Kalecgos and his kind by its original name: *the Dragon Soul.*

The other Dragon Aspects were wary of this idea. The Dragon Soul was a dangerous thing. Long ago, it had been enchanted so that none of their race could touch it without painful, and possibly fatal, consequences. Yet Kalecgos had a solution in mind: Thrall. He was not a dragon, and so he was immune to the relic's enchantments. Not only that, but he could infuse the element of earth into the artifact, which would make Deathwing especially vulnerable to its power.

Kalecgos's logic was sound, but the Dragon Aspects faced an even greater problem. The Dragon Soul was no more. The only way to use it would be to recover it from the past, an act that they could only perform with Nozdormu's blessing.

For Nozdormu, retrieving the Dragon Soul went against the very purpose of his existence. His duty was to protect the sanctity of the timeways, not interfere with them, no matter how noble the reason. It was only after much soul-searching that Nozdormu realized that venturing into the past was the world's sole hope of averting the Hour of Twilight.

Nozdormu knew that the first step to claiming the artifact was breaking the infinite dragonflight's control of the timeways. That meant facing Murozond. As mighty as Nozdormu was, he feared that he would not have the strength to fight this warped future version of himself. It was through the Horde's champions that he found courage. They, too, believed that the Dragon Soul was the answer to ending Deathwing, and they volunteered their lives to join Nozdormu on his quest.

Together, they ventured into a bleak sliver of the timeways, a future where Murozond and his infinite dragons had twisted reality beyond all recognition. Inspired by the iron will and bravery of his mortal allies, Nozdormu helped the Horde face his shadow self and end Murozond.

The victory was bittersweet for Nozdormu. Azeroth was safe, but he knew that he would one day fall to corruption and become Murozond. That fate was inescapable. He took heart in the fact that, when that terrible destiny came to pass, heroes would rise to strike him down and end his subversion of the timeways.

OVERLEAF: THE LANDS OF AZEROTH FOLLOWING THE CATACLYSM

TIME ANOMALIES

The decision to take the Dragon Soul from the past was not an easy one for Nozdormu. His purpose was to protect time, not meddle with it. Nonetheless, he was prepared to do whatever was necessary to stop Deathwing. If the Hour of Twilight came to pass, there would be no timeways left for him to protect.

Plucking the Dragon Soul from the War of the Ancients caused disruptions in the timeways, but Nozdormu knew that they would be short-lived. After the artifact was used against Deathwing, it returned to the past, thereby restoring order to time.

With the timeways freed of the infinite dragonflight's control, Nozdormu opened a pathway to the War of the Ancients, the era of the Burning Legion's first invasion of Azeroth. Traveling to this period would be dangerous, but it was necessary. The Dragon Aspects needed the Dragon Soul in its purest form, not long after Deathwing had crafted it and convinced his former friends to infuse it with their energies.

This time, it was heroes from the Alliance who rose to the challenge. Alongside Nozdormu, they ventured into the broken battlefields of the past. Demons swarmed across a land smoldering in fel fire and choked with bodies. Narrowly, they avoided becoming victims of the war themselves. They helped Nozdormu recover the Dragon Soul and return it to the present.

The Dragon Aspects set out for Wyrmrest Temple to infuse the artifact with their combined might along with Thrall's shamanic power. Their actions did not go unnoticed. Deathwing had agents throughout the world, and they had learned of the Dragon Soul's return and the plans to empower it.

If his enemies succeeded, Deathwing would perish. And so, he released all his fury at Wyrmrest Temple.

THE HOUR OF TWILIGHT

Deathwing held nothing back.

The force of twilight dragons and cultists he had rallied at Wyrmrest Temple was larger than any army he had ever mustered. From the ground and from the air, his servants surrounded the sacred tower. Even N'Zoth sent its own minions to aid the assault. At the Old God's command, nightmarish creatures called the n'raqi, or "faceless ones," arrived at Wyrmrest Temple just as the Dragon Aspects and their allies did.

The noble Dragon Aspects and the champions of the Horde and the Alliance did not face these enemies alone. Members of the red, blue, green, and bronze dragonflights gathered at Wyrmrest

Temple to fight for control of the area. They clashed with the twilight dragons, their winged forms blotting out the sun.

The costs on all sides were horrific. Hundreds of cultists and twilight dragons lost their lives, including the Twilight Father. Just as many of the temple's defenders fell in battle.

Yet the red, blue, green, and bronze dragons did not die in vain. Their sacrifices allowed the Dragon Aspects and their allies to focus their wrath on Deathwing. For all his might, he could not best his unified enemies or prevent them from empowering the Dragon Soul. Thrall and the Dragon Aspects unleashed the artifact on Deathwing and drove him from Wyrmrest Temple.

Wounded and enraged, Deathwing fled toward the Maelstrom in the hope that he could reach Deepholm through its swirling depths. Taking refuge in the elemental realm was his only chance of escaping the Dragon Aspects and recovering from his injuries.

The defenders of Wyrmrest pursued Deathwing through the skies and slowly whittled away his strength. N'Zoth sensed that its servant was on the verge of defeat. The Old God's plans were unraveling, and it made one final, desperate attempt to turn the tide. N'Zoth infused Deathwing with more of its power—more than the Old God had ever given the black Dragon Aspect before. The influx of energy was so great that Deathwing's unstable body wrenched apart, and molten tentacles unfurled from his broken hide.

Thrall turned the Dragon Soul against this aberration. To ensure that it would destroy Deathwing, the Dragon Aspects sacrificed all their remaining power to the artifact. Their essences, combined with the element of earth that Thrall had woven into the weapon, seared through Deathwing. The explosive power annihilated his tormented mind and body.

In that moment, N'Zoth's campaign to bring about the Hour of Twilight collapsed.

Azeroth was spared, but it had changed forever. The Cataclysm had reshaped the world and claimed countless lives. It would take years for Azeroth's nations to recover from the damage. For some, there would be no going back to the way things had been before.

The Dragon Aspects had sacrificed their energies to overcome Deathwing. They would remain active in the affairs of the world, but with their powers diminished, they could no longer serve as Azeroth's protectors. They passed that sacred duty on to new defenders.

They passed it on to mortals.

The age of Dragon Aspects and the Guardians of Tirisfal was over. The Horde and the Alliance had proved themselves capable of facing any force that threatened Azeroth.

The world was now theirs to watch over, but whether they were ready for this responsibility was another question. The cycle of hatred that had consumed the Horde and the Alliance remained unbroken. Vanquishing Deathwing did not cause the two factions to reflect on their warmongering. To the contrary, with the black Dragon Aspect and the Twilight's Hammer defeated, the Horde and the Alliance now turned all their attention, all their wrath, on each other.

TO BE CONTINUED...

REBUILDING PARTS OF STORMWIND CITY AFTER THE CATACLYSM

INDEX

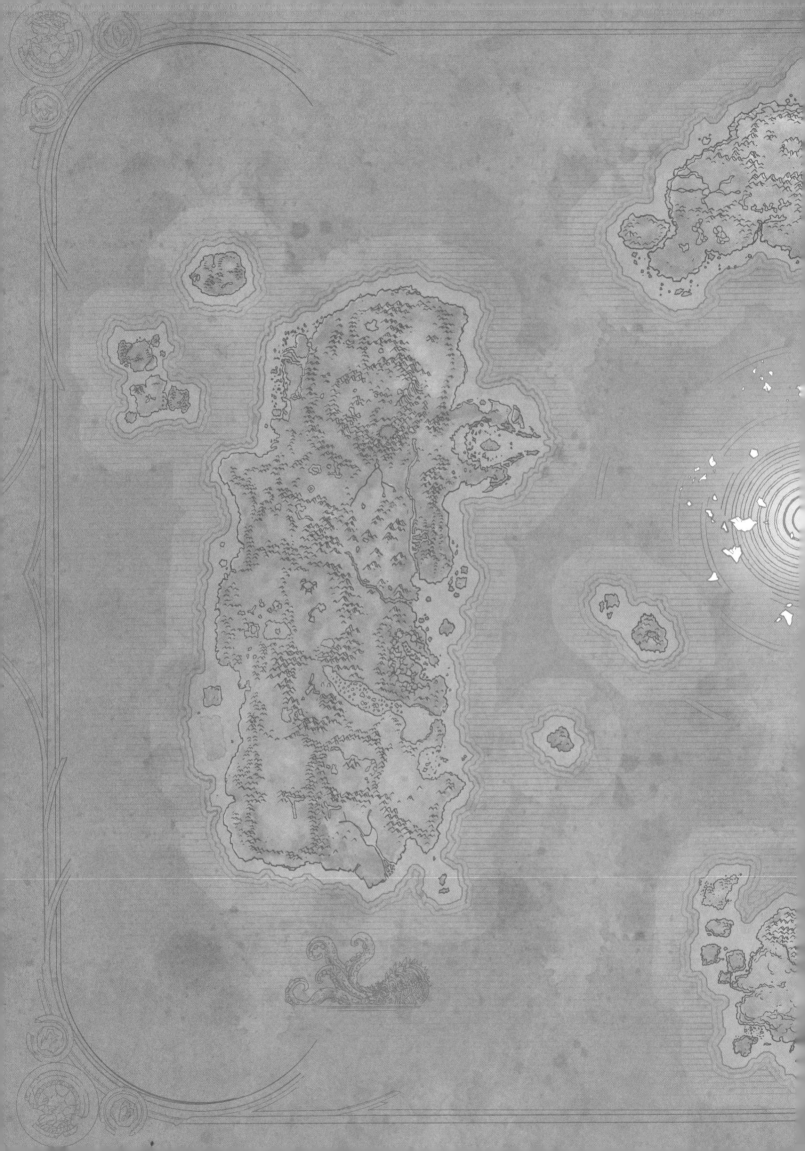